MURDER
BELOW
MONTPARNASSE

MURDER
BELOW
MONTPARNASSE

CARA
BLACK

Published by
Soho Press, Inc.
853 Broadway
New York, NY 10003

Library of Congress Cataloging-in-Publication Data

Black, Cara
Murder below Montparnasse / Cara Black.
p. cm.
ISBN 978-1-61695-215-0
eISBN978-1-61695-216-7
1. Leduc, Aimee (Fictitious character)—Fiction. 2. Women private
investigators—France—Paris—Fiction. 3. Murder—Investigation—Fiction.
4. Mystery fiction. I. Title.
PS3552.L297M785 2013
813'.54—dc23   2012032374

Printed in the United States of America

10 9 8 7 6 5 4 3 2

Dedicated to Madame Fauvette, true citoyenne of the fourteenth arrondissement, and to the ghosts

In hopes that I will bring away with me a snowflake from days gone by... —GEORGES BRASSENS

Truth arises from a conflict of opinions.

—FRENCH PROVERB

Monday, Late February 1998, Paris, 5:58 P.M.

AIMÉE LEDUC BIT her lip as she scanned the indigo dusk, the shoppers teeming along rain-slicked Boulevard du Montparnasse. Daffodil scents drifted from the corner flower shop. Her kohl-rimmed eyes zeroed in on the man hunched at the window table in the café. Definitely the one.

Gathering her courage, she entered the smoke-filled café and sat down across from him. She crossed her legs, noting the stubble on his chin and the half-filled glass of *limonade*.

He sized up her mini and three-inch leopard-print heels. "Going to make me happy?" he asked. "They said you're good."

"No one's complained." She unclipped the thumb-drive from her hoop earring and slid it across the table to him. "Insert this in your USB port to download the file," she said, combing her red wig forward with her fingers. "*Et voilà.*"

"You copied the entire court file to that?" The thick eyebrows rose above his sallow face.

"Cutting-edge technology not even patented yet," she said with more confidence than she felt. She wished her knees would stop shaking under the table.

"How do you do it?"

"Computer security's my business," she said, glancing at her Tintin watch. This was taking too long.

"We'll just see to make sure, *non?*" He pulled a laptop from his bag under the table, inserted the thumb-drive. More tech-savvy than he'd let on. Thank God she'd prepared for that.

"Satisfied?" She fluffed her red wig.

A grin erupted on his face. "The Cour d'Assises witness list with backgrounds, addresses, and schedule. Nice work." He'd lowered his voice. "Perfect to *nique les flics*." Screw the cops.

She grinned. Glanced at the time. "Don't you have something for me?"

Under the table he slipped an envelope, sticky with lemonade residue, into her hands. In her lap she counted the crisp fresh bills.

"Where's the rest?" Perspiration dampened the small of her back. "You trying to cheat me?"

"That's what we agreed," he said, slipping another envelope under the table. Winked.

Thought he was a player.

"Count again," he said.

She did. "No tip? *Service compris?*"

"Let's do business again, Mademoiselle. You live up to your reputation. Glad I outsourced this." He smiled again. "I couldn't be more pleased."

She smiled back. "Neither could Commissaire Morbier."

His shoulders stiffened. "Wait a minute. What . . . ?"

"Would you like to meet my godfather?" She gestured to the older man sitting at the next table. Salt-and-pepper hair, basset-hound eyes, corduroy jacket with elbow patches.

"Godfather?" he said, puzzled.

"Did you get that on tape, Morbier?"

"On camera too. Oh, we got it all," Morbier said. Two undercover *flics* at the zinc counter approached with handcuffs. Another turned from a table with a laptop, took the thumb-drive and inserted it.

The man gave a short laugh and pulled a cell phone from his pocket. "*Zut*, that's entrapment plain and simple. It'll never fly in court, fools. My lawyer will confirm. . . ."

"Entrapment's illegal, but a sting's right up our alley,

according to the Ministry's legal advisor." Morbier jerked his thumb toward a middle-aged man at a neighboring table, who raised his glass of grenadine at them. "Don't worry, I had the boys at the Ministry of the Interior clear the operation technicalities, just to err on the side of caution. Makes your illegal soliciting, paying for and reading confidential judicial documents airtight in court. "

"Lying slut," the man said, glaring at Aimée. "But you're not a *flic*."

She shook her head. "Just another pretty face."

"To think I trusted you."

"Never trust a redhead," she said, watching him be led away. Aimée removed the red wig, scratched her head, and slipped off her heels.

"Not bad, Leduc." Morbier struck a match and lit a cigarette. The tang of his non-filtered Gauloise tickled her nose.

"That entrapment business, you're sure?" She leaned forward to whisper. "I won't get nailed somehow? *Alors*, Morbier, with such short notice. . . ."

"Quick and dirty, Leduc. Your specialty, *non?* I needed an outsider."

"Why?" What hadn't he told her in his last-minute plea for help?

"But I told you." A shrug. "He broke my last officer's knees."

She controlled a shudder. "You forgot to tell me that part."

He shrugged. Not even a thank-you. And still no apology for what had happened last month, the lies he'd told about the past, her parents. A hen would grow teeth before he apologized. But she'd realized it was time to accept that he'd protected her in his own clumsy way. And make up for her outburst—she'd thrown caviar in his face at the four-star *resto*.

"So we're good, Leduc?" The lines crinkled at the edges of his eyes, the bags under them more pronounced. His jowls sagged.

She blinked. Coming from Morbier, that rated as an apology.

She pulled on her red high-tops, laced them up. Scratched her head again.

"*Au contraire.*" She stood, slipped the wig and heels in her bag, buttoned the jean jacket over her vintage black Chanel. "Now you owe me, Morbier."

Monday, 7:30 P.M.

IN THE QUARTIER below Montparnasse, the Serb shivered in his denim jacket, huddled in the damp doorway, watching Yuri Volodya close and lock his atelier door. Why do they lock the doors and leave the windows open? Just foolish.

Yuri Volodya walked across the wet cobbles and disappeared up the dark lane. The old man kept right on schedule—he'd be out for the evening. Now for this simple snatch-and-grab job. The Serb noted a few passersby taking the narrow thread of a street—the shortcut to the boulevard—the general quiet and cars parked for the night. Perfect.

He peered over the cracked stone wall of the back of the old man's place—part atelier, part living space. A small garden wreathed in shadows, the windows dark. He heaved himself up and over.

The garden was redolent with rosemary. The Serb waited a few seconds, then moved without making a sound on his padded soles to the side window. He slid it fully open and slipped in. He reached into his pocket and checked the syringe filled with the tranquilizer, just in case the old man came back. All capped tight.

"Don't kill him," they had said. Would have been easier.

A couple of lamps were lit, so the Serb didn't need his flashlight. The atelier was small enough to search quickly. He looked behind the worktable and under it, too—but *nyet*—no one would store a painting flat.

He had to think . . . *What was wrong here?* His eyes scanned the room and he noticed some fresh scuffing in front of the armoire, as if it had been moved back and forth—more than once, too.

He moved the armoire aside to find a locked door. He searched the armoire drawers for a key, and when he found it, he put it into the lock.

Then he heard a switch click, and the room plunged into darkness. The Serb sensed someone behind him. He flung out an arm, hoping to strike before being struck, but he tripped instead. Someone kicked him in the stomach. He felt gut-wrenching pain and the hypodermic needle rolled in his pocket.

His attacker went down on his knees and roped him around his neck, but the Serb fought him off. That was when he felt the jab in his rear. The liquid ran cold into his muscle, and he felt the freeze go up his body. He went limp.

His attacker let him go, thinking his job was done. A small penlight went on and the key turned in the lock. The wall cabinet opened to reveal . . . nothing. The painting was gone.

The Serb's attacker turned on his heel and walked out. The Serb, disturbed by the strange buzzing in his ears, knew he had to leave too. The simple snatch-and-grab complicated by a rival intruder, and then no painting. He stood, unsteady, and realized it was much harder to breathe. He needed to go outside into the fresh air. . . .

He managed to unlock the door and stumble onto the sidewalk before he realized he couldn't catch his breath at all. A rock-like weight pressed into his chest. Gasping, he reached out between the parked cars. His sleeve caught on something and the world went black.

Monday, 8 P.M.

IN THE OVERHEATED *commissariat*, Aimée signed her police statement. She took the last sip of Morbier's burgundy, then dabbed Chanel No. 5 on her pulse points and slipped the flacon into her bag.

"You'll need to testify against him, Leduc," said Morbier from behind his desk. "So the rat won't get up the drainpipe again."

"Not part of our deal, Morbier." She shook her head.

He waved his age-spotted hand. "Legally you're covered. Sanctioned from the top. It's all in my report."

"Against the Corsican mafia?" She snapped her bag shut. "My identity becomes public knowledge and then a thug appears on my doorway. I disappear. Didn't you tell me his history of intimidating witnesses?"

"Your testimony takes place in closed judges' chambers. No leaks. No media." Morbier stabbed out a Gauloise in the overflowing ashtray. "For three years the rat's boss has evaded every conviction. Now the Corsican's going down and I need you as a witness."

She figured this was linked to the corruption investigation that had almost cost him his career.

"More like someone you can trust," she said. And someone he could dupe into assisting him. It always went like this with Morbier. As if she didn't have enough on her plate right now after losing her business partner, René, to Silicon Valley.

The light of the desk lamp on Morbier's sagging jowls illuminated how he'd aged. Despite her annoyance with him, her heart wrenched a little.

"Then you double owe me, Morbier." She kissed him on both cheeks, then grabbed her jean jacket from the rack. She nodded to an officer she recognized from his undercover unit before she noticed Saj de Rosnay, the cash-poor aristocrat and Leduc Detective's part-time hacker, standing at reception.

"You need bail, Aimée?" Saj worried the sandalwood beads around his neck.

"*Non*, just a ride, Saj. And I borrowed your thumb-drive—owe you a new one. We've got work to do tonight. Feel like takeout?"

"But I thought you'd been arrested." He sniffed. "Drinking?" His jaw dropped. "What the hell have you been doing?"

"Morbier and I made up, but I had to play his game."

"Didn't look like poker to me." His eyebrows rose.

"He needed last-minute help with a sting. Long story."

Outside on the dark, narrow street, the locked exit of the Catacombs glowed under a street lamp. The car was parked in front of an old forge, horseshoes visible high on the façade. Saj unlocked the door for her. He took the wheel of René's beloved vintage Citroën DS, a classic entrusted to Saj temporarily until René had a chance to settle in San Francisco. Saj readjusted the custom seat controls, which were usually fitted for René's short legs. A pang went through her.

"You know, that could have gone very badly," Saj told her. "You took my technology without asking—what if I had had important client files on that drive? Warn me next time, Aimée, when you're putting the business at risk."

Her cheeks reddened as the Citroën's heated leather seat began to warm her derrière. "*Desolée*, Saj, I didn't think—"

"*Comme toujours*," Saj interrupted, exasperation in his tone. "Isn't it time you started thinking of the consequences before jumping into these dangerous schemes?"

Guilt assailed her. This was worse than her usual tactlessness—she'd been plain stupid. She needed Saj more than ever right now; she couldn't afford to lose him. Or stress him out. "Saj, I only had two hours to put this together. But you're right," she said, trying to sound contrite.

"What about my thumb-drive prototypes? I'm supposed to test them."

"I only borrowed one." She unclipped her hoop earrings, wondering how to make it up to him. "*La police* kept it as evidence. You'll get it back with the court files erased and good as new."

A crow cawed from outside the car window. There it was, looking down on the church, perched on the charcuterie's façade. She caught its beady black-eyed stare. Bad luck, her *grand-mère* would say.

"I won't hold my breath," Saj said, shifting into first.

"Consider the thumb-drive a rental. Morbier needs me to testify." She cringed at the thought. She hated the cold marble-floored tribunal, the smell of fear and authority.

Saj didn't reply, just nudged the Citroën out into the street. Aimée ran her fingers through her blonde-streaked shag-cut hair, wishing she hadn't run out of mousse. An evening of reports stretched ahead. They were barely coping with René's workload.

"It's a good time for you to start being honest with me about your other side-jobs." A thick envelope landed in her lap. The second tonight.

"What's this?" she asked, surprised.

"You tell me," Saj said.

Inside the envelope she found a bundle of worn franc notes and a card embossed with YURI VOLODYA, 14 VILLA D'ALÉSIA and a phone number. On the back: *Accept this retainer. Contact me. Urgent.*

She had no idea who this Yuri Volodya was. "Out of the blue, this man gives you . . . when?"

"This afternoon."

"*Une petite seconde*, did you speak with him?"

Saj said, "I told him to call you."

She'd turned her cell phone ringer off. Now she checked for messages. The same number had called twice but left no message.

"Some scam?" Another five thousand francs tonight. "We're busy. How could you accept this without an explanation?"

"I didn't—he mentioned being a family friend. Protecting his painting. Said you'd understand."

"Understand?" She shook her head. "What did he mean, family friend? You think an old colleague of my father's?"

"Your mother, he said."

For a moment everything shifted; she felt the oxygen being sucked from the car. Her pulse thudded. Her American mother, who was on the world security watch list? "How did he know my mother?"

Saj downshifted. "So he's trouble, *non?*"

She hit the number. No answer. "What else did he say?"

"That's all." Saj shrugged. "Even if his money's good, this smells bad. *Alors*, Aimée, we need to keep on track. We need to spend our time figuring out how to juggle all René's projects and keep our existing clients happy. We don't have time for whatever this is."

Anxious, she tried the man's number again. She needed to know more. A friend of her mother's? But no answer.

"We will sort it all out, Saj. But turn around. Let's meet this Monsieur Volodya."

"Didn't you say takeout?" Saj said.

The last thing Aimée was in the mood for was food. But she needed to do something for Saj. She also needed to talk to this man Yuri, and return his money. Her nerves jangled.

"Yes, takeout," she said. "My treat."

Saj downshifted off the boulevard into the honeycomb of

tiny lanes of small houses, ateliers, and old warehouses. A long-time resident, he knew the best routes to take at this time of night. The quartier was a less well-heeled bourgeois-bohemian version of adjoining Montparnasse, complete with mounting rents. Saj complained that the former ateliers of famous Sur-realists and Picasso now belonged to bohemian-chic residents whose trust funds couldn't quite afford the 6th arrondissement.

Twenty minutes later the couscous *végétarien* takeout sat on the backseat, the turmeric and mint smells reminding Aimée she'd forgotten dinner. But she had no appetite. Yuri Volodya still didn't answer his phone. Was it worth going to the address on the card? Part of her wanted Saj to drop her off at the Métro so she could head home and collapse in her bed. The other part knew she wouldn't be able to rest until she discovered why he'd sent this, and what his connection was to her mother.

The Citroën bumped over the cobbles. She wished Saj would slow down. He unclipped his seat belt, reached in the backseat for his madras cloth bag. Popped some pills from a pill case.

"What's wrong? Your chakras misaligned again?"

"Try some." He dropped a fistful of brown pellets into her hand. "Herbal stress busters. Works every time, remember?"

"*Bien sûr,*" she said, chewing her lip. His fungus-scented pellets reminded her of rabbit droppings. "We'll make it work without René," she added. "We should think of his amazing job offer. This opportunity for him."

Inside she thought only of the hole he'd leave. *Selfish Aimée, as usual.*

"René didn't trust me or the business, Saj. *Avec raison,*" she said, hating to admit it. She couldn't compete with René's job offer—six figures, stock options, and the title of CTO, Chief Technology Officer.

"Maybe René doesn't trust himself right now," Saj said, pensive. Apart from the purring motor, quiet filled the car. He was right; René had moped around, couldn't concentrate after his broken heart.

"We should do some more asana breathing sessions," Saj went on. "It will expand your awareness and you'll feel less stressed."

Not this again. She almost threw the pellets at him.

"Make a right here, Saj." She hoped they hadn't made a wasted trip.

He turned into Villa d'Alésia, a tree-lined lane lit by old-fashioned lampposts. Suddenly, a white van lurched in front of them. Saj honked the horn and downshifted. The van shot ahead, its hanging muffler scraping the cobbles, and turned out of sight.

Aimée scanned the house numbers for number fourteen. From the corner of her eye she caught a figure flashing in front of the Citroën's grill. A man's blue jean jacket shone in the headlights' yellow beam.

"Look out, Saj!" she shouted.

Horrified, her right arm shot out against the dashboard, while out of instinct she threw her other arm protectively across Saj's chest.

Saj punched the brakes. Squeals and then a horrible thump as the man hit the windshield. For a second the man's pale face pressed against the glass, his half-lidded eyes vacant, his palms splayed.

The man crumpled off the side of the car as Saj veered to the side. Too late. The Citroën jolted, hitting an old parked Mercedes. The metal screeched as it accordioned; the car shuddered. Cold air tinged by burning rubber poured over her face.

The impact set off the alarms of parked cars, a shrill honking cacophony. A hiss of steam escaped the Citroën's crushed radiator.

Her bag had fallen from the dashboard—mascara, keys, and encryption manuals spilling on the floor. Saj's body hung over the steering wheel. Good God, he'd taken off his seat belt.

"Saj, can you hear me?"

He stirred, rubbed his head.

"The *mec* came out of nowhere," he said. And before she could struggle out of her seat belt, Saj pushed open the dented door. He staggered in shock, his pale dreadlocks hanging in the yellow slants of the headlights. "*Mon Dieu,* I killed him."

Aimée's door jammed against the Mercedes. She climbed out of the driver's seat, then realized her phone was somewhere on the car floor. Stunned, she tried to take in the dark, wet lane, the body lying beside the car. Saj limping and clutching his neck.

A woman down the street, gripping a gym bag, ran toward them. Green surgical scrubs showed under her short brown jacket.

"Call for help," Aimée shouted. "Ambulance!"

"*Quelle catastrophe,*" said the woman. She pulled out her cell phone. "And I just finished my shift at the hospital."

The nurse knelt down beside the steaming car, the hem of her green scrubs trailing on the oil-slicked cobbles. With the nurse attending to the victim, Aimée hurried toward Saj. "What hurts? Can you move your neck?"

"Where did he come from? I didn't see him until he. . . ."

Dazed, Saj touched his temple. Grimaced in pain. She realized he was in shock, and guided him to a low stone wall.

"Stay here, Saj," she said.

"Help's coming," the nurse was saying to the motionless man. Apart from the cuts on his face, the man could have been asleep. "The hospital's two blocks away. Can you hear me?"

Not even a groan.

It had happened so fast, one minute she and Saj were talking and then . . . Aimée realized she might be in shock herself. She struggled to focus, became aware of the nurse's thrusts to the man's chest. The whining echo of a siren. Approaching red flashes splashed the walls. Lights went on in the windows of the adjoining alley.

Suppressing a shudder, Aimée watched the nurse put her index and middle finger on the man's carotid artery.

"No pulse," she said.

Aimée gasped. She looked closer at the man's pallor, his fresh facial cuts and scratches. "But he's not bleeding anywhere."

The shifting of the fire truck's gears swallowed the nurse's reply. The red lights reflected on the water pooled between the cobble cracks and on the roof tiles of the two-story ateliers.

Saj shivered in his thin muslin shirt, his sandalwood prayer beads tangled with his dreads. He had a glassy look as he spoke to the first response team. As if in a nightmare, Aimée watched the helmeted *sapeurs-pompiers* confer with the nurse beside René's Citroën. The arriving medic tried for vitals and shook his head.

They lifted the body onto the stretcher. The man's torn jeans were oil-spattered; his lifeless, pale arm fell limp, exposing the blue tattoos peeking from beneath the rolled-up sleeve of his Levi's jacket. Cyrillic letters intertwined in an elaborate figure of a wolf.

Нада и вера

"He's Russian?" she said to the medic who was putting a blood pressure cuff on Saj's arm.

"Worse," said the medic, a thin-mustached twenty-something. "A Serb."

Shivering, Aimée stared closer at the tattoo. "How can you tell?"

"Believe me, as the son of a Ukrainian dissident, I'm supposed to hate both Russians and Serbs." He pointed to the script. "See there? Serbian uses Cyrillic and Latin script. The Serb mafia tattoo themselves like that in prison."

Her blood ran cold. *Serb mafia?*

The medic clipped a Styrofoam brace around Saj's neck, then draped a blanket across his shivering shoulders. Then he took Aimée aside. "You look pale. We'll bring you in for observation."

"I'm fine." Aimée was loath to share how shaken she felt. How her stomach churned at the image of the man's white face, his half-lidded eyes reminding her of the fish on ice in the market. His palms splayed on the windshield. His tattoo.

"If we hadn't driven up this street to find. . . ." Her words left her. It spun in her mind that a man she didn't know who knew her mother had sent her an envelope of cash.

"Fate. Accidents happen, terrible," the medic said. He took her vitals. "Your blood pressure's a bit high." He put a stethoscope to her chest.

"But we ran him over," she said, hesitating. "There's something wrong—"

"You feel guilty, that's natural," he interrupted. "But if it happened as you say, it's not your fault."

Her shoulders shook. She couldn't get the words out, but any medic should be able to see the Serb didn't look like a man who'd been hit by a car.

"Alors." The medic leaned forward. "We've treated Serbs who were injured after bar brawls and knife fights here in the quartier."

"How's that supposed to make me feel better?"

He scanned the street, nodded to a colleague who assisted Saj toward the ambulance. "Between us," he said, lowering his voice, "I'd say watch your back."

But who was this Serb? Why hadn't anyone come out to identify him after the sirens, the commotion?

Her jacket whipped in the rising wind. She turned to see the van waiting for the corpse, engine running, as the flics arrived. Before she could get past the crowd, the medic bundled Saj into a waiting blue-and-white SAMU van. The engine rumbled, backing out down the lane.

Too late.

A *flic* escorted the nurse to a police van that had been set up for questioning. Aimée followed. "Wait your turn, Mademoiselle."

"But my friend's hurt." Shaken up, tired, and cold, she wanted to get this over with. "I need to get to the hospital."

"Where he's going you can't visit him."

The hair stood up on her neck. "You've taken him in *garde à vue?*"

"*C'est de rigueur*, questioning and treatment, Mademoiselle."

She knew the criminal ward at Hôtel-Dieu, the public hospital.

"But it was an accident, this man came out of nowhere and landed on our windshield."

"That's up to our investigation," he said, checking for messages on his cell phone. "Right now we're calling it a *homicide involontaire*."

Her heart dropped. Saj could face a charge of manslaughter. Saj? A gentle soul who meditated and spent months in ashrams in India. A hacker genius who could paralyze the French bourse, bring a Ministry database to its knees, but wouldn't hurt a fly. It made her sick to think they suspected him.

"*Zut alors*, Saj swerved trying to avoid this man."

"So he'd had a few drinks, eh?"

Again, the *flic* was off base. "Saj drinks green tea."

"Immediate blood tests and alcohol level analysis will confirm that." He nodded to the crime scene unit to tape off the area. "What's your worry?"

"The victim's injuries." She pointed to the dry cobbles. "Do you see any blood here?"

But he'd already gone to join several officers near the ambulance.

She hated waiting. Hated thinking of Saj being questioned in the criminal ward. The Mercedes' smashed grill leaked water;

escaping radiator steam hovered cloud-like over the hood. At least the car alarms had subsided.

A stocky man of medium height, bundled into a black lamb-fur coat—the kind she hadn't seen since the seventies—and a Russian fur hat ran toward them. His gaze took in the ambulance. Short of breath, he paused and shook his head. "*Mon Dieu.* Someone hurt?" There was shock and concern in his voice.

"Dead," muttered someone in the crowd. A finger pointed at her. The Mercedes.

"My car? Think you can get away with smashing my car, too?"

Aimée flinched.

Just what she needed. René's insurance would go sky-high. Another layer of guilt descended on her. René hadn't been gone twenty-four hours and they'd run over a Serb and totaled his prized car.

"An angry little Cossack," said one of the firemen under his breath. "The only things missing are his boots."

"*Restez tranquille,* Monsieur," Aimée said. "I'll take care of the damages."

Aimée noted a long-haired young man, a cell phone to his ear, rushing up behind the older man. An armband encircled his khaki jacket sleeve. "What's happened to your car?"

The old man waved him away. "I'll handle this, Damien."

His brows knit in worry. "But you need my help."

"Go back to the hospital," the old man said. "Your aunt's more important."

"You're sure?" said Damien, his tone conflicted.

The old man nodded. Aimée heard the slap of Damien's footsteps as he disappeared into the shadows.

"So you don't have insurance, Mademoiselle?" The man's face flushed. "I know your type, you want to rip me off. Offer to fix my car but sell the parts. You some gypsy?"

"Do I look like a gypsy?" He grated on Aimée's nerves. Saj injured, a man dead, and now this callous car owner. "I'll have your car repaired."

"Think I'll fall for that old trick?" Suspicion showed in his watery blue eyes. He gave a quick shake of his head. "Don't think you're leaving, Mademoiselle."

She had no intention of leaving—not until she had done everything she could to save René's insurance. But before she could respond, a *flic*, notepad out, asked for the car registration. She opened the intact door on the driver's side and reached into the glove compartment. Felt René's kid leather driving gloves. Size *petit*. A pang went through her.

After handing the *flic* René's car registration and scooping up the contents of her bag from the floor, she shifted on her high-tops, awaiting questioning. The crime scene unit photographer's flash emitted bursts of light. She caught sight of the old man a few meters away—he was opening the door to Number 14. He had to be the man she'd come to see, Yuri Volodya! She hurried after the old man just as he disappeared behind the gate.

"Monsieur . . . Monsieur Volodya?" she called out.

No answer. As she reached the darkened front door of the atelier, Aimée heard the tinkle of broken glass. A cry. She reached out but felt only cold air.

"Monsieur?" Her eyes tried to adjust to the dank vacuum in front of her. "What happened?"

"My door was open, the lights don't work," he said, his voice quavering. "I've been robbed."

Aimée's spine tingled. Smart thieves short-circuited electricity these days. With a tickle of intuition, she wondered if this was connected to the Serb they'd run over outside his door.

She rooted in her secondhand Vuitton bag until she found her penlight. Shined it on the man's confused face. A trickle of blood trailed on his cheek. He'd cut himself on broken glass.

"Where's your fuse box, Monsieur?"

"What good will that do?"

Did he want to argue now? "I'll try to switch the power back on."

She followed the old man across the creaking floorboards, glass crackling underfoot. A musty scent of paper emanated from the shadows. In the thin yellow beam she saw the problem right away. She pulled on her leather gloves and with a quick flick switched the fuse box levers upright.

Light flooded the sparsely furnished turn-of-the-century atelier. A worn velvet armchair had been overturned. A vase lay on its side, orange marigold petals scattered and water pooled on a long worktable.

Horrible. She pitied the old codger. His car, now his house.

"Monsieur Volodya? That's you, non? I'm Aimée Leduc, you sent for me. I'm so sorry about your car, but I hope—"

"Forget about the car." He grabbed at a dark wood beam in the wall, his bony white wrists shaking. Reminding her of her grandfather. She righted the chair, took his elbow to help him sit down. Dazed, he resisted, refusing to sit. With his thick fingers he smeared the blood on his cheek. Shock painted his face.

"I think you should see a doctor."

"Wait . . ."

With surprising agility he hurried to the armoire, which had been shoved aside. She followed, noticing the small door behind it. Like a broom closet. A dark red stain smeared the wood door.

Blood.

He pulled the creaking door open. Empty. Anguish painted his face. "You're too late. My painting's stolen."

"You kept a painting in a broom closet? A valuable painting?"

"But I locked it. It was only until the formal appraisal tomorrow." His lip quivered. "My legs feel not so steady."

His face had gone white. This time, he let her help him to the chair. "Let me get you water."

He shook his head. "Vodka." He pointed to the galley kitchen. A show of bravado, or to calm his nerves? But he looked like he needed it. She'd humor him until he explained. Then alert the *flics*.

The dark wood-walled atelier held an open mezzanine above, a cramped kitchen off to the side, an alcove with faded flowered wallpaper, and a bed covered by a rumpled duvet.

At the empty sink she wetted an embroidered towel, noticed the dish rack with a single plate, cup, and fork. The old man lived alone. Tidy. In the one cupboard she found a bottle of Stolichnaya, two glasses.

Could the Serb have been the one who robbed the old man? Caught in the act, she figured. But he hadn't been carrying anything. Definitely not a painting.

"Now how do you feel?" She uncapped and poured the vodka. Handed him the towel.

"A scratch," he said, clinked her shot glass. "I'm Yuri Volodya."

"I know. You sent me five thousand francs." She set down her card on the side table.

"So of course you came," he said. "But too late. Hand me my glasses."

Stubborn old Cossack, all right.

"There's a pair hanging from your neck," she said. "What's this all about?"

He put on his glasses, and his voice changed. "You look just like her."

Hope fluttered in her heart. "*Maman?* She's alive?"

He shook his head. Winced in pain. "Forgive me. I thought you could help. You see, I owe your mother."

"I don't understand. Help how? And owe my mother what? When did you last see her?"

He averted his eyes and swigged the vodka. "I'm a book-binder, I craft special editions. A commission takes a year." He rubbed his thumb and fingertips together.

Why had he changed the subject? Nerves? He seemed anxious now, worried. Like he was saying one thing but meaning another.

"*Alors*, Monsieur Volodya, if we could talk about my mother, this painting. . . ."

"My craft's for *les connaisseurs, vous savez*," he said, as if she hadn't spoken. "A certain clientele who appreciate the feel of a hand-bound book, the presentation of prints inside. Salvador Dalí commissioned my work, *des gens comme ça*." Apart from his odd sentence structure—as if he translated from Russian construction—he spoke with a pure Parisian accent.

Under her boot she felt something hard and round. A brass button embossed with LEVI'S. Like the brass buttons on the Serb's jean jacket. Her heart skipped. "What if this fell off the Serb's jacket?"

"That man you ran over?" Yuri's teary blue eyes widened. "Blame it on the Serb curse."

"Meaning?"

"We have a saying about Serbs: An unfortunate man would be drowned in a teacup. But of that man I know nothing. Nothing."

She doubted that. "I think this button came from his jean jacket. Maybe he trashed this place and came up empty."

Yuri's shoulders sagged, and the lines framing his mouth grew more pronounced. A quick scan told her the intruder knew exactly what to look for and where. The leather-bound books lining the shelves were untouched, as was an antique iron book-press on the worktable. An open calendar and note-pad lay undisturbed on the desk.

"Life kicks one in the gut and we're surprised?" he said. "As if one is the exception, not the rule?"

Since when do people refer to themselves in the third person, she wondered. *An old-world thing?*

"Monsieur Volodya, I'm here to return your money."

"Keep it. Find my painting."

"Art recovery's not my line of work," she said, suspecting he'd mentioned her mother as a ruse. This smelled off.

"I'll make up a list, tell you everything."

Everything? "Tell me how you know my mother."

His left hand trembled slightly. "Please, in my own way. Give me a moment."

It was foolish to rush him. Of course he was still in shock. He'd seen a man die, his car damaged, and his home burglarized all within a short time.

"Damien, my neighbor, the political boy, just brought me back from dinner at Oleg's place. Oleg's my stepson, as he calls himself. My wife's child. Not mine." Yuri's voice rose, petulant. "Oleg's wife served burnt blinis, like cement—can you imagine?"

Aimée contained her impatience with effort. "Why contact me to protect your painting?"

"Pour me another."

Frustrated, she reached for the bottle. His liver-spotted hand clamped on her gloved one with surprising strength. His confusion was gone.

"If the Serb left empty-handed," he said, "someone else didn't."

He knew something. She saw it in his eyes. Suspicion filled her.

"So you claim a painting is missing, but the man who appears to have broken into your house didn't have it. Strange, Monsieur. And I still don't understand what any of this has to do with my mother." She sipped the vodka. "Why do I feel all this is some ruse?"

There was fear in his eyes. He downed the vodka. His hand clenched in a fist, his knuckles white. "I've been rude to you, I'm sorry."

He was wasting time she should have been using to help Saj. "*S'il vous plaît*, Monsieur Volodya, quit the guessing games." She was angry with herself for getting caught up in this, for buying into his fishy story just because he'd mentioned her mother.

"So help me. I know you're a detective. I wanted to hire you to protect the painting, but now it's too late for that. I'm hiring you to get it back for me instead."

Like she needed to add to Leduc Detective's workload. They were already drowning. "Like I said, Monsieur, we don't do art recovery." She couldn't resist adding, "You didn't really know my mother, did you?"

"Of course I knew your mother. The American."

Aimée gripped his hand. "How?"

"It's complicated." He stiffened. "I didn't know her well."

Aimée didn't know her well, either. Sydney Leduc had abandoned them when Aimée was eight years old. "But you knew her. When?" Hope fluttered despite his vagueness.

"Of course, she was much younger then. Changed a little, but . . . it's been years."

Years? Her heart sank. "Where . . . how?"

"Now I want to make good on my debt."

"Debt?" Why wouldn't he give her a straight answer? "Is this about the painting?"

Footsteps crackled over the glass, and a draft of cold air rushed through the atelier. "Monsieur?" It was the *flic* with the clipboard.

"Please, Monsieur, how do you know my mother?"

"Not now." Yuri put his finger to her lips. Dry, rough skin.

She'd had enough. She reached into her bag for the francs, about to tell him to forget involving her, when he whispered,

"I'm being watched." He held her hand. "Tomorrow. Wait for my call. I'll tell you about her."

"But I can't take your money—"

"Recover my painting."

"Monsieur, I need your car registration," said the *flic*. He glanced around, noticing the scattered objects. "Your house was broken into as well? Is anything missing?"

"My wife. She died last year."

"*Desolé,*" he said. "But I'll need to take down the accident details before I make a robbery report."

"No report," Yuri said, shaking his head. His defiance belied the fear in his eyes. "I'm remodeling."

She wondered why the old man was lying.

The *flic*'s eyes narrowed. Maybe he wondered the same thing. Yuri pulled open a drawer in the Art Nouveau chest, the most expensive-looking piece in the room. Took out a folder and handed it over.

As the officer noted the vehicle info, Aimée watched Yuri sit hunched in his chair, his mouth set, the blood clotting on his cheek. She wasn't sure she believed him about her mother, or trusted him about his missing painting, but she felt pity for him.

"Let me ask a medic to look at your cut, Monsieur."

He waved his wrinkled hand in dismissal. "Now both of you get out."

OUTSIDE YURI'S DOOR on narrow Villa d'Alésia her hands shook. A man dead, her friend injured and in police custody, an old man who claimed to know her mother, and now a stolen painting. A sour aftertaste remained in her mouth and it wasn't from the vodka.

The day had gone from bad to worse after René's departure. She wanted this all to go away. To go home, crawl under the duvet. But first she had to help Saj.

Aimée needed her laptop case and reached for the car door handle. Couscous *végétarien* dripped all over the back floor.

"Not so fast, Mademoiselle," said a balding *flic*. "I'll need to search the car. And you."

They suspected her now? "Search the car? I tell you, the man ran into us. Not our fault." She hoped to God that René hadn't left his unlicensed Glock under the seat.

"If you're in such a hurry, better give me the details at the *commissariat*, Mademoiselle."

A "midnight special" in a wire-frame holding pen? Forget it. Weren't they supposed to offer her a trauma counselor?

"You call that procedure?" She flashed her *détective privé* license at him. Time to pull out the big guns. "I'm sure my god-father Commissaire Morbier will be interested, since that's his dinner all over the floor." A little lie, as Morbier's appetite ran to *bifteck-frites*. But a way to take the focus away from her—and maybe divert it to Yuri. She gestured to the spilled takeout. "Care to explain to him why you think picking up takeout some-how involves me in the robbery of an old Russian man's atelier?"

The *flic*'s mouth tightened. "Morbier's into couscous *végé-tarien* now?"

So he knew Morbier better than she'd guessed. Oh well, she had to roll with it now. "Part of his new healthier lifestyle." One could always hope.

"Robbery of the old Russian, you said, Mademoiselle?" The *flic* didn't miss a thing.

She nodded. Let him draw his own conclusions when he saw the blood behind the old man's armoire. "Too bad you can't ask the Serb about the robbery. Right place, right time for him to know something." She shivered, pulling her jacket tighter. "Don't you find it strange the victim didn't bleed? There's no blood here on the street. Do you understand it?"

"No, I don't." He shrugged. "Maybe there was internal bleeding. We'll know after the autopsy."

The tow-truck driver's horn shrieked a blasting echo off the stone walls. "Finished?" he yelled out the window to a crime scene tech. "Last run tonight. I need to hook up the cars and process them at the yard before it closes."

"Take your things, Mademoiselle." The *flic* waved to the crime scene tech and hurried ahead. "Open them up, show the officer." He paused and turned back, his shoe squeaking on the stone. "And the trunk."

AFTER FINALLY GIVING her statement, Aimée hurried down the cobbled lane. In the brisk chill, she searched her old address book for the fifth-floor criminal ward phone number in Hôtel-Dieu. She hoped her contact, Nora, a nurse, was working the night shift.

"Nora's off," said an older female voice laced with irritation. "Who's this?"

She needed to know Saj's condition and hated dealing with the notoriously close-mouthed police medical unit. She thought quick. "Traffic division in the fourteenth arrondissement. Any status update on the man injured in the collision fatality on Villa d'Alésia?"

"But I don't even have your report yet. Why so eager?"

"Make my life easy tonight, eh? The medics checked his vitals and took him for observation. Didn't even list suspected concussion, head injury, whiplash, or superficial injuries. I need a possible diagnosis for my report."

Yells and shouts came over the line.

"We're busy tonight," she said, "must be a full moon. I'll get back to you later."

"New regulations," Aimée said. "We need to fill in all the boxes and I've got a few empty. Please."

Sigh. "Just a moment. The patient's here. I'll ask his doctor."

"*Parfait.*" She had an idea. "I know you've got other patients. Put me on speakerphone with the doctor, it's faster."

Another sigh. The click of a button. A rush of background noise. "Doctor Robler speaking," said a crackling speakerphone voice. "The patient shows possible shoulder muscle and neck injury."

Poor Saj. "The patient's with you? You're taking him for X-rays?"

"*Bien sûr*," said Doctor Robler, "but after his questioning."

Alarm spread over her. "Saj, only give your statement," she said, hoping he was in earshot.

"Aimée?" It was Saj's voice, tired and confused.

"There's a robbery involved. Say nothing else until. . . ."

A loud buzz. The speakerphone disconnected.

Monday, 9:30 P.M.

MORGANE WATCHED HER accomplice, Flèche, peer out the half-open blue shutter. In the moonlight, tendrils of ivy curved over the potted geraniums on the window ledge. Morgane hated working with amateurs. Amateurs with hairy palms, her uncle would say, so lazy they grew hair on their palms.

Where the hell was Servier? Twenty minutes late already and they didn't have much time to hand over the goods. Her ears perked up as the gate clicked open below.

Flèche shook his head. "Just the hipster with a new conquest, like clockwork." He yawned, running a matchstick under his fingernail. A pigeon cooed from the low rooftop of a two-story house across the courtyard. "Bores me stiff."

"That's a good thing," Morgane said. Her shirt collar, damp with perspiration, weighed on her neck. She gathered her lank brown hair in a twist and clipped it up on her head.

"Too quiet. I don't like it."

Wary, she checked the walkie-talkie signal. All bars lit. "Nothing from control. Nerves got you?" Was he worried about the talkative owner of the *café-tabac* around the corner, where he'd bought cigarettes an hour ago? Like she'd told him not to. Never leave a presence, she'd warned him. "You think there's a spotter?"

"I mean it's dead here," Flèche said. "Old people, kids practicing piano after dinner, the retiree on the ground floor who never goes out. Spooks me."

"She's agoraphobic." That was the one Morgane worried about. An insomniac who telephoned her brother in Marseilles every night. A watcher with eyes like a crow's. "You're correct. It is dead quiet. The perfect place to hide." She'd told him time and again. The 14th arrondissement was ideal, residential, a mix of working-class and arty types. "You know, at the turn of the century, the tsar's Okhrana had more secret agents hidden in this quartier than in Saint Petersburg."

"Merde. Don't start with the history lessons again."

"Hasn't changed much. These people mind their business. Working-class solidarity."

He flicked his cigarette ash in the Ricard ashtray, stuck the cigarette back in his mouth and inhaled. In the dark, the red-orange glow from the burning tip made his face look ethereal. "A bunch of Commies."

She rolled her eyes. The Wall came down in 1989. "Who calls anyone Communists any more?"

Nearby lay Parc Montsouris, sloping grass hills and the reservoir, just beyond la petite ceinture—the abandoned and overgrown rail tracks edging the old Montrouge quartier. She'd grown up in the clustered lanes of small houses. Generations of her family had been dairy farmers here. Now almost all the farms were gone.

But she knew the quartier in the marrow of her bones, from the Montparnasse artist ateliers on rue Campagne Première—including famous ones, like Gaugin's and Picasso's—where publishing bohos now lived, to the Catacombs at Place Denfert-Rochereau, the only tourist attraction. The screams piercing the night from the psychiatric hospital of Sainte Anne. The nineteenth-century prison of La Santé hunkered scab-like on the fragrant lime-tree-lined Boulevard Arago.

A good place to lie low. Wait for the drop. And strategic. Access to the Périphérique ring road less than two kilometers away. A quick twenty minutes to the baggage handler connection at Orly Airport. Morgane could almost taste success.

The walkie-talkie squawked. "Painting arrived?"

Morgane's lips pursed. "Not yet," she responded. Late. Even using the van, he was late for a simple snatch-and-grab. She hit the talk button. "Complications?"

"Unclear. We're in a holding pattern."

But the cargo plane wasn't. This was their only chance until next week.

"Keep me updated." The walkie-talkie channel went yellow.

"Something's wrong," Morgane said.

Flèche checked his watch. "I'll say. He's not the type to go drinking. But I'm going to find out."

Dumb. How in the hell did he ever get the nickname Flèche, "sharp arrow"? Slow and dull were more like it.

"Wait until—"

"My cut disappears?" Flèche shook his head. Picked up his shearling jacket.

"You'll ruin the plan, Flèche," she said. "Screw up the timing."

"Since when are you my boss?"

She wished he'd shut up. Hated working with a loose cannon.

"We all want this to go smooth, perform our roles. Yours is to. . . ."

She paused. They both heard the click from the courtyard door below. She put her finger to her mouth. Footsteps padded on the wet pavers, mounted the staircase until they stopped outside the door.

One knock. The signal. He was here.

Tuesday Morning

RAPHAEL DOMBASLE'S NOSE twitched as he studied the small painting in the Montparnasse gallery's back room. His nose hadn't twitched like this since he recovered the stolen Renoir in 1996 from a battered suitcase in the Gare du Nord left luggage. But he kept his face blank as he turned to the art dealer Luebet.

"No provenance? Or certificate of authenticity, Luebet?" he said, his fingers running over the painting's carved frame. "So it's stolen?"

"That's why I alerted you, Dombasle." Luebet gave a tight smile. Long white hair framed his hollowed face and brushed the blue jacket collar of his tailored pinstripe suit. A little *phhft* escaped his pursed lips. "The seller gave me a verbal agreement to furnish the painting's provenance, of course, like they all do. But I knew right away."

Of course he did. Small figure studies like this rarely came on the market or through an art dealer.

"But I'm acting in good faith, Dombasle."

Dombasle figured Luebet had only alerted him because he'd been unable to sell the painting fast, before Interpol consulted the Art Data Registry. Luebet kept hands in both pots, as the saying went. The kind of informer who delivered when it suited him. Dombasle wondered at the timing.

"You'd rather a recovery fee than prison. Come out on the right side this time."

"I thought we had an agreement, Dombasle." Luebet's voice tightened. "We share information, like last time. Why insult me when I follow the law?" Luebet shook his head.

"You haven't heard me insult you. But I could." Dombasle pulled out his tape measure and assessed the small canvas, but it was just a formality. He recognized the painting, which had been stolen during the bold daylight heist of a Left Bank townhouse. This painting was a perfect match, even to the stained signature. An early Berthe Morisot. A jewel of delicate brushstrokes, a charcoal-and-aquarelle study of a mother and child under a garden trellis—her signature subjects. The *comtesse* had allowed it to be photographed for the glossy architectural magazine's ten-page spread of her townhouse collection—stupid. When the rich advertised what they had and where they kept it, what did they expect?

Luebet shrugged. Lit a cigarette and hit the air filter machine, which erupted in a whirr. "A cigarette is the perfect type of a perfect pleasure," he said. "Exquisite, and it leaves one unsatisfied, to quote Oscar Wilde. What more can one want?"

Dombasle watched the dealer expel a stream of smoke. "So the *comtesse's* other stolen works. . . ."

"Went the way of the ghost. Vanished. Or so the rumor goes."

"Care to elucidate, Luebet?"

Luebet shrugged. "Use your imagination."

"Any Baltic accents attached to the rumors?" Dombasle asked. Eastern Europeans exchanged stolen paintings for arms or jewels or drugs—not so picky. Last year a Serbian militant was caught pulling Chagalls from his Zagreb basement to trade for a fleet of armor-plated Land Rovers. In turf wars, art was a gold bar of exchange for such gangs, who cared nothing for it but as a commodity.

Luebet, who had been prominent in the art world for forty years, sighed. "Or they've gone to Moscow-on-Thames." The Russian oligarch billionaires bought up country manors around

London with irritating efficiency. Kept the UK economy afloat. Too bad that hadn't happened here since the eighties with the Japanese château-buying frenzy. "The young breed operates pipelines outside my sources." Luebet shrugged. "We're old, *compris?* There's a new generation."

True. Dombasle wanted to get this over with, but sensed Luebet had another agenda. "*Bon,* I'll contact the chief, he'll inform the *comtesse.*" Dombasle grinned. "The usual drill. Tell your seller you've found a client who wants a verbal provenance. Arrange a meeting. Say you'll bring the money. We'll do the rest." A cut-and-dried sting operation.

Luebet seemed to weigh his options. "*D'accord,*" he said finally. That hesitation in the dealer's look indicated he had more information—a tip, a name.

"Something else on your mind, Luebet?"

"Rumors."

"Concerning what, Luebet?"

"That's just it, rumors," Luebet said. "Years ago a story surfaced about a Modigliani that went missing in 1920—only shown once. Whispers only, you understand. That it's been found in France. Worth . . . well, for years its existence was the stuff of dreams. Now the whispers say right after it was discovered it went missing."

Dombasle knew the art dealer was fishing for something. Teasing the story out to find what Dombasle knew. But he wouldn't play.

"Luebet, is there a point to you spreading rumors?"

"Word goes a fixer, *une Américaine,* runs a network transporting certain *objets d'art.*"

Dombasle's nose twitched in full gear now. "The Modigliani?"

"Just rumors, as I said."

"I need more than rumors, Luebet," he said.

"*Alors,* I told you everything. . . ."

"Cut the act," Dombasle said. "You owe me, remember?"

RENÉ FRIANT'S HIP ached after the eleven-hour flight
and the long line at US immigration. Four feet tall, he stood
on tiptoe at the glass booth to pass over his French passport.

He smiled at the immigration officer. *"Bonjour."*

"You're a tourist, Mr. Friant?"

His promised work visa hadn't come through. Perspiration
dampened his shirt. Nervous, his mind went back to Tradelert's
last fax, which he'd memorized on the plane: *No problem, H-1B
visa's in the works. Soon as the green light comes, we whisk you over
the border at Mexicali, you come back in legal to work. Meanwhile
say you're consulting on a project for the week from Paris, no visa
required.*

René preferred to follow the rules and laws, at least more
than Aimée did. But the less said the better.

"For now, Monsieur."

A loud thump and TOURIST stamped on his passport. "Enjoy
your vacation."

Then an endless walk through the terminal with his bags,
goading the hip dysplasia pain. But currents of excitement ran
through him as he waited at the airport curb. The air felt different, the colors—the newness of everything struck him. Fog
settled over the taxis, the huge American cars.

"Over here, Tattoo," Kobo, Tradelert's rep, yelled from a
battered Volkswagen.

René grinned. "Where's the sun, Kobo?"

"You're thinking of LA." Kobo, tall and gangling, bent to give René a high five. A matchstick of a man, René thought, smelling of onions. Kobo tossed his bags in the backseat.

"But *Zeelakon Vallaaay*. . . ."

"We call it 'The Valley,' Tattoo," Kobo interrupted.

"What's with 'Tattoo'?"

"*De plane, de plane!*" Kobo laughed. "From the TV show *Fantasy Island*. Get it? You're wearing the same suit, too."

Wasn't Kobo too young to have seen that eighties show? Strange, but René recalled that Americans watched the *télé* all the time. René's aunt in the countryside stayed up late watching old reruns and made the same joke. Not that he found it funny. "Suit? *Oui*, but the weather doesn't cooperate." René smoothed down his beige linen jacket, wishing he'd packed his wool pinstripe.

The cramped VW was littered with food wrappers. "Andy's meeting with our investor angels." Kobo ground into first gear. "So I'll drop you off at the car rental and meet you at Tradelert later, okay?"

René needed to fire his brain cells for the meeting. Hit the ground running. There had to be a café somewhere.

The drive-through, as Kobo called it, served brown piss for coffee. Back on the highway, everything spread out before him was giant—the quadruple lanes, the cars, the sprawling flat buildings, the signs and billboards advertising lawyers to call if you've been in an accident. It all felt more foreign now than it had on his brief weekend trip for the interview.

He'd made the jump to a new life in a new country: a job—writing code, designing mainframes, running security—his métier—and a mission: to meet a woman, preferably a tan, leggy Californian who would sit with him under the palm trees and eat hamburgers. He felt the thrill of possibility. Time to leave the ghost of Meizi, that heartbreak.

"Everyone's so glad you're on board, part of the team."

"Me, too." René felt a flutter of pride.

"You're our distinguished French connection!" Another laugh as Kobo nudged him. He pulled into the parking lot of a car rental agency, let René out, waved, and took off in his battered VW.

Excited, René imagined the awaiting Jeep Cherokee he'd reserved. The job recruiter had raved about company bonding powwows in the countryside, "off-road"—wasn't that the term?

"Your reservation's confirmed for tomorrow," said the car rental agent, "not today, Mister Free-ant." René peered up at the Formica rental-car counter. The voice continued to boom like a loudspeaker above him. The gist of it was that the car with adaptations for his height hadn't arrived. He needed to clear his jetlag-fogged brain and think. He had a meeting with Tradelert's CEO in an hour. Thank God he'd gotten the international cell phone.

Kobo didn't answer. Time to call another friend.

"WELCOME TO THE Valley, René," said Bob, one hand on the baby-blue steering wheel of his big, finned 1974 Cadillac, the other draped over the passenger seat's shoulder rest. René had met Bob, a fellow programmer, last year when he'd come to Paris to work on a Netscape project. They had discovered a shared passion for vintage cars.

"Smart to snap you up," Bob said. "But why the hurry?"

"Seems everybody's gone into overdrive," René said. "New venture capital interest, so the agenda's on warp speed. We've got to get the security system up now. Such a challenge and thrill to get in on the ground floor."

"They're offering you stock options, right?" Bob turned down the radio, which was blasting Creedence Clearwater Revival.

René nodded. "I'm more interested in the work visa. I came in on a tourist—"

"Whoa, René, look out the window. See that temple?"

A gated block, the peaks of a tiled Japanese roof hinting at the wooden temple.

"No time for the scenic tour, Bob."

"A twenty-four-year-old owns that. Took it apart, brought it over piece by piece from Japan and reassembled it."

René nodded. "It's a gold rush, eh, Bob?"

"More like a bubble. Make your millions and get out. That's the smart thing."

As they drove south, the fog evaporated into piercing blue sky. To the west, clouds like tufts of cotton hovered over the range of coastal blue-purple mountains. Again he was hit by the immensity of everything.

"All this feels like CinemaScope. The colors like Technicolor. But I thought California would be hot."

"We're in the land of microclimates, René." Bob pulled into the motel off Alameda de las Pulgas. "Translates to 'Avenue of the Fleas.'"

A bilingual country—would he need to learn Spanish?

Bob grinned. "The fleas thrived here, sucking the conquistador's blood. But anyone can thrive here, René." Bob flicked the transmission into park. "No matter who you are, where you're from, or where your daddy went to school. Parlay your concept into money—that's what talks here. That's the Valley—never forget."

René checked into the motel. The receptionist shook his head. "We have your reservation booked for tomorrow."

Again?

"Alors, there's some mistake. I reserved one room."

"Mister Free-ant, right now the honeymoon suite's all that's available."

Complete with pink Jacuzzi.

René shrugged and passed over his credit card.

Ten minutes later, Bob dropped him off at Tradelert. "How about dinner where Steve and Larry eat sometimes?"

Bob spoke fast and René had trouble keeping up. Half the time he didn't catch what Bob meant and had to pretend otherwise. Had Bob mentioned these *mecs* before? "Your friends, Steve and Larry?"

"When anyone mentions Steve and Larry. . . ."

René caught himself before he gasped. Swallowed. "You mean Jobs and Ellison."

"As in Apple and Oracle, René. You need to pick up Valley lingo."

A different language all right.

Full of excitement at the vista opening up before him, René adjusted his new silk tie, the cuffs on his handmade Charvet shirt, and walked into the former Buick showroom, now Tradelert's new suite of offices. Bob had told him start-ups scrambled for space, often operating out of warehouses, attics, and garages until funded by venture capitalists; after they hit it big, they bought the building. Like Tradelert had.

The ceiling loomed over him, lost in popcorn stucco and fluorescent lighting. Everything was so high up. The office directory loomed several feet above his head on the wall. He bit his lip, wondering how he'd find his office and the meeting room. Of course, he was supposed to have been there five minutes ago. What about that special-needs accommodation, or whatever they called it, that he'd read about?

Feeling self-conscious, he grabbed an orange plastic chair and climbed up to read the office directory sign. But his name wasn't there. His nerves overtook him. Had he made a mistake, or had they changed their mind and hired someone else? Here he'd left Aimée and flown thousands of miles from his home and life.

To the left, on a corridor wall, in bright brass shone SECURITY DIVISION MEETING ROOMS 101–106. ROOM 104—RENÉ FRIANT, CHIEF TECHNOLOGY OFFICER. Pride coursed through him. He stepped off the plastic chair and ran down the corridor.

My new life's beginning, René thought. Forget the old, the past. Forget that momentary tug for Aimée, wondering if she was all right.

Of course she was.

Tuesday Morning, Paris

THE MIST CURLING on the Seine furred dawn's silver glow. Rain pattered on the grilled balcony outside Aimée's bedroom window. Miles Davis, her bichon frise, nestled on the silk duvet beside her while she monitored security reports on her laptop. Sleep eluded her. Images of the Serb on the windshield, the horrible thump, and that prison tattoo spun through her head.

Down on the quai a car's engine whined, a door slammed, and she heard a loud curse. Just the reaction René would have over his damaged car. The repairs would consume a big chunk of their bank account, but she had little choice. Volodya's refusal to report the robbery and his connection to her mother played in her head. A lie? If not, what was his debt to her? Had he been a snitch or some criminal involved in her past?

It smelled like ripe, three-day-old cheese. *When it smells,* Aimée's father always used to say, *sniff it out.*

Her phone rang. So early—but it was nine hours earlier in California. René calling to let her know he'd landed?

"Satisfied you've made me the laughingstock of the department, Leduc?" Morbier growled. "Count your favors used up."

Aimée cringed. So soon? She had to whip up a counterpoint defense for using his name last night. Deflect him. "*Bonjour* to you too, Morbier. Meaning what, exactly?"

"*Moi, un végétarien?*"

That's all? Miles Davis's wet nose nuzzled her elbow.

"Morbier, you're in desperate need of a healthy lifestyle to lower your cholesterol. Just listen to your doctor."

A snort. "Doctor? But I haven't seen him in. . . ."

"Two years. You keep putting off that appointment. But that's what he'd tell you."

"Seems you killed someone last night and involved me."

She chewed her lip. Word traveled fast. "Quite the way with words, Morbier," she said. "But you don't understand."

"Giving up meat, that's . . . that's so. . . ." Morbier's words failed him for once. "I've got a meeting in two minutes," he said. "Start talking, Leduc."

She hit SAVE on her laptop, pulled the duvet closer, took a breath and told him.

"Wait *une petite seconde*." Morbier sighed on the other end of the line. "You discover a Russian's sent you a retainer, *c'est ça?*"

"It's not like I planned this, Morbier. . . ."

"Then in front of this Russian's place Saj plows over a Serb with prison tattoos, damages René's car and the Russian's Mercedes. The Russian insists his painting was 'stolen.' Now he wants you to recover it." Another sigh. "That sum it up?"

Almost. She'd left out the part about her mother. Ever since the GIGN intelligence service had tried using her to find out whether her mother was alive, she trusted no one.

"The old man, Volodya, refused to report the robbery," she said. "Yet we hit a Serb in front of his place fleeing the scene. Strange, *non?*"

"You're implying a snatch-and-grab gone wrong? Easy to find Serbs for hire, a franc a dozen," Morbier said. "But not my call."

She didn't care for his brush-off, but it made her think. "Serbs working for a big cheese, you mean? If the Serbian mafia wants vengeance, that puts Saj in trouble."

"Manslaughter's what I call trouble, Leduc."

He had a point.

"What's the matter? It's not the first time you've knocked someone off, Leduc."

She wanted to hit him. "You call an accident knocking people off, Morbier?"

"Shaken a chink loose in your couture armor?"

Last night had rattled her more than she cared to admit. Why couldn't Morbier show sympathy? She jumped out of bed and hit the ancient steam radiator. For once it responded with a cranking noise and a welcome dribble of heat.

"I'd appreciate a flicker of sensitivity for once, Morbier." If only René hadn't left, if only the knot in her stomach would go away. Somehow her heart wasn't into toughing it out as usual. "The man fell on the windshield, we didn't run him over. Saj is injured and is being held in *garde à vue*. It's wrong."

"Traffic's not my territory, Leduc."

She wouldn't let him off. He owed her. "Who's the lord of the traffic division?"

"*Mais* you know him, Leduc, the officer who thinks I'm *végétarien*."

She groaned inside. "Put in a good word for Saj, eh?"

"Over lunch while I watch him consume a *bifteck?*"

"Amaze him with your power salad, Morbier. It's the new lunch. Get Saj released."

"Nothing happens until the autopsy report. You know that, Leduc," he said. "Like I haven't got enough on my plate without you restricting my diet. *Compris?*"

Over the phone came the familiar whistling of his old kettle in the background. How many times had she heard it in his kitchen as a child? The little girl inside her ached to question him about her mother's past, how Volodya might have known her. To throw away caution and endanger their rocky new reconciliation.

"The old Russian says he knew my—"

A woman's voice—"Coffee's ready"—interrupted her in the background.

She almost dropped her phone. Morbier with a woman? Only a few months after his lady friend Xavierre's death? "Did you get lucky last night, Morbier?"

He hung up.

Tactless again. She should be happy for him. Not let it jar her.

This conversation had done little to further Saj's cause. Yet despite Morbier's usual gruffness, she'd learned he had a new girlfriend, and that the Serb had probably worked for hire. That wouldn't help much with Saj's defense.

She speed-dialed her pathologist friend Serge's extension at the morgue. Voice mail. Frustrated, she left a detailed message asking for his assistance. Saj needed her help right now.

She scouted for something clean to wear in her armoire, settled on a Lurex metallic T-shirt under a ribbed oversize black cashmere cardigan, threw it on over leggings and ankle boots, and added her flea market Hermès scarf. At the porcelain sink in her bathroom, she scrubbed her face with a new bar of black clay soap guaranteed to ward off wrinkles, rimmed her eyes with kohl and smudged the lids, then accentuated them with mascara. She shoved the laptop in her leather bag and grabbed her agnès b. leather coat. With Miles Davis in tow, she hurried down the deep grooved steps of the marble staircase into the puddled courtyard. Patches of azure among the clouds promised a respite from the rain. She deposited Miles Davis with Madame Cachou, her concierge. From the courtyard's garage, once the carriage house, she walked her scooter across the cobbles. A jump on the kick-start pedal and her Vespa roared onto the quai.

"SAJ DE ROSNAY? He's in stable condition. No visitors," said the nurse at the criminal ward of Hôtel-Dieu. The ward, which was guarded by police, smelled of antiseptic and despair. What if the *flics* pressed manslaughter charges? Saj needed to keep his mouth shut. Not say anything the *flics* would use against him.

"So I'll leave a message." She glanced around the reception area. The scuffed green walls, the grilled metal gate. "It's urgent."

"Much as I'd like to help. . . ." The nurse glanced at the blue-uniformed police by the doors. Shrugged. "We're not allowed."

Panic flamed in her gut. "Nora still working nights?" She hoped she could leave a message for her friend.

"Nora switched to the day shift."

A spark of hope. "We're friends. Any chance you could let her know I'm here?"

"Not a good time." The nurse gave a harried glance down the green-tiled corridor.

The phone rang at reception. Aimée hated to press her, but she had to get somewhere. "*Desolée*, I know you're busy, but when's Nora's break?"

The nurse expelled air. "Who knows? The X-ray technicians went on strike. We're run off our feet." She hurried off to answer a doctor's call from the corridor.

Great. The season of *grèves*. Spring must be coming.

She recognized the *flic* near the elevator from Morbier's team a few years back. A quick glance at his name badge— Delisle—and she rustled up her courage, determined to give it her best shot.

"Officer Delisle?"

He was olive skinned, dark-haired, and muscular. He snapped his notebook shut, favoring his left wrist, which was covered with a brace. Irritation and indifference suffused his expression. "The public's not allowed here, Mademoiselle. Follow the signs to the patient wards, if you don't mind."

"But we met a while ago. I'm Aimée, Commissaire Morbier's goddaughter." She gestured to his brace. "Carpal tunnel? Awful, I know the feeling."

A snort of laughter. "I wish. Scuffle on the ward this morning."

She wondered at that, and at why, as a seasoned officer, he was on a rookie posting at the criminal ward. Demoted? Injury? "Inmate patients, you mean?"

He rocked back on his thick-soled shoes. "Big eyes. Now I remember you. How's Commissaire Morbier?"

Too much gray in his hair and a shuffle to his gait, but she kept that back. "Mismatched socks and a brain like a laser, as usual."

Delisle smiled. His upright stance relaxed—he'd thawed. She'd said the right thing for once.

He shot her a meaningful glance. "You're not allowed here, you know. I need to escort you out."

What else could she try to get him to bend the rules? She could go with the truth and get nowhere. Or lie and try to worm out info. Stall and hope that Nora would . . . what, go on a break? With a strike going on?

"I just visited my neighbor, a stroke victim," she said. "Thought I'd see if my old roommate Nora could have coffee on her break." She tried for her most sympathetic look. "But what happened to you?"

A quick shake of his head. "Doing my job."

"Hazard pay, that's what I'm always saying to Morbier," she said. "You men on the front lines deserve it."

Delisle shrugged. But she could tell he liked that. He thawed more and grew talkative, revealed that a slick operator had taken advantage of the normal chaos of a shift change to talk his way in.

He'd be on his guard, then. She had a feeling that with this one her best bet was laying it on thick. "But how?" she said. "I mean, you're so on top of it. The floor's a locked facility."

She hoped she hadn't overdone it.

Delisle's pager beeped. Eager to answer his page, he hit the elevator button. The door swooshed open. He gestured her inside.

So far her attempt at charm had gotten her nowhere. Aimée got off on the next floor and hiked back up the concrete stairs to an EXIT sign. She figured Nora still hit the coffin nails. On the fire escape outside the EXIT door, several nurses stood smoking. The Seine, khaki green below, crested with waves from the gliding *bateaux-mouches*.

Good luck, for once. Nora, a petite brunette, was crushing out a cigarette on the metal slat. Thank God.

"Nora?"

Nora looked up, grinned. "Didn't you quit smoking, Aimée?"

"Three days short of two months," she said. "But who's counting?" Aimée wished she didn't want to snatch a drag so much. "Nora, can you do me a favor?"

"Now?" Nora said. "We're short-staffed, there's a strike. I'm not even supposed to take a break." Nora opened the EXIT door to the back stairway. "I've got to get back or there'll be trouble."

Aimée needed to probe, and quick. "My colleague's a patient, Saj de Rosnay. Know of him?"

Nora thought a moment. "The blond with dreads, like a Rasta? Indian clothes?"

Aimée nodded.

"Not hard on the eyes, either," she said. "His vitals look good, X-rays normal, no fractures, under normal observation for his neck injury, took his pain meds."

Nora's pager vibrated.

"*Alors*, forgive me, Nora, but they're trying to nail Saj for manslaughter. Now robbery's involved. This Serb—"

"Serb?" Nora interrupted, frowning. "A Serb showed up demanding to see the accident victim—your colleague."

The hairs on Aimée's neck rose. The Serb's partner? "That's what the scuffle was this morning?"

"That's not half of it," Nora said as Aimée followed her up the stone back stairs. "The angry Serb was trying to visit his brother. Or so he said. Then claimed there was some family emergency. Lied through his set of whites."

All kinds of fear spun in her mind. "The Serb got Saj's name?"

"Who knows? Change of shift's always chaotic," Nora said. "Still, even if he did, no one gets in the ward unless they're part of the medical staff or law enforcement. *Tant pis.*" She glanced at her watch. "Gotta go."

"What did he look like?"

"Never saw him."

"If he caused a scene, someone would remember. Markings, accent, his clothing?"

"Smelled like a barnyard, they said." Nora shrugged. "That's all I know."

Aimée wrote down a message on the back of her card. "Can you get this to Saj, please?"

"I'm not supposed to, Aimée."

"Please, Nora. If this Serb's looking for him, he needs to be warned. Moved to another ward."

"Why?"

"Saj ran over his brother last night."

"'Ran over' as in the brother's dead?"

"As in an accident," Aimée said. She had to enlist Nora's aid. "It was like he was dropped on the windshield. His ashen face, white hand . . . I can't stop seeing him in my mind. But the odd thing, Nora—no blood. But one Serb is dead, and now another is asking for Saj. . . ."

Alarm crossed Nora's face. She nodded and slipped the paper in her pocket. Her clogs clipped over the stone and then she was gone. Aimée's insides churned. Even under police supervision, Saj wasn't safe.

* * *

IN THE CAFÉ below Leduc Detective, Aimée cupped her bowl of *café crème*, the froth swirling over the cup's lip. Like the whirlpool in her mind.

The café windows were fogged up and the whole place smelled faintly of damp wool overcoat. The radio was tuned to the soccer scores. But she could only think of how Yuri Volodya owed her mother. Or so he said. But how? Was her mother alive? Or was he using her? And if so, for what?

And Yuri Volodya wasn't answering his phone.

Last month Morbier had alleged her mother had gone rogue— dealt with arms dealers and terrorists. But Serbs? Art theft?

Aimée had nothing to go on but nightmares involving tattoos. So many questions. She could kick herself for not insisting that Yuri explain everything then and there.

The milk steamer whooshed. Zazie, the owner's red-haired preteen daughter, rinsed glasses before going to school. Businessmen and workers from the nearby Louvre downed espressos, slapped francs on the zinc counter, and rushed out into the pearl-gray morning light.

What had Yuri revealed, except that he knew her mother was American? And what could that possibly have to do with a dead Serb or a stolen painting? She shuddered. What in hell had this terrible accident gotten them all into?

She had half a mind to mount her scooter and go over to Volodya's place, but she held back. Too much work waited upstairs, and with Saj in the hospital . . . and Yuri Volodya still wasn't answering his phone.

Last night her cell battery had been low so she'd turned it off. But Leduc Detective's office number was on the card, too. What if Yuri had called her at the office?

"René forgot this the other day, Aimée," Zazie said, pushing something across the newly wiped chrome counter. "Mind giving this to him?"

His classic car magazine. Aimée dropped her demitasse spoon.

"What's that look, Aimée?"

"René got an amazing job offer from Silicon Valley," she said, trying to sound enthusiastic. "He's gone."

"Just like that? Wow." Zazie whistled. "René never mentioned it last time I saw him."

"So incredible, they sent a private jet. They needed him right away." Who could compete with that? Aimée pulled out her Chanel Red and in the gleaming reflection of the coffee machine reapplied her lipstick. She wished her hands didn't shake. "Aren't you late for *l'école?*"

"I'm in *collège*, Aimée. Remember?"

Almost twelve, or was it thirteen? "Of course."

Zazie pulled her red hair back in a scrunchie and grabbed her book satchel. Paused. "Do you miss René?"

More than she cared to admit. Right now she wished she could talk with René, her sounding board and best friend. Hash out what had happened. "Zazie, he's their new CTO—that means chief technology officer. Call me thrilled for him."

"I miss him too," Zazie said. She knotted her foulard, snuck a look behind the counter. Virginie, her mother, had her back turned. "May I try your lipstick, Aimée?"

Aimée slipped her the tube. "You're growing up."

"*Fluctuat nec mergitur.*" Zazie dabbed her lips and rubbed them together.

"My Latin's rusty," Aimée said. Drizzle pattered on the café's street awnings.

"Means, 'It is tossed by the waves but does not sink.'" Zazie grinned and placed the recapped lipstick on the counter. "That's the motto on the Paris coat of arms. We learned that yesterday. Remember that, Aimée—tossed by the waves but does not sink."

A wink and Zazie was gone in a gust of wet wind. A young boy with a book bag and an umbrella greeted her in front of the café door. Growing up, all right.

Aimée checked her phone for messages; still no word from Yuri Volodya or Serge the pathologist.

Time to head to work, check if Yuri had left a message on the office machine. And finish the report she and Saj should have worked on last night. She had a business to run, office rent to pay, and the rising cost of Miles Davis's horse meat.

INSIDE HER UNHEATED building foyer, she bypassed the creaking wire-cage elevator and mounted the winding stairs. She needed the exercise. And time to steel herself for an office empty of René. And, she realized, no Saj either.

"*Bonjour,*" she greeted the new cleaning woman mopping the stairs, then continued up, keeping away from the banister to avoid snagging her leggings. She wished her waistband didn't feel so tight.

A dim glow showed from behind the frosted glass-paned door of Leduc Detective. Hope filled her. Had this been a bad joke? Had René changed his mind?

"René. . . ." The words died on her lips.

"He gave me his key." A rail-thin, mop-headed young man looked up from behind the keyboard at René's desk. "I'm his student. He told you, *non?* A replacement."

Her heart fell. No one could replace René.

She eyed the scuffed Beatle boots, which matched the tousled Beatle bangs fringing his eyes, the skinny jeans and the black turtleneck. This kid was René's star hacker? He looked twelve.

"You're Maxence, I presume?"

A lopsided grin showed braces. "*À votre service.*" She guessed Québécois from his accent. A Canadian.

She hung up her leather coat, tossed her secondhand Vuitton bag on the recamier. Unfurling her scarf, she flicked on the chandelier for more light. The crystal drops gleamed, thanks to the new cleaner's feather duster.

"Tell me you're at least sixteen and I'm not breaking the child labor laws."

Maxence nodded, his hair in his eyes. "If you want."

Anger burned in her. "If I want? I want to follow the labor code. Does René know you're . . . how old are you?"

Maxence pulled out his wallet. "Sixteen, eighteen, twenty-two, whatever you'd like." He fanned out a number of *cartes d'identité* like a hand of playing cards.

She wanted to smack him. Slammed down her keys instead, almost upsetting the vase of daffodils. René had brought them in; every spring, he bought bunches from large-fisted Eastern European vendors at the Métro entrance. He wouldn't be refreshing this vase anymore.

"So you're an outlaw, eh," she said, "some boy genius? Let's see your student card from the Hacktaviste Academy." She scanned it. "According to this you're eighteen."

The new radiator emitted blasts of heat. Almost too hot. He gave another lopsided smile. "This work experience will be great for my new gaming company. I need to learn on the job, juggle tasks, set goals. Like I will for my own company."

Her stomach churned. She debated telling him to put on his Beatles jacket and hike out the frosted glass door. "No room for interns here, *desolée*."

He swallowed. His Adam's apple bobbed. "Please give me a chance," he said, his cockiness gone. "I'll do anything. René thinks I'm good. Let me help your part-timer, Saj."

She knew the *flics* might hold Saj in *garde à vue* longer. Or his injuries could slow him down; he might need to take medical leave.

Maxence's hopeful eyes bored into her skull. After all, René recommended him. Did she even have another option? Might as well try him to see what he could do.

"On a trial basis," she said. "But you might take an early and permanent lunch."

Fifteen minutes later, she'd checked the mail stacked on the marble fireplace ledge and started running the virus scans, checking the monitors for daily security contracts. All put in place by René. The whole operation could almost run itself.

"Keep your eyes on the systems and print out the reports and spreadsheets," she said.

Maxence nodded, eager now. "Then shall I download the info onto René's desktop files, make a backup?"

She nodded. Not so green after all. Her heart wasn't in this day-to-day stuff; she'd let the kid handle grunt routine and monitor his work.

Ongoing reports filled her desktop screen, and she took her laptop from the drawer. On it, she pulled up the old files she'd digitized from her father's dossiers. She'd transcribed his notes during the long November evenings after his death in the bomb explosion in Place Vendôme. A painful exercise in hopes of finding some clue to the explosion. But the leads had all gone up with him in a ball of fire and smoke.

All those years in the police force had instilled in him the habit of recording names, places, descriptions of people he interviewed or investigated—any memorable characteristic or quirk—in pocket-sized leather-bound notepads. Each entry, each date and name or initial, constituted a piece of a case her father had worked on. A detail he'd rechecked to fit pieces together. His scent clung to the notebooks. The pain lessened over the years, but never completely went away. For that reason, she kept his original notebooks rubber-banded together in the safe. Touching them hurt too much.

Now, she searched her father's case files under V for Volodya, and Y for Yuri. Nothing. She kicked off her ankle boots, rubbed her stockinged feet on the smooth wood floor, and wished she had an espresso. René had forgotten—correction, she had forgotten to buy coffee beans.

Quiet reigned, apart from Maxence's clicking fingers and

the distant thrumming of traffic outside on rue du Louvre. With the report summaries done, she concentrated on refining her search. She limited the parameters to her father's cases involving *indicateurs*, or snitches. Problematic, since her father often referred to his informers by initials or nicknames. Again, nothing under V or Y.

Her grandfather's cases went back to the thirties, a few from the Sûreté he'd carried with him as private clients when he'd founded Leduc Detective. She hadn't gotten to digitizing those yet.

"Quite a history here," Maxence said, gesturing to the wall with her grandfather's sepia photo, complete with waxed mustache; Leduc Detective's original license, circa 1925; her father's first case in the newspaper; the old sewer maps of Paris.

"Nice that you've kept it in the family," he said.

Looking down on her from the wall was her grandfather's commendation from the Louvre for service to la République in recovering a Degas. Another stolen painting. She had her grandfather's notes on the case. Somewhere. Fascinating, but not what she was searching for—she needed to find some connection to Yuri Volodya and her mother.

Think. Think like her father.

Trusting her gut feeling that Volodya had dealt with Leduc Detective in the past, she continued cross-referencing dates, names, and initials. Thirty minutes later, after eliminating the non-matches, she sat back, rubbing her big right toe along her left ankle to help her think.

"Remember your first impression," her father had always said. "Nail it down or it comes back to nail you later." Often all you had were first impressions to go on. She thought back to her first impression of Yuri Volodya, the old Russian—"a little Cossack," one of the medic crew called him. Belligerent, scared. But a criminal?

Under RUSSIAN in her father's case file, she found a

photocopied *Le Parisien* newspaper article of a Trotskyist rally and conference in the 14th arrondissement. Dated 1972. A grainy photo showed what appeared to be an abandoned Regency-style townhouse splattered with graffiti, slogans, and banners with the hammer and sickle. A squat, according to the article, housing assorted anarchists and radical leftists in *Action-Réaction*. More photos showed smiling members with armbands holding posters. Her eye caught on a younger man, with more hair but stocky then like now. Yuri Volodya.

The connection—murky but there. So did her father know him? Or. . . .

She read further. The article detailed doings of the leftist squatters who'd played host to the German Haader-Rofmein gang—radical seventies terrorists—before a security forces raid.

Her throat caught. Several years ago she'd learned her American mother—Sydney Leduc—had been captured with the Haader-Rofmein group after she'd abandoned Aimée. Sydney had been imprisoned and deported in a deal wangled by her father. Her father never talked about it, refused to speak her mother's name.

The hurt that never went away surfaced. Her hands shook.

Here was the connection. Why had her father kept this in his files?

She punched in Yuri Volodya's number. Busy. She counted to sixty, tried again. Still busy. She pondered his logic of leaving her an envelope of cash with an urgent note about a priceless painting that needed protection, then going out for dinner, trusting a broom closet for security. Some elaborate ruse? But his anguish and fear had seemed genuine.

Tense, she glanced at the time. At Maxence, working at René's desk. Wondered if she should chance leaving him alone and visiting Yuri.

Her cell phone trilled, startling her.

"Oui?"

"Since when do you run over Serbs, Aimée?" said Serge, her pathologist friend from the morgue.

"And live to tell?" She put Yuri's information in her bag, switched gears and grabbed her ankle boots from the floor. "At first I thought he had a death wish, attempted suicide, or that he was drunk and confused, but. . . ."

"It didn't feel right?" said Serge.

"All wrong. Tell me you've gotten results. His ID?"

"Besides the little Eastern European dental work he had?"

"That's rhetorical, I assume."

"Can't talk, I'm finishing the autopsy." In the background came the unmistakable whirring of a bone-cutting saw.

She grimaced. But with Saj facing a prospective manslaughter charge, his future teetered in the balance. Serge just loved to bargain; she would have to humor him. "*S'il te plaît*, Serge. I'll babysit the twins."

Pause. She heard the pumping spray of water pressure hoses. She cringed, unable to stop herself from picturing how the hoses were being used.

"*Bon*, twenty minutes. The usual place."

SHE'D BEEN SLEEPWALKING since René's departure yesterday, numb with the shock of hitting the Serb, Saj's injuries. But now she needed to wake up and take action, figure out the dead Serb's story and get Saj out of hot water. René would have warned her against getting involved and given valid reasons— a business to run, rent to pay.

Too late for that. Saj was in trouble. And there was no nagging finger to stop her.

But she also needed to figure out this Yuri Volodya. She'd checked Leduc Detective's answering machine. Empty.

"Ever used Xincus database for a person search, Maxence?"

"Cut my teeth on Xincus," he said.

"So dazzle me." She wrote down Yuri Volodya's name and

address. "Find everything you can about him: birth, schooling, family, organizations he belonged to, politics, his bookbinding business, something with Salvador Dalí."

"The works, Aimée?"

She nodded, rummaging in her drawer for a fresh cell phone. Thank God René kept them charged. She found a midnight-blue one and inserted her SIM card.

"Can you handle things?"

"I'm on it, Aimée."

"Keep in contact with me at this number. Check with me on the hour. Don't forget to monitor the reports." She double-looped her scarf, grabbed her metallic ballet flats and stuck them in her bag. It was time to test Maxence's efficiency and get to what needed doing. To where Leduc started. Grass roots.

"Good luck holding down"—she paused—how did they say it across the pond?—"*le fort.*"

A shrug. "If the Indians attack?"

"Arrows in the back," she said over her shoulder.

AIMÉE KEYED THE ignition, popped into first gear, and wove her faded pink scooter through the congested traffic on Quai de la Mégisserie. Ten minutes later, she parked on the rain-dampened cobbles near the redbrick Institut Médico-Légal entrance. In the morgue's waiting hall, busts of medical pioneers looked down on her, impassive and marble-eyed.

Last night's incidents replayed in her mind with slow clarity: arguing with Saj, that white van pulling out, the terrible thump and those dull eyes of the Serb, his splayed palms pressed on the windshield for what seemed like forever but was only a few seconds.

The image was burned onto the backs of her eyelids.

Her trilling cell phone interrupted her thoughts. Yuri? But her caller ID showed Martine, her best friend since *lycée.*

"My publisher commissioned me to write a book, Aimée," Martine said, excited. "A guide to looking chic."

The last thing she wanted to hear about right now. "Congratulations, Martine."

"I think I've got the main theme down. *Alors*, fashion sense involves mix and match," Martine said. "Like you—it's never just one look."

"*Moi?*"

"But you're the one who taught me to assemble outfits, make magic with two scarves. How to stock the definitive armoire. *Zut*, you schooled me in all the must-haves: a man's jacket, *le trenchcoat*, a black sweater," Martine rattled on. "A simple tank top, white silk blouse, a little black dress, jeans and, of course, a leather jacket. And Converse sneakers."

"You know my feelings about tank tops," Aimée said, shaking her head. "But you're a serious journalist, Martine."

"So I should refuse an outrageous advance?" Aimée heard the flick of a lighter. "I can write this in my sleep," Martine said. A short intake of breath. "Not to mention I can use you, Aimée. Your mix of classic styles, *déconstruit*, that thrown-together look with a whiff of vintage. A touch of whimsy."

"We share clothes, Martine. *C'est tout.*"

"But it's how you throw them together, Aimée," Martine said. "Tell me you'll give me tidbits, help me do the tie-in spread for *ELLE*. Okay?"

Now, of all times.

"Martine, René took the job in Silicon Valley. *Phfft*—gone. Just like that," Aimée said. "*Compris?* I've got a business to run."

Not to mention saving her colleague from manslaughter charges. Or from the dead tattooed Serb's partner.

"But René told you about his interview," said Martine. Aimée heard a long exhale. Imagined the gray spiral of smoke, the taste of nicotine, the jolt. "*Alors*, they recruited him, those Silicon Valley . . . *quoi?*" Martine searched for the word. "'*ead'unters.*"

"Headhunters, you mean?"

"Open your eyes once in a while, Aimée, before it's too late," Martine said. "Are you coping okay?"

All alone now. That old feeling of abandonment rose. Aimée bit her lip. "I want the best for René."

A sigh. "Put yourself in René's size twos. He's gutted after losing Meizi. And haven't you always worried over his health, how the cold worsens his hip issues? Never mind the money they offered." Martine exhaled again. "He's brilliant. You had to let him go."

"As if I'd stop him even if I could," she said. "Look, I'm at the morgue."

"Who did you kill now?"

"Not me." Pause. "We had an accident."

"*Et alors?*" Another exhale of smoke. "There's more. I hear it in what you're not saying. Spill."

Aimée could never keep anything from Martine for long. She sighed and then gave a quick version of what had happened the night before. "And to top it all off, I've let myself get so flabby and out of shape. Some fashion icon you'll think I am when you see how tight my waistband is lately."

"Saj totaled René's car?" Martine said. "Get it fixed. But *mon Dieu*, are you saying now you can't fit into the Dior?" She meant the blue vintage Dior they found at the winter sales. "Bad enough René is missing your cousin Sebastien's wedding; now you have nothing to wear to it either?"

"That's all you can say, Martine?" She hitched up her legging. Examined the scuff on her boot heel.

"Serb mafia, an old Russian, a painting?" Martine exhaled. "I'd say concentrate on what's important. Sounds like that's getting this *mec* off Saj's tail."

"You have a bead on this? Know a Serb who trades in art?"

Why hadn't she asked the old man about the painting's value? She didn't even know who painted it, whether it was someone famous. Stupid.

Martine sucked in her breath. "Watch yourself, Aimée. Serbian tough men score low on finesse points. I wrote an article on them last year. We know they contract out. It's the employer to watch out for."

Morbier and the medic had cautioned the same thing.

"But what's really important is that you're not making a mistake with Melac," Martine said. "He's moving in with you, *non?*"

Typical. Only Martine could be thinking about Aimée's love life at a time like this. "Only if Miles Davis agrees," she said. "It's complicated as usual."

Melac, Aimée's *Brigade Criminelle* detective boyfriend, was never around these days; he'd been seconded to an assignment he couldn't talk about. Only his citrus scent clung to the sheets.

"But if you still need an escort to Sebastien's wedding, let me suggest a man. He reminds me of the chocolate you like; deep, dark, and yes, somewhat decadent. I'll introduce you."

Always the matchmaker, Martine.

"Meanwhile, I'll contact my seamstress," she continued. "A perfect magician with Dior alterations."

Serge beckoned from the lab door.

"Got to go, Martine," she said. "Date with a cadaver."

She hung up. A little shudder ran through her. *Put yourself in René's size twos.* Was Martine implying that her selfish streak had surfaced again—the self-absorbed eye-blinkered mode? Had she driven René away, put too much pressure on him, relied on him too much? She'd made it all go wrong, as usual.

Practice your profession but also have a life, her Papa always told her. Morbier had no life—correction, even he had a woman making him morning coffee and she could imagine what else. In the end, René, her best friend and partner, had left her. The agency needed to be kept afloat. Yet dwelling on that right now would get her nowhere.

Aimée followed Serge down the stairs to the lower level,

past the cold storage room and to the lab. The frigid air sent shivers up her neck.

Serge paused on the steps outside the morgue lab. The dark hairs below his knuckles were powdered with talc dust from his surgical gloves. "So you agree to help with the twins on their half-day holiday, Aimée?"

The usual price for any favors—babysitting his energetic twin boys, whom she likened to shooting balls of mercury.

"Your mother-in-law's busy?" she said glumly.

He nodded. "Away for once at my wife's sister's in Sceaux."

Jeanette, his wife's mother, was a blue-coiffed, white-gloved *ancien régime* general's widow with steel in her veins. Poor Serge. His mother-in-law ruled their life. Of course, *Grand-mère's* iron fist might be exactly what the twins needed in a babysitter.

At least Aimée wouldn't have to take them to the pediatrician this time.

"There's an exhibit at Cité Universitaire near Parc Montsouris," he said. "My wife's been meaning to take them."

Fat chance. She'd bribe them with Orangina and *pommes frites*. As usual.

"Deal."

In the Institut Médico-Légal corridor, a linoleum-tiled affair, Serge looked both ways and then pushed open a nondescript brown door. "Meet me at the dissection area. Second door on your left."

She swallowed. Her mouth was dry as sand. "Why? Can't you tell me here?" But the door closed with a whoosh behind him.

The formaldehyde fumes and the sweetish smells of decomposition met her in the long white-tiled room. Cadavers in various stages of autopsy lay naked on the trough-like aluminum tables. This was the part she'd hated about her first year of medical school. The part she couldn't take, that compelled her to drop out.

"Is that necessary, Serge?" He had put on a mask, and was handing her one.

She avoided looking directly at the body, which lay face-down, and focused instead on the adjoining counter and the pair of rib spreaders resting on it. Serge consulted a clip chart, his brows crinkling.

"*Intéressant.*"

"That's all you can say?"

"He the one?" Serge's big eyes, behind his black-framed glasses, were wide. "Make sure, Aimée."

She steeled herself and looked down. Flaps of the peeled-back scalp were draped over a portion of the exposed base of the skull. Beside the head, a blue bucket held the brain. The Serb's back was white as aspirin but his arms were covered with blue tattoos. Crudely needled Cyrillic letters. "I'd recognize that tattoo with the wolf anywhere." And she wished she hadn't.

A tag hung over the dirt-ridged nail of his big toe: FELIKS.

"I hadn't started the autopsy yet when you called. So I drew blood prior to opening him up," Serge said. "I sent it for an expedited analysis, ran tests for the usual drugs of choice: opiates, cocaine, amphetamines, benzodiazepines, barbiturates, and alcohol." He consulted the clipboard again. "A slow day, so for once they expedited the tests. All negative."

"So he wasn't high or stoned?"

Serge shook his head. "Notice those incisions I made in the neck and vertebrae. Not the optimal way to remove the spinal cord." He shrugged. "But a way to look for subtle injuries to his neck." Serge pushed his glasses on his forehead, moved forceps out of the way. "But I found nothing."

Was that good? Or bad?

"You want the good news first?"

Hopeful, she nodded. "You found something else in the blood test, Serge?"

"First, explain your interest in this tattooed Serb, Aimée," he said. "And why I'm helping you out again."

"Saj ran over this Feliks," she said, motioning to the toe tag. "Killed him, or so the *flics* think. I'm not so sure."

Serge moved the scalpels and knives to the next cutting board. "A little difficult to argue, given the tire tracks on his fractured arm."

"But the lack of blood bothered me," she said. "And his expression—blank, even as he hit the windshield. Seemed so strange." She made herself look down again at the scraped, tattooed torso. "Sounds stupid, since my closest experience to seeing someone get run over by a car was a rabbit René ran over near Charles de Gaulle once."

"A rabbit?" He lifted his arm. "Never mind, I don't want to know."

The whole scenario from last night smelled, and she needed to air it out. "Can't you give me the autopsy results now, Serge? I need ammo to shove in the *flics'* faces to clear Saj."

"Clear him?"

Why did he pretend not to understand? His pager buzzed. After a quick glance he shook his head. "I've got to make a call. Let me get back to you later."

"Saj could sit in *garde à vue* under suspicion for involuntary homicide while. . . ." She took a deep breath. A nauseating sickish-sweet filled her nostrils. Bad move.

"What if I throw in overnight babysitting, *chez moi?* You know, twelve uninterrupted hours of freedom for you and your wife." He wouldn't be able to turn that down. But she didn't own a TV. Somehow she'd figure out how to entertain the twins. Or take them to Martine's.

Serge set the autopsy report down near the bucket containing the liver. "Make it quick. You were pre-med—figure it out yourself. And I never did this, *compris?*"

After the door closed, she picked up the clipboard and concentrated on trying to decipher the autopsy-ese:

1. Right forearm fracture, with relatively little hemorrhage.

2. Abrasions on front and back torso, arms, face consistent with scraping on street cobbles, again relatively bloodless.

3. In terms of the head, no hemorrhages beneath the scalp, skull fractures, or collections of blood around the brain— epidural, subdural and subarachnoid hemorrhages, or contusions of the brain itself. No lacerations in the ponto- medullary junction where one might expect.

She looked up as Serge entered.

"*Zut alors,* we ran over a dead man?"

Serge gave a small nod.

What the hell had happened? What had they gotten into? Between this news and the nauseating smells, her knees went weak. She grabbed at the table. Felt the corpse's leather-cold flesh, gasped and let go.

Serge cleaned his glasses with the edge of his lab coat. "The medic reports the victim was still warm upon resuscitation attempts, no rigor mortis or lividity until later. His heart could have stopped anywhere from five minutes to an hour before."

He turned the corpse over.

Aimée stared down at those half-lidded eyes. They looked exactly as they had when pressed against the windshield in front of her. Dead. "That accounts for his expression. No look of pain. No blood from the cuts on his face."

Serge pointed his ballpoint pen at the pale bruise on the Serb's shoulder. "I'd say he bounced off the windshield here. After he landed, his arm was run over, as the fracture indicates."

"But if Feliks the Serb was already dead, how could he fall in front of the car?"

"Good question. The whole thing bothers me. Let's look at the prelim crime scene photos." Serge rustled through a folder. "This one shows the angle. Do you recall any parked cars, a tree, a motorcycle—anything he could have fallen off of?"

"It happened so fast, although it felt like slow motion at the time." She studied the photos. The position of René's Citroën. "A white van pulled ahead of us. . . ." Her index finger stabbed at the photo. "Here. If the Serb was standing between this parked truck and this motorcycle. . . ." She paused to think for a moment. "He could have caught his sleeve on the truck's side mirror. For reasons unknown, his heart stopped. Then the car's vibrations on the cobbles caused him. . . ."

"To fall." Serge nodded. "His accumulated weight could have torn his jacket pocket, and he landed as you drove by."

Serge pointed to the photo of the body on the cobbles. The ripped jean jacket pocket.

"Brilliant. No one dies twice. At least not as far as I know." Aimée grinned. "This puts Saj in the clear."

Serge didn't share her excitement. He tapped his pen. "Still doesn't give me his cause of death." His other gloved finger probed the Serb's jawline. "He presents no wounds apart from the crushing attributed to the injuries sustained after death from René's Citroën," Serge said. "No bullet holes, knife marks, or concussion or injury to the brain." He checked the autopsy clipboard. Turned some pages. "His organs, brain came out normal. No distinguishable cause of death."

Not her problem.

"Aimée, I've never issued an inconclusive autopsy report in my career."

"Perfectionist" was Serge's other middle name, after Pierre. He was thorough, a recognized expert in the medical pathology field.

"*C'est bizarre.* But before I throw my hands up, I'll do a microscopic examination of the organs for what could have caused sudden death. Inflammation in the heart, maybe, like myocarditis, or inflammation in the brain. Never obvious."

"What if he was using a new designer crack or injectable synthetic cocaine cocktail?" She shivered, and not only from the chill of the cadaver room. "They wouldn't show on the standard tests you performed. You should run one of those advanced tox screen panels for other drugs, too. Have you examined his tattoos for puncture holes? He's got enough of them."

"Speaking of crack, our department head's cracking down on our pathology budget," Serge said. "We're allocated funds for only standard blood screens and tests."

"Didn't you misplace that memorandum, Serge?" Aimée winked. "Or it got lost in the shuffle when you were at the medical conference in, where was it, Prague, *non?*"

His dark eyes lit up. "You want me to bend rules, like you?"

"Live dangerously, Serge. You've only got one life. Add spice."

"So you're adding spice with Serb gangsters? You need to watch out, Aimée."

Her hands trembled. She put them in her pocket. She was tired of hearing this. "Has his brother ID'd him?"

Serge took off his glasses again. Rubbed the other lens with the edge of his lab coat. "No family has claimed him so far."

Odd.

"How did the *flics* ID him?" Aimée asked. "Driver's license, *carte d'identité?*"

Serge paused, put on his glasses and consulted another chart. Flipped the pages. "You never saw this either, Aimée."

A smudged copy of a receipt from a kebob takeout on rue d'Alésia for Feliks. He must have ordered ahead.

"So his stomach contents corroborate this?"

"See for yourself." Serge gestured to a bowl.

"*Non, merci*," she said. "How soon will you file the autopsy, Serge?"

"I'm not finished, Aimée. First, I need the cause of death."

She wanted to grab him by the throat. Shake him. Didn't he understand?

"Until you send in the prelim," she said, keeping her voice even with effort, "Saj faces manslaughter for this *mec*. Please, Serge, you know it's wrong to leave Saj hanging. Get the prelim paperwork to the lead investigator's desk."

"What's a few hours? Saj still needs medical care."

"Didn't I tell you this Serb's brother tried to talk his way into *garde à vue*—"

"*Bon*," Serge interrupted, waving his rib cutters. "You're babysitting the twins while we take a weekend in Brittany."

"Wait a minute, I offered overnight—"

"A weekend alone with my wife, Aimée. Take it or leave it."

She stifled a groan. Saj better appreciate this.

SHE CHEWED HER lip as she opened Leduc Detective's frosted glass door. Saj wouldn't face manslaughter charges— a good thing. Yet, considering the snail's pace of paperwork required for a release, she couldn't hold her breath. She hated waiting for the catch-up.

Stacks of printouts, color-coded folders, and copies of faxed proposals lay neatly on her desk. Maxence had been busy. Nice job. "You're starting to dazzle me," she said.

Maxence grinned. "There's a message on the machine."

"From who?"

"Didn't hear it, sorry. I got wrist-deep changing the printer toner." Charcoal smudges ringed Maxence's fingers. "Think you need a new printer."

And the money to pay for it.

She hit PLAY.

Aimée heard a cough, clearing of the throat. What sounded

like running water. "Please pick up if you're there. Please, Mademoiselle." She recognized Yuri Volodya's voice. "I should have told you the truth."

A chill crept up her neck. She turned up the machine's volume. Listened close.

"I lied to you last night." She heard the catch in his throat. Fear edged his voice. "Come now." Another pause. "Please, if you're listening, pick up. Your mother told me things."

Her breath caught. *Go on, Yuri, tell me what things. Tell me what my mother means in this. To you.*

"You look just like her, you know. Those same big eyes. *Alors*, we need to talk in person."

Aimée wanted to scream. *What about my mother?*

"I have to trust someone," he continued. "A person on the outside." Still that sound of running water. "*Zut*, it's complicated, but I know who stole the painting. I need you to understand."

Understand what?

She made out a faint knocking in the background. "You should know . . . *Merde!*"

Go on, Yuri, she prayed.

The message clicked off.

"He a friend of yours?" Maxence asked, looking up.

"I wouldn't call him that." Frustrated, she tapped her chipped mocha-lacquered nails on the PLAY button.

Maxence nodded in a knowing way. "Your mother referred him and now you have to help the old fart, *n'est-ce pas?* I know what it's like."

She sat, stunned. A slap like a wave of cold Atlantic seawater hit her. "Say that again, Maxence."

"Don't I know it, Aimée." He shrugged. "My mom volunteers me all the time to help idiots who can't even turn a laptop on. Stupid."

Maxence didn't know her American mother was on the

world terrorist watch list. Or that she'd gone rogue. Rogue from whom, and why, Aimée didn't know.

Her fingers gripped the phone. She sensed in the marrow of her bones that her mother was alive. Last month she'd been convinced that figure standing on the Pont Marie was . . . But what did that have to do with the painting?

Aimée hit the callback button. Busy. Shivers of hot and cold rippled through her.

She heard the fear in that sad, feisty voice of Yuri's. Serb thugs had threatened him, he'd said as much. She'd found the Serb's jacket button, seen the blood. The Serb dead before they'd hit him. What in hell was going on and how did it involve her mother?—if it even did.

Some trap? A setup?

The phone rang.

"Leduc Detective," she said.

"I've changed my mind, Mademoiselle," Yuri Volodya's voice came on the line. "Forget my message."

"What? Why?" She tried to make sense of this. "*Mon Dieu*, you talked to my mother." Silence on his end.

"You two have history together, don't you? That squat in the seventies. Trotskyists, *non?*"

Water rushed in the background. "My damn sink's flooding. Don't . . . come. Too dangerous. Complicated. She doesn't want you involved."

Doesn't want . . . Her mother was here? So close?

But she was involved already.

"I'll be right over."

"Tell me about it!" Maxence was saying. "So if he calls again, shall I tell him you're swamped with 'real' work?"

From her bottom desk drawer, she took her Beretta. Checked the clip to make sure it was loaded. Maxence's jaw dropped.

"*Non*, tell him I'm on the way."

* * *

BEFORE EXITING HER building's foyer, she pulled on a black knit cap, shapeless windbreaker, and oversize dark glasses. She'd been warned three times this morning about Serbs; she'd exercise caution. On the rue du Louvre she scanned the parked cars for a telltale tip of a cigarette, a fogged-up window indicating a watcher. Nothing.

Tension knotted her shoulders. On the side street, rue Bailleul, she unlocked her Vespa and walked it over the uneven cobbles. For a moment, she wondered if she had overreacted. Nothing seemed out of place on the busy rue du Louvre except for a lone squawking seagull on a pigeon-spattered statue. He was far from the water. As lost as she felt.

She shifted into first gear and wove the Vespa into traffic, passing the Louvre. Fine mist hit her cheekbones. She shifted into third as she crossed the Pont Neuf. A *bateau-mouche* glided underneath, fanning silver ripples on the Seine's surface. Swathes of indigo sky were framed by swollen rain clouds over Saint-Michel. The season of *la giboulée,* the sudden showers heralding spring.

Too bad she'd forgotten her rain boots.

Cars and buses stalled as she hit road closures on the Left Bank. Bright road construction lights illumined crews excavating the sewer lines. Street after narrow street.

Frustrated, she detoured uphill, winding through the Latin Quarter, then zigzagging across to the south of Paris, former countryside squeezed between wall fortifications now demolished; past the old Observatoire, two-story houses, remnants of prewar factories leaving an urban patchwork.

Clouds scudded over the slanted rooftops, the chimney pots like pepper shakers over the grilled balconies. Avenues led to tree-lined lanes in this neighborhood, fronting hidden village-like pockets of what her grandfather called "the Parisians' Paris."

Her shoulders knotted in irritation. She didn't have time for this scenic detour. Down wide Avenue du Général Leclerc, through the nodding shadows cast by trees and clouds of chestnut pollen, past the Métro signs and the steps of l'Eglise Saint Pierre de Montrouge. Into a logjam. Horns blared. Protesters chanting "Stop the developers!" and wearing La Coalition armbands blocked part of rue d'Alésia, a street known to fashionistas for designer markdowns. Of course, a demonstration!

Great. No way she'd get through this banner-waving crowd on her Vespa. She downshifted and wove through protesters, desperate for a parking place. It took a good five minutes, then another five until on foot she turned into cobbled Villa d'Alésia. She paused where the narrow lane twisted to the right, past the two-story ateliers. Quiet. A world away from the street protest. Clouds above fretted the cobblestones with a patchwork of light.

Further on, she saw a woman rattling Yuri's front gate. What was going on? Her stomach churned.

The older woman, in a mink coat over a purple jogging suit, gripped the grilled gate with one hand, beckoned her with the other. "*Viens*, Mademoiselle."

"Something wrong? Is Monsieur Volodya all right?"

The woman, her dark penciled eyebrows at odds with her thinning brown hair, stared at Aimée, her mouth pursed. "All that yelling! Disturbed you too, *non?*"

Nonplussed, Aimée nodded.

"It's overcast and you wear dark glasses?"

"The optometrist dilated my eyes this morning," Aimée improvised, removing them and sticking them in her pocket. "But Yuri. . . ?"

"Worried me, too," the woman interrupted. "His water pipe's flooding my wall and balcony again. A mess. Not the first time. But I've called. . . ."

The screech of a police car's brakes coming to a halt in front of them drowned her out.

"You reported this, Madame?" asked the arriving *flic*,

motioning to his partner. Aimée wondered how they'd gotten through the congested demonstration.

"The commotion disturbed her too." The woman gestured to Aimée. "All this yelling in the middle of the morning."

The woman took Aimée for a neighbor. She kept talking, but the *flic* and his partner ignored her. With a sense of foreboding, Aimée followed them inside, her ankle boots sloshing in water. A flood all right.

"Monsieur?"

Over the blue-uniformed officer's shoulders, Aimée saw Yuri bent over the gushing kitchen sink. His bloody arms were tied with a necktie to the faucet. She gasped. Rivulets of red-tinged water streamed onto the floor, eddying around her boots.

The first *flic* rushed to turn off the gushing taps. It took him several attempts to unknot the tie and hoist the old man down. Yuri's blackened eyes were swollen shut, his face cut and bruised, his distended tongue thick and blue. His hair, plastered to his head, dripped water.

"*Mon Dieu.*" Aimée's hand flew to her mouth. "I'm too late."

"What's that, Mademoiselle?"

She shook her head. Instinct told her to keep her mouth shut. She wondered who'd tortured the old man in broad daylight.

Trying to piece it together didn't stop her knees from knocking or the shivers from running up her spine. A familiar floral note—like *muguet,* lily of the valley—floated in the damp atelier. Her mother's scent. Then a piercing scream—Aimée jumped as the woman in the mink coat appeared in the hallway, pointing, her face crinkled in horror. The *policier* called for backup, speaking into the microphone on his collar.

"Take your neighbor outside, will you?" he said. "We'll talk to you both when backup arrives."

Her unlicensed Beretta felt heavy in her bag. A good time to make herself scarce. Guiding the sobbing woman, Aimée

sloshed through the ebbing water. Just last night she'd sat here
with Yuri. The vodka bottle and glasses were still on the table.
But the card she'd left was gone.

Good God, what if the killer had taken it?

A broken chair, waterlogged books, and the armoire on
its side showed evidence of a struggle. Had the thieves come
back for the painting they hadn't found last night? Or had her
mother? And if her mother was involved in this, who was she
involved with—Yuri, or whoever killed him?

Chilled, she pushed that thought away.

Only forty or fifty minutes had passed since she'd spoken
with him. It made no sense. Last night his shock over his stolen
painting had seemed genuine. Why torture him for a painting
already stolen? Why had he called her and changed his mind?
Saddened, she thought of her last image of Yuri Volodya, holding her card in his hands. Now she'd never get to ask him any
of her questions.

"Just like in the war," the woman said, her shoulders heaving.

Tense, Aimée put her arm around her. "What do you mean?"

"Standard torture by *les Boches*," the woman said. "That's
how they got information from my brother. They tortured him
in a bathtub on rue de Saussaies. Left him on our doorstep."

Aimée only had a few minutes before backup arrived. She
and her Beretta needed to be as far from here as possible. "Let
me take you home, they'll want to question us."

She escorted the woman up her stairs. "You heard Yuri yelling?"

"But you heard it too," she said.

"*Bien sûr.*" Aimée needed to keep the woman talking. "It
bothered my dog, but I couldn't understand what they were
saying."

"Who could, unless you speak Russian."

How did this add up? "You speak Russian, Madame?"

"*Les Russes* filled the quartier once," she said. "A generation or two ago, I don't remember."

Lining the walls of the stairwell were faded amateurish watercolors of pastoral countryside and villages with canals. Painted long ago on holidays, she imagined.

"My brother painted those," the woman said, noticing Aimée's gaze.

Aimée nodded. "So talented, your brother."

"Then, in 1943, that afternoon, gone. . . ." Her words trailed off.

Outside, Aimée heard car engines.

Both the woman's brother and Yuri had been tortured in the same way. A link? Or maybe someone wanted it to appear that way? She'd think about that later. In the few minutes before the *flics* arrived she needed to pry information out of this woman. "Poor Yuri. He had so little. . . ."

"'Sitting in sweet butter,' Yuri said to me," the woman interrupted, reaching the first-floor landing. She opened her door and hung up her mink coat. Warmth and the smell of apples drifted from inside this atelier, which was similar to Yuri's. Aimée guided her toward a chair as the woman dabbed at her eyes with a tissue. "*Bien sûr*, his wife's son, he's been sniffing around. The type who wants the butter and the money to buy it."

An old saying of her *grand-mère*'s. Aimée hadn't heard it in years. She remembered Yuri's comment on his daughter-in-law's cement blinis.

"Mark my words, look to family," the woman said. "That's what those crime shows say."

"What sweet butter?" Aimée fingered her bag's leather strap. "Yuri won the lotto?"

The woman dabbed her eyes again. Shrugged.

A painting so valuable Yuri had been tortured for it. Did that make sense? Aimée needed to press. This woman might have more information, a crucial detail.

74 CARA BLACK

"*Mais* following his father's funeral, he acted differently," the woman said. "Didn't you notice? After he visited the old Russian nursing home?"

A knock sounded on the door. The *flics*. Flustered, Aimée took a stab in the dark. "Ah, you mean that painting he inherited from his father, *non*? Seemed to worry him?"

"Not too much. Talked big after that, don't you remember?" Her eyes narrowed. "Where do you live, eh? I haven't seen you around."

"*Juste à côté*," Aimée said. Time to get the hell out of here. "May I use the ladies' before we talk to the *flics*, Madame?"

More knocking.

"End of the hall."

Aimée found no window in the bathroom. Cursed under her breath. She peeked out the door. Saw the woman's back. Tiptoed to the small kitchen and the back door, opened it to the dripping-wet balcony.

One floor down. She grabbed the metal balcony bars, let her legs dangle in the late morning air. Next door she saw Yuri's lighted atelier through a tall window. She took a deep breath and dropped, landing in wet grass. Mud and grass caked her boot heels.

Great.

A walkway led through the small courtyard. She scanned the back building windows for neighbors. Lace panels covered many of the closed windows. Too cold and wet for hanging laundry. Satisfied no one was looking out, she passed through an old gate and scaled a cracked stone wall to land on mud. Again.

A damp, trampled rosemary bush lay in her path. The fragrance enveloped her.

Her view at the garden's rear gave onto Yuri's kitchen. She could crouch down undetected—but for how long? Arriving blue uniforms filled the atelier. At any moment they'd start taping off the apartment, spread into the garden.

Something wet and fragrant brushed her cheek. A broken sprig of rosemary stuck from the wall. Rosemary for remembrance, and she had so much to remember. Stalling, she picked up the rosemary and examined it. Wound around the stem was a bit of yellow grass. Straw? No, more like hay. She had a sudden intuition it was the murderer who had trampled this rosemary, perhaps coming over the wall the same way she just had. She stuck the hay-tangled sprig in her pocket.

Right now only one thing was clear: She had to find this painting Yuri was tortured for that somehow led to her mother. Saj was in the clear for the accident now, or would be once Serge filed his report. Yet Aimée couldn't be sure he was safe until she knew who the Serb who'd tracked him down to the hospital had been. She couldn't shake the feeling that the dead Serb and the missing painting were linked. Besides, even if they weren't, she was caught up in this case now—she'd missed the old man's call, and now he was dead. His five thousand francs sat in her bag. She couldn't shake her feeling of guilt, not to mention her regret at losing her one link to her mother.

The neighbor's window opened. A finger pointed. "She's over there. . . ."

Aimée took off and didn't hear the rest.

Monday Afternoon, Silicon Valley

"WE'VE BUILT THE mainframe. Your job's maintenance so we can go back in and tweak it. Anything you need, René." Andy slapped him on the back, then followed up with a hug. *So California men like to hug?*

As if reading his mind, Andy laughed. "We're not kissers, like you froggies. But we're totally jazzed to have you as our CTO. Just remember, we need that back door for routine maintenance." He hugged René again. "Anything you need, dude."

Excited, René nodded. Dudes, cowboys—*alors*, this was the Wild West.

Andy peace-signed his way out.

Andy the long-haired CFO and Rob the investor angel were two of the most brilliant people René had ever met. Within five minutes of meeting them, he'd known there was no one like them in France. The company had algorithms a year ahead of any he'd seen. Their one problem was keeping people from getting in. His job: to make their security top-notch.

René cranked up his ergonomic chair at his new desk in what had been the car dealership's assistant's office. The room emanated fresh paint and glue from newly laid carpet. A leftover Buick Skylark calendar adorned the wall.

With his chief tech officer position came the company laptop, two desktop terminals, and keys to the former coffee room, which now housed the bank of computers. The beating heart of their stock-trading search-engine start-up. His start-up, too—he owned shares.

René glowed inside. Their genius concept was perfectly timed to crest the oncoming wave of stock trading. He kept wanting to pinch himself.

A few more algorithms, and he'd complete the security firewall. A real beauty. He savored a challenge.

He rubbed his hands together at the keyboard. *Splat!* Warm liquid dripped from his cuff-linked sleeve. He'd knocked the cup of what they called "coffee" over.

Merde.

By the time he reached the restroom, he'd figured out part of the code for the next algorithm in his head. But the big problem right now was the sink's high faucet—out of his reach. Had they built this for giants?

Non, just big Americans. He'd need a stool to reach it so he could wash off his stained, dripping sleeve. Hunting for anything to stand on, he ended up in the back storeroom. The cooling system whirred.

"He's perfect. The mainframe security's almost there."

René stopped in his tracks. Someone was speaking of his work. Pride filled his chest. The voice spoke at intervals. Like a cell phone conversation.

"He's brilliant but we won't. . . ." Loud whirring drowned the rest. René's gaze caught on a Pepsi crate. "He's set up. . . ." More whirring. ". . . front running." With all the background noise, he couldn't recognize the voice. "The dwarf's got no idea."

René's hands paused on the crate. What did that mean?

He walked through the storeroom, following the sound of a door shutting. EXIT. He opened the door, blinked into blinding sunlight to find the parking lot. He couldn't see over the hoods but heard an engine start up. By the time he reached the middle of the lot, the car was gone.

Had he misunderstood with all the noise? Or his bad English? But the thumping in his chest didn't go away.

Courtesy of the Pepsi crate, he cleaned up at the sink. He mulled over what he'd just heard while scrubbing out the stain. Wished he understood English better, and that his other Charvet handmade shirt wasn't in the motel on the street of fleas.

He cleaned his cuff as well as he could and returned the crate. Waiting for him in his office stood a Nordic-looking blonde. He did a double take. She held a steaming *café au lait* in a Styrofoam cup.

"We knew you'd prefer this, René." She grinned. Handed it to him and squeezed his arm. Wide hazel eyes, legs to forever. "We're here for you. I'm Susie, head programmer. My personal mission is to make sure you're happy."

He fell in love right there. His dream of California in the flesh. A *coup de foudre* standing in that car dealership garage-*cum*-office still emanating oil fumes. "I'll drop by your office later, okay?"

Back at his desk his mind spun in love. Or lust. He didn't know. He sipped the *café au lait*. It tasted perfect, like he imagined she would. Her hair would smell of sunshine.

Why couldn't his English be better? His mind went back to the storeroom. Of course he'd misunderstood.

He finished writing the algorithm. Tested it. But he couldn't get the phrase he'd overheard out of his mind—*The dwarf's got no idea.*

Tuesday Midday, Paris

HEAD DOWN, AIMÉE hurried down rue d'Alésia, merging with the chanting protesters. Her midnight-blue phone rang. Maxence.

The security reports, the systems monitoring . . . good God, she'd entrusted it all to a kid. Worried, she pressed TALK. "Anything wrong, Maxence?"

"No, but the funeral mass for Piotr Volodya—"

"Who's that?" she interrupted.

"Yuri Volodya's father, who died at one hundred last week," Maxence said. "Big to-do out at the Russian nursing home. *Le Figaro*'s obituary makes him out to be some kind of art connoisseur. Instrumental in the art movement in the twenties, apparently. That's the most recent hit I found."

Not bad, this kid.

"What did the old Russian say?" Maxence asked.

Her heart clenched. "Tell you later. If anyone calls, you don't know where I am. Take a message." She took a breath. "Keep researching. Find out how active Yuri was in political groups in the seventies." Her mother's time. "How's it going with the reports?"

She spied her scooter where she'd left it. A police car turned into the street ahead of her. She kept her head low as it passed.

"Printed out, filed, and backed up on René's computer."

Already? The kid took initiative. "Mind running the next batch? And give me a status update midway, *d'accord?*"

En route to her scooter she had an idea. "Maxence, where's that Russian nursing home?"

MORE THAN AN hour and two wrong turns later, Aimée located the Château de la Cossonnerie, outside Paris, now the nursing home adjoining the Russian cemetery. She down-shifted past the grilled gate into a circular gravel-lined drive-way and parked her scooter to the side of the tall limestone building. Her pulse raced. She was determined to discover how Yuri got "in butter" and then murdered. And how it involved her mother, if it did.

The deserted reception area—dark maroon chairs and matching wallpaper under a high ceiling bordered by faded gilt woodwork—exuded dim gloom. The back office lay dark. Paprika aromas drifted from the hallway, a low hum of clink-ing cutlery. Lunchtime. Didn't old people eat early? Not a bad idea. Her stomach growled. But she saw no computer to search for patients' names and rooms. Under a vase holding heavily scented freesias, she found the visitor log.

She wished the reception area offered more light as she searched the dates. But going back a few days she found a *Piotr Volodya, Room 34,* and Yuri's scrawled signature. Better to question a fellow patient who'd known him. She'd get more info that way than from a staff member bound by confidential-ity and privacy laws.

An orderly in white appeared in the hallway pushing a lunch cart. Behind him a woman, wiping the sides of her mouth with a napkin, bustled in from the dining room.

"You wish to tour, make an appointment?" Red, flowing curls framed her round, highly blushed face. Buxom and sealed into a green dress with shoulder pads, she could have stepped out of the eighties. "I'm Madame Gobulansky, *la directrice.*"

"Aimée Leduc. It's regarding the late Piotr Volodya's estate."

Madame Gobulansky played with her drop earrings. Wary.

"Estate? The man lived on charity here the last twenty years. Who do you represent?"

From her tone it sounded like Piotr had overstayed his welcome. Aimée flashed her *détective privé* card.

"A private detective?" Her lipsticked mouth pursed. "No crime's been committed here. I don't understand. Unless you're some vulture hired by his son."

Aimée kept her impatience down. "Madame, could you talk with me about Piotr Volodya?"

"We've got seventy-eight beds," Madame Gobulansky said. "And a waiting list. Neither I nor my staff discusses former patients."

La directrice covered her derrière. Yet, after coming all this way, Aimée wouldn't give up.

"But I can speak with residents who knew Piotr, his friends. No regulation against that?" Aimée smiled and kept on talking. "Perhaps the resident across from Piotr's room, number thirty four. Yuri spoke fondly of—"

"The only time we saw his son, Yuri, was before the funeral." Her lipstick smudged on her teeth.

"I'm acting on Yuri's behalf. He's the heir. . . ." Aimée looked down the hallway. Still deserted for lunch. "*Alors*, I wouldn't want to cause any unpleasantness or create unnecessary paperwork. Or raise a judicial complaint."

"We're a private foundation, Mademoiselle."

Aimée smiled. "Then you won't object to me having a casual conversation."

Madame Gobulansky sighed. "If you mean Madame Natasha . . ."

Madame Natasha? Aimée nodded. "*Mais oui*," she said. "Where is she?"

"Where Madame Natasha always sits at lunchtime." *La directrice*'s features became impassive. "For the last five years while Piotr was bedridden, she remained his companion. I'll introduce you."

Helpful now, Madame Gobulansky guided her across the hallway. Either Aimée had scared Madame *la directrice* or she'd cooked the wrong rabbit, as her father would say, and was getting fobbed off. "Just a moment, *s'il vous plaît.*"

Companion? Aimée wondered.

The nursing home was a museum. To the right swept a nineteenth-century staircase, brass rods holding dark maroon carpeting in place. Lining the hallway were oil portraits of Empress Catherine II, Emperors Alexander I, II, and III, a marble bust of Nicholas II, and an oil painting of tight-lipped Alexandra Fédorovna. In the corners clung a musty old-world smell. From another age, a vanished tsarist Russia of long ago. The only things missing were the cobwebs and Cossacks.

Her nose crinkled at the old-people smell that the disinfectant didn't cover.

Madame Gobulansky beckoned her inside before disappearing in a rustle of polyester.

The high-ceilinged salon held a cloying old-lady rose scent and a large *télé*. On the screen played a ballet—vintage black-and-white reels without sound.

"*Bonjour*, Madame, maybe you can help me."

"*Moi?*" Madame Natasha, in a wheelchair with an oxygen tube clipped to her nose, was applying mascara. "God blesses those who help themselves." A fine dust of wrinkles covered her otherwise taut, translucent face. Her clawlike fingers wavered. Aimée wanted to reach out and guide the mascara comb.

"Not bad for ninety-eight, eh?" She gave a quavering laugh. "Go ahead, tell me I don't look a day over eighty."

"You don't." Aimée smiled. Must have been a beauty in her day. Clear sapphire eyes, erect posture in the wheelchair. Hopefully her mind was as clear.

"May I take a few minutes of your time?"

"Time? But that's all I have now." She pointed to the *télé* screen. "Of course, you came to hear my stories of the Ballets Russes at Monte Carlo. That's me, the third from the left."

Aimée stifled a groan. "Fascinating. But I'd like to know about Piotr Volodya. I hear you were his companion."

"Where's Piotr gone?" She tugged a crocheted throw over her withered legs. "He's late."

Late?

"His son Yuri sent me." A semi-truth.

"That son who never visits him?" Natasha put down her mascara. "I outlived four husbands." Natasha gave a theatrical sigh. The corners of her wrinkled red lips turned down. "We're engaged. See my ring from Piotr." Natasha flashed a blue-veined hand with a garish red stone like a cherry on her swollen, arthritic middle finger. Not even glass.

"Exquisite." Aimée stared, her heart sinking.

"Spoils of the tsar." Madame Natasha leaned over her wheelchair arm. "We must speak in code. They're listening."

No wonder Madame Gobulansky had complied, Aimée thought. The old biddy drifted through time with a good dose of paranoia.

"Who's listening?"

"The Okhrana. The tsar's secret police." She put a thin finger to her lips. Nodded. "Piotr knows. Lenin told him."

The white-tutu'd ballerinas flickered on the screen. Great. A ninety-eight-year-old ballerina with dementia.

Natasha's lips parted in a wide smile. For a moment the years fell away. "Men have always given me things."

Aimée scanned the dull gold icons on the walls, an assemblage of pastel and watercolor paintings. In the corner a bronze samovar bubbled and steamed.

"Can you tell me about Piotr and Yuri's relationship?"

"After we have tea, Mademoiselle."

Aimée contained her impatience as Natasha wheeled herself

to the samovar. She passed Aimée a steaming cup of tea with a cube of sugar. "Suck. Like this."

Aimée followed suit, propping the cube between her tongue and teeth as Natasha did. The Kusmi Russian tea trickled down her throat like a sweet, wet, smoky breath.

Natasha opened a worn scrapbook with yellowed ballet programs, thrust it at Aimée. The last thing she wanted to see.

"Diaghilev worked us hard, let me tell you. Olga, my garret mate, married Picasso, you know. They met while he was designing our ballet," Natasha said. "He ignored me, thank God, the little toad with a barrel chest. Diaghilev's buried out in the cemetery. Nureyev too, that upstart. Rudi was charming when he wanted to be, but I heard he was a devil to work with."

Sad, but Aimée hadn't come for wistful historical remembrances. The fact that Yuri had been murdered so soon after his father's death meant something.

"Let's get back to Piotr's relationship with Yuri," Aimée said, setting her cup down. "Wasn't there a painting?"

"Shhh. Piotr's on a mission."

And he wouldn't be coming back.

"But you must know the code or you wouldn't be here," Natasha said.

Best to play along with her. Learn something. "*Bien sûr*, but Yuri said. . . ."

"Yuri knows only part of the code. I let him think he understood. It's all in the letter."

"Letter?" Aimée took a closer look at the scrapbook. Opened the back pages. "One of these?" Stuck in between were yellowed parchment envelopes with old canceled stamps addressed to Mademoiselle Natasha Petrovsky.

"Not my old love letters." A flicker of the gamine crossed her eyes. "*Les pneus.*"

A code? So far she'd gotten nowhere. And then, wedged

in the scrapbook, she saw a letter addressed to Monsieur Piotr Volodya postmarked Paris, March 1920.

Natasha glanced toward the samovar. "More tea?"

"*Non, merci,*" said Aimée, slipping the letter in her pocket. "*Les pneus?* I don't understand."

"A pity. The two hadn't spoken in years. But Yuri was in such a rush that day."

Aimée saw an opening. "That's why I'm here. Piotr told you his stories, *non?* He left Yuri a painting from his collection."

Natasha took another sugar cube between her teeth. A good set of dentures, Aimée figured. Natasha's gaze wandered. Her neck muscles quivered under thin white skin.

Aimée leaned forward. She needed this old woman to open up. "Wasn't Piotr instrumental in the twenties avant-garde art movement?"

"Instrumental? Piotr was a penniless Russian émigré from the shtetl. Just a classic émigré story." Natasha waved her thin blue-veined hands. "In those days, after the Revolution, you'd find a prince driving a taxi." She sighed. "Piotr served . . . how do you say it, like a waiter in a bistro where destitute artists—all famous now—paid for meals with their paintings."

Natasha sounded rational. As if she'd heard this story many times.

"Worth a fortune now, I'd imagine," Aimée said.

"A franc a dozen then. You call that instrumental in the avant-garde?" Natasha's tone turned petulant. "Piotr's supposed to help me. Awful man, late again." She pushed her wheelchair back. "But you young know the price of everything, not the value. See art as merchandise to trade and sell."

Surprised, Aimée shook her head. "I don't understand. Didn't Piotr pass his painting collection to Yuri?"

"You sound just like Yuri's stepson."

Aimée's mind went back to Yuri's neighbor's words—how Oleg the stepson had been buzzing around him like a fly lately.

"Oleg's no friend of mine," Aimée said. How could she make sense of the strands running through the old woman's words? To do that, she'd need to gain her trust. "As you know, Piotr's on a mission. I came to assist."

"But the code. . . ." Natasha's eyes narrowed in suspicion. "I thought you knew."

The old woman went from rational to irrational in seconds. Would Aimée have that to look forward to if she lived as long?

"There are more letters, *n'est-ce pas?*"

"Like everything else, I had to keep them for him. They're somewhere, of course."

Letters that should have been given to Yuri. Letters that could authenticate the painting, she imagined.

"All his talk about drinking *la fée vert*," Natasha said.

La fée vert, the green fairy, the old name for absinthe. Where did that come from?

"Absinthe's been outlawed a long time," Aimée said.

"All those drinks at la Rotonde with the artists, poets, revolutionaries, anarchists," Natasha said. "Montparnasse in the old days. The good old days. As if Piotr knew."

Aimée started to put things together.

"Tall tales, eh? Or you believed him?"

"Piotr loved recounting how Lenin bounced him on his knee. The way Modigliani wore a red scarf and danced on the table."

Aimée remembered that lesson in history class about the Russian Revolution. 1917. She calculated mentally that Piotr, if one hundred years old, would have. . . .

"I'm tired," Natasha said. She clicked the remote and the *télé* went dark.

Instead of leaving, she could go along with the old biddy and search for more letters.

"Let me take you to your room," Aimée said.

* * *

NATASHA'S ROOM GAVE off that same cloying rose scent she'd noticed before, coupled with disinfectant. A hospital bed with a stained duvet, old Russian newspapers piled on a *secrétaire* desk with an old-fashioned inkwell—all bathed in light streaming in from the tall window. A small armoire and chest of drawers were topped by china figurines, giving off a sense of genteel disorder. Framed sepia-tinted ballet posters covered the walls, which were fringed by a ceiling of carved wood boiserie. So many places to hide letters.

"They're listening," Natasha whispered, gesturing to the ceiling. "They put special devices in the wallboards."

Aimée gave a knowing nod, determined to get some sense out of her. Appeal to her somehow. "Between you and me, Natasha, I'm shocked Yuri and his father didn't get along," she said, trying again. "Any idea why?"

"Piotr always said he wanted Yuri to understand." She leaned toward Aimée conspiratorially.

"To understand what?"

Natasha shrugged her thin shoulders. "So sad. He trusted me with everything."

"The letters, that's what you mean?"

"It's all in the code." Natasha's blue eyes sparkled. "We celebrated Piotr's one hundredth birthday last month. Big celebration. Even the priest from the Alexander Nevsky church came."

Aimée knew the Russian Orthodox church on rue Daru—a gold cupolaed confection near the Parc Monceau. Nestled in an enclave called Little Russia in the chic 8th arrondissement, the church was well known for its Orthodox ceremonies. René had found a terrific freelancer, a dissident émigré hacker who went by the name Rasputin, on the job board at the side vestry. It was a Russian community hub.

Was Natasha dropping a clue here?

"Any bad blood between Yuri and Piotr?"

Natasha fiddled with the control on her oxygen tank. "Piotr

abandoned his wife and his son." A sigh. "I think Piotr wanted to make it up to Yuri. But never had the chance."

Or maybe he did. *In butter*, the neighbor had said. And Aimée had Yuri's cash in her bag.

"Didn't Piotr leave Yuri something special, Natasha? "

Natasha yawned. "Where's Piotr's key?"

"Key?"

"In his drawer. There was a key." A bell sounded from downstairs. "His son took it. But he didn't take everything."

"A key to what?"

"How do I know?"

"What did it look like?"

Natasha yawned again. Her lids drooped.

"Small, like for a bank safety deposit box? Or a bigger key, like to an apartment or storage? Try to remember, Natasha."

"Old-fashioned." Natasha rang a bell for the nurse. "I need my pills."

Aimée scanned the room. Handed Natasha the pink pills in the oval plastic cup. "These?"

Natasha shook her head. "I want the purple ones."

Now or never. She'd appeal to the paranoia. "I've got to find the cameras, Natasha."

"The cameras? *Mais, oui.* I want to dance," she said, her breathing labored. "Get my tights."

Aimée opened the drawers: mothball-tinged lace camisoles, graying leotards crumbling to her touch. In the armoire she found folded linens, hanging vintage wool coats, a pleated Fortuny pale lemon chemise. Timeless.

The *secrétaire* drawers yielded worn leather boxes of costume and paste jewelry. A gray, gummed tarnish came off on Aimée's fingers.

Perspiration dampened the back of Aimée's neck, the thin skin at the crook of her elbow. The old woman had become quiet during her search. Aimée shot her a glance.

Natasha's lids drooped. Short, shallow breaths issued from her. The oxygen tank meter level had dropped to the red range. What should she do?

Aimée twisted the oxygen meter knob, but the needle stayed steady on red. Her stomach clenched. The poor old woman wasn't getting oxygen. Thank God the red call light lit up on the wall. A bell rang from the corridor. She figured she had a minute at most.

She shook the Russian newspapers. No hidden letters. Desperate, she reached under the hospital mattress, looked under the bed and found dust balls. Footsteps pounded in the hallway. She ran her hands under the crisp cotton pillow. Inside the pillowcase she felt something hard and cylindrical, recognized an old-fashioned pneumatic tube. She stuffed the tube in her waistband.

Of course it made sense now.

"Madame Natasha?"

A nurse stared at Aimée. She stiffened. "What are you doing?"

"Quick. Her oxygen's. . . ."

"Low because she fiddled with the knobs again." A sigh came from the nurse who turned on the reserve. "It happens every day. Why are you in here?"

"I can't find her tutu."

Natasha sat up, wide awake, with a glint of fire in her crow's-feet eyes. "Stop her, she's the Okhrana agent. She's spying on me!"

Aimée fluffed the pillow, then shot the nurse a knowing look. "*Bien sûr*, Madame Natasha. Next time we'll decipher the code."

Aimée winked at the nurse on her way out the door. She took the stairs two at a time. Too bad the writing she'd glimpsed inside was in Russian.

But she knew where to start. She climbed on her Vespa, double-knotted her scarf, and headed back to Paris.

"Piotr Volodya? I don't know him," said the plump, black-cassocked priest with matching black beard. He sported a thick gold cross on his chest. "Can't help you, Mademoiselle."

He reminded her of a black bear standing on the Alexander Nevsky Cathedral steps.

"You're sure he's not one of your flock, Father?" She smiled. "The nursing home at Sainte-Geneviève-des-Bois mentioned that one of your priests visited for Piotr Volodya's one hundredth birthday party."

"The rector might know, but he's in Nantes until tomorrow, Mademoiselle. Check back then."

The priest stepped down the last step of the cathedral's wide staircase. He waved to several women setting out food on a table under an umbrella by budding plane trees. Young boys played nearby. A quiet islet of peace next to the church. Plates of smoked fish, thick black bread. Quite a spread. Reminded her she hadn't eaten since a yogurt this morning.

"If you'll excuse me, Mademoiselle?"

A dead end already?

"Sadly, Piotr passed away," she said, thinking hard. "Alone. But I want to inform his relatives in Russia. Or here. Speak with someone who knew him."

"Now I remember," he said. "That was Father Ninkinov. But he's down south for a retreat."

Didn't people confide in priests? Especially dying people? She pressed her card in the priest's big hands.

"The man died without family here. I'm just trying to help out. Please ask Father Ninkinov to contact me."

"A retreat of silence, Mademoiselle." He turned away.

Now she didn't hold out much hope. Her heels scrunched over the gravel, trying to keep up with him. As they passed the message board, paper slips with Cyrillic names and phone numbers fluttering in the breeze, she made one last attempt. "I need a translator. Who do you recommend, Father?"

He paused long enough to consider the board. "Marevna

or Valeria. Try either of these two." He tore them off. "Don't forget to mention Father Medveyed recommended you."

"You're a close community, Father," she said, biting her tongue before adding "closed against outsiders."

"Cautious," he said. "Introductions count within our community, just like in yours."

Did they have such different cultures? Not for the first time she felt she was stepping into another world, complete with a language and alphabet she couldn't decipher.

"*Merci*, Father."

A few pops of the gravel and he disappeared under the trees.

THE TRAIL HADN'T iced up yet. The first twelve hours after a murder—crucial in an investigation—yielded the most. Her father had drilled that into her.

But she could kick herself for not insisting Yuri reveal what made this painting so valuable that it was stolen before the appraisal. Why he'd begged for her help, then changed his mind.

She reached the first recommended translator, Marevna, who agreed to meet with her. At last, some luck. Aimée circled chic Place de Catalogne in the 14th arrondissement and wound her scooter down rue du Château, run down in places, passing narrow lanes marked by two-story workshops, a bakery, a cobbler shop. The old Paris.

A rustle of tepid wind enveloped her. This weather forecasted a hot, wet summer. This thought took her back to a long-ago humid August in the countryside. Her *grand-mère*'s candles had gone limp, leaving a trail of wax tears on the wooden farm table. Hunting in the oak trees for birds' nests of speckled blue quail eggs, the taste of *Grand-mère*'s cake perfumed with orange-blossom water. The hazy memory of her mother laughing in the orchard, kissing the fresh raspberry stains on Aimée's small fingers.

A barking Westie on the pavement brought her back to the present, to the sun-dappled, rain-freshened street, the passersby. The ache of longing remained, the buried sense of guilt that she'd caused her mother to leave. Her mother had been an artist, a sketcher and painter, who probably saw the world through a delicate artistic temperament. Aimée could only guess that she had been too much to handle. Once, just once, she wanted to see her mother again. This painting led to her mother, she knew it in her bones.

And then Yuri's battered face, his swollen tongue, filled her mind. Only a few hours ago she'd stood in bloody water and smelled that lingering floral note of *muguet,* lily of the valley, her mother's scent. Her mother . . . Yuri's murderer?

The light turned green. Horns blared behind her. She popped into first gear.

Le Zakouski, the meeting point, turned out to be part *resto,* part delicatessen—one red-ceilinged room with a glass refrigerator case crammed next to tables with red-checked plastic tablecloths. Old photos and bright paintings plastered the walls like wallpaper. Kiev kitsch circa 1967.

"You pay cash?" A woman's round face framed by long, straight, platinum hair poked up from the deli counter. Early twenties, Aimée thought.

Nice greeting. Aimée nodded. "Marevna?"

"Take a seat. We open later for dinner."

Aimée sat by the window, moving aside the red napkin holder. She set Piotr's letter and the funny tube down on the red-checked plastic cloth and studied it for the first time.

La poste pneumatique, or *"pneu,"* had been in use until the mid-eighties, a system for delivering letters, *télégrammes,* or cards. These cylinders were propelled along tubes underground by compressed air or partial vacuum to post offices, which delivered them for a few centimes. At one time the National Assembly linked pneumatically with the Senate—a precursor to the intranet—via tubes under the Jardin du Luxembourg. She had childhood memories of watching her grandfather slip a *pneu* in the narrow slot at *la poste*. But she wondered why Natasha had kept this ugly gray metal tube. Aimée unscrewed the end. The musty smell of paper came out with rolled-up creased envelopes bearing forty-centime stamps. Circa 1920, she figured. The fat one was written in Cyrillic. Aimée put the few in French addressed to Natasha, and the one from Natasha's scrapbook, to the side.

Marevna pulled up a chair. Sniffed. Her pink lipsticked mouth formed a moue of distaste.

"How much to translate everything?" Aimée pulled out her worn Vuitton wallet.

"You're kidding, *non?*"

"I need the whole contents. I have to know what's relevant," Aimée said.

"Relevant? Father said you're some volunteer at the nursing home trying to locate family back in Russia."

So she'd checked. Aimée wondered again at the priest's word, "cautious." Suspicious, more like it.

Aimée took out the other slip from her pocket and showed her. "Valeria, the other translator, didn't ask me questions. But Father said you're better."

Marevna's long-lashed eyes blinked. "What your meaning?"

"You do a simple translation. We keep this between us."

Aimée glanced around the deserted *resto*, the faded photos, the none-too-fresh tubs of orange salmon caviar in the cooler. Doubted Marevna earned much in salary or tips. "This now." She slid a hundred-franc note over the table. "Two more like this when you finish. You interested or not?"

Marevna's fingers clenched the hundred francs. "Deal."

Smart. She understood.

Marevna untied her apron. Pulled out a pen and a notebook from her pocket, opened the rolled papers. A few moments passed. Only the ticking of a clock, the thumbing of pages. A slab of sun warmed Aimée's arm through the window.

"Maybe I summarize, *da?* You looking for names and family in Russia?"

Aimée didn't know what she was looking for besides a reason for Yuri's murder. A clue to this painting. Or whether these old letters even led there. Two letters and several pages of writing on old, browned onionskin paper. Papers she'd stolen from an old Russian ballerina.

Far-fetched, maybe, but she couldn't help wondering if Natasha had remained lucid long enough to contract the painting's heist. Or more plausible that Oleg, Yuri's wife's son, had heard the stories and put it together. That's if there was something to put together. She hoped this wouldn't come back to bite her.

"Why don't you just read?" Aimée said, trying to control her impatience. "You can write it up later."

"*Da,* this from 1988." She scanned a few pages. "He switches back and forth in time. What you say, not linear events?" Marevna read more.

Through the window, Aimée caught sight of a teenage boy straddling his parked motorcycle, smoking. Relishing every puff and blowing smoke rings into the air. She wished her fingers didn't twitch for just one drag. Marevna was leaning forward, jotting down a word every so often. She was interested now. "Lucky for you. I study psychology."

Aimée sat up. "Why?"

"Therapist recommends Piotr explain an old letter to his son, to—how you say—make his guilt be less? Make amends for past, yes, that's better way to say. Do like an exercise in a journal for what he remembers. Write down as much as he can to flex brain muscles, prevent mental stagnation. For therapy."

"Like a chronicle of his life?"

"Russians tell stories. That generation, like my

great-*grand-mère*, that's how they teach us about the past."
Marevna sighed. "Wars, siege of Stalingrad, all those things."

"Piotr was born in 1898," Aimée said. "How far back in his
childhood does he go?"

"First he write about coming to Paris. Hungry, his own
father looking for work. His father dying. That kind of thing
you want to hear?"

The story was probably fascinating, but she didn't have
time. Aimée thought back to Natasha's words. "Look for mentions of Lenin. Paintings." For the first time, she noticed pages
had been folded back. "What about here?"

"Lenin?" Marevna shook her head. "Vladimir Ilyich Uly-
anov Lenin?"

"That one, *oui*."

Marevna flipped through the journal pages, scanning for the
name. Aimée, suddenly irritated, wanted to snap at her to be
careful with the thin paper.

"Piotr says he the second wave of *Russes* immigrants. I'm the
fifth or sixth, depending how you count."

"That doesn't seem important," Aimée said.

"Important you understand background." Marevna's face
flushed. "Must understand Russian psychology to do with
French. Make more sense for you to know."

Aimée gave a quick, impatient nod. "*Et alors?*"

"Russian aristocrats at tsar's court learned French, spoke it
to each other instead of Russian," Marevna said. "The elite
had a love affair with French culture. French reciprocate—you
know *bistrot* is a Russian word?"

Aimée didn't much care.

"Tsar's troops occupied Paris in 1871, but nobody served
meal fast enough. 'Bisto, bisto,' meaning 'faster, faster,' they
shouted in Russian. It became *bistro*—you know, for fast food."

It was too much. "Look, can you just check if there's anything about—"

Marevna huffed. "I try to tell you about why are Russians in Paris. You don't know this, maybe his stories here don't make any sense."

Aimée sighed and nodded. The withered caviar was starting to look delicious.

"This Piotr." Marevna tapped the pages. "He was poor in Russia. But you know even before the Revolution so many Russian aristocrats come to Paris. In 1900, the Exposition, they settle in little *palais* and give parties for French nobility. Later, Lenin and Trotsky, the revolutionaries, they come to Paris, and the tsar's Okhrana, his secret service, also comes, to watch them."

"Okhrana?" The ones Natasha feared. "How do you know all this?"

"Mandatory revolutionary teaching, before the fall of Soviet Union. Everyone my age learned history of our country and yours. We know white *Russes* aristos fled Revolution of 1917— dukes, counts leave everything. Now penniless. Drive taxis— you know about white Russians who drove taxis. Lana, the owner here, her uncle drove a taxi."

Marevna pointed to a wall photo of a middle-aged woman and older man posing self-consciously in front of the restaurant.

"Then Jews before the Great War. After Great War, POWs and more Jews, who escaped Stalin's stalag. Stalin say all POWs are traitors. After that, a wave of dissidents in the eighties, and like me, after the Wall tumbled, we came here." Marevna shrugged. "The old white Russians look at us like trash. Soviet trash."

Aimée had no idea.

"But essential you understand importance of Lenin in Paris." Marevna's voice rose, growing passionate. "This is where he . . . how do you say? Where he formulate his ideology. Like idealist. All his writings, he did in Paris. Cradle of Revolution, we learned. Right here."

Enough of the Revolution. "Of course, but getting back to Piotr and Yuri. Does he mention Lenin?"

"*Da*. You see." She pointed to the slanted Cyrillic letters, meaningless to Aimée. "That's why I'm telling you. After his father died, Piotr and his mother lived on rue Marie Rose."

"How's that important?" Aimée wanted to explode.

"Piotr lived below Lenin's apartment," Marevna said. "He writes how Lenin bounced him on his knee."

Aimée nodded. Natasha had quoted that almost verbatim.

"Lenin's wife, Krupskaya, made Piotr *borscht*," Marevna continued. "Lenin helped Piotr's mother get work as a cook. His father had died, the mother was so poor. *Da*, here he mentions Lenin," Marevna said, pointing to a sheet. "He's writing now how Lenin never had children. Piotr writes about him with affection, saw a human side."

Aimée watched as Marevna read more, jotted notes. Laughed. "Piotr's describing his first taste of absinthe, when he's eighteen. 'Green like firewater,' he write. At la Rotonde in Montparnasse, Modigliani buy him drink. Modigliani would sketch in the café for five francs. Then buy drink for everyone."

Aimée blinked. The ravings of Alzheimer's or. . . ?

Drink, drugs, women, the legends and myths of Modigliani in Montparnasse. Or Modi, as they called him, rhyming it with *maudit,* cursed. A drunk lunatic.

That was when Aimée noticed a photo sticking out from the pages. Much-thumbed, black-and-white and grainy. Three men stood squinting at the sun. One wore a bowler hat, another a scarf, and both towered over the short man between them. Aimée recognized the sign of la Rotonde café behind. And the men. Her heart skipped. She turned it over to see what was written on the back.

André Salmon, Amadeo Modigliani, and Pablo Picasso, 1916, signed Cocteau.

Stunned, Aimée turned it over again. Studied the faces. Happy.

She picked up an envelope stamped UNDELIVERABLE—RETURN TO SENDER, addressed to Yuri Volodya with an old forty-centime stamp, a café name imprinted on the upper left. From days gone by, when cafés supplied writing paper to their patrons, who could count on twice-a-day postal service. Or *la pneu* delivery. She stared at the faded blue paper covered with Cyrillic—wondered where a salutation would go. But most of all, whether this involved Lenin.

This was taking too long. Too much payout and no real information. Unless this photo had something to do with the letter. She opened the envelope, handed it to Marevna. "Do you see a date here? Anything about a painting or Lenin?"

"Patient, please. June 2, 1925. This letter say, *To my son Yuri*." Marevna's eyes scanned intently. "Piotr writes about his bistro job when he was twenty-two, in 1920. Just married. About to have him, his son Yuri."

Marevna read further.

"Piotr writes Modigliani was terribly sick. Tuberculosis. Like a plague, if people knew. Everyone avoided you."

Like AIDS today.

"Modigliani hid disease, Piotr says, few knew. Or understood him." Marevna looked up. "He wants Yuri to understand. Here it's very sad."

Her voice had changed. Aimée leaned closer, struck by Marevna's tone. "Go on."

"Piotr says no one saw Modigliani for several weeks. Piotr worried, so he snuck a pot of cassoulet from bistro to Modigliani's atelier, on rue de la Grande Chaumière. Found Modigliani in his studio, in a very cold December, burning with fever. Coughing blood. No heat. Only ashes in the grate. He wished he'd brought coal. He saw empty wine bottles, moldy sardines in a tin. Modi's mistress helped feed him but she was very pregnant, like his own wife. Difficult for her to get around. Modi said—to thank him—for Piotr to take a painting, anything he wanted."

The *resto* fell away and Aimée felt the cold, the worry a twenty-two-year-old Piotr knew for this genius, this man who'd been good to him.

Marevna shook her head. "Here I try to quote. 'Modi was always generous and kind to me growing up. The man lived to paint, to express. A purist. Genius. It pierced me to see him forgotten in this freezing room, surrounded by art he barely made a living from, shivering with fever. But Modi says then I must take the portrait of my old friend, Lenin. The one Lenin commissioned in 1910 but didn't like.'"

"Didn't like?" Aimée interrupted.

Marevna scanned the page. "An argument. Modi said they'd had some kind of fight. Lenin left for Switzerland and never took the painting."

Aimée sat up. A portrait of Lenin by Modigliani? Rare, unique, unknown. But if Modigliani painted this portrait as a commission in 1910, before Lenin returned to lead the Revolution, who else knew about this? What did this mean?

"He writes Modi was coughing, coughing," Marevna continued. "Blood over the blankets but Modi insists to sign the painting to him, 'For my friend Piotr.' He writes, 'Modi said to me, "This means something to you, Piotr. You must have it." And that's the last thing he ever said to me. Two days later he died at the Hôpital de la Charité. Next day his mistress, big with child, jumped off a roof.' Tragic."

Aimée noticed Marevna's hands quivering. The paper was stained with a watery blotch of faded ink. As if Piotr had cried while writing this.

So Piotr had a portrait of Lenin painted by Modigliani. A gift from the artist. Unless this letter had been forged afterward to give the painting a provenance. But the feel of the old blue letter, the stamps, the café address told her it hadn't.

"Is there more?"

Marevna translated on. "'That night you were born, Yuri, all I remember was the cold wind on my way to fetching midwife. And your pink, wrinkly face hours later. That's what I want to explain—this painting belongs to you, too, Yuri. The painting was of Lenin, the man who lived above us, who talked to me when my own papa died. I will try to make things up to you since I had to go away.'"

Go away? Aimée checked the faded postmark. She made out 1925, the letterhead of Café de la Gare in Marseilles.

"'When you are older, can appreciate, the portrait belongs to you.' That's all." Marevna looked up. "If the painting exists, it's very sad. Very rare."

The painting existed, all right. Yuri's murder attested to that. But who had stolen it last night?

Piotr had written this as a testament, kept this letter for Yuri as an authentication. Yuri, not Natasha, should have had it. Why hadn't it come to light while old Piotr was alive?

Questions, so many questions.

She figured Oleg, his stepson, knew of the painting's existence—that was why he'd been snooping around for money lately. Were there others? She'd start with him.

A door slammed in the back. Marevna jumped. Fear flashed in her eyes.

"I have to work. You go, please."

"But there's another letter," Aimée said.

"Not finished yet, Marevna?" came a voice from the kitchen.

"Leave before Lana asks questions." With a quick motion Marevna piled the papers together.

"Careful. That's delicate." Before she could stick them in her apron pocket, Aimée gripped her hand. "Not so fast."

"But I translate more after work."

She'd discovered what she needed for now—the rest later. "We'll meet then," she said, noting Marevna's mounting uneasiness. "I might need these."

Did Marevna see another avenue of cash? A conduit using the Russian grapevine—the tight community—to broker the information? A portrait of Lenin by Modigliani . . . and the letter to prove it. One needed the other. But then Aimée knew zero about the art world.

A priest's referral didn't guarantee she could trust Marevna, but she had to keep her options open. Aimée stuck two hundred francs in Marevna's pocket. "That's for now."

She paused at the Trotsky photo by the door. A piece of the puzzle clicked in the back of her mind. "Lana's political, a Trotskyist?"

"That's all so passé," Marevna said, glancing back at the kitchen. "It's her old uncle's."

"He around?"

Marevna tipped an imaginary bottle to her mouth. "Fond of the drink. Like all that generation."

Like Yuri.

"Ask him to call me, will you?" Aimée handed her a card and another bill. Yuri's money. "But this we keep between us, *d'accord?*"

Marevna nodded.

Tuesday Early Afternoon, Paris

AIMÉE KNEW LITTLE about art, even less about the art world. But she knew who to ask.

"Lieutenant Olivant?" said the receptionist at the *préfecture de police*. "He works out of OCSC now."

She never remembered the meaning behind those acronyms for various police branches. The terms changed all the time.

"He still works with stolen art, *n'est-ce pas?*"

"*Bah ouais*," came the typical Parisian reply. "That's what they do there, Mademoiselle."

"Mind transferring me?"

A click. Another receptionist, who transferred her to the third floor, then another series of clicks. A bland recording of extension numbers. Finally, after punching in Lieutenant Olivant's extension, she got his voice mail. Didn't anyone answer their office lines anymore?

She got as far as giving her name and number before the recorded voice came on. *Message box full.*

Great. She'd try later. Right now a big, fat zero.

The old man's letter hadn't shed any light on one mystery, though. How did Yuri know her mother? Dead, he couldn't tell her. But if there was any chance to learn something about her mother, she'd find it.

By now the *flics* would have questioned people on the street, the inhabitants of Villa d'Alésia. The mink-coated neighbor knew something—even if she didn't know she did. She'd heard the raised voices. Aimée had to risk going back there to find this Oleg. She didn't even know his last name.

"You again?"

Yuri Volodya's neighbor, Madame Figuer, whose name Aimée discovered by reading the mailbox, stood in her door in a black jogging suit. Her red-rimmed eyes darted under freshly applied black eyebrows. "The *flics* want to talk to you, Mademoiselle. Ask you why you ran away."

"Please, Madame, I need your help," Aimée said. "I'll explain."

Madame Figuer gripped a pink cell phone. "May I help?" She punched in a number. "Explain it to them."

Aimée reached out and hit END. "*Pardonnez-moi*, Madame, but no phone calls. *Desolée*, it's important."

Alarmed, Madame Figuer stepped back. Started to close her door. "Leave me alone."

Aimée stuck her foot in the door. "Please, we need to talk."

"They said you could be an accomplice." Her voice rose. "Dangerous."

"Can you keep a secret?" Aimée shouldered her way inside, going with her plan B: on-the-fly improvisation—approaching plausible, she hoped. She needed to keep this woman quiet and glean information.

"Madame, my unit investigates stolen art of national cultural importance," she said, reaching in her bag. "Not many know of us. We work out of 3 rue de Lutèce."

At least her contact did. Unless the bureau had moved. Openmouthed, Madame Figuer stared at her.

"Art investigator? In that outfit?"

Aimée noticed a nick on her Prada boots. The pair she'd borrowed from Martine.

"You think we wear uniforms? Forget those crime shows you watch on the *télé*, Madame," Aimée said. "Nothing exotic. Our cases involve painstaking investigation. Any detail could lead to recovery."

Madame Figuer pulled herself ramrod straight. She was about to throw Aimée out the door.

"We work independently, but often in tandem with police," Aimée said. "Our interest coincides here, but I'm working another angle."

"Likely story. You ran off."

Aimée nodded. "I'm undercover. But I shouldn't have told you."

"So I should believe that? Show me your credentials, your ID."

Undercover never carried ID. Too compromising if they were rumbled. But Madame Figuer wouldn't know that. She pulled a card from her alias collection.

"Ministry of the Interior?" asked Madame Figuer.

"Thefts from cathedrals, state museums. In certain cases we investigate robbery from private collections. But that's all I can say." Aimée leaned forward as if in confidence. "I've told you more than I should. Yet your brother was an artist. Talented." She gestured to the watercolors in the hallway. "You of all people will understand. That's why I came to explain. Enlist your aid."

Madame Figuer blinked several times. Cheap to use the dead brother? But Aimée had struck a nerve.

"You can't think old Yuri possessed . . ."

"A national treasure, Madame Figuer?" she said. "We do." Suddenly she noticed a wonderful buttery smell emanating from the kitchen. Her overwhelming hunger, which she'd forgotten in the excitement of the letter, came roaring back.

"Yuri was tortured and murdered for it?" Madame Figueur's hands shook.

"I'd rather talk here, but we can go to headquarters."

Madame Figuer adjusted the jacket zipper of her jogging

suit, played with the snap on her coin purse. "But I'm late for the market. The melons. Then the plumber's coming to repair the water damage."

"We'll make this quick." Aimée gestured to Madame's kitchen.

By the time Aimée had eaten half the plate of Madame Figuer's fresh-baked crisp almond *financiers* plus leftover *pain perdu*, she'd gleaned an outline of Yuri's movements for the past three days.

"The *flics* questioned me," Madame Figuer said, "but then I didn't volunteer much. Couldn't. The shock. I took one of my pink pills."

"Pills?" The woman was elderly but seemed clear and alert to Aimée.

"For my nerves, you know. When I think of Yuri tortured next door . . . just like my brother was betrayed and tortured in forty-three . . . it's all so. . . ." Her voice trailed off.

Coincidental? But Aimée kept that to herself. Perhaps Madame's retelling over the years had, like such stories steeped in shame, become unspoken common knowledge?

Madame Figuer shuddered. "Do you think *la police* will ask me more questions?"

"Possible." Aimée needed to work fast. "Let's go back to when you noticed Yuri got 'in butter,' as you said."

According to Madame Figuer, Yuri had borrowed her wheelbarrow from her garden shed four days earlier to clean up his father's cellar—that was how she knew his father had died. But when he'd returned it, he'd brought her a bottle of wine. "Soon we'll be celebrating," he'd said.

Saturday he'd driven his old Mercedes somewhere with Damien Perret, the young long-haired man from the printing shop on rue de Châtillon. A nice boy, she added, in spite of his radical politics, but then everyone's young once, *non?* Yuri's stepson, Oleg, visited in the afternoon.

But of last night's accident she knew nothing, having stayed at her sister's. She'd returned this morning to a flood in her apartment and loud voices from his open window across the courtyard wall.

Aimée thought back to earlier that morning; she'd been at the morgue when Yuri had left that message. Not much later, he called to take back his words. After contact with her mother? An acid taste filled her mouth. She took a deep breath. "Did you hear a woman's voice?"

Madame Figuer shook her head.

"Didn't you say Russian before?"

She shook her head again. "Thought so at first, but no, that I'd recognize," she said. "The quartier used to be full of them. Thick with artists, too. Giacometti used to live here. He was like a stick man, the wild hair. . . ."

More stories of the past?

Madame Figuer gave a little sigh. "Everything's changed. So different now."

Aimée compiled a list of everyone Madame Figuer mentioned. Oleg—at the top of the list—wasn't answering his phone, so she left a message. Damien's name was next. It was time she spoke with him.

RUE DE CHÂTILLON, the next narrow street over, paralleled Villa d'Alésia. Earlier, climbing Yuri's back wall, she'd noticed little of it, except the bit of hay she found clinging to the rosemary.

Now, trying to figure out how the killer escaped, she eyed the *maison de maître*, typical bourgeois townhouse shutters framing its tall windows. Why did it strike her as familiar? It was fronted by what would have been a rose garden in the nineteenth century, now weed-choked patches of grass and wild lilac. The sign at the gate indicated the house's current function was a youth job training center.

She found Damien's printing shop further in, beyond an open-gated courtyard. On the cobbles under the chestnut tree, a man in blue overalls loaded the back of a *camionnette*. A few stacks of playbills for theaters, concert posters, and ads for a traveling circus. Posters emblazoned with STOP THE DEVELOP-ERS in red were bundled against the wall on wood pallets.

The pounding of the printing press competed with the chirping of birds in the bushes.

"Monsieur, I'm looking for Damien Perret."

"Come to pick up the posters, eh? All ready, Damien made sure."

He mistook her for someone from the demonstration.

She shook her head and smiled. "Where's the office?"

"Inside and to the left," he said. "But he's with his aunt at the hospital."

Great. "Any idea where he went Saturday?"

"You mean deliveries?" The man rubbed his neck. He was bald and overweight.

She thought quickly. "That's it, regarding a delivery order we received Saturday."

"I don't think so." His eyes narrowed.

"Can you check?"

"Don't need to. Today's our delivery day."

Stupid to lie when she didn't know the schedule.

"Damien used the *camionnette* that afternoon," he said. "Helped the old man."

Yuri.

He eyed her legs. "Maybe I can help."

Not the help she needed.

"Florent!" A shout came from inside the glass-roofed print-ing works.

He dusted off his thick palms. Winked. "Don't go away."

Like hell she'd wait for him. But she stared at the inside of the *camionnette*. Stacked full to the roof. She peered through the open front window. Old newspapers on the floor, Styrofoam cups, candy wrappers, and detritus strewn below the passenger seat. She looked closer at the newspapers; something was unusual. They were copies of *Le Matin*, yellowed, the typeface faded. A newspaper her grandfather had read that didn't exist anymore. She reached in, unfolded a crumpled portion. The date—February 1920—above an article about horse cart traffic dangers on Boulevard du Montparnasse.

No doubt this came from Yuri's father's belongings. What if there was more? She glanced around. No Florent or other workers. She opened the passenger door, went through the trash on the floor again. Nothing else of interest but a parking ticket. She dropped it, then picked it up again. A hefty one hundred francs. She looked at the date. Saturday, issued at 3 P.M.—the time Damien and Yuri had gone out. The address: 34 rue Marie Rose.

"Guess you'd like to ride on my deliveries with me, eh?"

She felt hot garlic breath in her ear. The texture of Florent's grease-stained overalls on her arm.

"In your dreams."

Then a knee was shoved between her legs. Rough arms shoving her onto the seat. Hands pinning her legs. Panic raced through her. The way he had eyed her should have put her on high alert. His thick fingers dug into her skin.

"You know you want it," Florent said.

How could she be so stupid?

Monday Early Evening, Silicon Valley

RENÉ GRIPPED THE leather armrest as Bob backed the
Cadillac into a narrow-looking spot in the gravel parking lot.
"Can't beat this place. Best burgers in the Valley, René."

A weathered neon sign read GROVER'S above a diner off the
Avenue of the Fleas.

"Millionaires eat here?"

"They weren't always millionaires." Bob grinned. "You
wanted Americana—where real people and geeks eat. Doesn't
get greasier or more authentic than this."

René noticed the meal portions as they walked by the booths.
Gigantic. A single plate looked like it could feed a whole table.

On the wall of their plastic-upholstered booth was a juke-
box. Bob slotted in quarters and hit some keys. "Green River"
by Creedence Clearwater blasted from speakers overhead.

"The usual, Bob?" asked the waitress, an older woman.

Bob nodded. "And two Buds. For my friend here. . . ."

"What'll it be, hon?" she said, slapping down a menu.

René's chest hit the edge of the Formica table. "What he's
having, Madame. But a smaller portion."

"Kid's cheeseburger, all right?"

René nodded.

She winked a blue-shadowed eyelid. Scribbled on her order
pad. "Got it. My cousin's married to a man of your stature, they
own a ranch in Morgan Hill." She gave an approving cluck.
"Prize dairy cows."

He swallowed his embarrassment. "I suppose you have phone books?"

"What you waiting for, Bob? Your friend needs some vertical assistance. Phone booth's in back."

Bob stood, all six feet of him, a sheepish look on his face. "Sorry, René, I didn't think."

"Just don't come back with one of those children's booster seats."

René finished half of the child's plate. How did people eat such great quantities, and all in one sitting? And no cheese course to follow. But he kept that to himself.

"How's it feel after your first day as CTO?" Bob grinned, wiping ketchup off his chin. "Spot any blondes yet?"

René leaned back on the phone books. "I met a programmer who makes a perfect *café au lait*. Two in one, Bob. Legs to forever. I'm in love."

"Three in one, René. Love, lust, no difference, eh?"

Bob, twice divorced, complained of child support and alimony.

"But tell me," René said, leaning forward. "I train at dojos, but I'm not into team sports. Am I expected to do *le jogging* with my boss?"

"What?" Bob said. "I don't follow. Start-ups are all hustle. No one's got time for team sports."

"But this front running, it means *faire du sport, non?*"

Bob dropped his fork. "Front running? Explain."

René told him the little he'd overheard.

"Hard to say, but front running involves a kind of insider trading," Bob said. "There's different ways to spin it, but say a financial search engine provides trading services. Somehow, for example, they set up access on the mainframe to stall data transmission by a few seconds—that's a big no-no."

"I don't understand, Bob." René's cheeks flushed. The beer and Bob's reaction got to him.

"Did you program a relay and delay code?"

René nodded, worried. "I need to for security and maintenance."

"But for a financial search engine that uses portfolio tracking and a stock screener, this kind of front run could provide a few seconds' advantage in online stock trading," Bob said, playing with his napkin. "So you can manage to get a lower day-trading guarantee. Millions of dollars' advantage in trading, René. What the hell did they tell you?"

"That's just it, nothing. I patched and vented the mainframe back door, the usual. Secured the system."

"Maybe you heard wrong," Bob said. "Tradelert's got top investors. Generating a lot of buzz. I don't know."

Had he done their dirty work?

Bob paid the check.

"Nothing jumped out at me after I double-checked all systems," René said.

Or had jetlag clouded his brain?

"It's your ass, René."

AFTER BOB DROPPED him off at the motel, René hung up his suit jacket and trousers on the plastic hanger and stepped into the pink Jacuzzi. He needed to ease the ache in his hip joints after the plane ride. He allowed himself to float in the water, feel the massaging jets, empty his mind.

His head cleared, he played back the algorithms. After he dried off with the largest and thirstiest pink towel he'd ever used, he unpacked his handmade Charvet shirts and hung tomorrow's suit up in the closet.

At the laminate wood motel desk, complete with Gideon Bible in the drawer, his gaze fell on the empty, dimly lit parking lot outside the window. His thoughts drifted—had Saj garaged and waxed his car? Did Aimée remember the client meeting he'd scheduled, or Miles Davis's grooming appointment? For a moment he felt alone. So alone in this room with the king-size bed, so oversize he needed a chair to reach it.

Stop it, he told himself. He booted up his laptop, stuck in the second prototype thumb-drive he'd neglected to tell Saj he'd borrowed, got ready to work. But that phrase niggled in his mind: *The dwarf's got no idea.*

Had he heard wrong?

He'd call the Nordic blonde. Test his suspicions.

"Susie, it's René, sorry to call so late."

"What happened to you after work?" She almost purred. "I failed in my mission to serve you."

"But you can redeem yourself, Susie," he said, envisioning her long legs. "I planned on checking the mainframe again," he said, "but without remote access I'll need to take care of that tomorrow."

"Didn't you get your token?" A little gasp. "My fault. I forgot."

The token allowing him remote access to the mainframe. Tokens were guarded like the Holy Grail. Had she really forgotten?

"Security would allow that? I mean, in France we work on-site only."

"This is the Valley, René," Susie said, a smile in her voice.

Something bothered him. And he wished he knew what.

"I'm so sorry I forgot, René. You needed it tonight? I'm still here working, and I just ran the systems. We're all good for tomorrow. Drop by my cubicle before the investor meeting," she said. "I'll set you up. *Café au lait* included."

René imagined her tan legs, long blonde hair, and hazel eyes. Big eyes like Aimée's. A pang went through him. All these miles away and her scent lingered on his jacket. Chanel No. 5. But he was nothing to her but a friend.

"Don't worry, René, someone's here twenty-four, seven if you have questions," Susie said.

After hanging up, he worked off the backup he'd put on Saj's thumb-drive. It was smaller and more efficient than floppies or CDs. He hadn't tested Tradelert's hardware security—not a priority with the meeting looming tomorrow—but he'd noticed plastic pillars like the ones they have at department stores to stop theft. Saj's thumb-drive hadn't set off the alarm.

First rule, as always, he'd backed up all his work. He examined the firewall hole he'd patched—necessary security for the investors Rob stressed would join in the next round of financing, and for the product launch, even a possible IPO.

Secure. Then he examined the back door he'd engineered. Tested the code. All good. He clicked into the safety net backup. And then his fingers froze on the keyboard.

Tuesday Afternoon, Paris

AIMÉE GRASPED THE truck door handle and spit at Florent. A sharp slap stung her face.

"You know you want it," Florent grunted.

"Not what you've got." She twisted her body, wriggled, trying to push him off her. His dirty fingernails clawed her thighs. Raked her skin. Her heart pounded in her ears.

With all her might she shoved him against the window. Kneed him in the groin as hard as she could.

Florent fell back with a loud groan. She scrambled out the driver's door. Slammed it. Ran.

Two blocks away, beyond Alésia, she stepped into a corner café. Shaking and berating herself, she hurried down the dark wooden stairs to the WC. In front of the soap-splattered mirror, she ran hot water—washed her legs, arms, and face with shaking hands, intent on scrubbing off Florent's smell, his filth clinging to her skin. She put her head down, took deep breaths until she stopped trembling.

Feeling cleaner, she brushed mascara through her eyelashes. A swipe of Chanel Red over her lips and a spritz of Chanel No. 5 from her bag to complete the repairs. Next time she wouldn't be so stupid.

Not far from the Montsouris reservoir she found rue Marie Rose, a short-sloped block of six-story stone apartment buildings across from the red-brick church. Quiet after the bustling roundabout of Alésia. But even if she knew what to look for—a cellar where a Modigliani had been hidden—the idea of entering each building and questioning dwellers was daunting.

Scouting midblock, she found a plaque at Number 34 attesting that Lenin had lived there, and that his apartment was now a museum. From Piotr's letter she knew Lenin had lived upstairs from him. She'd struck gold.

This route to the painting led her backward, but in some cases, she remembered her father saying, going to the beginning helps you find the end. Feeling more hopeful that she was close to finding another piece of this jigsaw, she entered the light-filled foyer.

Scents of pine cleaner lingered on the brown encaustic-tile walls and the staircase banister's burnished mahogany. Clean, utilitarian, no frills. The working-class aura remained. For a moment she imagined the Russian émigrés here at the turn of the century.

No answer to her knock on the concierge's door or any of the ground-floor apartments. Voices came from above. She hoped for better luck there.

At the Lenin-apartment-museum entrance, several people listened to a serious-faced young woman. She wore her brown hair in a bun and wore no makeup. "The father of the Revolution lived here from 1909 to 1912 with Comrade Krupskaya, his wife, and her mother," the guide explained. "As you will see, every effort's been made to document his life here and provide as many furnishings of that period as possible. Austere, by our standards today. The Revolution's architect lived simply, focusing on formulating Revolutionary theory."

Before Aimée could duck out, she felt a pamphlet pressed in her hand. An image of Lenin shrouded in a greatcoat, saluting Revolutionaries from a train. A heroic man-of-the-people pose.

"Welcome, Comrade, the tour's just beginning."

What planet did this woman live on? The Wall came down

in 1989, almost ten years ago. "Sorry, but I didn't reserve for the tour," Aimée said. "I wouldn't want to take another's place."

That sounded weak.

"Join us, *s'il vous plaît.*"

Reluctant, Aimée smiled. The guide was no doubt a red-diaper baby from one of the few surviving red suburbs. Once, Paris had been enclosed by the "red belt" hotbed of unions and Communists.

"The new socialist Russia," she said in a reverential tone, "and the movement that changed the world, were born here."

A hush descended.

So out of touch, this young comrade. And passé. But the possibility of hearing more about Lenin—the man who'd bounced Piotr on his knee—held Aimée's interest.

"Comrade Krupskaya wrote in her journals of their life in these two rooms. They held meetings and discussions right here, forging the doctrine."

The guide gestured to notebooks piled along the burnished orange walls under portraits of Marx and Lenin's mother. Her voice droned on. Aimée stared at the French translation above Krupskaya's journal.

> To get the gas connected I had to go up to town three times before I received the necessary written order. The amount of red tape in France is unbelievable. To get books from the lending library you must have a householder to stand surety for you, and our landlord, seeing our miserable furniture, hesitated to do so.

AIMÉE IDENTIFIED WITH Krupskaya's frustration at French bureaucracy—some things never changed. She scanned more of the translations. Krupskaya wrote about Lenin's daily routine of bicycling to the Archives to do research. How on the weekends they joined other émigrés at Parc Montsouris—"a little Russia," she wrote, her tone wistful. How she and Lenin kept their bicycles in the cellar, her struggles with the steep cellar steps and the keys.

An article published in 1960 detailed Khrushchev's visit to Lenin's museum, or "shrine." A local seventy-three-year-old resident interviewed for the piece spoke of his childhood:

Lenin? Mais oui, I knew him. His cleaner, Louise, was my neighbor. I saw him cut his hand two or three times on his bike lock, he always seemed preoccupied. The police watched him and his friends, les émigrés, constantly. On Sundays when I rode my bicyclette I'd see him on his. Ah, but in those days I was young.

And it hit her. The cellar the comrade kept her bike in—the old-fashioned key Natasha mentioned—could it be the key to a cellar storage space? The cellar Madame Figuer lent her wheelbarrow to Yuri to empty out? Aimée needed to get down there.

She passed the visitor log with the signatures of Khrushchev and Brezhnev and tiptoed out before the tour guide noticed.

At the concierge's loge she didn't have long to wait. A young man wearing jeans set down a Darty shopping bag.

"You're early," he said. "My mother's showing the apartment in twenty minutes."

"No problem," she said, improvising. "I want to rent space for my bike. Can you show me?"

"The cellar space goes with the apartment. *Desolé.*"

She sighed. "I'm tired of having bikes stolen. The third one in two months. I need it for work. Really, it doesn't take much room. I'd share."

"Talk to my mother."

She was desperate to get down there. "But I heard an old man's storage got emptied. My friend helped clean it out, a real mess he said."

The young man took out his door key. "That's the truth. Like a dump. Left for years."

Her ears perked up.

"Gave my mother a real headache, trying to get his son, the old man, to empty it."

"But I don't care. Can't I just see it? You'd really help me out."

"She's in charge, *desolé*, not up to me." He opened the door.

She couldn't let him go.

"Could I measure it? We'd go for the apartment if I knew I could fit the bikes and an old chest down there." She smiled. "I love this street. Had my eye on the building. I know I could convince my boyfriend, but . . ."

"The soccer match on the *télé* starts in three minutes." He picked up his bag.

Poor *mec*, she hated to push but couldn't lose this opportunity. "Would you mind giving me the cellar key?" She gave another smile. "Won't take me but ten minutes. Then I'll tour the apartment with your mother."

A sigh, then he reached for something inside the closet. Handed her an old-fashioned, rusted key. "Number C-twenty-four. Watch out for rat droppings. Don't say I didn't warn you."

He wanted to get rid of her and watch the game. Fine by her.

Her penlight beam wavered over the dirt floor in the cellar tunnel. A row of water-stained coved doors with numbers stretched along the cellar tunnel. Only a single naked bulb illuminated the space.

C24 opened with the key and a wave of musty air hit her. What was she looking for? A sign that Yuri had found a Modigliani that had been left here for more than seventy years? All she discovered in the shadows were rat turds and a broken chair on the hard earth floor.

"Mademoiselle?"

A plump black-haired woman shone a flashlight.

"I've already rented the apartment." Her words rolled with an Italian accent. "The storage goes with it. You'll need to find another place for your bicycle."

"A shame, but *merci*, Madame," Aimée said, racking her mind for a way to prolong the conversation. This woman might offer some insight. "Nice cleanup for a space full of seventy-something years' worth of garbage. Least that's what your son—"

"*Porca miseria*, don't get me started," the woman said. "A health hazard. I could do nothing until that old buzzard's son finally came. He should thank me, he should. Found a master-piece, or so he claimed."

The woman liked to talk. And used her hands, evidenced by the flashlight's yellow beam waving over the damp stone walls.

"By masterpiece you mean a painting?" Aimée shook her head. "Like a Rembrandt?"

The woman shrugged. "I don't know. He seemed excited enough. These things happen, *sì*? People find treasures at flea markets, in attics. Down here all that time, wrapped up. Wouldn't surprise me if it's worth a fortune, that's how it always happens. But you only know for sure if you get it appraised."

Aimée followed the flashlight beam back up the steps, glad to leave the whiffs of decay and humidity behind her. Mortar crumbled under her feet.

"That's what I told him," the woman continued. "Let an expert examine it. Take it to an auction house, or an art gal-lery, a museum—I don't know." She laughed, a deep laugh from her stomach. "He says to me, Madame Belluci, you're right. I promise to buy you a nice dinner."

"He took your advice! Did he buy you that dinner?"

"That's the funny thing," Madame Belluci said. "We have reservations tonight at La Tour d'Argent. He told me we'd have champagne with the art dealer."

Reservations Yuri couldn't keep. "Lucky you. A prominent, well-known art expert, I assume?"

"I don't know."

Aimée paused. "Then I won't keep you, you're busy." She glanced at her Tintin watch. "Eight o'clock comes early, I know. Keep me in mind if a space opens up for bikes, okay?"

Madame Belluci ran her hand through her curly hair, blew a gust of air out of her mouth. "But I didn't say eight. Dinner's at nine."

Now Aimée knew what to do. She forgot the unpleasantness of Florent's groping—finding the parking ticket had led to the cellar and the concierge. Now the art dealer.

No one got reservations at La Tour d'Argent at such short notice unless they were connected. Yuri wasn't, so she figured the art dealer must be.

Ten minutes later, she entered La Tour d'Argent on Quai de la Tournelle. Afternoon light spilled over the gold sconces, red carpet so thick it muffled her footsteps, the red-velvet-flocked wallpaper soaked up conversation. The place exuded privilege.

An entrée cost the price of a pair of gently worn Louboutins. Even if she won the lottery, not her type of place. A tuxedoed maître d' took one look at her outfit. "Mademoiselle, our last seating for luncheon's full."

She pulled out her father's police ID doctored with her photo. Shot him a measured smile and gestured to the tall reception podium.

"No fuss no muss, Monsieur. Please cooperate and show me the dinner reservations for this evening."

He hesitated. Adjusted his tie. "Anything I should know?"

"Pre-security detail," she said. "I'm sure you know what that means."

President Chirac, while notorious for being a palace homebody, had a proclivity for spontaneous visits to *restos* of this caliber with his daughter. It drove his bodyguards and security detail nuts, but, according to one she knew, it was the best possible security—if no one at the restaurant knew he was coming, no assassin would either. Reservations would be made under a false name, but contingent on a green light from security, who'd make a quick sweep a few hours prior.

"Extra measures, Monsieur. I'm sure you understand, *n'est-ce pas?*"

The maître d' gave a knowing look, inclined his distinguished white head. So Chirac had dined here before.

"*Bien sûr.*" He turned the thick vellum pages toward her.

"We're wondering about an old friend, an art dealer."

"Monsieur Luebet, party of three, at nine P.M."

"And his gallery, Monsieur?"

"Laforet on Montparnasse."

Maître d's knew everyone. That was their job. Only three people—Yuri, the art dealer Luebet, and the concierge. Yuri hadn't invited his stepson.

"Most helpful. *Merci,* Monsieur."

He smiled and executed a little bow. "I'll drop a word to the chef to have *aiguillette de canard et foie gras, gelée de porto* on the menu. His favorite."

"You do that."

A WORLD-CLASS FOUR-STAR dinner tallied for an art dealer expecting a fat commission on a Modigliani. Several scenarios spun in her head: Yuri, following the concierge's suggestion, takes the painting to Luebet, with Damien driving the *camionnette*. Luebet, recognizing a true Modigliani, this unique lost treasure, strikes a deal with Yuri to handle the sale and perform a professional appraisal for authentication the next morning. Meanwhile Luebet, counting his *poulets* before they hatched, lines up potential buyers, interested museums, and makes a reservation to celebrate.

But if that had been the case, wouldn't Yuri have lodged the painting with Luebet for safekeeping? She remembered his stricken look when he opened the pantry to discover it empty.

And the fact that he was tortured—none of it made sense. But Luebet would know something.

Gunning her scooter, she reached the Boulevard du Montparnasse and found Luebet's gallery closed. She tried the gallery number. Only voice mail. She left a message.

Who stole the painting? Who tortured Yuri? Not her job to find out, but she couldn't put it out of her mind. Nor could she forget the Serb who'd found Saj's name. But she had a business to run. She called to check in at the office.

"Any Indian attacks, Maxence?"

"Only a few sales calls, if you call those—"

"*Attends*, Maxence." She didn't feel good about a kid assuming René's position and making sales pitches for their security. "I'll handle those."

"*Bon.* Iridium and Netex faxed the proposals back and accepted," he said. "I was about to fax them contracts, but I'll leave it for you."

Two new contracts? He'd just faxed the proposals out this morning. The kid impressed her.

"All right, go ahead and prepare contracts. Use the template in my file and just fill in the parameters from the proposals. Anything else?"

"Virus scans have been run. I'm digging more in Xincus on Yuri Volodya. All quiet on the western front."

"Good job. See you later." She hung up.

Maxence had it under control. She tried to ignore her feeling of superfluousness and concentrate on the problems at hand—Yuri's murder, this painting, and Saj.

She was still holding her phone when it rang again.

"*Oui?*"

"Mademoiselle Leduc, I'm Monsieur Luebet's assistant," said a smooth voice. "He's unavailable today but I can schedule an appraisal tomorrow."

Didn't the inherited Matisse she'd lied about on her message merit more consideration? The longer she waited, the worse her chances of ever finding this painting. And then another scenario hit her—what if Luebet had arranged the robbery? Contracted it out to the Serb to steal the Modigliani so he could show up pink and innocent for the appraisal? But the Serb was dead, the painting gone. She could only spin theories until she spoke to Luebet.

"I'm afraid that's too late," she said. "Two dealers have already expressed interest in the Matisse."

This should put fire under the receptionist to contact Luebet.

"*Alors*, Mademoiselle," the receptionist said, her voice now rushed. "Let me see what I can do."

"But if he's not in Paris, I can't wait," she said. "A shame, I heard he's the best."

"As soon as his curating meeting finishes at the Musée Bourdelle . . ."

Aimée clicked off. Now she knew where to find Luebet. It was vital that she glean more about the Modigliani from him. She might even show him Piotr's letters in exchange for information.

AIMÉE POCKETED HER scooter key, smoothed down her cashmere cardigan, and took a deep breath. That hint of spring hovered in the pocket of warm air engulfing the Musée Bourdelle's open garden. Passing the garden's massive, ample-figured female sculptures made her think of the kilo she'd gained lately. She wondered if she would have completely let herself go by the time Melac came back from his new assignment—one so hush-hush he couldn't reveal its nature—*if* he ever came back. Her life was such a mess lately. She needed to figure out how to cope better with the constant worry over Melac's safety, the danger he faced every day on the job. Not to mention she'd been neglecting poor Miles Davis. She made a mental note to straighten out her priorities. Later.

Aimée paid her fifteen-franc admission. A yawning member of the museum staff tore her ticket in half at the door. She hurried by the wall history explaining Bourdelle's apprenticeship under Rodin and his mentoring of Giacometti, continued out through the rose-pink portico and turned left. A brown wooden door labeled ATELIER, then an arrow to LES BUREAUX ADMINISTRATIFS.

Inside she found not an airy, light-filled studio but damp, peeling walls, a rusted charcoal stove, aged wooden beams, and old metal sculpture tools, illuminated only by gray slants of daylight. She shivered, missing the sun-drenched garden she'd just come from. The cross-hatched wood-slatted floor creaked under her heels. Each step echoed, filling her with the sense of having stepped into another time.

"Takes you somewhere else, *non?*" A man spoke from the shadows. "As if the sculptor will walk in and take up from where he left off on that arm." The stranger pointed to the half-finished marble figure. "Just as Bourdelle left it in 1929."

True. She wondered if the dank cold had given the artist chilblains. Not her idea of prime working conditions.

She walked toward the shadow. A guide. "I'm looking for the administrative offices, the director."

"Keep going."

Aimée followed the directions, taking her through an ivy-walled walkway leading to a warren of offices. As archaic as the rest of the museum.

"Monsieur Luebet?" said the young secretary. "But you just missed him, Mademoiselle."

Again, too late.

An older man in a suit emerged from a back office waving a folder. "Luebet rushed off and forgot this. Stick it in the mail for him, *s'il vous plaît.*"

Aimée sensed an opportunity.

"Monsieur Luebet's gone?" Aimée said. "But he said to meet here."

"And you are?"

Prepared, Aimée pulled out a card with a generic company name. "Lisette. We specialize in packing artwork. Custom crating, shipments."

The man shrugged. "Something urgent came up at his gallery."

"*Vraiment?* That's a problem, since he's not answering his mobile."

"Try the gallery."

She shrugged. "If he took his car, I'll never make it in time."

"You're in luck, Mademoiselle. Luebet took the Métro today," the man said. "He complained he couldn't drive in because of all the street demonstrations."

"*Merci,* Monsieur."

The older man returned to the office, the secretary to the fax machine grinding out papers. Aimée slipped the file under her jacket. She'd hand it to him in person. Forget negotiating the Vespa through a demonstration and the underpass; faster to go on foot.

Minutes later she approached the side entrance of Montparnasse, the octopus-tentacled station with multilevel rail lines—the TGV, the suburban RER, and the deep Métro. Luebet might get off at Edgar Quinet station and walk up to his gallery on Boulevard du Montparnasse, or direct to Vavin. Either route offered a stop with a short walk to his gallery.

Two different lines and tunnels. Which one to take?

Hell, she didn't even know what he looked like.

Or whether he'd told the truth about an urgent summons to his gallery. But she had to start somewhere. She took the closest tunnel, jumped on the first train—the Number 6 line toward Place d'Italie.

On the softly rocking train, she opened the file. Read the contents; scribbled lines from a curatorial committee on a grid-lined pad. Notes to himself about a Bourdelle sculpture exhibition at his gallery. Behind it a small, metal-clasped manila envelope labeled M—*Find it this time.*

What did that mean? Curious, she wedged her fingernail under the clasp, opening the envelope to find a wallet-sized Polaroid photo, overexposed and stained by emulsion. In it she could just make out Yuri standing before a small canvas spread on a worktable, and a tall man in a pinstripe suit holding the canvas's corner—she took the man for Luebet. Both men were half turned toward a painting. Yuri's atelier window framed them in the background.

The painting leapt out of the blurry detail of the photo. A younger Lenin with more hair—a bicycle in the background— holding a book, a paper? Its vibrancy shone through.

Luebet had been in a hurry all right if he'd forgotten this. Rattled—by what? But this was proof Yuri had shown Luebet the painting. She wondered who had taken the photo.

M—*Find it this time.* More pieces clicked together in her mind. Uneasiness ground in her stomach. If her hunch about this note was right, Luebet, a respected art dealer, was after this Modigliani, too. Could he have hired a thief himself?

Whom had he rushed off to meet? A buyer? Her thoughts spiraled. M—the thief he'd hired? The one who'd tangled with the Serb, caused his death somehow? She didn't know how Feliks had died, but she was certain now that his death was directly linked to the painting's theft. Two people, Feliks and Yuri, had been murdered over this painting. She remembered that white van that had pulled in front of them moments before the Serb fell on René's windshield—was it connected? She was guessing the Serb had been interrupted in an attempted robbery by whoever had succeeded in stealing the painting, then killed him; but that person would have had no reason to come back and torture Yuri. That meant there were at least two ruthless parties involved in this mess, and still no painting. A web growing more complicated and dangerous—and somehow Luebet was involved.

René, always cautious, would have told her to pull out before getting too involved. Forget this while she could.

By now Luebet might have discovered he'd left this envelope behind. She imagined him irate on the phone with the helpful curator at Musée Bourdelle. Guilt invaded her for a moment.

But she had Yuri's cash in her bag. And no other way to find her mother. She needed to reach Luebet. Talk to him.

The train jerked. Brakes squealed. A moment later it shuddered to a halt in the tunnel, throwing Aimée and her fellow passengers against the seats. Lights flickered. Her arm cracked against a bar before she grabbed it. Bags skittered across the floor; an old woman cried out.

The train car plunged into darkness—like night. The air filled suddenly with the smell of burning rubber. A loudspeaker crackled and buzzed. "Mesdames, Messieurs, due to an *accident grave de voyageur*, there's an interruption on the line. Service is at a standstill. We ask for your patience."

A murmur rumbled through the passengers in the darkness. Aimée imagined the knowing looks they would share if they could see each other. *"Accident grave de voyageur"* was the standard euphemism for a track jumper. A suicide.

Notorious on the Number 6 line, which served three hospitals, one of them Saint Anne's, the psychiatric facility.

This could take God-knows-how-long, she thought, rubbing her bruised arm and imagining the grim scene ahead. With her feet she felt for her bag, which had lodged under the next seat, then recovered her penlight. She shone it toward the old woman huddled on the floor, whimpering and gasping for breath. With another passenger, she helped the old woman to a seat and tried to calm her.

After what felt like a long time, the lights flickered. The doors cranked open to another wave of burning rubber odor. Passengers were instructed to step down in the pitch-black

tunnel to the narrow service walkway hugging the wall above
the track. Taking the old woman's arm, she eased her down
onto the dark ledge and guided her along the blackened tunnel
walls. Ahead Aimée could see lights reflecting on the gleaming
white tiles on the wall of the platform at station Edgar Quinet.

"Not far, Madame," she said.

It looked like a messy accident, requiring a scooper train
especially elevated to clean the electric rail lines. With sad
incidents like this, it took forever to reestablish service and
reroute the disrupted network. Usually they herded passengers
back along the track walkway to the previous station to give
room to the emergency crew. But Montparnasse, webbed by
four lines, was a vast maze.

Enveloped in the close, stifling air shared by too many people, she wanted to get out. She had almost pushed ahead in
line behind a mother helping her toddler when she froze at a
shriek. To the side of the iron steps leading to the platform on
the tracks lay a severed arm still in its pinstriped suit jacket.

Aimée gasped. The arm ended in a bloody clump where the
shoulder had been. She averted her eyes too late. Bile rose in
her stomach at the metallic scent of blood. Her gaze crept back
to the hand, fixated on the pinkie ring. That large stone-like
class ring in an engraved mount.

The driver and scurrying staff attempted to block the track
view, to shield passengers from the scene and move them along.
Mutters of "heart attack . . . slipped . . . *quel dommage.*" A frisson of fear prickled her neck.

By the time she mounted the Métro steps to the boulevard,
she knew where she'd seen it before. She grasped the pole of an
awninged market stall and gulped lungfuls of late afternoon air,
hoping she was wrong. Feeling cold and alone in the middle
of the bustle of merchants setting up for the evening market,
she reopened the envelope. In the photo, Luebet's hand was
clearly visible on the canvas, complete with that distinctive,

large-stoned class ring on his pinkie. He wouldn't be dining at La Tour d'Argent tonight. Nor would Yuri.

She doubted he'd suffered a heart attack. More like been pushed. Again, she'd been too late.

Her gaze darted among the shoppers threading the stalls. Whoever had pushed Luebet could be watching her. Whoever had killed Yuri was clearly willing to kill again, and she'd retraced too many of his steps. Head down, she dove into the crowd.

Tuesday Early Morning, Silicon Valley

DAWN BLUSHED ROSE-ORANGE over the mountains fringing the bay and over the Buick logo still visible under the Tradelert sign. Five A.M. René, goosebumps running up his arms, had logged into Susie's terminal using his sysadmin access. Nervous, he scanned yesterday's protocols. He was drinking instant General Foods International café mocha cappuccino. Even though he'd doubled the packets, it still tasted like brown piss.

With that bad taste in his mouth, he dug deeper into the admin program to find who held the tokens for remote access. Susie had added him last night at 11:45 P.M.

He took one more sip. Clenched his teeth and started with her drawers. Manuals, zip drives. Finally he found the envelope marked René with his token.

He inserted the token, verified his log-in—she'd written in red marker with a heart—and accessed the whole program.

He'd entered Ali Baba's cave. The workings, up-to-the-minute reports and scans—everything. With mounting anxiety he wondered why this access hadn't been provided to him yesterday. It would have streamlined his work, saved him a lot of time. Had Susie forgotten or deliberately left him out? But those overheard words came back to him—*the dwarf's got no idea.*

There had to be more tokens. After some searching in her drawer, he found one. Now he'd clone it and. . . .

"Early, eh? Didn't see you." A tall figure shadowed the breaking dawn. "Signed in yet?"

René smiled up at the blue-uniformed rent-a-guard. "They haven't even printed my business card. I'm René Friant, chief technology officer."

"Don't see your name here, sir."

He had to buy time. "You're sure?"

René reached down to tie his shoe.

"Sorry, sir." The guard came closer. "We're obliged to check."

"Then check the bronze CTO office plate with my name, René Friant."

After scanning the empty offices and corridors, René finally found two programmers at workstations. Doughnut crumbs trailed from the youngest one's sparse goatee. "Like one, my man?" he asked René, offering him a cardboard box assortment.

René hesitated, eyeing the icing-laden circles of fried dough. "Thought that was *flic* . . . I mean, police food."

"Cop food—good one, my man. Nice you appreciate fine distinctions in American cuisine," he grinned. "I'm Brad. Night shift." He yawned and glanced at the time. "I'm outta here in ten minutes." Brad swiveled his chair back to the terminal screen and clicked a few keys. "I love French movies. Those shots of the Eiffel Tower and girls in berets. Accordian music."

"*Mais oui*, Parisian girls, striped shirts, berets and baguettes." *We live to be stereotypes*, he almost said. Then he thought again. "Brad, before you go, mind doing me a small favor?"

BEFORE THE INVESTOR meeting, René found Andy at his laptop in the bright fluorescent-lit boardroom of the converted Buick leasing office.

"All systems go, dude. Brilliant work."

Andy's smile blazed. Charisma, wasn't that what they called it? He lit up a room, made you feel like the most important person in the universe. Megawatts of charm in a two-piece suit over a Hawaiian shirt and sandals.

"Afraid there's an issue you need to know about, Andy," René said. He gathered his courage. Tried to figure out the right words.

Andy's brow rose. "Issue? I checked the system minutes ago, it's all good." He shook his sun-bleached surfer curls. "Nerves? That's it, isn't it? Your first presentation as CTO. Dude, I get it."

René hated disappointing him.

"My baby . . . our baby's hatching into the world," Andy said. "Be proud, René."

He needed to know before the investors arrived.

"Not proud of this." René hit keys on Andy's laptop, opening the program. A few more strokes and René pointed to algorithms popping up on the screen. "This back door allows pre-trading advantage. Like front running. Illegal, Andy. It violates every stock exchange standard."

Andy shrugged. "It's business, René."

Shocked, René stumbled against the boardroom table. He didn't understand. Didn't want to understand.

"You knew, Andy?"

"Forget about it, René. I've got the term sheet."

"Term sheet?"

"Everyone in the company wants this term sheet," Andy said. "It's our offer from three venture capitalists to invest thirty million. We'll go public within two months and be worth two hundred million." Andy squeezed René's arm. Smiled. "Your two-dollar stock will go to eighty dollars, then twenty million."

"Twenty million dollars?"

Andy winked. "And a lot more in francs. It's all worth it to us if you can patch and tweak before we launch the product for stock trading. And to keep you here. Okay, dude? We're good?"

Astounded, René felt his eyes widen. Serious, Andy was serious.

"But you can't think this won't be discovered," René said. "Anyone in securities will recognize this scam."

Andy gave a big laugh. He slapped René on the back. René felt his world caving in.

"Don't worry, we're talking about a stock trading advantage of a second or two to three seconds. Harder than bullets to prove. The work's brilliant. Beautiful, dude," Andy said. "Hell, you did it yourself."

Andy pulled out his cell phone.

"So we're good, right, René?"

"I'm not an employee," René said, shaking. "I came in on a tourist visa. This has got nothing to do with me."

"Did you forget the fax you signed and accepted for the CTO position, René?"

One step ahead of him. The whole time. A bitter taste filled his mouth and it didn't come from *faux* cappuccino. Their rush employment offer, the private jet, the stock options lured him here, trapped him. Idiot.

Andy had used him. A scapegoat to take the fall if he squealed. René doubted Andy needed him anymore except to keep his mouth shut.

René's phone trilled in his pocket. He answered automatically.

"*Ça va*, René?" Aimée's voice an echoey reverberation as the call pinged over the ocean. "Made your millions yet?"

Little did she know. "I like my millions clean," René said in English.

Andy folded his arms, planting himself in front of the door.

"Not dirty, Aimée," he added, looking Andy in the eye.

But he'd lost the connection.

Tuesday Afternoon, Paris

I LIKE MY millions? Aimée kicked the matted lime-tree blossoms littering Boulevard du Montparnasse's zebra crosswalk. Not there forty-eight hours and René had gone *Zeelakon Vallaaaay* all the way. She hit dial back. No connection.

Just when she needed to talk to someone, throw ideas back and forth like they always had. She needed help reasoning out why Luebet got shoved in front of the Métro.

No doubt René had the corporate jet at his beck and call. She walled up the disappointment. No time for that now. The sky opened and she ran for shelter in a doorway.

La giboulée issued an intense pelting shower, then five wet minutes later layers of blue sky appeared. She shivered in her damp boots. Now confident no one had followed her, she hurried along the rain-spattered boulevard to Luebet's art gallery. Shuttered and dark. He'd been lured out of a meeting and murdered.

But she couldn't prove that. The only documented connection between Yuri's torture and murder and Luebet's supposed Métro accident was the painting in the photo. Yuri and Luebet were the only ones who could have verified the Modigliani's existence except whoever took the photo. No doubt the same person who'd stolen it.

Oleg, the stepson? The dead Serb's partner, the brother?

Or Aimée's mother?

Whoever had known that Yuri had dined at his stepson's last night also knew what time to steal it.

Her cell phone blinked with one message. The insurance company giving her repair quotes for the cars' damages. She sighed, tempted to ignore this particular problem, given René's millions and the fact that Yuri was gone. But that wouldn't make it right.

Nearby on Boulevard Raspail, inside the AXA insurance office, she stared at the estimated vehicle damages. The base of her spine went weak. She could blow a kiss goodbye to a chunk of the incoming Arident check. Doing the right thing would cost her.

But she nodded assent, signed the triplicate form and handed it back to the clerk, a young woman all in brown, which only highlighted her already mouse-like appearance. Brown—the new black?

Now she had another reason to reach Oleg—the insurance money. No one turned down the offer of money.

She rang the office. "How's it going, Maxence?"

"You sound different," Maxence said. "Something wrong?"

Should she tell him, confide in this young kid?

"Just worried about Saj," she said, crossing Raspail again and realizing she'd left her scooter at the museum. *Merde.* "Any word from him or the hospital?"

"Not yet."

She walked by the small tree-lined park on rue Campagne Première, which fronted the glinting tiled art-nouveau façade of artist ateliers. When she had been in the *lycée,* their art teacher brought the class here for a vernissage, an art opening. She and Martine had snuck out to smoke. And gotten caught.

"Contracts faxed, Aimée. Backups made. Files complete," Maxence was saying. "Have to go to my evening class now."

"Call me impressed, Maxence," she said. "I'll finish up."

"You'll find printouts concerning old man Volodya on your desk," he said, that Québécois roll to his words. "Did a Damien Perret call you?"

Just the man she wanted to see.

"I gave him your number," Maxence said. A long pause. "Do you, I mean, want me back?"

Poor kid, on the job by himself all day. Wondering if she'd left him at sea.

"Maxence, consider yourself our intern," she said. "You've impressed the hell out of me. See you tomorrow."

Aimée checked the cell phone, scrolled through the numbers. Found Damien's—no answer—and left him a message. She'd give him an earful on his employee Florent after she questioned him.

Gravel had lodged in her damp boot. Great. Leaning against the fence, she shook out the gravel and reminded herself to breathe. Her mind drifted to their *lycée* art teacher telling the class how in the eighteenth century this had been a country path leading to fields and farmland. How Montparnasse took its name—*Mont*, or hill, and Parnassus, the mythological home to Greek muses—from the seventeenth-century Sorbonne students who came here to recite poetry. The hill and students both long gone.

Now she wished she'd paid more attention to his stories. She remembered something about cabarets dating from the Revolution, *les guinguettes*—the dance halls all *lieux de plaisir*—where the bourgeoisie mingled with the artisans and working class in what had been an outlying quartier. Later, the avant-garde came, attracted by the cheap rents and blossoming Surrealist costume balls. Then, as now, the Breton presence near Gare Montparnasse, the station linking Paris to Brittany, established a Breton culture in the quartier. And the best crêpes in town. She remembered her teacher telling of the *marché aux modèles*, the street market where artists hired grisettes—women working as seamstresses or milliners—to model. The market had been held at the boulevard's end before the First World War. Modigliani's time. The going rate for models to pose was five francs for three hours.

She passed a rain-beaded plaque that listed Man Ray and Marcel Duchamp as one-time residents on the painted geranium-fronted hotel. A former one star, the hotel had now jumped to three stars for the remodeled ambience.

She couldn't ignore the present: two deaths, a missing Modigliani. Her mother, mysteriously returned after more than two decades? What did it all mean? But she knew in her bones finding the Modigliani would lead to her mother. She had to find it.

And to pick up her scooter. With no taxi in sight, she headed to the bus stop. She pulled on her cap and her oversize sunglasses, walking briskly past the dark cream stone enclosing the Montparnasse cemetery.

Five minutes later she emerged from rue Delambre by Café du Dome, where aproned men shucked oysters on ice and waiters added lemons to platters of *fruits des mer*. She crossed Boulevard du Montparnasse. Patrons grouped on rattan chairs under the red façade of Café de la Rotonde, the fat thirties-style neon letters of its marquee a beacon.

She thought of Piotr Volodya's faded blue letter in her bag, the letter Yuri never received. Tried visualizing the ascetic Lenin huddled with Trotsky; Modigliani with a red scarf dancing on a table; his model, sloe-eyed Kiki, once dubbed "Queen of Montparnasse."

But the black Mercedes pulling up in front of la Rotonde brought her back to the present as it ejected a shouting group of footballers onto the pavement. Though not a sports fan, she recognized the drunk soccer star swinging from the Mercedes door. His face was plastered on every sports page on the newsstand. This young man from Marseille was the star of Les Bleus, the national team, who were aiming for the World Cup, which would be held this summer at the new Stade de France.

Traffic snarled at a standstill. Her eye caught on the blonde miniskirted girlfriend and groupies behind the footballer. A dark-suited bodyguard herded them back toward the limo. One of the blondes threw her arms around the bodyguard, kissing him. Aimée's heart jerked. She recognized this bodyguard who was now energetically returning the blonde's long kiss.

Melac.

She stood frozen on the pavement, watching the door shut and the limo pull away down Boulevard du Montparnasse. A passerby snorted in disgust. "The team's goalkeeper, partying . . . typical."

Had her dark glasses deceived her? Melac, former *Brigade Criminelle* detective, the man she was supposedly in a relationship with, who'd taken a new assignment he couldn't talk about? Gone incommunicado. The man who just last week had wanted to move in with her?

SHE SAT IN Leduc Detective alone, cocooned with memories, warming her feet at the sputtering radiator. Looking down on her from the nineteenth-century wood-paneled wall was an old photo she'd discovered of her *grand-père* and Papa as a young boy fishing on the misted quai, a haze of black and white. She was surrounded by ghosts.

She wondered how she could keep the agency afloat. If she even wanted to. First René gone on to greener pastures. Now Saj injured—if he could even return. She was reduced to counting on a teenage intern, who seemed capable of running her business well enough without her. How long could she even keep him?

And the deeper sting, this charade played by Melac. To think she'd fallen for it.

The chandelier's light suffused her mahogany desk in a soft glow. She stared at her mocha-lacquered toenails on the radiator. Too long since they'd had a touch-up, too.

Melac kissing the blonde at la Rotonde replayed in her mind. She turned over what she knew about his supposed promotion, which would ease his alimony payments—his hush-hush position linked to the ministry, or so he'd implied.

Lies. He worked both jobs, by day still a *flic*, moonlighting as a pimp handler for sports celebrities. It made her sick.

Nothing new. She'd witnessed men in the force with her father lose their families, gamble, remarry, and moonlight more to pay more alimony. A spiral of debt and divorce.

Useless to sit and dwell on Melac's gray eyes, those warm arms around her, his lime scent that lingered on her sheets. The weekend in Strasbourg they'd planned. Never trust a *flic*, it never worked out.

She debated, then punched in his number, hating herself. Hated herself more when it went to voice mail. Forget leaving a message—better to tell him off in person. Or not. Expose herself to face-to-face humiliation? Forget it.

He'd found a long-legged football groupie. Every male's dream. And she'd thought, what? That he was different?

She had to admit it, she'd scored another relationship train wreck. She should have listened to that little voice of doubt. So different from Guy, her eye surgeon ex, who'd wanted her to forgo detective work, go suburban and be a doctor's wife in Neuilly. Giving luncheons. Not that she'd considered it. Or Yves—she'd thought he was "the one," but his ashes lay in Père Lachaise. She still wore his Turkish puzzle ring on her finger. But here she'd fallen for a *flic*. Against her own rules. What did she expect?

She pushed the hurt aside, determined to get over him. Feeling sorry for herself would get her nowhere. As her *grand-mère* said, *spilt milk doesn't fill the pitcher*.

She'd start on her list right now.

Damien Perret's number was busy. She tried Oleg Volodya again. Only voice mail. People didn't answer their phones. It made her crazy.

With a sigh she picked up the printouts Maxence had left and started reading about Yuri Volodya. Engrossed, she didn't notice the shadows lengthening in the window from rue du Louvre until the phone rang, startling her.

"Leduc Detective," she said, reaching for a cigarette in her bag before remembering she'd quit. A glance at her watch told her in three more hours it would be two months.

"Aimée Leduc? It's Damien Perret. I've been trying to reach you since you came to my. . . ."

"Printing works?" *And your worker Florent attacked me?* But she left that out. She popped a stick of cassis gum in her mouth. "Let's meet at a café. Say fifteen minutes?"

A breath of expelled air came over the line. "I've been gone all day, we're still running orders. I can't leave."

"Your deliveryman Florent around?"

"Florent? I fired him tonight. Why?"

Good.

"See you in twenty minutes," she said and hung up before he could put her off.

At this time of night the Métro would be faster. She'd finish her reading later. She laced her red high-tops and headed for the door.

Until the bulge in her coat pocket reminded her to return her unlicensed Beretta to the desk drawer, and leave the old papers in the safe. She felt for her Swiss Army knife stowed in her bag's makeup kit. Just in case. She double knotted a green leopard-print scarf around her neck and she was off.

AIMÉE SNEEZED AT the tang of hot oil and ink permeating the printing workshop. Two large presses pounded out colored sheets. With the loud chopping noises of industrial paper cutters, she couldn't hear herself think.

"Damien around?" she shouted.

An older man in grease-stained overalls looked up and hit a lever. He gestured to another white-haired codger to take over the press. She followed him past a stairway leading up to a storeroom, then through a dark wood hallway. He pointed to an open door with a sign: CHEF DU BUREAU.

Harsh white light illuminated a scuffed wood desk, file cabinets, and streaked glass windows that looked unchanged since the fifties. Banners and posters she recognized from this morning's demonstration were piled in the corner. The only concessions to the nineties were the desktop computer, fax machine, and laser printer.

She knocked on the open door. Damien, whom she recognized from after the accident, looked up from his desktop. Bags under his eyes, swollen red lids. He'd aged overnight. She contained her shock at this twenty-something's haggard appearance.

"So you're the one Madame Figuer called about. The art *flic?*"

Madame Figuer couldn't keep a secret. The busybody. On top of that, Aimée had an awkward feeling she'd intruded on his tears.

"Then you know about Yuri," she said.

"I can't . . . believe it."

Aimée sat on a wooden plank chair and watched him blow his nose with a blue bandanna. He reached for a water bottle and poured two glasses full, his hands shaking. She noticed the La Coalition armband by his computer.

Shaken over Yuri's murder?

"Been gone all day and we've got to fill this order tonight before I. . . ." He took a breath. "*Un moment*, I'm sorry," he said, scanning an invoice on his laptop.

Shaken all right. She reached for the glass and drank.

Done, he shut down the desktop. "Can we make this short? I need to handle an order."

Having come all this way, she wouldn't let him off before he answered her questions. "This won't take long, Damien. It's important we talk," she said. "You know about what happened on Villa d'Alésia?"

He nodded.

"Did Yuri seem worried?"

Damien rubbed his cheek. "My aunt's in the hospital, maybe I didn't pay attention. I don't know." He was lean and muscular with wavy black hair that went down the nape of his neck. Handsome, wounded—her type. Well, maybe not bad boy enough.

Then she thought of Melac. Look what bad boy had gotten her.

She decided to test her hunch. "Did you not return my call because you're scared of the Serb?"

"Serb?" Surprise filled his face. "*Zut!* Three hours ago I returned from my aunt's hospital bed and found *flics* waiting to question me over Yuri's murder." His shaking hands spilled the glass of water. He wiped at the puddle with his bandanna. "Then they quizzed me over a painting."

Aimée had no concrete reason to suspect him of anything, just his proximity to Yuri and the uneasiness in her gut. But he must know something, even if he wasn't aware. She practiced her concerned look.

"Talk about a bad time," she said. "I know it's difficult for you now. But the police investigation is focused on a Serb, the man we ran over, in connection with the stolen painting."

A lie, but they *should* be focusing on that.

"That Serb? The dead man in the street?" he said, trying to piece this together. "But how could he murder Yuri this morning? That makes no sense . . . unless you're saying he was working with others?"

"I'm saying nothing," she said. "Tell me about the portrait Yuri recovered from the rue Marie Rose cellar."

Sadness filled his eyes. "Yuri told you, didn't he?"

If he'd lived he would have. She nodded.

"Yuri's the only one who believed in me," he said, his voice choking. "It shouldn't have happened."

Alert to the different tone in his voice, she looked up. "What shouldn't have happened?"

"If only I had. . . ." His voice trailed off.

Again that fear in his face. Then it was gone. Blaming himself?

"Done what, Damien?"

"Yuri called me this morning. Left a short message on my phone saying he didn't need a ride to the art appraiser. But my aunt is dying, and I didn't. . . ."

Aimée gripped her glass of water. "Did he say why he didn't need a ride anymore?"

"He told me not to worry. That's all."

Odd. "But his painting was stolen last night."

"That's what he told me, too." Damien shook his head. "So I just stayed at the hospital with my aunt all day. What an idiot I was. I should have gone to his studio."

She understood his feelings of guilt. If only she'd arrived earlier herself. Those damn detours on the Left Bank. The protesters blocking rue d'Alésia.

Damien's knuckles whitened on the edge of his desk. "The doctors gave my aunt days to live. That was a month ago." A look of pain crossed his face. Genuine, as far as she could tell.

"*Desolée*, but if you could answer a few more questions?"

"My uncle left me this printing business tottering on its last legs." Damien sighed. "Yuri mentored me. Now I've built up a clientele and have more orders than we can keep up with. I can keep the staff on. Support what I believe in." She saw a hint of pride in the way he gestured to the posters.

Political, like Madame Figuer said. She needed to lead this back to Yuri. But a file with Florent's ugly mug sat on his desk. She remembered Florent's knee between her legs, his garlic breath on her neck, his strong arms.

"Your employee Florent. . . ."

"Him? Gone," Damien said, his mouth pursed. "Turns out Florent was robbing the till. Yuri had suspected him all along. Turns out he was right."

She sat up. Florent, the murderer. A straightforward revenge?

"So Florent held a grudge against Yuri?"

"Against me, *bien sûr*." Damien expelled air.

"Why's that? Aren't you his boss? The one who gave him a job?"

"Called me a Commie. Jeered at our goals in La Coalition. Complained that I print the posters and banners for free to support the cause. But he liked Yuri."

"Or until he found out Yuri suspected him," Aimée said. "They argue, it turns nasty, and to stop him Florent—"

"I told the *flics*," he interrupted. "Florent made deliveries in Levallois all morning."

"You're sure?"

Damien stood, a file tucked under his arm. "Believe me, the shop owner called complaining. The *flics* checked." Damien's fingers played with the file. "Florent's father and grandfather worked here. No matter our differences, it made me sick to fire him."

Aimée slammed down her empty water glass. "You're naive. Florent attacked and almost raped me."

"What?" Damien's voice rose in shock.

"Open your eyes," she said. "No one told you he was the type, eh?"

He shook his head. "Florent's always caused trouble, but attacking you. . . ." He ran his ink-stained fingers through his hair. "I had no idea. That's terrible. *Désolé*."

She believed him.

"In 1900 this was a Russian press employing deaf mutes," Damien said, his brow creased. "Yuri never let me forget. He insisted we had to continue, stay loyal to the quartier, the workshops. Hire locals. But now commerce has dwindled down to us, Dupont the *chauffage* manufacturer across the street, and Yuri's bookbindery."

A leftover nineteenth-century industrial Paris full of artists, publishers, bric-a-brac traders and craftspeople who saw themselves as the memory keepers of a time now forgotten.

Underneath the peaceful and almost timeless look of the place, however, ran dark currents.

But she didn't need a small business lecture.

"Granted, you're not selling chocolates," she said. She had to draw him out. "But the quartier's still bohemian, cheaper but with a certain Montparnasse cachet."

"Yuri said that too." His lip quivered. "I just don't want to believe Yuri's gone."

She needed to connect the dots. If she didn't press for information, this would go nowhere. Time to appeal to his bond with Yuri. "Damien, this is important. Someone tortured Yuri to find the painting."

"Tortured?" Damien's mouth dropped open in horror.

"Madame Figuer didn't tell you? We found him tied to his sink—beaten, tortured, then drowned."

Shame, guilt, and something else crossed his face. "Who would have . . . hurt him like that?"

"Damien, I'd say you're in danger, too."

"Me?"

"Do the math," she said. "Two of the three people who saw the painting are dead. You're the third, non? You took this Polaroid."

His intercom rang. Instead of answering he headed to the door. "Look, I've got orders to fill."

"You helped Yuri clean out his father's cellar, and he found this painting. Then you brought him to the art dealer to see if it was genuine."

Damien turned. The printing presses chomped in the background. "Not me."

"Then who did?"

"Why does it matter now?" He shook his head. His shoulders sagged as if in defeat.

"Someone shoved the art dealer in front of the Métro this afternoon."

She couldn't prove that.

"You should talk to Oleg," Damien said. "He took Yuri to see the art dealer."

Oleg. Her next stop. "Don't you want to help me? Wasn't Yuri your friend? Tell me everything you know."

Damien rubbed his eyes. Hurt and bewildered, he looked out the window into the courtyard. Loaders filled stacks of posters into a *camionnette*.

He took a deep breath. "I'm sorry. Saturday Yuri asked to borrow our *camionnette*. That one. To clean out his father's cellar. I offered to help. You know, given his medications and all the times he's helped me."

Damien paused.

Aimée reined in her impatience. She knew all this. But maybe there was more.

"All full of garbage, old newspapers," he went on. "But in the corner we found this small canvas, unrolled it. Amazing the rats hadn't chewed it. A man wearing a green jacket. On the back it said, 'For my friend Piotr,' signed Modigliani."

Just like in the old man's letter. "Forgotten in a cellar. But why would Yuri's father leave it there all these years?"

"I don't know."

Damien's intercom bleeped again. "Shipment's ready," said a voice over the pounding of the printing presses. "We need your sign-off."

Damien shrugged. "I've got work to do."

Aimée followed him through the hall, waited until he'd signed off on the order. He motioned her outside.

The courtyard was dark except for the glow from the warehouse splashed on the wet cobbles. The chomping machines receded in the night.

"Yuri wanted the painting appraised. I told him to keep quiet until he knew the value. Hide it. But *bien sûr* he had to go opening his mouth, telling people."

"Like who?"

"Besides his stepson, Oleg? Oleg's wife, I'd imagine. The concierge who let us into the cellar, an Italian woman. The art appraiser. Then I don't know who else."

She needed to prod him more. "Oleg and Yuri didn't get along, did they?"

"Yuri called me when I was at the hospital with my aunt to give him a ride home from Oleg's. Oleg and his wife had invited him over for dinner—that was unusual. The dinner was a disaster, he said. They always wanted something, those two." Damien glanced at the lighted windows of the printing works, checked his watch.

"Whoever tortured him won't give up," she said.

"Oleg schemed and plotted with that wife of his behind Yuri's back," Damien said.

And he hadn't returned her call.

"Wanted him to make a new will, he told me. Yuri always complained about the wife, Tatyana. She's the type who wears *faux*-designer clothes, always bragging of her connection to some oligarch's wife. How they went to school together. One of those super-wealthy women with bodyguards, limos."

Aimée didn't understand how this fit in. "You're saying there's some connection?"

Damien shrugged.

But the painting had been gone by the time Yuri returned from dinner.

"Do you know where Yuri hid the painting?" she asked, trying to feel him out.

"Where he always hides . . . hid things. So he'd remember." Damien's lip quivered. "He usually forgot things. Even to take his medication."

Yuri Volodya had seemed sharp enough last night, after the initial shock at finding his studio ransacked.

"And this morning when you spoke, did he mention a Serb?"

Damien shook his head and shrugged.

"Did you know when he was younger he was political, a Trotskyist? Did he talk about it? Stay in touch with those people?"

"Yuri?" A little laugh. "Never spoke about the past. Not to me anyway. More apolitical."

Was that disappointment in his tone?

"No time for politics, he said. The books he crafted took up his life, even more so after his wife's death."

Frustrated, Aimée pulled her scarf tighter against the chill. "Didn't anything about Yuri strike you as out of the ordinary in the past few days?"

Damien thought. "That's right, he bought a disposable cell phone."

"The kind that won't get traced?" she said, interested. "That struck you as unusual. Why?"

"Yuri hated cell phones. Never wanted one."

If the murderer hadn't taken the phone, it would be in the police report.

She sensed more. "What else, Damien?"

"He carried on conversations in the garden, never inside. I asked him why. . . ." Damien paused, pensive. "Said the fixer wanted it that way."

"The fixer? Did he explain?"

Again Damien shook his head.

"But you think this fixer is involved with the painting somehow?"

"How would I know?"

Aimée's phone vibrated. Oleg's number showed up. A message.

"Letterpress rotor's jammed," a voice shouted from inside the printing works.

The last thing she saw was Damien's shadow filling the doorway before he disappeared without a goodbye.

* * *

After listening to Oleg's message, Aimée took the Métro two stops and emerged into the clear, crisp evening in front of the spotlighted Lion de Belfort statue, the centerpiece of the Denfert-Rochereau roundabout. The bronze lion's cocked head was wreathed in a wilting daisy chain—a student prank.

To her left lay the shadowy, gated Catacombs entrance.

Her mind went back to another rainy day in early spring— the week after her mother left, when she was eight years old. Her father was working surveillance—like always, it seemed, during her childhood. That day, Morbier picked her up late from school. A trip to the Catacombs, he promised, for a special commemorative ceremony. She remembered the fogged-up bus windows, the oil-slicked rainbow puddles, arriving late to the ceremony in the Catacombs. The old woman describing how the Resistance had used the tunnels as a command post in the days preceding liberation.

As if it had been yesterday, Aimée could still feel her wet rainboots and heavy school bag on her shoulder. See those walls of bare bones illuminated by bulbs hanging from a single wire. Feel that jolting terror at the mountains of skulls. So terrified she wanted Morbier to carry her. But he'd ducked his head under the timbers. Afraid he'd call her a baby, she tried to keep up, tramping through the web of limestone tunnels lined with hundreds of thousands of bones. So scared, wanting to close her eyes. Wrinkling her nose at the musty dirt-laced odor of the departed. Shivering at the chill emanating from the earth.

"Were you a soldier, *Parrain?*" She'd called him godfather until she was ten. She tugged his sleeve until he slowed down.

"I was only a boy during the war, but my father helped the Resistance," he said.

"But you said your papa worked on the trains."

"So he did. But in secret he brought Colonel Rol-Tanguy the rail plans to sabotage the Wehrmacht freight in the Gare de Lyon yards."

"Did they hide here?" she asked, wondering why anyone would.

Morbier ground his foot in the packed dirt. "You could hide here forever."

"Weren't they scared?"

"Scared?" He shook his head. Then his thick eyebrows knit. He opened his mouth to say something. Didn't.

She watched him, surprised, her fear forgotten now. "Why are you sad, *Parrain?*"

"It happened a long time ago now. People forget."

"So we're in this smelly cave piled with bones to remember?"

"Something like that." He paused, his eyes faraway. "They say if you don't remember the past, you're condemned to repeat it, *mon petit chou.*"

She'd taken his big hand with her small one and squeezed it.

Aimée shook off the memories. On rue Daguerre, a lighted pedestrian shopping street, the evening air carried pungent aromas from the cheese shop. Below a whipping awning stood the butcher Alois in his bloodstained apron. He waved at her. She stocked up here on Miles Davis's horse meat.

This evening, Café Daguerre's outdoor café tables bustled on the terrace. She picked her way past the crowded tables to the interior, scanning the patrons: locals, middle-aged women, old men with baguettes and chives poking from their shopping bags—drinking an aperitif before heading home for dinner.

For a brief moment, she thought about how she'd intended to cook more—but since boiling water presented a challenge to her culinary skills, she discarded the thought.

"*Un express,*" she said, sitting at the counter and catching the scurrying white-aproned waiter. Next to her a young woman cut into a scallion-fringed croque-madame, on a thick-crusted slice of Poilâne bread. Tempting.

Instead she opened her agenda to the to-do list she'd begun after reading that *Marie Claire* article. Plan, set goals, and prioritize. She ticked off "proposals filed," "security checks run"—thanks to Maxence—and "butcher's for Miles Davis." Under the pending column, she crossed off "René's tuxedo" and added "autopsy findings," "fitting for the Dior bridesmaid dress," "pick up software encrypter." She also added "Yuri," "Serb," and "car repair," and considered whether telling off Melac warranted inclusion on the list.

No doubt she'd get his voice mail if she tried calling again. She put "Melac" in the future column; she'd deal with him later. Now to Oleg. She'd escaped before the police questioning—he'd be ignorant of the fact that she'd discovered Yuri murdered or that she had Piotr's letters. Two up on him. Always a good thing when facing a suspect.

"Aimée Leduc?"

She turned to see Oleg, tousled brown hair, corduroy pants and denim jacket—an academic air.

"The *flic* told me you were in the car that smashed Yuri's Merc," he said. "Ran over and killed a man in front of his house."

Belligerent and breathless. Not even a *bonsoir*.

"We had an accident. I've filed the insurance claim, everything will be handled. But your stepfather wasn't hurt." What's that to you, she wanted to say, moving away from his crowding elbow.

"Maybe you had something to do with my father's murder this morning."

He'd turned the tables. Accused her.

The waiter slid Aimée's *express* in front of her. "Monsieur, something to drink?" he asked, poker-faced.

Oleg pointed to Aimée's cup. "The same." The waiter nodded and moved down the counter.

"Yuri told me you're the son of his wife," she said, unwrapping a sugar cube and plopping it in her espresso. "So you have no legal grounds in any of this. I'll deal with his lawyer about the car."

"I'm the only family Yuri had." Oleg drummed his nail-bitten fingers on the counter. "We've kept him company since my mother passed. He was lonely, had bad health."

And you'd been sniffing around for an inheritance, according to his neighbor and Natasha at the nursing home. Oleg might qualify as extended family, but everything told her to keep Piotr Volodya's letters in her bag.

"Not that it's my business," she said, taking a sip, "but Yuri intimated otherwise last night. Nine times out of ten, it's the family the *flics* find guilty of crime. I'd keep that in mind before you accuse me, a stranger."

Oleg stared as the waiter set down a *salade niçoise* in front of a young woman wearing slim, black cigarette pants. Aimée recognized them from the latest agnès b. collection. Eating salad—no wonder she could wear size two.

But Oleg looked hungry. Why didn't he order one? Cheap.

"Robbery. Murder." She took another sip. "Your supposed inheritance, I'd imagine, would be their line of inquiry. It comes down to motive."

"But he was at our house for dinner just last night. My wife cooked his favorite dish."

"Yuri's place was trashed," she said. "He told me a valuable painting had been stolen."

Oleg stared at her. "So you're the detective he asked to help."

He'd put things together fast.

"Quite a coincidence, eh? Running someone over, hitting Yuri's car." Oleg leaned closer. "Maybe you set him up, robbed him, and appeared to offer your services with a nice cash reward."

This man was geting on her nerves. His affected academic

air, his insinuations. His incessant drumming on the counter with his nail-bitten fingers. Ignoring café etiquette.

"Funny, that never crossed my mind," she said, clenching the demitasse spoon. She wanted to slam it on his drumming fingers. "My colleague's up for possible manslaughter, Yuri's murdered, and you're accusing me? Turn it around—say you hired someone to rob Yuri and it backfired?" She paused. "You don't seem upset over his murder."

Oleg's mouth parted in surprise. Deflated, he stared at the water rings on the zinc countertop.

"What happened?" She needed to know his take.

"You won't understand." He shook his head.

"Try me."

"Yuri abandoned me," Oleg said, "like his father had done to him. Some role model. My mother sent me to boarding school when I was six. It broke her heart." He shrugged. "Still, we're the only family each other has . . . had, now. *Alors,* he liked to complain about Tatyana's cooking but he ate it."

Hurt showed in Oleg's eyes. She believed him. The only thing he'd said that rang true.

"*Mon Dieu,* such a big mouth, he told everyone about that painting. Damien, the art dealer. . . ."

Just what Damien had said. Poor Yuri, his big mouth had gotten him killed. And yet, she hadn't been able to get the story out of him. Sad and frustrating.

"You took him to Luebet, the art dealer, when?"

"Sunday. We warned him to put the painting away. Hide it. At least until this morning."

Part of her wanted to believe him. The other part figured he was telling a version of the truth.

"He called me after the accident last night," Oleg said. "Told me he'd spoken with you. Hired you."

She chose her words. "Hired me?"

"To recover the Modigliani."

"A Modigliani?"

"Don't play dumb. He called you, didn't he?"

"Not dumb, cautious." She decided to trust him. A little bit.

"But why would someone torture him for a painting that was already stolen?" Oleg said, his brow creased.

Aimée wondered the same thing. She pulled out Luebet's Polaroid. "Of the four people who've seen the painting, only you and Damien are still alive." She left out his wife. "Did you take this?"

Oleg stared at the photo.

"Doesn't do the painting justice," he said. "Even in the humidity, that dim light, the shadows, the painting . . . it spoke." Oleg's eyes glowed.

"Go on." Oleg seemed more than acquainted with the art world, from the way he spoke. "You're an artist?"

"When I was at boarding school, every Sunday I was the only boarder who never went home." Self-pity stained his voice. "The art teacher used to take me to the *musées* in Bordeaux."

"Now you're an art teacher, that it?"

"You're a detective, all right," he said with sarcasm that could have sliced stale bread.

The mirror behind the counter reflected the gauzy, fleecelike light from rue Daguerre's street lamps.

Oleg reached for his espresso. "This glimpse into Lenin moved me." He turned and his eyes pierced her. "Where is it?"

She almost choked on her espresso. "Like I know?"

His cell phone vibrated on the polished wood counter, but he ignored it. Oleg patted his jacket pocket, turned his back to her. In the mirror behind the counter, she saw him checking something from his pocket—what looked like a glossy hotel brochure with a logo she couldn't make out.

She averted her eyes as he turned back.

"Your stepfather wouldn't make a robbery report," she said,

switching to another tack. "That only makes sense if he feared something."

Oleg ground his teeth. "Do you speak Russian?"

She shook her head. "Do you?"

"My wife, Tatyana, is from Ukraine."

"Meaning you don't and she does."

He didn't deny it. She had no idea why he had asked her in the first place.

"I don't know why, but he trusted you." Oleg hung his head. "More than me."

And then she understood. "He knew my . . . mother." The word caught in her throat. Sounded strange coming out of her mouth.

"How?"

"I don't know."

"Come on, you just said—"

"We never got that far, Oleg."

Her mother—words never spoken by her father, never used while she grew up. This phantom spirit in the house no one ever talked about. Like the elephant in the salon everyone pretended not to see.

She came back to the conversations in the café, the hiss of the milk steamer, what Oleg was saying. "Yuri asked me to find a buyer."

Should she believe him?

"I've got someone who's interested."

His cell phone vibrated non-stop.

"What do I do?" Oleg looked lost.

He was asking her?

"Besides ignore that call?" She leaned closer. "If you didn't steal the painting, who do you think did? Your stepfather hired me before he discovered it was missing—why? Threats, extortion?"

"He told me he owed someone."

Yuri's words about owing her mother thudded through her mind.

"Like who? Any specifics?"

"A woman—*oui*, that's right."

"Did he let on why? Their connection?"

"I thought you were the detective," Oleg said, standing up abruptly. "Fat lot of help you've been to me."

A swish of air and he'd gone. Left half his espresso and her with the bill. Her gaze followed him to an idling late-model Peugeot, a blonde at the wheel. She glimpsed a flash of something red as he opened the door. Then the car roared away down Avenue du Général Leclerc.

Aimée's mind spun. Was Oleg playing an elaborate game? Had the painting been stolen while Yuri dined at his house? Was he pretending he didn't have it to force her hand, find out what she knew, what Yuri might have confided in her? But that was all conjecture.

When you hit a wall, think of the opposite scenario, her father always said.

What if Oleg figured she knew the painting's whereabouts? And he clutched at her connection because of what Yuri had led him to believe?

Had her mother stolen the painting? Aimée's stomach clenched. In Yuri's last message, he had been adamant that she leave it alone. Too dangerous.

Crazy. She had to stop these crazy thoughts.

But she'd learned that he had a buyer. A buyer and, she was guessing, no painting. That's why he'd met her.

In his shoes, she'd be off to stall the buyer. Hold him or her in the wings until the painting surfaced. Or, if he was the one who stole it, until attention died down and it was safe to sell it.

Oleg hadn't even hounded her for money for Yuri's damaged Mercedes.

A race to recover the Modigliani and she'd gotten ensnared in it. She downed her espresso, caught the waiter's attention, and slid some francs over the counter.

"Your friend uses our café as a meeting place," the waiter said as he made change. "But he doesn't pay for his drink?"

She pushed the coins back at him. Waiters knew the clientele in the quartier. "But I bet his father Yuri did."

A shrug. "Old Russian, gray hair?"

"The bookbinder," she said.

"That's right." He nodded and smiled. "All that Russian winter of the soul."

A waiter quoting literature? She tried to remember if that had been a question on the baccalaureate exam. Or had René, a voracious reader, quoted that from a crime novel?

He noticed her quizzical look. "Tolstoy."

RIDING THE MÉTRO back, she took out her to-do list, wrote down:

Damien
Oleg—nervous
Letters

Off rue de Rivoli, she stood in line for takeout *salade niçoise*, thinking of those black agnès b. cigarette pants. She needed to lose a kilo before she'd be back to her normal size. Awful. She'd never let this happen before. Time to swim laps.

For the second time she called Morbier to check if he'd pulled strings for Saj. Only voice mail. She left a message for him to call her back. Frustrated, she tried the criminal ward at Hôtel-Dieu. A new nurse who refused to give her any information.

Tired of voice mail and people who gave her the runaround, she headed to her office. She had reports to finish up, a security scan to run. And Maxence's printouts on Yuri Volodya to go through. But when she punched in the entry code on the keypad, no answering click opened the door. *Merde.* On the blink again.

She searched in her bag, dropped the boxed salad, and found the old key after a minute. Picking up the salad, she inserted the key, turned it twice, and finally the tumbler turned. She'd complain to the concierge. First the lift didn't work, then the door. Always something. And a long, empty evening of work ahead.

She hit the timed light. Nothing happened.

Then she heard scuffling, felt a whoosh of cold air.

"What the . . . ?"

Before she could turn in the darkness, something was pulled over her head. And then everything went black.

Tuesday, Silicon Valley

RENÉ'S HANDS SHOOK in his jacket pockets. He faced Andy and Susie, who towered over him on strappy sandals and tanned legs. Only one door out of the back supply room, and that was blocked by the rent-a-guard.

"Reconsider, René. Two new investors fly in tomorrow. The pot's growing. With the three we've got so far, that IPO gives you twenty million, give or take. Put that against two hundred thou' a year, René." Andy shook his head. "Why would you say no to a two hundred percent profit increase? Doesn't make sense."

"Andy, it's wrong."

"Sounds right to me. Do the math."

"You can't think—"

"Think all you like," Andy said. "You've set the relay and delay mode. It's all your work."

"While you monitored me, and never even provided me access to the whole system. It says 'Chief Technology Officer' on my door, yet you used my work and froze me out." He glared at Susie. Her cool hazel eyes met his for a moment, but she had the grace to look down. "You had me do the dirty work."

"Check this out, René," Andy said, handing him the business page of the *San Jose Mercury*. "Detained corporate French spy awaiting trial. Just last month. Caught at the airport. Terrible. Looks like San Quentin for him."

San Quentin, the prison?

"You've set me up."

"More like we took out insurance, René," Susie said, her voice thin. "We bought you, now finish delivering. Make nice."

He had to figure out how to blow the whistle on them. And get out alive. "Give me some time," he said. "I've got to think."

"What's to think about?" Susie said, edging forward.

"You engineered the back door, René," Andy said. "If you talk, we deny all allegations. Report you to immigration. They'll be watching for you at the airport. Detain you."

"What?" Fear flooded him.

"Just another foreign corporate spy detained for questioning at immigration."

Andy lifted his phone and checked a message. "Hurry up, René. The meeting's starting."

"Front running's illegal," he said, hating how weak he sounded.

"Don't want to play? Think you'll blow the whistle on us?" Susie said. "But no one understands all the technical jargon, René. Of course, if you try we'll tell them it was you, some idea you wanted to show us on our platform. How we had no clue you tried to sabotage us."

Andy flicked off his phone. Jerked his thumb at the guard, who put a cardboard box on the floor. Inside was René's coffee cup, the brass plate with his name, a blank memo pad, and his own laptop. The motherboard open and exposed.

"You're out of here, René."

René realized that was Andy's plan all along.

Susie opened the supply room door, glanced down the corridor. "All clear. The guard will escort you out."

In shock, René picked up the box. Threatened and now fired—what could he do? They'd covered their tail. Shut him up for good.

But he had an idea. They'd be preoccupied with the looming investor meeting—if he hurried he could do it.

"Dude, I'm so sorry. I wanted us to work together. You know, be friends," Andy said, that rocket-bright smile back on his face. At the door he paused, turned to the guard. "One more thing, empty his pockets."

The guard took René's token and office key.

"You're walking funny, René," Bob said from his Cadillac window. "Did they beat you up?"

René ducked out of the El Camino Real bus shelter and slid into the passenger seat. "This car's got eight cylinders. Use them, Bob."

Bob hit the gas. "What the hell's going on?"

"Not right now. Just get me to the motel before they discover what I stole and change the passwords."

He reached down in his shoe. The token he'd cloned using Susie's ID bit into the ball of his foot. He unlaced his shoe, moved it to the side. Safest place for now.

They wouldn't be able to change the pass codes for a while. René figured that, given all the reconfigurations that would be required once they did realize what he'd done, it would take a minimum of twelve hours. Bare minimum. But if they didn't catch on to his cloning the remote access token, he'd have twenty-four to forty-eight hours.

"Bob, I need to get out of the country."

"I can drop you at SFO, no problem."

Bluff or not, he wouldn't chance them tipping off immigration. Ruining his chance of ever working in this country again.

"No commercial airport, Bob. Ever hear of Mexicali?"

"That bad?"

Bob pulled up in front of the motel.

"Keep the engine running," René said. "Call me if. . . ."

"I see suspicious people? Sure, René. Never knew about your flair for the dramatic."

René slammed the car door, slid the key card into his room

door. He threw everything in his bag. Reached for his laptop and backup drive. His phone rang. Bob.

He ran into the bathroom near the pink hot tub, found the plastic Aéroports de Paris duty-free bag and stuffed the laptop and backup drive inside. From the bathroom window overlooking the back door of a Mexican restaurant came the smell of refried beans.

The phone rang again. René hurried back to the front window and peered out a chink in the drapes. Bob's big-finned, baby-blue Cadillac was nowhere in sight. Only two big men at the door with baseball bats.

Tuesday Night, Paris

AIMÉE HEARD THE sea, the lapping water. Her mind went to white sand, the pine scrub near the shore at Cassis. Was she on holiday? Dreaming?

A wave of dizziness overtook her. She blinked and realized she couldn't see because a blindfold was covering her eyes. Nausea rose in her stomach. She gagged, but her mouth was taped shut.

Panicked, she tried to kick but a sharp cord cut into her ankles. Tight bands on her wrist tied her to something flat and hard. She struggled for air through her nose, terrified she'd choke on her own vomit.

A loud rip and the tape came off. Stinging needles tore her face. She gasped for air. Gagged again.

Hot and cold rippled over her. The smells around her took over her senses—pine, and leather. She realized she must be bound to the armrests of her office chair. With luck, she'd be near her desk and the drawer containing her Beretta.

Fat lot of good that did with her hands tied up. More nausea; she gulped for air. What did the sea sounds mean? Through her own choking and coughing, she heard footsteps, the fluttering of papers.

"Mademoiselle, we need to talk," said a man's voice, distorted by the telephone line. It must be coming from the speakerphone on her desk.

"Who are you?"

"Introductions another time."

In the background, she heard the whooshing of tires on wet pavement, footsteps. A call from a public pay phone?

"What do you want?"

How could she stop them? Or the flashes of dizziness from whatever they'd drugged her with?

"Tell the fixer we'll meet her price."

Fixer . . . price? "I don't understand."

"Yuri told us your connection."

The hair on her arm tingled. A Parisian accent, but she couldn't place the voice. "I don't know who you are," she said, "or why you're playing games, but—"

"Your mother and Yuri have had certain dealings recently," the voice interrupted.

She broke out in a cold sweat. The bile rose again.

"Then he's seen her more recently than I have," she said, catching her breath. Saliva dripped from her chin. Her damp sweater was plastered to her back. "What kind of dealings?"

"Not over the phone."

"Why should I trust you?"

"Up to you, Mademoiselle."

Her heart thumped in her chest. "What do you want?"

"What I'm paying for. So tell us before—"

A ringing interrupted the voice. Another call coming in on her office console. Grunting noises. Her wrists and ankles were untied. Before she could reach out for the drawer, she was dragged away across the floor by her hair. Her knees hit something hard and strong arms plunged her head into a bucket of water. She swallowed a huge mouthful of water, tried to hold her breath and choked, her lungs exploding.

And then she was yanked back up by her hair.

She sputtered, her throat and lungs burning. The phone was ringing again. She heard the speakerphone voice saying something in a language she didn't know.

"He'll do that again," the voice said. "Unless you contact the fixer and furnish the Modigliani."

She had to deflect them, stop this.

She coughed. "You're off base. Don't you—"

The hands gripped her hair, plunged her head again in the cold water. She gulped another lungful. The hands pulled her up again, coughing and shivering. A sob escaped her.

She couldn't take any more. "Please stop." She trembled with intense cold. "My mother left when I was eight years old." She gulped. "Walked out. I never saw her again. Ever. Don't you understand?"

Pause.

"Then I suggest you find her," the voice said. "Before we do to her what she did to Yuri."

Her mother?

"You're lying." Prickles of ice cold ran up her spine.

Another voice was leaving a message on the answering machine.

"Going to thank me, Leduc?" said Morbier. "What's so important that we need to talk?" Pause. "Answer if you're there. I'm working late at the *commissariat*."

Morbier? Her mind clicked into gear.

"That's my godfather," she said. "If I don't call him back, he'll come over."

"Then we'll make it a party." Her hair was grabbed again; she felt those thick, strong fingers push her face toward the bucket. "My boy will take care of him." Her nose touched the water's surface. "Play host."

Her breath came in spurts, gasps, fear constricting her lungs. She couldn't take another dipping. Couldn't hold her breath long enough.

"So you've got a death wish?" she shouted, struggling as the finger pushed her down. Her forehead touching the water. Her hair clinging to her neck. Quick, she had to come up with something. "Morbier's with RAID, the antiterrorist unit."

"Tell me another one."

"Want to find out? Call that number back. He'll answer at the *commissariat*." She had to get them to stop. "Hurt me. . . ." she gasped, spitting water, "and Morbier's team will be on you like hair clogging the drain."

A bark of words in that other language. All she could make out was "Morbier" and "RAID."

The hands pulled her head out of the bucket.

"You've got twenty-four hours."

Tuesday, Silicon Valley

RENÉ DRAGGED THE huge armchair to the motel door, propped it in front of the handle like he'd seen in films. Should buy him a few minutes. If the two giants outside didn't smash the door like a twig.

He was a black belt, but no Jackie Chan. He had one option and it was dimming by the second. Perspiration beaded his forehead. He hooked the duty-free bag containing his laptop and backup drive over his wrist and climbed onto the toilet seat lid. One hand on the tile wall, he stretched a wobbling foot to the edge of the Jacuzzi tub. *Merde*. The curse of short legs.

He reached it, balanced on the slippery chrome faucets. A splintering sound came from the motel room. Beads of sweat dripped into his eyes as he slid open the panel of the double aluminum-framed window.

Over the sharp ledge he draped a pink towel, wishing his arms were longer. He hoisted himself through the narrow window. A tight squeeze, but wiggling himself sideways, one leg then the other, he scraped through. The duty-free bag dug into his wrist, cutting off his circulation, but nothing compared to what a baseball bat would do.

Thank God the room was on the ground floor, he thought, as he fell sideways, landing on a wooden crate of green chilies. The screened back door to the Mexican restaurant's kitchen was his way out.

Every second mattered. He punched in Bob's number, pulled the pink towel over his head, and made his way into the steaming kitchen. All he could see were concrete floors, bins of tomatoes, and the flanged struts of a stove. The sizzle of frying and blaring Spanish-language music made it difficult to hear the phone ringing. He hurried through the kitchen, sweat drenching his shirt. They'd remember the pink towel but not the little man inside. He hoped.

"Bob, I'm in a Mexican restaurant. Tell me you're—"

"El Toro, right? No time for tacos, René."

A cool blast of onion-laced air hit him—a fan. He realized he was in the dining area. Pulling the towel back, he saw the blue fins and red tailights outside the window.

"*Qué pasa?*" A surprised young waitress with a full tray blocked his path.

No time to explain, not that he could anyway. He ducked under her arm and ran.

At the Cadillac's open door, he swung himself into the seat, panting. "Let's get the hell out of here, Bob."

René looked in side-view mirror and saw the two goons emerging from El Toro. One was speaking on a cell phone.

Merde.

Moments later, Bob was cruising down tree-lined side streets of ranch-style houses.

"Going to tell me about it, René?"

"As soon as we get out of here." A fugitive with no papers, a tourist visa on his passport, on the run. He had no way out. "There must be a small airport around here."

"We'll go to San Jose Airport. . . ."

"I told you, I can't take chances. Immigration's on the look-out for me. Remember the goons at the motel? They work fast."

"Stay here," Bob said. "Anyone can get lost in America. You can live here swallowed up for years."

At what price? Always hiding, a *sans-papiers* living

hand-to-mouth, joining the army of California's illegals? "Like people of my stature don't stick out, Bob?"

He could hear Andy saying "Find the dwarf." Not difficult if he were standing in line at an airport, rental car agency, or train ticket office, if people even used trains here. Everyone drove.

"I need to get back to my office. In Paris."

"Pink suits you, René," said Bob, turning onto a multi-laned freeway.

René realized the thick pink towel was still draped over his shoulder, fragrant with onions and chopped tomato.

Ribbons of another multi-laned freeway arched over them like a maze of concrete arteries, everyone going somewhere. Pumping fast. Yellow scrub dotted by oak trees carpeted the hills that flashed by.

"I've only got about twenty-four hours if the security cycle's set on the standard. Forty-eight max. Mexico's close. I need a plane and no customs. You know people like that?"

Bob stared straight ahead, concentrating on the road.

"Then call me screwed, Bob." René took a deep breath. "Hate to say it, but you, too—this Caddy's hard to miss."

Bob punched a number on the speed dial of the cell phone mounted on the blue leather dashboard.

"I may not know people like that. But I know people who do."

"NO TIME TO act fussy, René," Bob said in the rear of the Cessna. "Just a little cargo of bud."

Smuggling? He felt a flutter of fear, but Bob was right. No time to worry about breaking another law. He had to get out of here. Now.

"This Bud, is that Budweiser you mean?" Didn't Mexico brew good beer?

Bob grinned. "Herb, René. Our golden state's largest export apart from microchips."

And then René realized what the plastic-encased burlap sacks filling the small passenger area contained. Even in plastic, the contents reeked. "But I thought Mexico exported marijuana."

"For the connoisseur, René. California gold rates as top quality, if we say so ourselves. Mexico's just the distribution point."

René peered over a sack, caught a whiff. Then another. The silver-haired pilot, who was wearing aviator shades, a khaki camouflage T-shirt, and parachute pants, grinned. "Gentlemen, fasten your body harness, sit back, and enjoy the flight. I apologize, no movie today."

The pilot taxied the Cessna over the rutted runway somewhere in the next valley. Hills of orange poppies and oak trees disappeared into a mountain of dark green redwoods. "But for our inflight service, help yourself to Humboldt Hog. Primo harvest."

He passed René a joint.

René's eyes almost popped out of his head.

"Sit back and chill. I'm your captain, Phil. Delighted you're flying with us at Milehigh. We appreciate your patronage. We know there's a lot of other flights you could take. . . ."

Bob elbowed René. "You pay him now."

René placed the bunch of bills Bob had rubber-banded together near the hi-tech control panel. It looked like a video game.

"Glad to do business, gentlemen."

"I owe you, Bob."

"Sure do, René. Line up four-star restaurants every night I'm over next time."

Captain Phil turned a dial, checked a control, then reached under his cockpit seat. Pulled out a nine-millimeter handgun. "Always good to prepare, just in case."

René swallowed. "In case of what?" he managed.

"All under control, don't you worry." Captain Phil grinned

as they took off. "Learned in Nam that you always need to plan for the worst-case scenario."

Right then, René knew he would die—engine trouble, a desert crash, angry drug runners who didn't speak French. Rattlesnakes.

The plane dipped but his stomach remained in the air. Terrified, he grabbed the door. This was it—they were going down.

"Take a hit, René. You need to chill," said Bob. "And you need to pack." He passed him the handgun. "Keep this handy in case the second pilot gets . . . finicky."

"What?"

"We take two planes to land at Santa Lucia in the southern suburb of Mexico City." Bob sat back against a burlap sack, checked the cartridge. "A small airport used for medical transport. Then the van driver takes you to the Air France terminal. Hand the Glock to the van driver when you arrive at the terminal. Got it?"

René nodded.

"A smooth and professional operation," said Bob, exhaling a stream that made René choke. "Not like in the Antonio Banderas movies. This is commerce, René. Business."

Andy had said that too. René checked his cell phone. No service.

"What about you, Bob?"

"Me, I'll lay low on the beach in Zihautanejo."

René reflected on meeting the blonde. A toxic experience. Maybe next time he'd concentrate on the beach, if there ever was a next time.

"I'm crashing with a friend," Bob continued, "using his computer until this thing passes over." His eyes were hooded. For the first time, René saw his nervousness. A programming director like Bob couldn't take extended leave on the spur of the moment. "It will pass over, right, René?"

René showed him the backup drive and clone he'd

made. Managed a small grin. "Once I hook this to my tools in Paris. . . ."

"You'll make their front running history, right?"

"Count on it, Bob." He prayed he could close the greedy bastards' back door. God knew what they'd aim to manipulate if he couldn't stop them. Why stop at Wall Street? He shuddered at the global implications—markets in Brussels, London, Hong Kong.

If he ever wanted to come back to this country, he had to make it right. And he had to make it up to Bob.

FOUR HOURS AND fifteen bumpy minutes later after landing at the San Lucia Airport and transfering to Mexico International, René handed the van driver, a mustached grandfather with white hair, the Glock.

"*Buen viaje,*" the driver said and slammed the door.

"Any bags to check, Monsieur Friant?"

René looked at his duty-free bag, then up at the smiling blue-uniformed Air France woman at the counter.

"Only carry-on, Mademoiselle," he said.

"Good, because they wouldn't make this flight. We're pre-boarding."

"This is nonstop?"

"*Bien sûr.*" She passed his boarding pass across the counter. He tiptoed to reach and palmed it in his sweaty hand.

"What's the flight time?"

"With a good tail wind, the flight's expected to take ten hours and twenty minutes."

And then he'd be home. Almost six hours since Andy kicked him out of Tradelert.

She glanced back at her computer. "You've got the last ticket. I've alerted the boarding gate, but you'll have to hurry, Monsieur Friant."

At Immigration, the official thumbed René's passport. "I see the US arrival stamp but none for Mexico."

René's heart dropped. Why hadn't he thought of that?

If the official detained him, he'd never make it to Paris in time.

"Monsieur, we entered through Mexicali. My friend drove, I didn't pay attention. Should I have insisted. . . ." René shrugged. "It's my first visit to your beautiful country. Sadly, a family emergency cut short my visit. . . ."

A loud thump as his passport was stamped.

"Come back again, Señor, stay a bit longer."

René could have sworn the immigration official winked.

As he ran down the long terminal to the far gate, he heard the announcement. "Final boarding call for Flight 813 to Charles de Gaulle."

René pumped his legs, clutching the duty-free bag to his chest and ignoring the pain in his straining thighs. "Courtesy alert to passenger René Friant, last call to Paris. . . ."

Panting, he ran into the deserted waiting area as the attendant was about to close the gate.

"Please hold that plane," René yelled, waving his boarding pass.

"Thirty more seconds and you'd have been out of luck, Monsieur Friant." She swiped his pass and reached for the interphone all in one movement.

"Ground crew, keep the door open," she said, her voice terse, "the last passenger's boarding in the jetway now."

Exhausted, his legs trembling, René stumbled in the jetway. His hip seized up and he collapsed in pain. Alarm crossed the flight attendant's face at the plane door. "I'll alert the medical crew, have you taken to the airport clinic."

"Not while I can crawl," he said.

"Monsieur? But you're ill and aviation regulations. . . ."

With the last ounce of his strength, every muscle cramping, René pulled himself up the jetway wall. Sweat streamed down his face. He gritted his teeth.

"Just an old sports injury. Flares up once in a while." He made a rictus of a smile. Limped forward and took her arm. "Champagne, the extended leg room, adaptors for laptops and Bose headsets," he said. "First class in Air France never disappoints, am I correct?"

Wednesday Morning, Paris

BELLS CHIMED. SOMETHING soft and wet pressed Aimée's cheek. She cracked open her eyes and squinted at the sunlight streaming in her office. Morning. It was morning.

Nearby rang the bells of Saint-Germain l'Auxerrois. She'd slept on Leduc Detective's recamier and drooled on the silk duvet.

Groggy, she sat up and rubbed her sore wrists. Beside her lay the concierge's blue wash bucket, half full of water. A grim reminder. But the rest of the office looked untouched.

Last night floated back to her—that voice, those large hands ripping her hair, plunging her head in the bucket. Her roots tingled. She remembered the deadline, passing out, then coming to, alone, her hands untied, wet and shivering on the floor. The office in darkness. Her head throbbing, knees weak. Remembered phoning her concierge to keep Miles Davis for the night. What else? Beside her, on the silk duvet, a page of notes she'd jotted down last night before she'd passed out again.

She heard footsteps on the landing outside. They were coming back. Controlling her panic, she crawled across the office floor to her desk.

A stab of nausea hit her as she grabbed the desk drawer. Her hand slipped. Tried again, yanked it open and felt her Beretta.

Leduc Detective's frosted-pane door opened, bringing a gust of lemon-polish-tinged air. Saj entered wearing a neck brace, dreads twisted in a ponytail, army jacket over his stained muslin shirt. His habitual grin faded when he saw her.

"I'm all in one piece, Aimée," he said, "but it doesn't look like you are. Mind putting the gun down?"

She wanted to run to Saj and hug him. Instead she laid the Beretta in the drawer by her mascara. "You're all right, Saj?"

"Apart from a strained tendon. I'll live," Saj nodded. Winced. "*Zut!* Whatever magic happened at the Serb's autopsy made my day."

Serge had come through.

"Ready for more good news?" she said through a wave of dizziness.

"To prepare me for the bad?"

"Something like that," she managed before everything slipped away and went dark.

SHE'D COME TO later, then fortified herself with a double espresso and a fresh brioche from Saj's foray to the *boulangerie.* Halfway through a second double espresso, queasiness rose in her stomach again, and a bitter taste filled her mouth. She pushed the demitasse away.

"You're still reacting to the drugs," Saj said. "You'll have to take it easy today, Aimée."

Then a wardrobe change in the back armoire: black leather leggings, ballet flats, retro Pucci silk tunic topped by a flounced jacket. Feeling slightly better, she finished filling Saj in.

"At least I know I didn't kill the Serb," Saj said, sipping green tea next to her on the recamier. "This Feliks."

"The autopsy proves the Serb's heart stopped before he fell on the windshield," she said. "Hence your release."

"But the robbery and now the old man's murder complicates everything, Aimée. Not a *fait accompli,*" Saj said. "I'm still on the hook."

"What do you mean?"

"The *flics* questioned me again and again last night—did I

know this Yuri, asked about a painting, implying the accident was a screen for a getaway."

As usual, they gravitated toward the first person they met with any connection to the crime as a suspect. Sloppy police work.

"You kept mum, right?"

"Not difficult on painkillers," he said. "But the last thing I want is to be a suspect in a robbery when they've dropped the manslaughter charge."

"That's the least of your worries," Aimée said. "Another Serb's entered the equation and knows your identity."

"Your friend the nurse warned me," Saj said.

Nora had come through.

But now what? The Serb asking after Saj didn't know Saj hadn't killed Feliks—and if everyone who'd warned Aimée to stay away from Serbs was right, that could be a deadly misunderstanding. Meanwhile, she still had a dead man's money. Yuri had hired her to track down that painting, and so many other people were after it, she knew she had to move fast.

She was tied up in this thing, past the point of just walking away. Someone had broken into her office to torture her for information about the painting. For her own safety, she needed to find the thing, or at least figure out who was behind the theft. Decide whether she wanted to turn the whole thing over to the authorities, whether they could even protect her or would only get in her way. Whether she'd be putting them on the trail of her missing mother, a wanted woman.

Aimée needed advice. She reached for her cell phone, hit speed dial. Then realized René wouldn't answer. Stupid. She clicked off. *Get a grip. Helm the ship, step up*—all those trite phrases, but she better follow one. Focus on helping Saj deal with this.

"I need more green tea."

On the espresso machine he pressed the steamer button,

held a cup under as the vapor whooshed out. Pensive, he sat back down next to her on the recamier.

"So the Serb's brother, or partner or whoever, didn't find the painting that night, came back and tortured the old man to find it?"

Her hands shook. "I thought the same." Sadness filled her. "Yesterday Yuri asked for my help. Then changed his mind. I wish I knew why."

Saj took off his neck brace. Did a cautious neck roll. "Something tells me there's more," he said.

"Luebet the art dealer 'falls' on the Métro tracks, but that doesn't explain what he'd left behind at the *musée*."

She showed Saj the photo, the envelope with the note, M— *Find it this time*.

"I'd say there are more crooks in the pot, Aimée. Bad ones." Made sense.

"There's something I'm not seeing," she said.

"What about Oleg? You think he could have held his stepfather under the water to make him reveal the location?"

She thought. Shook her head. "Oleg didn't tell me everything. But a murderer? Besides, he claims he told Yuri to hide the painting until it was appraised."

"Didn't Yuri tell the world? Must have been lots of interested people. You're talking a Modigliani, Aimée."

"Of the four who I know saw it, two have been murdered. Oleg has a buyer and he thought I had the painting. Or so he said."

Saj moved to his tatami mat, set down his tea, and opened his laptop.

Aimée related more of what happened—about seeing the Serb's Levi's jacket button on Yuri's floor, the blood smear on the pantry wall, Serge pointing out the telltale bruises on the Serb's corpse.

"Sounds like a fight." Saj sipped his tea. "Perfect timing, with the old man out."

"But it bothers me why, if he worried over the security, he left me cash and an urgent note, but accepted a dinner invitation and left a Modigliani in the broom closet."

Saj shrugged. "Put that aside for now. Go back to the Serb. He comes in to get the painting, but someone else beat him to it. They fight, the painting snatcher escapes. Let's go on the assumption the Serb wasn't the only one searching for the Modigliani," Saj said. "Luebet for starters. Do you think Luebet could have been the one to hire the Serb?"

Aimée shook her head. "It's possible, but then who is 'M'? The Serb's name was Feliks, and besides, he was already dead. So who was Luebet's note to?"

Saj pondered for a moment, then began to tick off fingers. "Oleg and Damien both knew about the painting, and might have tried to steal it. Piotr Volodya's concierge knew there was a painting, maybe a valuable one, although probably not where Yuri would have kept it, and you don't suspect her. Perhaps Madame Natasha, although you think she's too paranoid to tell anyone. And the neighbor, Madame Figuer, she knew Yuri had come into something, but you don't think she knew it was a painting. Do we know of anyone else who might be involved?"

Aimée hesitated, knowing the more Saj knew, the more dangerous it was for him. But then the Serb had already found his name.

So she told him about her mother. The deadline.

The color drained from Saj's face.

"We're installing an alarm system. Now." Saj picked up the phone. "My friend wires security systems." He paused. Fingered his beads.

"Did your mother torture Yuri?"

And for a moment she couldn't answer.

Her own mother, a supposed terrorist gone rogue. Aimée kept coming back to her mother's scent, *muguet*, which she had recognized at Yuri's. That scent that clung to the wool sweater her mother forgot in a drawer. The sweater Aimée slept with until she was ten, when her father discovered and burned it.

Conflicting emotions swirled. Love and pain.

Saj punched in some numbers on his phone. He organized an appointment quickly and turned back to her.

"You ready to answer, Aimée?" he said. "Do you know if it was your mother who tortured Yuri?"

"We're not exactly close, Saj." Her hands shook.

"According to Yuri, he 'owed your mother,' *non?*"

"If she brokered Yuri a deal, why murder him?" she said. "The goons see me as the link to her. Bait. But they're wrong. The Modigliani is the bait."

"What do you mean?"

The stakes had risen—this threat, the deadline. "We're all ensnared. I need the Modigliani."

"*Et alors?* By what logic?"

"The painting's my only shot to find her."

"Does she want you involved? *Non*, think about why." Saj blew air from his mouth. "Have you any idea what she's like now?"

If she'd ever known. Aimée felt a shiver run down her spine.

"And our work, the business?"

"Maxence and I have survived so far," she said. "The kid scored two contracts yesterday."

That stopped him. Saj shook his head, his dreads coming loose.

"Good idea to alarm the office, Saj," she said.

"So Maxence stays as intern?" He pointed to the neat piles of proposals, invoices, the color-coded files.

"René's star pupil. A go-getter. Brilliant." Almost too brilliant. "Why not? One thing less for us to worry about."

Saj sipped. "But there's one thing I don't get."

"Only one?" Right now she was bobbing like a cork in a flooded gutter.

"Old Piotr's living on charity for twenty years in the Russian nursing home. Why? When he stored a priceless painting in the cellar?"

She'd wondered the same thing. "Piotr's letter shows it carried a sentimental meaning. He counted both men, Lenin and Modigliani, as friends. He wanted Yuri, his son, to have it. But . . ." She chewed her pencil. "Could he have sold off other art over the years, then forgotten this one?"

"Forget a Modigliani?"

"Alzheimer's, or dementia. I don't know."

"Who would let him 'forget' this if they knew it existed?"

Good point. She doubted Natasha would have understood the painting's value, with that silly red rock on her finger— wait. What if the ring was real, after all?

She had to put herself back on track. "Say he'd kept this for the son he abandoned. He's guilt-ridden in his later years, like he writes in the journal. . . ."

"But would guilt have been enough of a reason to hang onto a valuable painting while he was living in poverty?" Saj interjected. "My grandfather sold his Rembrandt before he gave up his race horses, Aimée. Off-loaded his Picassos to repair the roof. Kept the Rodin to pay for my sister's debutante *cotillon.*"

Open-mouthed, she stared at Saj. "I had no idea."

"And they wonder why I visit only once a year," he said with a little smile. "Moldy tapestries and crumbling châteaux aren't my thing. Or those living in the past who expect me to recoup their lost fortune and carry on the family name."

Saj never talked about his aristo background.

Aimée's phone vibrated in her pocket. The men who had threatened her last night? Her fingers shook as she hit answer.

"You left a message for Lieutenant Michel Olivant," said a man's voice. "He's *en vacances.*"

Michel, her contact in the art squad.

"You're handling Michel's cases?"

Pause. "I assume you have info on the Cézanne?"

Cézanne?

"I didn't get your name," she said, trying to stall. Come up with something.

"Raphael Dombasle."

Her mind went back to meeting with Michel last year, the photos of him and his unit lining his office. "Of course, Michel's partner."

"We work on a team." His tone was brusque.

"Monsieur Dombasle, we need to talk."

"Concerning the Cézanne?"

Pause. The clink of silverware, the blare of a horn.

"No Cézanne, eh? Make a report, Mademoiselle," he said, bored. "I've got fifty cases on my desk right now."

"But this involves a homicide."

"That's *Brigade Criminelle* turf," he said, businesslike. In a rush. Like all of them. "We're overloaded with cases, *desolé*. I'm due at Thirty-Six in fifteen minutes."

"Thirty-Six," as they all referred to it, was 36 quai des Orfèvres. But across the street from 3 rue de Lutèce, where the art theft division of the BRB, *Brigade de Répression du Banditisme*, shared the building with the RG, *Renseignements Généraux*, the domestic intelligence. Not her favorite people.

Before she could say Modigliani, Dombasle had rung off.

Saj sat on his tatami mat, scrolling through files on his laptop. "The kid's good, Aimée." He nodded in appreciation at the neatly stacked work on her desk. "Got us up to speed. Gives me time to work on the new project."

"René trained him," she said. "We couldn't hope for better."

Saj turned his neck, stretched. "The Serb bothers me, Aimée. I feel disturbed auras."

"More than disturbed auras, Saj," she said. "Yet I don't know what."

"Then find out."

Yes, she could do this. She wasn't lost at sea without René anymore; the office wheels were now running with irritating efficiency thanks to Maxence. And Saj was back on board. Thank God. Now she had to get to the bottom of this so he no longer had to fear vengeance from the Serbian mafia, and so she could clear her guilty conscience about Yuri, who had needed her help and ended up dead—possibly at her mother's hands.

In her bones she knew that, like a bloodstain, the traces of this tragedy wouldn't disappear.

DOWN ON RUE du Louvre, she stopped at the newspaper kiosk. "Anything earth-shattering, Marcel?" Aimée handed Marcel, the one-armed Algerian vet, two francs. In return he handed her a morning copy of *Le Parisien*.

"*Et voilà*, in the seventh month of the Princess Diana inquiry, the lead investigator reveals . . . the investigation continues." Marcel shrugged. "Rumors of the Russians reneging on aerospace contracts at the trade show." He gestured to the line of limos parked on rue de Rivoli. "At least the oligarchs' wives don't renege on their shopping sprees."

The scent of the budding plane trees mingled with diesel exhaust from the Number 75 bus on rue du Louvre.

"No strikes today, Marcel?"

"Only one, the TGV."

Good thing she hadn't planned a railroad trip. "Mind taking Miles Davis to the groomer's and dog sitting tonight?"

A flicker crossed Marcel's face. "Hot date?"

She wished. "The glam life, Marcel. Work."

Ten minutes later, she reached the corner café on Île de la Cité frequented by *flics* and administrators. A few doors down stood 3 rue de Lutèce. An anonymous door, no sign. Nothing to indicate the nest of vipers working here.

Notre Dame's bell chimed. Right on time, a tall man in his late twenties rose from the café table, grabbed a briefcase, and took a few steps. She recognized him from the photo Michel kept on his desk.

"Raphael Dombasle?" she said. "I'm Aimée Leduc, Michel's friend."

"How did you know that . . . ?"

"Forgive me, you're in a hurry," she said. "Let's talk while we walk."

"Try taking no for answer, Mademoiselle," he said. "I need to brief them on the dossier for tomorrow's hearing. The lawyer's got thirty minutes. . . ."

"A Modigliani's worth more than a Cézanne. I checked. Especially one that's been hidden for seventy years."

Dombasle's shoulders jerked. "What's your name again?"

"Aimée Leduc, *détective privé*."

He glanced at his sports watch. "Give me thirty-five minutes. But it better be worth it."

She nodded. "Back here." She pointed to the café table he'd risen from.

"Too many people I know." He lifted his chin. "Café du Soleil d'Or on the other corner."

Too many ghosts for her there. But she nodded.

AIMÉE TOOK AN inside table at the window. Memories drenched the old bistro—the back banquette where she'd done her geography homework while her *grand-père* bantered with the owner over a bottle of wine. Her father had been denounced by a colleague at the bar, humiliated in front of off-duty officers. They'd engineered for him to be thrown off the force.

She'd vindicated him, but only years later, after his death.

"Mademoiselle Aimée?"

She smiled up at Louis, the owner and her grandfather's drinking partner. "How's your wife, Hélène?"

Louis's eyes clouded. "Her funeral was last month. We held the wake here, didn't Morbier tell you?"

"I'm sorry." Saddened, she took Louis's hand and squeezed it. A generation was passing. "I would have come if I'd known." Would she have? She averted her eyes.

"Couldn't face them, could you?"

"The old-boy network who accused Papa?" She caught her breath, wishing she'd bitten her tongue. Her father's supposed friends, who kicked him when he fell. Yet all of them were still in power at 36 quai des Orfèvres.

"Then why come here today, Mademoiselle?" He set a carafe of water on her round marble-topped table. "Seems you can't forgive and forget."

"I'm investigating, Louis."

"So you want to bend a *flic*'s ear?"

"He better bend my ear." She winked. "Information."

A little smile cracked his wrinkled face. "Just like your *grand-père*. You learned from the best. But a *fille* like you should be having babies. Your *grand-père* wanted. . . ." He paused. "Women do it all these days, they say, juggle a job, children."

Not this again. She'd heard those words often before. "I need wider hips, Louis."

But Louis snapped his finger at the waiter smoking on the pavement and motioned to a table with patrons waiting to order. Always hands-on. "The usual?" Louis asked.

She nodded. A few minutes later, Louis set a Perroquet on the table. She diluted the intense green mint syrup with water from the carafe, and sipped the anise-flavored Pernod. From the window she watched the sun-drenched balconies of the blackened stone *préfecture*, the mid-morning throngs in line for the Sainte-Chapelle, workers spilling from offices to smoke on the pavement or heading to the bus stop. Pulsing with energy like always.

"That seat taken?"

That deep voice shook her to the core. Surprised, she looked up to see Morbier.

He held a cigarette between his thumb and forefinger in one hand, a cell phone in the other. Today the bags under his eyes were less pronounced, his clean-shaven chin showed less pallor, and he looked almost relaxed. Morbier, relaxed?

The ironed blue shirt, the tie, the whiff of Vetiver cologne, no stains on his corduroy jacket for once—it all spoke of promotion. Had that case been closed with her help?

"Nice outfit, Morbier. Nominated for an award?"

A flicker of surprise. "Nothing like that." He paused. "No happy face for me? I went *végétarien* and put myself on the line for Saj's release. Why that look, Leduc?"

It broke out before she could stop herself. And she didn't care. She needed the truth.

"She's alive, isn't she? The fixer?"

He blew a plume of smoke that hovered in the sunlight slanting in from the window.

"Can't say it, Morbier?"

"Say what, Leduc?"

"My mother."

His thick brows knit in his forehead. "Didn't we handle that?"

What kind of jargon was that? "How about the real story, Morbier?" Her lip trembled. "The truth?"

His cell phone rang in his hand. A brief check and his eyes softened. He turned away to answer. "Jeanne, I'll call you back. . . ." The rest she couldn't hear.

"Ah, *cherchez la femme*," she said when he turned back to her. "The woman who makes you morning coffee, irons your shirt."

Hurt hazed his eyes, then disappeared. He stabbed his cigarette out in her Ricard ashtray.

"Jeanne's my grief group facilitator, Leduc. Cheap shot."

Morbier, in grief counseling?

"She's helping me deal with Xavierre's loss." A shrug. "But that's off point."

"*Désolée*, I didn't know." Why did she always feel like a little girl with Morbier? That inner compulsion to throw him off balance. Hurt him, like now.

But she knew why. All the secrets he'd kept from her. She needed his help again.

"Last night someone broke into my office, drugged me, and almost drowned me in a water bucket," she said. She chewed her lip. "They called my mother 'the fixer.' Demanded I contact her."

"Who did this?"

"I don't know," Aimée said. "She's in danger. I need to reach her."

"Let the past go, Leduc."

That's all he could say?

"Leave it alone for once. It's over, you know that. She's gone."

"That's not what I've heard," she said. "I'm in over my head. They almost killed me, Morbier. They gave me twenty-four hours."

"For what, Leduc?"

She told him what happened. Finished up with his voice message on the machine. "*Zut alors*, your irritated message saved my skin."

An unreadable look crossed Morbier's face. "How?"

"Your name carries weight. It's not like last time. No one's using me to get to her. She's involved."

"How can you be sure of that, Leduc?"

"Yuri was an old Trotskyist." She thought quick, putting her assumptions together. "They knew each other from the raid in the seventies, when she got caught. My father kept a file—"

Just then, Raphael Dombasle entered and waved to her at the café door. What timing.

"What do you know, Morbier?" she said.

"Never kept tabs on her history," he said. "Take a vacation, Leduc. Sun, sand, and surf."

"That's all you can say?"

He shrugged. *"Cherchez l'homme?* Melac not bad boy enough for you?"

"You know him, Morbier?"

"I wish I didn't."

What did that mean?

"Don't think you can suck me in, Leduc." Morbier chewed his cheek.

And then he stood up, nodded at Dombasle, and went out the door to be swallowed up in the crowd. Just like that.

"You're well connected, Mademoiselle Leduc." Raphael Dombasle hung his coat on the rack, sat down.

"Morbier's my godfather," she said.

Dombasle pointed to the Perroquet and called, "I'll have the same, Louis."

Louis winked. "You two make a nice pair."

Aimée's cheeks reddened.

Dombasle tucked his briefcase under the round table. "Word goes you're an investigator with a knack for manipulation."

"You say it like that's a bad thing," she said, determined to concentrate, to forget the sting of Morbier's abandonment. He hadn't even blinked when she'd told him her life was in danger. Why did she keep trying to bridge the distance between them when he cared this little about her? "But my job's computer security, Monsieur Dombasle."

"Michel vouched for you, or I wouldn't be here," he said. He'd checked her credentials.

She studied him. Slim. Intense dark eyes, tousled russet hair curling over his collar. Not the typical *flic.* More of an art historian, a tad *intello.* An interesting mix of *flic* and bobo.

"What do you have to tell me?"

Right now she had no way to find the painting unless the art cop gave her a lead—she'd parse the details, avoiding her mother. She gave him an edited version.

"Please, call me Raphael." Dombasle loosened his tie. "But we're talking about an unknown Modigliani, which I imagine has no authentication or provenance?"

"Hypothetically, if the painting had authentication, documentation and all that, what's the value?"

"Why do I feel I'm missing something?" Dombasle sipped his drink.

"Michel I trust. You I don't. Yet," Aimée said. "But I'm sure you'd like to find it. So would I. And so would some Serbs."

Dombasle grinned. For a moment he relaxed. "*Et alors*, you don't beat around the bush, do you?"

"I don't have the time."

"In our field, it's word of mouth, trust, relations built up over the years. The art dealers' world is hermetically sealed, apart from small fissures from time to time."

"When greed takes over?"

He nodded. "Usually. If our department recovers ten percent of the art stolen in a year, we consider that good. The number of thefts, private and national, is immense. But the profit's enormous too."

Only 10 percent? Her heart fell.

"But people don't fence a Modigliani on the corner," she said. "This painting warrants an elite type of buyer, *non?*"

"You want Interpol statistics? Three quarters of stolen art end up transited through a minimum of three countries, exchanged for goods including arms and gold. Recently, someone traded art for a restaurant chain in Slovakia."

A means to an end. A kind of currency.

"Collectors comprise less than one percent of art theft. A focused hit is rare." He paused. Angled his fingers toward hers. "A Modigliani—say one of the several he painted of Jeanne Hébuterne, his last lover—would go for seven or eight figures."

Dombasle's cell phone vibrated on the table. He glanced at the number.

"Museums shy away, since the authentication process would eat up a good portion of their funds. Modigliani is one of the world's most forged artists. Not worth the connoisseur's effort, to be blunt. Your Yuri Volodya might have had a fake."

Luebet hadn't thought so.

"Sounds like you're chasing smoke."

Little did he know. She hadn't learned much from this conversation. Frustrated, she fingered the cardboard drink coaster.

"My office investigates robbery claims," Dombasle said. "Where's the robbery? There was no report made."

"To investigate, you need a dead man to make a claim?"

"Why do I think you want my help, yet aren't telling me the real story?"

Time to give him something. Figure out how to work an exchange. Use him.

She brushed back guilt. Less than twelve hours remained and so far she'd come up clueless. If he was smart—and there was no doubt on that score—he'd use her too.

"Say an old man found a forgotten Modigliani in his father's cellar," Aimée said, glancing around for listeners. Only at a far table, a woman talking into her phone, a bulldog at her feet. "He's unsophisticated and runs his mouth. He contacts a renowned art dealer—you might know him, his name is Luebet—for an appraisal. But before the appointment, the painting's stolen. The old man, Yuri, is found tortured and dead the next morning. Later, Luebet 'falls' on the Métro tracks. I can't prove any of this except they are both dead."

"Then it's the *Brigade Criminelle's* territory. Not mine."

Didn't the forces work together? Collaborate? "People don't murder for fakes, do they?"

"You'd be surprised." Dombasle shrugged. She noticed the gold flecks in his dark-brown eyes.

"Then time for show-and-tell. I show and you tell, *d'accord?*"

"Depends on if you'll accompany me to a reception tonight. A vernissage."

Was he flirting with her?

"An art opening, that's your tell? Would I find it interesting?"

"You might learn something."

"Meaning?"

"A respected world authority on Modigliani will attend," he said.

"That's all?" she said, disappointed.

"Then you're afraid this supposed Modigliani will crumble under an expert's scrutiny?"

Smart-ass, she almost said.

Instead she placed the Polaroid over the Stella Artois cardboard coaster.

Dombasle pulled out an eyepiece like a jeweler's loop. Adjusted the magnification and added a small lens. Like an optician.

He read out loud. "'For Piotr, a keepsake of your friend Vladimir. Modigliani.'"

"Still think it's fake?"

"Where did you get this?" He leaned forward and covered her hand with his.

Aimée grinned. "With your hair poking out like that and your eyepiece, you remind me of a mad scientist." She pointed to the Polaroid. "You know one of those men, don't you?"

He nodded. "Luebet." He stared closer. "Taken when?"

She took a guess. "Sunday."

"How are you involved?"

She had her story—a version of the truth—ready. She showed him the message written on Luebet's envelope.

"So Luebet wanted the Modigliani," he said, glancing at his insistent vibrating phone. "He'd contacted some person or persons to steal the painting for him before he performed a professional appraisal."

Her thoughts, too. Brought it back to the theory that there were two teams on the playing field. But the ball had already been stolen.

"But a respected art dealer. . . ."

"Seen it before. No surprise. He'd contact someone who's ripped him off before—a thief who knows his métier—say 'Let bygones be bygones, I've got a job for you.'" He lifted the photo to look at the painting again. "Any idea who stole it?"

"Would I be meeting with you if I did?"

Dombasle's phone rang again, and he excused himself to answer the call outside. She counted on him, as a member of the art squad charged with recovering stolen national art treasures, to investigate. She knew Michel's team kept more irons in the fire than she could imagine. Contacts, information, a network she hoped to access. Right now, with no leads, she didn't see another option.

Doubt gnawed her insides, raw and festering. It would never be completely gone until she located the painting. And she didn't have much time. The painting was the only key to her mother.

And to finding out if her mother had tortured Yuri.

She tried to keep those thoughts at bay and had almost drained her Perroquet by the time Dombasle slid back onto the rattan café chair.

"I've got a proposition," he said.

She saw excitement in his gold-flecked eyes. Whoever had contacted him on the phone had changed his mind.

"Twenty minutes ago, an *antiquaire* at the flea market showed my colleague the same photo," he said.

"So you believe me now?" she said.

"We propose to stage a buy. Use you as the client. Interested?"

"*Moi?*" She sat back, her leather leggings rubbing on the rattan chair rungs. "You trust this *antiquaire?*"

"They're all crooks at Marché Sainte-Ouen, but this one's my informer," Dombasle said, downing his drink.

"He gives you a little info and you look the other way?"

"Works for both of us."

She'd heard of the pipeline, how antique dealers moved stolen paintings, furniture, and jewelry for thieves in a hurry. Wished she'd thought of it herself.

"But fencing a Modigliani in the flea market? Sounds unprofessional."

"Two years ago, I nailed a Velázquez there by the *frites* stand," Dombasle said. "Still in the eighteenth-century frame. Idiots, thank God. They didn't know what they had. Didn't much care either, after the quick cash."

Aimée's mind clicked over everything she knew. What about Oleg's buyer?

"Has your *antiquaire* sparked any interest?"

"My colleague intimated as much," he said. "First I need to check the painting against our database of stolen art."

She doubted he'd find it.

"Modigliani's daughter inherited nothing," he said. "Not a single painting."

Aimée shook her head. So unfair, when her father's work fetched millions today.

"A sad, broken woman." He paused. "I met her once before she died. You'd never have known she'd run a Maquis network during the war."

"Part of the Resistance?"

"In the South. Then a long affair and children with a married man who kept a double life. In the end, too much of the bottle, forgotten by her last lover. Her body was found days after she died. Tragic. Like her father."

But what about the Serb? All kinds of questions rose in Aimée's mind; the blood smeared on Yuri's wall, his Levi's jacket button—all evidence of a fight. Who was this phantom thief who supposedly stole the painting first and somehow murdered the Serb in Yuri's house? The Serb's "brother"? But then why would he pursue Saj? To tie up loose ends? Or, less likely, a flunky of Luebet's? But that didn't make sense, according to what Luebet wrote on the envelope.

Dombasle's buy complicated things.

"I'm confused," she said, "too many threads. You haven't told me the plan."

He explained over another round of Perroquets. "We're organizing a buy. Setting the wheels in motion. All the more reason for you to attend the reception tonight. I'll know more details. The drop schedule."

She'd bartered her info for what . . . a Modigliani expert? That was it? And now she was a pawn in a buy? "This could work?"

"If the thief's desperate, and thieves usually are, it works nine times out of ten. A hot piece for quick cash, that's what they want." He paused. "Worried?"

"I'm guessing you involved *la Crim* and the art cops at BRB."

"You know I can't say."

"But you're asking me to stick my neck out, wanting to use me as a patsy?"

Had word of her involvement in Morbier's sting gotten around the *préfecture?* She couldn't fathom Morbier compromising his case or talking when he'd promised "no leaks." But she still wanted to kick him.

Dombasle looked down at his drink. "Let's just say all law enforcement involved would appreciate your assistance. That do it for you?"

All frothing at the mouth, too.

She needed to think how to use this to her advantage. No matter what happened with the painting, she needed to make sure Saj was safe, and learn the truth about her mother. But showing Dombasle the Polaroid had at least gotten her on the inside of the formal investigation, or some layer of it. Like an onion, her father said of cases involving more than one juris-dictional branch, keep peeling and try not to cry.

She took the Polaroid back and stuck it in her pocket. "So in return I want the fixer."

"Who?"

"When you find out, Raphael, let me know."

She put down her card and threw twenty francs on the table. Stood, waved at Louis, and slipped onto the quai.

Wednesday

MORGANE RAN ACROSS the cobbles into the rainy courtyard. Shivering and wet, she glanced up at their curtained window. Untouched since she'd left.

Just as she feared, Flèche had gone out to locate the painting
his way. Intimidation, his usual métier. Now she'd insist they do
it her way or she'd let him loose.

"The new phone books arrived," said the agoraphobe, peeking out from her ground-floor window. "Every tenant takes
their own. Not my responsibility, as I told your husband on his
way out."

Always observant, this one. Morgane leaned down and
picked up the heavy plastic-wrapped directory. "I'll take it,
merci."

Water ran from the roof tiles, splashed in silver eruptions,
missing the rusted drain. On the damp landing she shifted the
directory under her arm to unlock the door, and a blow hit
her in the middle of her back. The air was knocked out of her.
She stumbled forward, the directory falling on her foot. But
not before her wrists were grabbed behind her and a bag pulled
over her head.

Stupid. Phone books wouldn't be out for a few months. Such
an old trick and she'd fallen for it. No doubt the attacker had
bribed the agoraphobe.

Hands pressed her shoulders down and plunked her on the
floor.

"You *salaud*," she said, "this won't get you anywhere, you. . . ."

No answer. Only the systematic sounds of drawers opening, the few pieces of furniture being turned upside down, taut mattress fabric ripping. Professional. Her neck stiffened.

"What the hell do you think you'll find?"

"The unexpected," a voice said. "Looks like you're in the dark in more ways than one. No clue to the painting, *n'est-ce pas?*"

"Who are you?"

Objects rained on her lap. Something damp leaked on her leg. The familiar smell of Miss Dior flooded her nostrils. Whoever this was had emptied her bag. She heard papers rustling, the jingle of coins, keys . . . her wallet?

Clicking. "I thought so. Two calls to Luebet, your boss."

"Who are you?"

"He can't answer anymore," the voice said. "They scooped what's left of him from the Métro tracks."

Panic filled her. "You mean you . . . ? Listen, he gave me orders by phone."

"Liar."

"Told me if we didn't find the painting, he wouldn't pay."

Sigh. "Tell me why I shouldn't shoot you right now."

Morgane's chest heaved. "Shoot me now and you get what? The painting's disappeared."

"So you're just a hired hand?"

"Luebet didn't hire me for my looks." Her thoughts raced. "You're some rogue *flic?*"

A short laugh. "Worse. I think you need to convince me, Morgane."

Nothing for it but to tell the whole story. "*Alors,* five years ago, I worked in his gallery, lifted a series of Chagall lithographs from him. Long story. After I got out of prison, my son was diagnosed with leukemia. Then Luebet called me a week ago, told me we're good now but he needs help. A job. He couldn't do it, but I could. Like I'd refuse?" The cold floor against her legs chilled her.

"This photo in your wallet," the voice said, "your son?"

A sob rose in her throat. "Please don't touch him . . . he's sick, please."

More rustling paper. "There's a Swiss Clinic bill. . . ?"

"My son needs a bone marrow transplant." Her throat caught. "I need money. I'll do anything."

"How did you plan to transport the painting?"

"But our man got there too late, there was no painting."

"Answer the question."

"My cargo freight contact at Orly."

A cough. "So, mother of the year, why threaten the private detective?"

"Who?"

"Don't play innocent."

"I don't know what you mean."

The key turned in the door.

"That's Flèche," Morgane whispered. "An amateur. He went off half-cocked last night. Wouldn't listen, uncontrollable . . . I don't know what he's done."

"Hope you're telling the truth," the voice hissed in her ear, "for your son's sake."

"Who the hell are you?" Flèche's words hung in the air. "Look, put the gun down, we'll talk about the painting. We don't have it, but I've got a lead . . . just calm down."

"What lead?"

"Plenty in the pot for everyone," he said. "The bitch will lead us to the fixer."

A short laugh. The door closed. Morgane heard footsteps. The rustle of fabric. Flèche kept a knife strapped to his calf under his jeans. If only she could get out of the way . . . but she couldn't see. Couldn't move.

"Why's the fixer important?"

"The old geezer hid the painting," Flèche said. "The bitch told me everything. We stuck her head under water like they did to the old geezer. . . ."

Morgane struggled but her wrists didn't budge. "Idiot," she said. "You won't find the painting that way."

As she'd feared, Flèche had rushed in headlong and now half the world would know. He'd brought attention and trouble to the door. If only she could cut her losses. Run.

"She's right," the voice said. Morgane realized now it was a woman's voice. Low, rasping, a foreign accent. "So that was you. Are you going to do that again?"

"I'm on that Leduc until she coughs up, or else . . ." Flèche said.

Morgane heard the hiss of a match lighting. A swift inhale. Could taste the plume of smoke Flèche exhaled. Idiot.

"Or else what?" the woman asked in that curious accent.

"I'll make her talk."

"Wrong answer. Pity, Flèche. Stupid nickname—for an arrow, you're dull as a post."

"*Tant pis,*" Flèche said, his footsteps moving past her. That smell of cigarettes that clung to his clothes. "You want a bigger cut, why do you deserve it?"

She had to warn this woman. Even though she'd attacked Morgane, bound her and threatened her, Morgane trusted her more than this idiot who'd get her killed.

"He's got a knife strapped to his leg," she said.

"That's too bad, Flèche. I don't like uncooperative types."

Morgane heard the unmistakable sound of a revolver cartridge clicking into place. An intake of breath.

"And no need to look for the fixer anymore," the woman said. "Here I am."

"What the. . . ?"

The rest was drowned in the crack of a gunshot. Morgane tried to make herself small. Sounds of shattering glass and a loud thump on the floor next to her. What felt like a man's arm—Flèche's—hitting her shoulder. Morgane shivered in terror. Then an oozing, warm wetness on her sleeve. That metallic smell. Her fingers came back sticky with blood.

She tried to scream but it froze in her throat. Nothing came out.

Her body tensed, expecting the gunshot. Expecting to die. But she couldn't force her mouth open to plead for her life. Could only sputter a few words. "My son . . . needs me . . . I beg you. . . ."

Only the chill draft from an open door answered her.

Wednesday

DOUBTS CLOGGED AIMÉE'S mind like the leaves stuck in the quai's rain-swollen gutters. Dombasle's informant *antiquaire* orchestrating a buy of a Modigliani at the flea market—it all seemed too easy.

Or maybe she was paranoid.

But it reminded her of the apricot tart her grandmother left to cool on the windowsill one long-ago summer afternoon—a flock of crows had swooped down and left not even a crumb. Was there a swarm of scavengers picking each other off for the prize?

She needed a plan, quick and dirty. Grabbed her cell phone.

Oleg answered on the first ring.

"Mademoiselle Leduc, you've thought of something? Want to talk?"

Still rude. He'd kept her number on his caller ID.

"Call off the Serbs and I'm more than ready."

A snort. "I don't understand."

Damp air laced with the fresh scent of rain hovered on the quai. Aimée shook the water off her Vespa cover, took out her keys, and shouldered her bag. The sporadic showers made one feel damp all the time, her *grand-mère* used to complain. Nothing ever dried.

"Didn't you send the goon last night to plunge my head in a bucket, like he tortured your stepfather?"

A swift intake of breath. "What?"

"Lucky my godfather's a *flic* and—"

"Nothing to do with me," Oleg interrupted. "You're wrong."

A bus whooshed by, spraying water from the puddles. She stepped back but not in time. Droplets shimmered on her leather leggings. "Act like that," she said, irritated, wiping herself off with a café napkin from her bag. "No information then."

"Either you have the Modigliani or you don't," he said.

This wasn't going well. Accusing him might not have been the best plan. But she had a feeling.

"Oleg, you're in the dark with a buyer and no painting," she said. "Guess we've got nothing to talk about."

"*Attends,* I never intended for this to get out of hand."

Her foot paused on the kickstart. Her hand gripped the phone. "What do you mean?"

"The buyer's anxious."

"So you hire someone to threaten me?"

"Never. You're crazy." His voice rose a notch.

"But to kill your own—"

"I'd never hurt Yuri. Ever."

"Expect me to believe that? He sent you away, never regarded you as his. . . ."

"Son?" Oleg said. "You don't understand. Tatyana—we never thought the Serb would die. That you'd run him over."

Realization hit her gut. "You hired the Serb."

"A fiasco." He'd admitted it.

"The Serb bought it before he hit our windshield," Aimée said. "His partner's an angry dog and I want him brought to heel or—"

"What can I do?" His breath caught. "A simple job. . . ." What sounded like a sob erupted. He sounded afraid. "But I never hired anyone to hurt you. Or Yuri. Don't you get it?"

She believed him. He sounded in over his head. But he was withholding something. She leaned on the quai's stone wall, overlooking the rippling Seine. Below chugged a long, open barge loaded with sand like she remembered from years ago. Didn't see many of those these days.

"Then explain. I'm listening, Oleg."

"Tatyana knew someone who knew someone," he said finally.

"Too vague, Oleg."

"A word here and there, back channels, I don't know," he said. "*Zut*, part of me wanted Yuri to keep it. A family heirloom."

His depiction of himself as a solicitous stepson contradicted Madame Figuer's, Natasha's, and Damien's accounts. Again, that suspicion niggled—had he stolen the painting and concocted an elaborate scheme to derail the *flics*? And now answered her call to find out what she knew?

"I wish we could have kept that painting. The Modigliani spoke to me, I told you," Oleg said. "But we're working people. Tatyana convinced me, said this buyer has a private museum, people would admire it. Yuri needed money for an operation. I thought he'd come around, given time."

She doubted that part. Yuri was a feisty old goat who wanted things his way. Hadn't he "hired" her?

"You invited him over for dinner, Tatyana cooked his favorite meal. But he refused to let you sell the painting," she said. "Ruined your plans. He'd found a fixer to handle the painting."

A sigh. "He told you all this, then you know. . . ."

She wouldn't disabuse him of the idea that Yuri had confided in her. Or reveal that she knew nothing.

"But someone stole the Modigliani before the Serb got there," Oleg said. "And now his brother's demanding payment. A job's a job, he insists, no matter the outcome."

That she could believe.

"Call him off, Oleg."

"Believe me, I want to," he said. "I tried."

"Tried, Oleg? Tell me how you contacted him."

"By cell phone, but he doesn't answer."

Why couldn't he just spit it out?

"Give me his number. He's gone vigilante on my colleague."

Pause.

She wanted to kick him. Raised her voice. "Now, Oleg. I need it."

Aimée reached in her bag, grabbed a pen from the car insurance company, and wrote the number on her palm. A seagull strutted down the wall, squawking. She covered her other ear to hear better.

"Tell me who else wanted the Modigliani," Aimée said.

"I don't know."

Holding back again.

"I think you do, Oleg," she said. "There was blood on the wall."

"Look, I'll give you a percentage," he said, sounding rushed now. "Think it over."

He thought she wanted in on the profit. Thought she knew the painting's whereabouts. Damien's words came back to her. "But Damien heard you argue that night."

"That bleeding heart?" Oleg said. "Damien should mind his own business. Yuri never gave me a chance whenever I tried to help him. But Mr. Do-Gooder's always at his beck and call, when he's not demonstrating, or at the hospital with his dying aunt. He wants first place in line for her inheritance."

"Funny, he said the same thing about you."

Oleg hung up.

As long as Oleg thought she had access to the painting, she had value. But he might have already told her everything he knew. The desperation in his voice sounded real enough.

Aimée tried the Serb's phone number. Out of service. A disposable phone. And a dead end.

She kicked loose gravel at the stone wall. Alarmed, the seagull took off, his wings making a flapping whoosh as he skimmed the dimpled surface of the green-brown Seine. The color reminded her of lentil soup.

She rang Saj. Gave him the latest.

"What did you expect, Aimée? Thought the Serb would answer and apologize?" Saj sounded worried. "Like a slap on the wrist would make any of them walk away? High stakes like this?"

She figured these were rhetorical questions. "*Bon*, Oleg lives not far from Yuri in the fourteenth. . . ."

"So pay him a visit," Saj said. "Meanwhile, since I don't have the thumb-drive prototype. . . ." He paused. "I'd like the anti-malware program that's in the drawer at my computer desk at my place. Can you stop by? Grab my stress busters while you're at it?"

Her neck felt hot with shame. "Don't tell me you came from the hospital to the office without even going home?"

"Good thing, too, with you getting attacked," he said. "Someone's got to mind the office with René gone. Look, I want to keep the business going, forget what I said before."

Guilt riddled her. Unlike René, loyal Saj stuck with her. And he needed help in return.

"*Bien sûr*, Saj."

After punching in 12 for directory assistance, she found Oleg's address. One bit of luck, thank God. First she'd stop at Saj's—the least she could do. And it was en route. She donned her helmet again and gunned her scooter to the Left Bank. Not ten minutes from Yuri's on Villa d'Alésia lay rue des Thermopolyes, a village-like street battling developers. She saw the jagged walls of half-demolished buildings with a faded Dubonnet sign, the abandoned plot an attempt at a community garden with a rusted pinwheel turning in the wind. Farther on, she passed pastel two- and three-story maisonettes, painstakingly restored, and the taffy brick walls of the occasional small workshop. Saj lived in one of these.

A churchbell chimed in the distance. Pastoral and quiet. She keyed in his door code and reached his studio on the second floor. Diffused light from the slanted glass roof bathed the former workshop in a clouded vanilla. On the oblong window facing the courtyard, something was painted in red, like graffiti. Art? But when she got closer, she saw the misspelled words slashed like blood spatter: *I'll get you murderrer.*

Her heart jumped into her throat. She gasped. Stepped back, and stumbled on Saj's pile of encryption manuals. She didn't need a high IQ to know the handiwork of a Serb bent on vengeance.

A creak behind her startled her and she turned to see a female figure in black Goth garb. "Can't get away this time."

Aimée dove under Saj's kitchen table just in time to avoid the swinging scythe. She scooted on her hands and knees as fast as she could over the tatami mat. "Hold on, I'm Saj's friend," she said, meeting the woman's heavily made-up eyes, black holes in her white face. "Who won't get away?"

"Like I believe you? I heard those noises this morning. . . ."

By the time she'd convinced this Goth neighbor—Solange, or Sheila, the Celtic name she preferred to be called by—that she wasn't out to kill Saj, five precious minutes had passed. But at least she could get some information, if Sheila had seen the Serb. "So you heard him. Did he speak? Have an accent?" she asked.

"I was rushing to work and heard loud noises. That's all."

Work, in the morning? Not some vampire party? Aimée blinked.

Sheila noticed her reaction. "Had to open my medieval shop on rue du Couédic early today for the confluence gathering. The tribes request it, you know," she said, her high-pitched voice at odds with her appearance—black lace, tapestry-festooned apron, and matching black fingernails. She resembled a milkmaid from Hades.

"Then I found the door open, and no Saj. I'm worried."

"Did you see who did this?"

"He ran away."

Obviously.

"What did he look like?"

"Everything happened so fast." She shrugged. "He took off through the courtyard."

Aimée was stuffing several of Saj's muslin drawstring pants and matching white shirts, an alpaca vest, and his mail in her bag. He wouldn't be coming back here. Of that she'd make sure.

"Try to remember something about him. Anything strike you?"

"A hat, a cap? But he ran, I . . . didn't see well."

Great.

"We're a community here, supporting the garden, keeping developers out. . . ." She sighed. "Hasn't Saj told you? We're the last bastion for artists and musicians, the way it used to be. The only thing that hasn't changed is people living on the margins." Another shrug.

This Goth liked to talk. Aimée wished her acute observations extended to this morning.

"The closer you get to the Périphérique, the cheaper," she continued. "We've never had trouble even with the squatters who live by the garden. The single men, the day workers, they even respect the families."

She painted a pretty picture, but the words dripping in red on Saj's window belied the harmony.

"We're a mix—old anarchists, poets, *intellos*, and film stars who like *la vie de bohème* without the prices closer to Mont-parno."

Montparno, argot from an old Jean Gabin film.

"Violence and sick attacks like this just don't happen here," she said. "At least La Coalition is militant and rabid to stop the developers. Those bloodsuckers."

La Coalition, those demonstrators who'd blocked rue d'Alésia.

"That so?" Aimée was half-listening, checking Saj's computer—untouched—and finding the malware program. She scanned Saj's tatami floor, the walls basic, white and untouched apart from the red letters on the window. "What about the Roma, the Gypsies on rue Raymond Losserand?" Many a time she'd seen women sitting on the street corner begging with a child in arms. Saj called it the shame of the quartier.

"From encampments beyond the Périphérique? Sad." Sheila shook her head. "The bosses drive them here in vans, drop them on the corner to 'work' begging. The bosses take it all when they pick them up. Beat them when they don't make their quota."

Horrible.

Just then, she remembered Saj's disgusting rabbit pellets, his stress busters. She found them by the window.

"Change the digicode." Aimée gave her a card—no Leduc Detective logo, just her name and number. "Keep your eyes open and call if you see anything, okay?"

Halfway through the courtyard, she bent down to examine something yellow in the cobble crack. A damp bit of hay.

Sheila's voice called from the upstairs window. "Maybe it's nothing but . . . I remember he had a long coat on under his jacket."

"Like a lab coat? Hospital worker?"

"Like that, but blue. And a blue cap."

But where had the straw come from? The last farm in Paris battling the wrecking ball lay not far from here, on Tombe Issoire, sheltering squatters and artists. She almost grasped the connection, felt it bubbling up then eluding her.

Write it down, her father had always said, even if it appears random. Then connect the dots later. Boring, tedious, and the way the investigations got done. Tiny details contributed evidence in the most banal way. "That's why we're called *poulets*, chickens in the farmyard pecking for a crumb," he'd say, "a seed sprouting into a detail." "*Non*, Papa," she'd reply, "you're called *poulets* because the *préfecture*'s built on the ancient chicken market." "True, *ma princesse*," he'd say, "but we still peck for details. Details nail your perp, make your case. Nothing else."

At her scooter, she jotted down notes, put the bit of straw in her pocket and Saj's clothes in her helmet compartment. She dialed Saj.

"Please listen, Saj. You're staying with me and Miles Davis for a while. No argument."

"Has something happened to my place?"

"It's not safe," she said, feeling inadequate. "I've got you a change of clothes."

A sigh. "I'll stay at René's. It's closer and he's got more equipment. He gave me the key. I should water his plants."

"*Bon*. The alarm installed yet?"

"As we speak. Any good news?"

"Straw mean anything to you?"

"Not off the top of my head . . . a Serbian farm?"

"More later. Keep the door locked and alarmed."

Suddenly she had a flash of realization. Stupid, why hadn't she put this together before? Oleg mentioned a buyer, admitted Tatyana hired the Serb. Tatyana bragged to Yuri about her old schoolmate who had married a Russian oligarch. What if the oligarch's wife was the buyer? A slim shot, but right now the only one to pursue. Time to speak with Tatyana, the brains behind this, to call off the Serb.

By the time she pulled up on her scooter at Villa Leone, her bad feeling mounted. Beyond the passage's Moorish arched gateway was a stretch of irregular cobblestones, geraniums and ivy trailing the walls of old wooden ateliers. A rustic, faded charm lingered on Villa Leone in a run-down nineteenth-century

way—forgotten ateliers and wash hung out under the dripping
vines.

On the corner, a Peugeot started up. Moments later Oleg
rushed out and jumped in the passenger seat. With a grinding
of gears, the Peugeot headed toward rue d'Alésia. The same
blonde at the wheel of the same car Oleg drove off in last night.
Evidently, Tatyana wore the babushka in the family.

Aimée followed, leaving two cars between them. At the
stoplight, she squinted to see into the car. Two heads bobbing,
hands waving. Oleg stepped out and slammed the door at the
Plaisance Métro, scowling. Looked like an argument.

Aimée kept behind the Peugeot, zipping through the yellow lights to keep up. Not fifteen minutes later, they crossed
the Pont de l'Alma, over the tunnel where Princess Diana's
Mercedes crashed, and past the heaps of fresh flowers
brought daily in her memory. Tatyana veered into Avenue
Montaigne, deep in the *triangle d'or*—the golden triangle,
or luxe land, as Martine called it—the wedge of wealth bordered by the Champs-Elysées and the Seine, showcasing
designer couture such as Yves Saint Laurent, Dior, Hermès.
These days, no self-respecting, budget-minded, fashion-
conscious French woman emptied her pocketbook on the
avenue of haute couture, according to Martine, who knew
these things. They left this province to the wives of sheikhs
and foreign billionaires.

The Peugeot pulled into the Hôtel Plaza Athénée drive. She
recognized the Plaza Athénée logo from the brochure in Oleg's
pocket. Red geraniums adorned the balconies, framed by stone
art nouveau carvings. Expensive taste. Odds were Tatyana was
visiting her old school friend and had disinvited Oleg.

Tatyana handed the keys to the valet and, with a swish of
her long red leather coat, flounced past the bowing doorman.
Too bad the hotel detective Aimée had known retired last
Christmas. But he had always complained that this five-star

hotel hadn't upgraded their video surveillance. Or staff rooms. A tightwad for a manager, he said.

Aimée parked on a side street. She exchanged her ballet flats for heels, her helmet for the red wig she kept in the customized storage compartment under the seat installed by her cousin Sebastien. Minutes later, wearing oversize Dior sunglasses, her trenchcoat belt knotted, she smiled at the doorman.

The lobby exuded privilege: fresh sprays of white roses everywhere, gleaming marble floors, crystal chandeliers, and Louis XV chairs. From the adjoining bar she heard Russian conversation punctuated by peals of laughter. A woman wearing tight jeans, open-toed snakeskin stilettos, and an enormous bored pout passed Aimée in a cloud of amber perfume. She held a cell phone in each hand. All she lacked was an entourage. This diva made even the mauve Givenchy she wore look tacky. Tatyana, sitting in this group of three women, leaned forward laughing and hanging on the diva's every word.

The third member, a sleek-haired brunette in a black pant-suit, scanned the bar and checked her cell phone every few minutes. A personal assistant, a trainer? Aimée hedged her bets on a bodyguard.

The diva nudged the bodyguard, who snapped her fingers at the waiter.

Aimée moved closer to hear. The bodyguard pointed to a menu. "*Da, oui*, please to order from the dog menu. *Steak haché* for Pinky. But first, please to take him for walk."

The diva deposited a Chihuahua with an eighteen-karat-gold collar into the hands of the black-vested waiter. Not an unusual task in his job, judging by his servile expression.

"*À votre service*," said the waiter, smiling at the little rat of a canine.

Aimée hoped the diva tipped well. The waiter deserved it. But the rich were different, *n'est-ce pas*?

The diva and Tatyana clinked frosted cocktail glasses together. Designer bags bunched beside them. The new Russia.

Aimée was dying to know what they were saying.

Instead of moaning that she hadn't taken Russian at the *lycée* like Martine had, she sat within earshot by the walk-in-sized butterscotch stone fireplace. Tried to figure out a plan.

"Madame Bereskova, *une petite signature, s'il vous plaît*," said another waiter, depositing a moisture-beaded bottle of Taittinger in the ice bucket.

The diva signed the bill with a flourish.

"Has Madame's husband's driver returned?" said the bodyguard.

"I'll check, Madame." The first waiter bowed out with Pinky under his arm.

"Our tour guide should arrive any moment. Please to ask her to join us."

Aimée had an idea. She pulled out her wallet, chose a card, then stood up.

In the lobby, by a potted palm, stood a young woman with a cell phone to her ear and a badge that read DISCRIMINATING TOURS.

"Mademoiselle Vanya?" Aimée said, reading her badge.

The young woman smiled and clicked off her phone. "You're Madame Bereskova's assistant I spoke with?"

She hesitated to get the woman in trouble. Thought fast. "May I speak with you in private?"

"Is there a problem?" Her eyes were unsure. "Where's the Russian woman who arranged the tour?"

Aimée took her elbow. Guided her behind a pillar. "Change of plans. You've taken ill. Food poisoning. Instead of canceling, you're sending in a replacement. Okay?"

Mademoiselle Vanya's jaw dropped.

"Nod if you understand, Mademoiselle."

"I *don't* understand. That's my job."

Aimée scanned the lobby.

"Who are you?" the young woman asked.

"I'm with Monsieur Bereskova's Paris security. Reports have alerted us to a threat. I'm to take over. He wishes me not to alarm Madame Bereskova. *Compris?*"

Aimée saw the questions spinning in the woman's mind. One was if she'd get paid for her time. Another was whether to believe Aimée or not.

"Not to alarm you, but it's imperative you cooperate," Aimée said, flashing the generic security badge she kept for emergencies. "The firm will take care of your fee, of course. Now make the call. Sound convincing and here's an extra hundred francs."

"Forget trying to bribe me," she said. Her jaw stuck out, a defiant look in her eyes. "I'm calling my boss."

Great.

"Then you're trained to deal with kidnap attempts? Trained to disarm *les explosifs?* Handle armed combat and martial arts?"

"But her husband arranged for lunch at the Ritz, a bilingual afternoon cultural tour, some sights—"

"Someone slipped up. You should have been told," Aimée interrupted, pointing to the one video camera in the ceiling woodwork. "We're private security hired to guard his wife."

"You?"

The woman needed more convincing and Aimée needed to hurry. Time for the matter-of-fact approach she'd gleaned from Chirac's security detail.

"As a woman, I blend in, people assume I'm a personal assistant," she said. "*Bien sûr,* I'm trained in firearms, protective driving, countersurveillance, and bomb search. But it's about being able to read a situation, identify threats—whether it's the paparazzi, a kidnapper, or an assassin—and get my client to safety. If it comes down to conflict, I've failed my client and myself. We like to defuse potential threats before they become issues."

Aimée pulled out her phone. Pretended to consult it.

"I suggest you cooperate before it's too late. The doorman, if you didn't notice, is one of ours."

She pointed to the uniformed doorman speaking into a headset. *De rigueur* in five-star hotels these days. She counted on the tour guide not to know that.

"Easy to say. How do I know you're a bodyguard, not a kidnapper?"

Smart.

"That's going to have to be your call, isn't it?" Aimée rolled her eyes. "At this moment we have a situation. A level-three threat." She continued making it up as she went on. "Wives of Russian businessmen make prime targets these days. Serbians pick them off like candy."

Horror filled the young woman's eyes.

"I'd prefer not to make a scene, but either make that call or—"

"Make it two hundred francs more worth my while," she interrupted.

Aimée cringed, hoping it would be worth it.

In return the woman handed Aimée her tour guide pin. Pulled out her phone and hit speed dial. "Mademoiselle. . . ." followed by several phrases in hurried Russian. *"Dosvedanya."*

She pocketed the money and disappeared without a backward glance. Aimée waited ten minutes, using it to read *Le Parisien's* business section, which she scanned until she found an article on the Russian oligarch business deals at the air trade show. The diva's hubby, Bereskova, was a major player. It seemed the oligarch's search for composite carbon parts necessary for plane fuselages had hit snags with the Ministry of Defense.

Putting aside the flea market *antiquaire*, Tatyana stood to gain from the Modigliani—a guaranteed entrée for a babushka girl from the village to ride with the nouveau riche of Moscow.

Tatyana would keep contact with the Serb's cohort, needing him to make good on the deal. Find the painting.

Aimée would have to get Tatyana aside, threaten her cover if she didn't call the dog off.

Russian oligarchs belonged to the select economic strata with enough disposable income for a Modigliani. Hadn't Marcel just pointed out the limos of the Russian oligarchs' wives—boutiquing while their husbands shopped for an air fleet? A Modigliani would be a plum treasure for a Russian collector.

She prayed she could pull this off. In the marble restroom scented by floating gardenias in a matching marble fountain, she used a gold-braided linen hand towel. Touched up her eyes à la *ELLE*, smoky shadows to smolder.

Smiling with an apologetic shrug, Aimée introduced herself to the women. "Your guide took ill," she said, re-explaining the situation.

Tatyana and the bodyguard looked her up and down. Did Tatyana's gaze linger a second longer before turning to the diva?

"The boring Ritz and some cultural tour?" The diva laughed. "No way."

Aimée's heart sank. Thought fast on how she could use this. "Actually, the tour company suggested me because I conduct shopping tours also. I'm collaborating with my journalist friend on her book—*Chic Pas Cher*—a fashion guide to what Parisians wear. We're doing a spread in *ELLE*."

That much was almost true.

"*ELLE?*" The diva sat up. "*Vogue's* my, how you say, bible."

Aimée beamed her a smile. "But *ELLE's* au courant for the young set like you."

The diva ate that up—Aimée could tell—cocking an eyebrow at Tatyana, who grinned back like a lapdog. "I like this idea. We go shopping. You take us to where *Parisiennes* go."

"Hermès, Vuitton, you mean?" Aimée asked.

"*Nyet*. Like you. You do good job, get good tip."

In the Mercedes limo, the chauffeur tipped his blue cap. Large shoulders, Slavic cheekbones, and an accent. "The Ritz first, Madame Bereskova?"

The diva leaned back in the seat and pointed at Aimée. "Change plans. Tell him."

Tatyana and the diva drank champagne from the bar in the back. The bodyguard, Svetla, poured and checked her cell phone. The women weren't much for small talk with the help. Aimée racked her brain for a way to engage them, turn the conversation to the painting somehow. But the diva, not one for culture, flashed francs like Métro tickets. The chauffeur, stocky and phlegmatic, interested her. Even more when she noticed the bulge under his jacket. The oligarch kept his wife protected. She doubted the chauffeur had a license for that.

"You with the KGB?" she winked.

"We don't call it that anymore. It's the FSB," he said. "Retired."

Great. His thin mouth set and he ignored her further attempts at conversation.

But he couldn't guard the diva in the changing room. Aimée hadn't thought this through, as usual, but she'd seize whatever opportunity she could. Doubted she could keep the charade up too long; the guide might have second thoughts and check with her boss. She flicked on the tape recorder in her bag.

The glass partition of the limo closed. Bad news. She had to bide her time until she got Tatyana alone. She directed the chauffeur to agnès b., then Lolita Lempicka, for starters.

Aimée steered the diva away from a strapless teal wide-legged jumpsuit, and the flamenco-inspired tie shrug. Guided her to a bronze metal-mesh tunic, helped her accessorize with a tasseled clutch and T-strap heels.

Tatyana stuck to the diva like glue, even in the dressing room. Two shops and several thousand francs later, Aimée understood none of what they said.

While the diva was in the dressing room, Aimée stepped outside and called Marevna, the translator. Busy.

"You are holding out," said the diva, her voice shrill, when they were back in the limo. "We want fashion must-haves for the *Parisienne*. Why we not find more accessories?"

Aimée cringed inside but smiled. "Excellent point. I can't fool you. But you must understand, a *Parisienne* builds a seasonal wardrobe. Invests in certain basics, the foundation—" What had Martine said? "A good bag, coat, or jacket and heels. Then it's simple to mix and match."

"Teach us accessorize," she said, accompanied by a burp.

The back of the limo filled with hoots of laughter.

The girls were out for a good time. How could she turn it around? Only a car seat away from Tatyana, who appeared to be having the time of her life. The champagne flowed. Meanwhile, Aimée's twenty-four hours were ticking away.

Had she gone up the wrong *allée*? She'd assumed the diva negotiated with Tatyana for the Modigliani. Time to push.

"Fashion's an art, you know. Style takes thought." Aimée pretended to think. "Think of building the perfect outfit as an artistic process. One must visualize the background, shade it with a working color scheme, accessorize to heighten the mood. Evoke a feeling. Think of a great painting. A Modigliani."

Tatyana's mascaraed eyes narrowed. Had Aimée gone too far? Had Tatyana finally recognized her?

The diva was speaking into her cellphone in loud Russian. Apparently someone on the other end was chewing her out.

"*Da*, Dmitri." She clicked off and her fuchsia mouth sagged in disappointment. "Must go Ritz hotel."

"But you booked the afternoon," Aimée said, trying to keep calm. "We haven't even hit Louboutin. His must-have red-soled heels."

The diva sighed. "For one time I having fun. With French woman, like friend, see real Paris. Not stupid boring Ritz.

Meetings, always business." A bitter laugh. "My husband Dmitri book me."

Dimitri kept his diva on a tight leash. For a moment Aimée
felt sorry for her. How sad, if she really regarded Aimée as a
friend.

"Your husband appreciates art?"

The diva snorted. "Dmitri buys culture. Like everything
else. Now he buys museum."

Like Oleg had said.

"Pay her." The diva nodded to her bodyguard as the limo
pulled up at the Ritz. But Aimée hadn't even talked to Tatyana,
had learned nothing. She couldn't let her get away.

A wad of francs were thrust in Aimée's hand as she emerged.
"Keep extra. It's your tip." The diva and Tatyana disappeared
under the portico.

Holding in her anguish, Aimée smiled at the bodyguard,
whose name she'd discovered was Svetla. "That's too kind. But
I'd like to give her my card. You know, for a more detailed tour."

"I handle that."

"Of course, please do. . . ." She played it another way. "I love
the ladies' room here. They wouldn't mind if I used it, non?"

The bodyguard leaned closer, placing her dry hands on
Aimée's . . . a fraction too long. Her scent of leather and champagne filled Aimée's nose.

No mistaking that body language.

"You like women?" A definite come-on. Aimée wanted to
crawl back into the limo and speed away. But it wasn't her limo
and it wouldn't speed away.

Aimée nodded. "And men."

"Bi, me too. Why frown on pleasure? A drink later, yes? I'm
off tonight."

Aimée had never been propositioned by a female Russian
bodyguard before. Always a first time.

"Give me your number." Aimée took Svetla's cell phone

and replaced it with hers before Svetla could object. "We'll key each other's number in. French numbers are so difficult." As she keyed in a number that went to an answering service, she casually nudged her bag with her elbow so it landed on Svetla's foot. "Oh, I'm so sorry."

As Svetla reached down, Aimée scrolled to the last three numbers dialed—all the same. Before she could memorize the number, Svetla palmed her phone. Shot her a look. "Tonight."

By the time Aimée entered the lobby, there was no trace of Tatyana or the diva. Conversations buzzed from huddled groups of men in dark suits, blue shirts, and red ties—the Ministry uniform. Definitely something high-powered going on. A hovering man, obviously a plainclothes hotel detective, had glided toward her.

"May I help you?"

Get lost, she wanted to say.

"Madame Bereskova forgot something in the limo," she said.

"I'll make sure Madame gets it," he said, blocking her way by the Hemingway Bar sign.

She brushed past him, flashing her father's old police ID with her photo on it. The only way with minions like this.

Hurrying down the long, plush carpeted corridor, she heard a hiss. A snap of fingers. "You! Here!"

Tatyana, her eyes narrowed in anger, gestured at her from an alcove. Her long, red fingernails stabbed the air.

"What do you want, spy?"

"Simple," Aimée said. "Call the Serb off."

Tatyana's mascaraed eyes crinkled. "Like I know what you mean? Get lost or I call—"

"Dmitri? I'd like to meet him."

Tatyana's thick foundation creased in a network of fine lines. Not as young as Aimée thought. Or else the woman had had a hard life.

"Maybe you want him and the *flics* to know you hired—?"

"Shhh." Tatyana gestured to ladies' restroom. "In here."

Tatyana checked the cubicles, the closet with extra hand towels and soap, the dish with coins for the attendant. Empty. "I make it quick before the *pipi* lady come back," she said, arranging her sleek blonde bob. "Quit hounding my husband."

"Oleg called me."

"I mean following us around, like yesterday and today," Tatyana said.

Yesterday? "You're paranoid, Tatyana. Give me the Serb's number. The contact."

"What do I know?" She shrugged. "It's his brother. He's pissed, out of my control. Right now you want a cut. Fine. Ten percent."

"Quit haggling," Aimée said. "Bereskova's your buyer, right?"

"He has museum." Tatyana pouted.

"He's a Lenin stalwart, or an art connoisseur?"

"What he knows about art fits in my toenail. Maybe the babushkas in his orphanage idolized Lenin."

"What does that mean?"

Tatyana's eyes glinted. "Fifteen percent?"

Aimée tried another angle. "Why is your diva friend unhappy?"

"So much money and still unhappy. I don't know."

"Quit the act, Tatyana. Cooperate or—"

"Dmitri not big oligarch now. More like a gardener," Tatyana said, glancing at her watch. A white Chanel. A gift from the diva or an imitation, Aimée couldn't tell. "He needs art, this museum."

"A gardener?"

"Dmitri plants seeds, adds fertilizer, water, like that."

"I don't understand." She wished Tatyana made more sense.

"Dmitri grows connections, like you say. Needs to make himself legitimate again. Now he have so many little projects, all seeds he's trying to plant to grow into something big, put him back on top. Museum is one seed."

Then it fit together. Dmitri was the buyer.

"So Dmitri wants the Modigliani to legitimize his museum and gain connections?"

"Who knows? But he owes *krysha,* we call it in my country—it's how you do business."

"*Krysha?*"

"Protection and patronage." Looking bored, Tatyana smoothed back an eyebrow in the mirror. "Maybe Lenin means something to him." A short laugh. "Dmitri comes from nothing. He was raised in a collective orphanage. Worked at a factory all the way up the apparatchik ladder. A self-made man. But last year he backed the wrong—how you say—Eurocrat? I give him credit. He wants to be back at the top."

Aimée's surprise must have shown on her face.

A bitter laugh. "No secret. The price of doing business. That's Moscow rules. Honor *krysha* if you want to stay alive."

"So you furnish the Modigliani and he owes you, *non?*"

Tatyana's cell phone rang. She checked the number. "I must go. He's pressuring me." Her tone went serious. "I need the painting. We make it work for everyone."

Aimée blocked the door. "The Serb threatened my partner. You're not leaving until I find him."

Tatyana hesitated, considering. "Avenue Claude Vellefaux, a *café-bar* by the hospital. That's all I know." Her eyes narrowed. "All right, twenty percent. But furnish it tonight."

"TATYANA GAVE UP the info too easily," Aimée said.

Back at Leduc Detective, she'd finished her account and a bottle of fizzy Badoit after handing Saj his clothes and malware program. The office was filled with the scent of sage still smoldering in the incense bowl—Saj's ritual of purification and cleansing of auras. After last night, she agreed to it. Aimée flicked her lighter and lit another bundled stick of sage, wishing she were lighting a cigarette instead.

"She sounds desperate if she offered you twenty percent," Saj said, sitting on his tatami mat, a program running on his screen. "Or she's playing the oligarch. On the other hand, he could be playing her, too."

"You mean he's got his own feelers out?"

Saj shrugged, then winced. "Aimée, tell the *flics*. That one from the art squad who liked you so much. The one who wants to set you up for a buy."

Dombasle. The one with the nice eyes. "He wants a patsy." Part of her wanted to confide in Dombasle, get his advice, but the other part knew she had to handle this alone. Finding the painting would lead to her mother. But first she had to deal with the Serb.

And the hours were ticking away, her deadline looming. A tingling sensation ran up her arm.

"But tell him what? That I ran away after I found Yuri tortured, and took the art dealer's photo before he was pushed on the Métro tracks?" She shook her head. Reached in her desk drawer and shuffled the reports until she found her mascara and kohl eyeliner. She needed a quick touch-up. "*Alors*, the Serb's brother made a fool of police security at Hôtel-Dieu, threatened you, who they regard in their own twisted logic as a suspect." She stood, headed to the back armoire. "I need to neutralize the Serb, and not in this outfit."

Behind the plumber's overalls, nurse's uniform, and other disguises in her armoire, she found jeans, a vintage charcoal Sonia Rykiel cashmere tunic, and a black chrome metallic jacket.

"Slow down, Aimée," Saj said. "Don't go this alone. Or run off half-cocked without a plan."

"Good point. I'll bring my bag of tricks."

"Act tough, then. Don't say I—"

"Didn't warn me? This *mec's* ruthless—you're injured, and what if you'd been home alone? He's carrying out a vendetta.

Until he learns you didn't kill his thief of a brother, he won't stop."

"You don't have to prove that to me. Or that you're brave."

Brave? The last thing she felt. "Look, my mother's involved and I need you safe."

And then she remembered. "Where's Maxence? Don't tell me he's playing hooky already?"

"Been and gone to René's for the cables I need. You need me working." She heard the smile in Saj's voice. "Someone has to be beside this kid. He's good, Aimée." Suddenly he looked a little bleak. "But don't forget, boss, I need you."

"Still hurts, Saj?"

He nodded. Winced. "What can I do from here? How can I help?"

She thought. "Find out what you can about this Bereskova. His business, the museum. Tatyana intimated it's a front."

"Odd, *non*, that she's so up-front on that score?" Saj said.

"That struck me, too." She pulled out her map and located Avenue Claude Vellefaux near the hospital where Serge gave pathology seminars. Why hadn't she heard the lab results from him? She tried his number again; his phone went to voice mail.

At the office door she paused. "What's our alarm code disarmer?"

"*Hare krishna hare krishna.*"

"A Hindu mantra?" She'd learned that much from Saj. "Feels like sacrilege or something."

"Krishna won't mind. Means we'll chant several times a day."

HER SCOOTER IDLED at the red light on Canal Saint-Martin. Irritated, she pulled on her gloves, watching the locks move the water slowly under the arched bridge. Like everything else today. Slow.

A barge made its way into the water, filling the basin with shushing ripples as a small heron winged its way over the bank.

She found the café across from the peeling stuccoed walls of Hôpital Saint-Louis, built in the seventeenth century to contain plague victims. The area still felt isolated. She noticed the young drug dealers on the corner of nearby rue Jean Moinon and a Chinese hooker emerging from a car, two blocks down from the hooker turf on rue de Belleville. Edgy and mixed.

The Serb mafia café fit right in. Soccer team pennants on the nicotine-stained walls, mismatched chairs at gouged wooden tables. The turn-of-the-century frosted-glass windows were fogged with smoke.

The clientele matched the decor. Several large-shouldered men, bouncer material, wore tracksuits and huddled over beer and dice at the half-zinc, half-Formica counter.

A shame to ruin the counter like that, she thought. And a bigger shame to see no espresso machine.

"Badoit, *s'il vous plaît*," she said to the man behind the counter. He looked up from the dice, revealing a craggy, pitted face and dark-knit brows. He was the size of a truck.

"No Badoit."

"*Bon,* something sparkling, as in water."

He popped the bottle top of a Knjaz Miloš.

"Nice label."

"From Serbia, my country," he said, as if challenging her.

"*Bon.*" She smiled, took a sip. Mineral-tasting fizz trickled down her throat. "We're off to a good start, you sharing with me and all."

"Eh?" His brows knit closer together.

One of the *mecs* jerked their thumb at him. "You raise or not?"

He inclined his big head with the barest of nods. If she hadn't been watching him closely, she wouldn't have noticed. She realized this crew communicated in subtle ways.

They'd sussed her out from the moment she walked in. At least no one had raised a gun. But she doubted the bulges in the waistbands of their jogging pants held packs of facial tissue.

"No need to waste time, eh? Tatyana. . . ."

"Who?"

Like he didn't know.

"Russian, blonde." That sounded generic. She racked her brain. "Sports a white Chanel watch—a client who referred me." Also lame. She took a breath. "I have a job for Feliks's brother."

She saw no reaction on his face.

"Job? You're in a café. My café. Go to the labor exchange."

"I mean a job for a specialist."

A smile spread over his jowls. An ugly smile that didn't reach his dull eyes.

"Construction, you mean—removals, concrete work. I refer you. But plumbers, you get Polish in their own café, or the soup kitchen outside Notre Dame de l'Assomption church."

"Not that kind of work." He'd make it hard. He didn't trust her. She felt the others looking at her. Better to leave a card and then . . . what? Hope word would trickle down and the Serb's brother would call her?

Her cell phone rang.

"Aimée, you've got to see this." Serge's excited voice on the other end.

See what? She turned away from the counter. "Can't you just tell me, Serge?"

"I asked the lab to expedite a broader screening using liquid chromatography-mass spectrometry."

She looked back and noticed the men throwing dice. One had his eye on her.

She lowered her voice. "So you found the cause of death?"

"It took a lot of doing," Serge said. "Let me tell you. This screen shows what peaks pop up, then we did a quantitative assay, looking at the peaks the compound fell in. Fascinating."

She turned away again, wishing he'd cut to the chase. "Say it so I understand it, Serge."

"Xylazine. An injectable horse tranquilizer. Not a high dosage, but the victim suffered an allergic reaction to it."

"Like anaphylactic shock?"

"Similar. His body shut down within minutes. But not before he'd gotten a few steps."

"So he staggered from Yuri's atelier. . . ." That fit. "And you think. . . ?"

"The lab tech's seen it before," he said. "For a home invasion the thief takes precautions. In this case, a syringe of horse tranquilizer to neutralize the occupants if they wake up or return home unexpected. Not a lethal dose, but enough to knock them out and give him time to clean out the house." Serge paused. "In this Serb, a portion of his bruising happened before death. I conclude he got interrupted, fought with someone, and stabbed himself by mistake."

"By mistake?"

"A small needle puncture in his derrière. Aligning with the back pocket of his jeans."

He'd killed himself.

"Brilliant." Her mind spun. "But where's the syringe?" ·

"Check the crime scene report," Serge said.

She thought back. It might be in the bushes, in the gutter where he got caught between the cars, or it might even have fallen in the atelier that night and washed away in the detritus of Yuri's overflowing sink.

On some report she'd find it. But what she needed most was the lab report to prove this to the Serb's brother. Suddenly, one more thing made sense. She reached in her jacket pocket for the straw she'd found at Saj's, thought of the matching straw twined in Yuri's trampled rosemary, and the barnyard smell Nora mentioned. "Where would he obtain this . . . what's it called?"

"Xylazine? Around horses."

"Meet me in ten minutes," she said.

She turned to the man behind the counter. Smiled. "I'm

looking for the *mec* who works with horses," she said. "There's money in it."

He pointed to the door. "Drink's on me. Go back the way you came in, Mademoiselle."

She ground her teeth. Wondered what the going rate for a hit ran to today. Took a guess.

"Five thousand francs' worth."

He pounded his fist. "For the long-haired freak who ran over his brother?" Shook his head. "You think money buys his brother back, stupid French bitch?"

Her spine stiffened. She'd hit a nerve. The men in back advanced further up the bar, crowding her. Their heads down. Like a pack of hounds waiting for the hunt master's command. Her damp shirt stuck in between her shoulder blades.

"Never," she said, hoping her voice wouldn't break. "But it would get him payback and help me at the same time."

A snort. "What the hell. . . ?"

"Let's call it two in one. I'd like him to take care of that *mec* who took care of his brother, *compris?*"

One of the men looked up.

"No love lost on my end," she said. "I'm willing to pay."

Another one cleared his throat. She saw a bare nod of his head. The *mec* caught his look. For whatever reason, they had decided to trust her.

"Why didn't you say so?" he said. "Bois de Vincennes stables, the Hippodrome."

"His name?"

"Goran."

"I'll tell him you're coming," he said. "Better have his cash ready."

Aimée met Serge in the back lot of the morgue, the elevated Métro clanking above their heads. The Seine flowed darkly to their right.

"You copied the report, right?"

Serge made a long face. "And no one will ever know. Promise me, Aimée." Serge looked around in the lot as if the authorities would swoop down any minute. Only a man wearing white boots hosing down a loading bay. Aimée didn't like to think what went down the drain.

"You've got my word," she said,

"And *you've got* the twins for next weekend," Serge said.

She cringed inside. Hyperkinetic three-year-olds? She'd have to take them to Sebastien's wedding. They could be . . . what, flower boys? Ring bearers? She'd beg her cousin. Better yet, she'd let Saj teach them computer games. Serge's wife never let them near a computer.

"*Bien sûr.*" She smiled.

A STABLE HAND in blue jeans poured water in a horse trough in the clear afternoon light. Flies buzzed; fragrant piles of manure steamed in the cold air. Aimée stepped around a bale of hay and jumped as she sent a nest of mice scurrying.

"Lost, Mademoiselle?" said a man in overalls topped by a three-quarter-length blue work coat. He had a pronounced Eastern European accent. "Public's not allowed in the stalls."

"But I'm looking for you, Goran," she said. "Your friends called, *non?*"

Goran straightened up. She saw piercing black eyes in a weathered face, a mustache, and thick brown hair graying at the temples. A face aged before his time, she thought.

"You're the one, eh?" He gestured to a back stall. "Make it good. I'm working."

She shook her head. No way in hell she'd let him box her in a rodent-infested stall.

Goran eyed the groom. "I'll deal with this and join you in the exercise ring," he said, gesturing the other man out. The stable door clanged behind him. Uneasy, Aimée breathed in the horse smells, took in the old wooden enclosure and the high, dark ceiling.

"Tatyana owes me and you're going to—"

"Show you the proof Feliks died by his own hand," Aimée interrupted. "His autopsy reports the cause of death is heart failure due to Xylazine. He injected it by mistake."

Goran slammed the half-door on a whinnying horse. "Liar."

"I thought you'd say that. Read it yourself," she said. "The same Xylazine you use to tranquilize horses here."

He pulled a bandanna from his overalls pocket, wiped his neck. "I know what it does."

"Of course you do," she said. "You stole it from the veterinary cabinet and furnished it to your brother for his job. A simple snatch-and-grab that went wrong."

"Xylazine doesn't kill humans," Goran said, his eyes hard and narrowed. "What's all this to you anyway?"

"Given a high dosage, it could. But you only gave Feliks enough to sedate the old man if needed."

"That freak killed my brother. Ran him down. I'll take care of him for you—a pleasure."

"Feliks died before he hit the windshield. Read the autopsy."

He looked up in alarm. "Who are you?"

"I was in the car, Goran. Your brother didn't bleed; his heart had stopped pumping."

"Bitch. It was you." He rushed at her. Only stopped when he saw her Beretta leveled at his kneecaps.

"Feliks suffered an allergic reaction to the Xylazine," she said, her heart pounding. "He died a few, maybe four, minutes after accidentally injecting himself."

"What?"

"It's all here."

"But I'm a veterinarian."

"So you say," she said.

"In Serbia I'm qualified, but—"

"Here you contributed to your brother's robbery jobs."

He stepped back. "Feliks was small-time. Go after the big players in the suburbs with Kalashnikovs."

Lay the blame on someone else.

"Feliks's body was covered with prison tattoos. He's Serb mafia, like your friends at the café."

A muscle in Goran's cheek twitched. "Ever walked on the wrong side of the street in Zagreb?" His voice rose. "Or get thrown into a cell with warlords—the mafia? You don't get out alive unless you join. We escaped, our family didn't." His lip trembled. "You wouldn't know what it's like to sleep on the street, on the floor of a café if we were lucky. No job. Feliks met up with former soldiers here. I told him to stay away from them." He sighed. "But he saw me, a qualified doctor teaching veterinary courses at the university, shoveling horse shit."

"Don't look for pity from me," she said. "Trying to attack my friend at the hospital, threatening him and defacing his home. What medical code of ethics do you follow? Injecting horse tranquilizer, taking a hit job for revenge and money?"

"Think I earn enough to bury my little brother?" His shoulders slumped. "I owe the café owner, we slept there. . . ."

Aimée's neck went hot. She hoped to God they wouldn't appear. But they'd smelled money.

"He's all I had left. But that freak—"

"The injection killed him, Goran." She thrust the autopsy into his shaking hands.

"*Non, non.* . . ." A low wail welled up from him. Then a searing animal-like cry of pain. Horses kicked the stall, whinnied. His cry raked her skin raw.

"What's going on?" A veterinarian in a lab coat rushed into the stable, followed by the groom. "Goran, what's wrong? You're hurt?"

The veterinarian leaned down and noticed the autopsy in the hay. "What's this?"

Should she let the vet read it? Goran would be fired. Arrested. Then she'd learn nothing from him.

And she could tell—from his sweating brow, the nervous toe movement of his boots—he knew something.

Before the vet could reach for the report, Aimée picked it up. "Bad news, I'm afraid. His brother. . . ." She let her voice trail off.

Goran crumpled against the wooden stall, destroyed. Despite everything, she pitied him.

"I'm with the Red Cross, doctor," she said. "May I speak with him alone?"

"Use the tack room. Jacky, get some water," he said.

Five minutes later, Goran was slumped on a chair by hanging bridles and horse brushes. A dazed look on his face. "I killed him."

"Take a sip." She handed him the water. "Now shut up and listen. I didn't turn you in, but you need to help me, understand?"

"Why?"

She thought of Yuri's saying about the Serbs—an unlucky man would drown in a teacup.

"Your plan went wrong and you're devastated. But you're going to call the café and tell them the hit's off. Go to Chantilly, where there are plenty of horses, and work there. Start fresh."

He looked up. "Why would you do that? I killed my brother."

"Then prison appeals to you?" she said. "Tonight the *flics* will question every stable in Paris and within a twenty-five kilometer radius."

His eyes bulged in fear.

"Accessory to murder and theft. Prison, deportation."

"Deport me back to Serbia?" The reality hit him.

"Or did I get it wrong—you returned the next morning and tortured the old man?"

"Me, why? What's the old man to me?"

Or had he attacked her in her office? But Goran spoke with a thick Serbian accent, unlike the voice over the speakerphone. She looked at his hands. Slim palms; thin, tapered fingers—not like the meaty paws that had grabbed the roots of her hair. Her scalp tingled.

"So convince me, Goran. Start talking." She kept her eyes locked on his. "Like I said, you can start over. In return for my not turning you in, you tell me everything—how you met Tatyana, Feliks's role—each detail."

"I don't know. Feliks worked alone. He wanted it that way."

"Lie to me and I turn you in," she said, pulling out her cell phone. "Tell your café friends you'll meet them later. Make the call."

He nodded, punched in a number. Mumbled something in Serbian. Clicked off.

"You were on Villa d'Alésia the night of the robbery, weren't you?"

A shrug. "Feliks didn't want me involved," he said.

Aimée thought back to the police report Serge had shown her in the morgue. The contents of the Serb's stomach.

"But Feliks ordered a kebob takeout from rue d'Alésia. The receipt was in his pocket." She took a guess. "You shared it, didn't you? Lie to me again and the deal's off."

Goran hung his head. Nodded. "He was so blasé. I worried about him. The danger. But he kept saying. . . ."

Blasé? "Just a routine job, non?" she said. "He'd done this a lot."

Goran's shoulders sagged again. "He shouldn't have been a criminal. Feliks was such a gentle boy when we were children. He changed after Pristina. The massacre in the town square, the roundups in the hills . . . our family thrown in a pit."

Pain creased his brow.

"You waited behind the old man's house by the wall in the rosemary bushes, didn't you?"

He nodded. "I worried for him."

"But Feliks didn't come out the back like you thought, right, Goran?"

He looked up. In his lined face, his eyes brimmed with tears. "I heard sirens."

"Did you see a white van?"

"A white van?"

"Think back. Which way did you run?"

"I went through the park by the wall. Then toward the Métro . . . *non*, I waited in the park."

Aimée nodded. A queasiness rumbled in her stomach. *Residue of last night's drug*, she thought, but the horses pawing in their stalls, the manure, the leather tang of the saddles didn't help. She wanted something to settle her stomach, but she couldn't stop. This went somewhere. She needed to keep pressing him.

She sat down cross-legged on the earthen floor, took a deep breath. Then shoved aside the hay, brushing away the mouse droppings with her boot. With her finger she drew a square and lines in the dirt. "Goran, think of this as a map. Here's the park, here's the wall behind Yuri's."

"Yuri?"

"The old man Feliks attempted to rob. But the painting had been stolen."

"Phfft," Goran expelled air in disgust. "Painting, jewelry? I don't ask. All I know is this Tatyana contracted Feliks for a job. Never paid him, you understand. Now she owes me. A job is a job."

His words echoed what Oleg had told her. She drew a circle. "See, here's the old townhouse with shutters. Show me where you were."

Goran stared. Then pointed. "Here, maybe there. I kept walking in the bushes trying to find somewhere to climb over the wall. So dark, and every place was so high." He blinked, shook his head. "I couldn't get out."

"You remember something, don't you?"

He put his finger in the dirt. Scratched an X.

"In the park I hid below the wall here. Looked for a rock, a tree. I saw a van drive by two, three times. That's right," he said, almost to himself. "Like it was circling the block."

Aimée started to nod, but every time she moved her head queasiness rose from her stomach. She kept still, willed it down.

"You noticed because you were looking out for your brother," she said. "You watched out for the *flics*."

"At first I thought it was the police," he said, his finger hitting the dirt. "But no blue light, no blue letters."

The pieces fit together. The person who fought the Serb—a member of Luebet's gang? Now it seemed everyone who knew of the Modigliani had tried to steal it.

"Where did the van go?"

"It pulled over, waited. . . ."

"How long?"

"The driver got out. . . . Wait, I remember, I heard metal noises. He was doing something on the back of the van."

Aimée remembered the white van shooting out in front of them, Saj downshifting and honking the horn.

"I don't know after that," Goran said.

What was she missing here? "So you left? Took the Métro?"

"I waited maybe ten, fifteen minutes. Climbed the fence, then I walked. Along here." He trailed his finger in the dirt along rue de Châtillon.

"What did you see? People, lights?"

He closed his eyes, thinking. "Some lights in windows, a small factory, but no one saw me. I avoided the Métro."

"Where did you head?"

"Tombe Issoire, a place full of squatters. I was supposed to meet Feliks there, but he never came."

"But where was Feliks supposed to hand off the painting to Tatyana?"

"He wouldn't tell me."

Aimée believed him.

"Did you see the van again?" she said. "You were nervous, *non*? Had an eye out for white police vans."

He shook his head. "I kept my head down. Walked fast."

One last try. "The van. Think again. You said it parked here on rue de Châtillon by the park. Then it drove on. Anything strike you? The lettering on it, the model or make, scratches or dents, old or new?"

"Was that who hurt Feliks?"

He'd registered the bruise marks from the autopsy.

"Someone beat him to the painting," she said. "Try to remember. Could the van have been a rental?"

He nodded. "Maybe. Maybe like those ones that service Orly."

Excited, she leaned forward. "A service van for catering, or packages like express post, or baggage handling?"

His brow furrowed. "Now that I think back, like those. Just white, square, wedge back . . . a Renault? Too hard to see through the bushes."

Like every other Renault van in Paris. But she made one more attempt. "I know it was dark, but try to think. An older model, even a partial license plate?"

"You're joking." He paused. Thinking. "*Non*, like new."

She nodded. "Go on."

"It had, like, you know, a temporary license until new plates come."

An itching feeling told Aimée he knew more. "But you haven't told me everything, have you, Goran?"

The smell of his fear and sweat mingled with the dust.

"I'm giving you a chance, a way to start over. Quit holding out," she said. "Feliks failed to show that night, so you returned in the morning, *non*? To find out what happened."

"What difference does it make? Feliks is gone."

"But that's how you knew, or thought you knew, that Feliks was hurt and in Hôtel-Dieu."

"Feliks died. No one told me. By a fluke I found out myself."

Her anger rose. "Punching a *flic* and being thrown out of the criminal ward—you call that a fluke?"

Goran looked shocked. "I want to go."

"Not until you tell me who you saw in the morning."

"What?"

"How early did you go to Villa d'Alésia?"

His mouth hardened. "You got what you wanted. Leave me alone."

"Had a coffee, maybe, at the corner café? Waited until people left for work to engage them in conversation like you were a neighbor?"

His eyes flashed. But by then she'd registered the tattoos just visible on his wrist where his sleeve was rolled up. Those prison tattoos, like Feliks's. She controlled her shudder.

"You're good at that, playing someone else—that's how you got your job here, *non?* You neglected to reveal your prison time, I bet." She pointed to his tattoo. "Almost talked your way past the reception at Hôtel-Dieu . . ." She paused for effect. Raised her Beretta again. "Cough up and quit wasting my time."

His lip curled.

"Feeling uncooperative? Then so am I." She shrugged. "The café's video surveillance shows the street movement. All I need to do is identify you to the *flics*. Let them deal with—"

"Eight A.M.," he said, his voice monotone now.

She'd made up the video camera, but he bought it.

"Give me the morning timeline." She drew another line, curved like Villa d'Alésia to rue d'Alésia. "Point out who you spoke with and where."

He'd only spoken to the café owner, it turned out. She thought back to Yuri's message while she'd been at the morgue, and later when he'd warned her off—around 9:45, according to when she'd checked her Tintin watch.

"I took the Métro around nine thirty, my job starts at ten," he said flatly. Glanced upward at the five time cards in metal slots behind the door. "Check my time card."

She did. Too late for Goran to have been the one to murder Yuri.

"But here at this house—did you see anyone enter? Hear shouting?"

He shook his head.

"Or see the white van again?"

He pointed to the X she'd made. "A little man with a Cossack hat went in there."

Yuri. Her pulse raced. "Would that have been nine or closer to nine fifteen?"

"Like that."

Loud voices came from somewhere in the stable. Had Serge's autopsy sparked the *flics* already? "Was he carrying something, like a package?"

Goran shrugged. "A taxi blocked my view."

"But you remembered him."

"I remember Russians in my country with hats like that. Then the woman got out of the taxi."

"You mean Tatyana, the blonde who hired your brother, don't you?" Battling her rising nausea, she realized one of the voices she'd just heard outside in the stable was familiar. A Serbian accent. Not the *flics*. Her throat tightened.

"No. Tall, thin." A snort of laughter. "Tatyana owes me my brother's funeral money. More." A smile spread over Goran's face. "Big connections with a rich man, she told me, nice commission."

No wonder he suddenly oozed cockiness. He hadn't called the Serbs off. Dumb to believe him. "You lied to me. Bad move, Goran."

From the corner of her eye, she caught his hand creeping under the straw to the pitchfork. She pulled a horse blanket from the stall over him. Instead of grabbing the pitchfork, he tossed the blanket aside, lunging forward to grab her arm. The move slowed him down, put him off balance for the seconds she needed. She kicked dust in his eyes, sidestepped him, then kicked his ankle. Hard. He landed on his back with an *ouff*. She cocked the Beretta's hammer.

"Want me to shoot your toes first, or your knees?"

"*Non, non.*" Sweat broke out on his forehead. He rubbed his watering eyes, which kept darting toward the stall door—looking for his backup.

"Now you're an accomplice to murder and robbery, and I'll be sure to implicate your friends."

"Good luck, bitch."

"No luck involved." She reached up to the alarm system box. Pulled it.

Silence. No piercing shrieks. *Merde.*

Only blinking red lights. A silent alarm designed to avoid frightening the horses? She hoped so.

At the half-door she turned. "What made you remember the woman who got out of the taxi?"

"Reminded me of you, bitch."

This is what she'd expected him to say, but bile rose in her throat nonetheless. But she couldn't think about that now. She grabbed a riding helmet from the wall and strapped it on. Panic filled her as she crouched down behind hay bales and shooed off buzzing flies.

Goran was shouting something in Serbian. She heard approaching footsteps and banging stall doors. Any moment now, they'd discover her.

On her left, a stable hand led out the last horse by the reins. Straightening up, and shielded by the horse's body, she kept pace with its front legs as the Serb thugs passed by the stalls.

She couldn't count on the silent alarm working. Once clear, she hurried through the side stable and found the fire alarm box.

Broke the glass and pulled the switch. Loud whoops blasted in the stable and barn. Horses neighed in the exercise ring.

"Where's the fire?" the stable hand shouted at her.

"No fire. Terrorists. Lock down the stable."

"Aren't you with the Red Cross?"

"Undercover." His mouth dropped open. "No time for explanations. Tell the team it's the Serbs. Give this to the vet." She handed him the autopsy. "Seems Goran ripped you high and dry."

By the time she made it to the bus stop, fire engines and unmarked cars were whizzing toward the stables. She took the first bus that stopped. Concentrated on breathing deep, the window beside her open to the pollen of the chestnut trees. The rest faded in and out, passing in a blur. Nerves, the residual effects of the drugs, and the revelation of her mother warred in her system.

She changed buses and boarded one in the direction Denfert-Rochereau. Why couldn't the driver go faster? She had to get back to the office. Somewhere ahead there had to be the Métro station.

From the window, she saw a van pull abreast of the bus, honking at straggling schoolchildren on the zebra-striped crosswalk. A white Renault van with temporary license plates, sporting a chrome muffler held to the bumper with wire.

And then it all came back to her—the dark lane, Saj honking at the white van with its bumper trailing on the cobbles. That's what she couldn't remember, what Goran heard but couldn't see. The driver had stopped to reattach the dragging muffler so he wouldn't be noticed or given a ticket.

Aimée had to get off the bus. She rushed toward the back doors, which were closing. She wedged herself through and got a mouthful of exhaust as the bus took off.

Worried, she looked around for the van. Traffic surged ahead at the green light. Where had it gone so fast?

The pavement shifted like sand under her feet. Passersby scurried around her. Didn't they feel this shifting, this rumbling from the Métro trains below? Or were the underground quarry tunnels fissuring, cracking open, the streets opening to sink-holes?

Blood rushed to her head. She put one foot in front of her, yet she stood stuck in the same place, under the globed street lamp glinting in the sun. Why hadn't anyone noticed? Why was she sinking to the pavement? Slipping into darkness. . . .

AIMÉE OPENED HER eyes. Sunlight streamed through shutter slats, warming her toes. She lay curled on soft pigskin leather—a toffee-colored divan—luscious. She stretched.

Then it hit her—the white van.

"You're pale, breathing shallow." A young woman with short red hair *à la gamine* and tortoise-shell glasses felt her pulse. "Eaten today, Mademoiselle?"

"But I have to catch. . . ." She tried to sit up. Her elbows slipped and her legs didn't cooperate. The tang of old leather-bound books and paper hovered in the warm air.

Where in the world. . . ? A ticking wooden ormolu clock on the wall read 1:20 P.M. Twenty or thirty minutes had gone by. The van was long gone by now. Hopeless.

"*Desolée*, but I don't know where I am." She shook her head. Felt a wave of dizziness. "Or how I got here."

"You fainted in front of the Observatoire's side entrance," the woman said. "A teacher on a school field trip brought you into my office."

Embarrassed, Aimée looked at the woman's name tag. Doctor Sylvie Taitbout.

"*Desolée*, doctor," she said.

"I'm just the PhD kind. Call me Sylvie," she said, smiling. "I study black holes between the stars."

Aimée became aware of the posters of planets and galaxies lining the walls. The notebooks piled on the desk beside framed family photos. "You're an astronomer."

"Guilty," she smiled. "I research planetary nebulae in the optical regions of external galaxies—finding tools to understand the late stellar evolution in varying galactic environments. That kind of stuff." Her mouth turned serious. "*Ecoutes*, you are exhibiting the symptoms my sister had—anemia compounded by stress. Unpleasant combo. Serious, too. Let me ring your doctor."

Children's voices drifted in from the window, along with jasmine scents and humid air.

"Thanks for your concern, but I feel better already," Aimée said. She had to get going. "My blood sugar gets low. Just need some air."

"Up to you," Sylvie said, but she handed Aimée a grapefruit juice from her bag. And a banana. "I insist."

"*Merci*."

"Have your doctor run tests," Sylvie said. "Does anemia run in your family? Any history with your mother?"

A pang hit her. This woman probably took for granted that all Parisian mothers take Sunday afternoon walks in the Luxembourg Gardens arm in arm with their husbands after the midday roast chicken—a classic *déjeuner de famille*. Well, not Aimée's. "No history to speak of."

Sylvie took off her glasses to clean them, revealing small birdlike eyes. "Mothers don't tell you everything."

So true. In her case, nothing. No road map. During the *lycée*, she'd observed Martine's mother and secretly recorded her observations in a notebook. Like they did in biology class, cultivating nuclei in a petri dish and recording reactions and behaviors. She made an effort to decipher this species down to each detail—from Martine's mother's tweed beige jackets to her effortless soufflés, from her warm living room cluttered with bright pillows and books to the way she wiped her toddler's runny nose while reminding the girls with a smile to say *"merci"* at the *boulangerie*.

"Is everything all right?" Sylvie asked. "Anything on your mind?"

Sylvie seemed like the type of counselor the *flics* should have assigned to her the other night after the accident. Aimée knew she should take better care of herself. Why had she quit yoga? But without René to insist. . . .

"Been under more stress lately?"

Apart from her best friend's defection to America, Saj's injury, the murder of an old man who'd known her long-gone mother, a stolen Modigliani, death threats from Serbs, being attacked in her office and almost drowned in a bucket. . . .

"A little more than usual," Aimée admitted.

And just when she'd stumbled on the van, she'd lost it again. Her chance to find the painting. Her mother, ever elusive, a vague shadow who loomed in the background.

"Try to relax."

With people out to torture her and only a few hours left? Aimée sat up with mounting dread and scrambled for her boots.

"You've been so kind," she said, standing with a wobble and pulling down her Sonia Rykiel tunic. "But I must go. . . ."

"Not before you share my *tartine* and I see you can function. We'll go to the garden."

Too weak to argue, Aimée nodded. She and Sylvie sat on a bench in the garden bordered by a gravel drive. An islet of peace bounded by green hedges and old stonework fronting the Observatoire, a blackened limestone-like château punctuated with a rounded verdigris metal globe roof, which dwarfed the trees. "When the king ordered the Observatoire built, this was countryside," Sylvie told her. "Far from the lights of Paris and perfect for the telescopes. By 1900 the street gaslights rendered them useless. Today we measure and calculate the heavens with computers."

"Vraiment?" Yet, didn't numerical equations and statistics neglect the allure of the night sky, of wishing upon a star?

Aimée munched the crisp *tartine* slathered with Brie, pear slices, and cornichons. She felt color returning to her cheeks. It had been stupid to forget to eat.

"Loaded up?" Sylvie shouted to someone behind the hedge on the gravel drive. It was a woman in a hoodie and jeans, loading file boxes into the side door of a van. Aimée noticed how the woman kept her head down. Noticed the white Renault van with a temporary plate. The grapefruit juice in her hand trembled.

But how many new white vans drove in Paris?

"She'll hit traffic. Running late as usual," Sylvie said.

"Who's that?" Aimée asked.

"Morgane delivers our instruments. Receives our air-shipped data drives."

"You use a service from Orly?"

"The van belongs to the Observatoire."

Could this be the one?

"So it's kept here at night." Yuri's place was in the quartier, only three Métro stations away.

"Why?"

Aimée shrugged. "Guess you've got a big budget."

"Think so? Morgane's only part-time. They're cutting back on everything, even research hours." Sylvie glanced at her watch. *"Desolée,"* she said, standing, "I've got an appointment measuring a black hole." She smiled. "Take care of yourself."

Morgane spoke on a cell phone, her gaze fixed on Aimée. A frisson went up her spine. Had she gone paranoid again? Or did this tingling mean something?

Paranoid or not, she wrote down the front license plate number with her kohl eye pencil. She'd need to get closer to see the bumper. Before she could make it to the driveway, the engine turned over, gravel spit, and she saw the muffler wired to the bumper as it took off.

She'd found it—the white van that had pulled in front of them on Villa d'Alésia, the one Goran noticed circling the block. By the time she ran back to the bench and got Dombasle on the phone, the van had gone.

"This might be nothing, but. . . ." Aimée said, hesitating.

"Anything to do with the Modigliani interests me," Dombasle prompted.

"Could you check for any traffic video surveillance installed on rue d'Alésia?"

"Mind telling me what I'd be looking for?"

"A white Renault van, license 750825693, belonging to the Observatoire, that could have circled Villa d'Alésia and rue de Châtillon the night of the robbery at, say, eight P.M.?"

"I'd need to call in favors," he said, the interest gone from his voice. "You're saying it's important?"

"I suspect it's the van that was used in the robbery." And she needed them off her back, but she kept that to herself. Hadn't Luebet addressed his message to M . . . Morgane? "Maybe Luebet was behind this. If so, Morgane's the woman to talk to."

"Several witness statements mention a white van. One of those statements has your name on it." Pause. "What haven't you told me?"

"It's complicated," she said. "But I think she broke into my office."

"Think or know?"

"The only sure things in life are death and taxes, Raphael," she said. "They blindfolded me and held my head under water."

"But Luebet's dead, and according to his message. . . ."

She couldn't be sure if Luebet's team had found the painting, and it had long disappeared. But she needed to light a fire under Dombasle. "His team's still searching," she interrupted. "You'd put it past them to kill Yuri? *Alors,* they gave me twenty-four hours to find the painting."

There, she admitted it. Hadn't wanted to, but she needed his help.

"So that's why you came to me," he said. "No goodwill involved."

Playing hurt all of a sudden? Hadn't he'd drafted her for a sting with a crooked *antiquaire?* A ploy she was more and more skeptical about.

"Raphael, didn't you tell me art thieves were up your alley and homicide up *la Crim's?"*

She'd burned her bridges with Morbier, who had deserted her. Couldn't expect Saj to run at full speed. If Raphael didn't cooperate, she didn't know who else to ask. Her options narrowed to zero. "Someone threatened me. Can't you check this out? Isn't this your job?"

"Morgane's known to us, that's if she's the same one," he said. "A Morgane Tulle came up flagged in the file. Luebet's former employee who served time."

The connection. "Does she work at the Observatoire now?"

"You want an answer off the top of my head?"

She brightened. "But you'll follow up?"

"Meet me at thirty four rue Delambre at six P.M." He clicked off.

She felt a tremor of relief—this should lessen her chance of torture—but it still didn't help her find the Modigliani. Or her mother.

AIMÉE TOOK A taxi, had it circle rue du Louvre three times. Satisfied no one was following, she overtipped the driver. Always good insurance for rainy-night taxi karma.

Back in the office, she popped open a Badoit and did some neck rolls. Better. She thumbed the report Saj had culled from details on the oligarch's dealings in Gazprom, the now privatized Ukraine petroleum giant.

"Bereskova took a fiscal nosedive into concrete last year but somehow reinvented himself, see?" Saj said, from his cross-legged position on the tatami. "Look at page eight. Seems he made himself indispensable to major players in the past few months."

"They call it *krysha*—rub my back big-time, I'll rub yours. Any more details?" She needed more. Something smelled wrong.

Saj readjusted his neck brace. "That's as far as I got."

"Didn't you work with that Russian hacker, René's friend, for a while?"

"Rasputin," he said. "The wild man."

A living Internet legend, Rasputin snuck into a missile engine testing facility north of Moscow with his hacker pack. They breached military security through a hole in the fence of a factory dating back to the Soviet era—still producing engines for Russia's space and military programs.

The Kremlin discovered Rasputin's photos of the Cold War-era facility with giant turbines, tunnels, tubes, Soviet emblems, and a bomb shelter. And his penetration of the missile system mainframe. Rasputin claimed his aim was to increase awareness over security.

"The man knows no fear," Saj said.

"So pick his brain," she said.

"Good idea." With ginger movements, he picked up his shoulder bag. "My acupuncturist squeezed me in, do you mind?"

She'd prefer to hash ideas out with him. But every time he turned, she noticed his body tighten.

"*Bien sûr*," she said. "I hope it helps."

"Before I forget, thanks for dealing with the Serb. You got my back. *Desolé*, I shouldn't have doubted you."

She'd called from the taxi and recounted what happened in the stables on the way back. "I pitied Goran—a refugee from a war-torn country, an exiled doctor reduced to shoveling horse muck. His brother's death devastated him. The aggressors were victims once." She stared at Saj. "But then I wasn't so sure."

"Talk about karma. You gave him a chance, showed compassion, Aimée." Saj shrugged, then adjusted his neck brace yet again. "Ever thought the whole thing was a lie told by a mercenary or a war criminal?"

She thought of Goran's anguish, so palpable it had raised the hair on her arms. "But if you'd heard him cry. . . ."

"Going soft, Aimée? You?"

"Soft as in not shooting his toes?" She'd wanted to.

Saj shook his head. "*Alors,* this circle of samsara, *c'est fini,*" he said. "Thank God."

She wished she felt the same.

"But the van, Saj. . . ."

"You alerted the art *flic,* didn't you?" he said. "Let him do his job. I'll alarm the door on my way out."

What more could she do right now but assuage her guilt and pull her weight? She'd review reports and ink the two new computer security contracts. A ray of light shone in the accounting: Leduc Detective was floating on a cushion this month, and would continue into the next. Made for a change.

Aimée sipped the Badoit, thumbed the printouts Maxence had left on Yuri Volodya. Apart from his Trotskyist leanings in the seventies, nothing interesting. Looked at the names on her to-do list and let them simmer.

She removed Piotr Volodya's letters from the safe. About to scan and copy them, she remembered Marevna's boss's interruption and their missed appointment last night.

She needed to see the big picture. Think big. Find the pieces and how they fit together.

She dusted off the dry erase board behind René's old desk and rustled up a working red marker. With the board propped on the velvet recamier, she wrote down the suspects, made columns—*Motives, Opportunities, Victims, Stakes*—to cross-reference. Like her father always did. Something she wished she'd done earlier. Now to fill them in: *Stakes*—*money, prestige, a priceless Modigliani, a commodity to trade. Robbery suspects—Luebet, Morgane; Tatyana and Oleg's crew; Damien; Feliks and Goran.*

But someone was missing. From Luebet's note, she knew he'd never gotten the painting. He could have had nothing to do with the team in the white van, who might have stolen the painting before Tatyana and Oleg's hired Serbs got there. But hearing Dombasle confirm Morgane once worked for Luebet, she couldn't shake her hunch that Luebet hired Morgane to steal the painting. So what was another explanation? Perhaps Luebet had hired Morgane, but she'd fenced the painting herself before turning it over to him. Or she never got it at all, because the painting was already gone. If Luebet's gang and the Serb found the broom closet empty—as Yuri had—who had stolen the Modigliani?

Back to the beginning again.

Or either Oleg and Damien could have taken it, in theory; they were the only people she was sure knew where Yuri had hidden it. But which? Damien had insisted Yuri forgot things, and Oleg and Tatyana had offered her a percentage.

Or had the fixer beat everyone to it?

The door alarm shrieked and she dropped her Badoit. Flecks of mineral water sprayed over the erase board. Terror thudded through her. They'd returned.

Why had she trusted Dombasle? She took out the Beretta, checked the cartridge. Aimed.

"*Merde!*" she heard from the other side of the frosted glass.

But she knew that voice. She punched in the security code and opened the door.

René leaned in Leduc Detective's doorway, his linen jacket stained, a large straw hat held in one hand and a duty-free bag in the other. Her heart jumped. She wanted to hug him.

"Forget something?" she said, finding her voice.

His brow knit in worry and pain.

"My common sense, Aimée. Mind setting your gun down? Look, I need to get the relay codes . . . don't have time. . . ."

His words tore her heart. Apparently he wouldn't be staying.

"So the corporate jet's waiting at Orly, eh? Need to rush back to your millions?"

He shook his head. "I don't like them dirty, Aimée. Look, I've got four hours, maybe six. . . ."

Her hurt bubbled to the surface. "Before you leave again?"

He limped inside and pulled out his laptop from the duty-free bag. "If I don't stop them, I'm in a little trouble."

His tone made her stand still. "Sounds like big trouble, René."

"Tradelert's front running and I secured the back door in their damn system. Now if I don't disable it. . . ." He hobbled to his desk. Must be his hip, she thought. "Please just let me work. I need my tools here. Can I explain later?"

"Go ahead," she said, surprised. "Why the sombrero?"

"Mexico City."

"I thought you. . . ."

"Long story, Aimée. I've had ten hours on the flight to prepare," he said. "Think I've found a shortcut to rewind the algorithms, circumvent the disabler. But it's all contingent on the clone providing me access. From here."

She understood less than half of what he'd just said.

"If I don't execute preventive measures, Wall Street will come after me and it'll be all my fault. Not now, maybe tomorrow. . . ." He opened his desk drawer. "Then I'll leave."

Aimée bit her lip. She'd never seen René so upset. Or with a stain on his jacket. "Can I help?"

René connected his laptop to the terminal, his eyes never

leaving the screen. "Call Saj. Tell him I need his eyes and his old relay and delay codes. Use my car."

His car. Aimée looked away.

She heard a buzz—the alarm had been disabled. Saj walked in with Maxence. "I forgot my herbs . . . René!" He shot Aimée a look.

She shrugged.

"Long time no see, René. At least three days."

René kept his eyes on the screen. "Still have your relay and delay programs here?"

"*Bien sûr*," Saj said.

"Let me help too, René," Maxence said, smiling. "No luggage? Means you're going to stay a while, I hope."

René looked up. His green eyes widened at Saj's neck brace, his arm in a sling. "Saj? *Mon Dieu*, are you all right?"

"Did you tell him, Aimée?"

"Not now, Saj."

A knowing look passed over René's face. "My car? Never mind, are you okay?"

"All systems go," Saj said, rubbing his good hand. "Two seconds for me to dig out that program. But I think you'll be more interested in the newer version."

Glancing at the time, Aimée reached for her scarf and left them to it.

TWENTY MINUTES LATER, on rue Delambre, she pushed open the tall green door into a courtyard. She felt like she'd stepped back in time. A cold dampness crept up her legs. Ivy trailed the walls of faded tea-stain-colored stuccoed workshops, timbered two- and three-storied ateliers roofed by zinc tiles. Tall windows, like dead eyes in the twilight, faced northern exposure—as favored by artists. Skylights dotted the slanted roofs, glowing patches swept by the beacon light of the Eiffel

Tower. A mustard-colored cat padded over the wet cobbles at her approach. Strains of a high-pitched *binioù kozh* bagpipe trailed from the *Ti ar Vretoned*, the Breton cultural center at the heart of the courtyard.

She wondered why Dombasle insisted on meeting here. What happened to the vernissage? Inside the large hall of the Breton cultural center, children held hands in a wide circle, dancing, concentration on their faces. The girls wore lace caps, kicking and performing intricate back steps. The sheepskin pipes wheezed in the background.

"Any luck on the white van?" Aimée said, sidling up to Dombasle by the Breton-language bulletin board.

"The traffic chief's daughter-in-law went to school with my sister," he said. "Life's a gratin, *non?* The white van with corresponding license plates clocked Avenue du Général Leclerc's traffic cameras at Alésia five times within an hour."

That confirmed what she'd thought. He'd come through. "*Et voilà.*"

The music and the dancers' pounding feet made it hard to hear. She edged closer and caught Dombasle's scent. A woodsy musk . . . Aramis? Stupid, she needed to focus.

"Morgane's on parole," Dombasle said. "A single mother, eager to talk."

"She confessed?"

"Nothing we can use."

Would Aimée have to drag each word out of him? But she smiled. "Meaning?"

"Luebet hired her to organize the job. She admitted to planning and hiring her accomplices: Servier, to break into Volodya's atelier, and a *mec* called Flèche to transport the painting to Orly. But someone else beat him to it, Servier says, no painting. A *mec* punched Servier, he returned the favor and ran."

"But you can arraign them on breaking and entering."

"After the fact."

Flics always worried about technicalities and judges.

"You don't call screwing up my building door, drugging and almost drowning me in a bucket in my office. . . ?"

Ahead of them, a mother with her child in her arms turned in alarm.

"Blindfolded, weren't you?" Dombasle said, his voice lower. "Can you prove who did it?"

Her head hurt—the music and the dense air made it hard to think.

She forced herself to remember. Felt those large hands shoving her head down as she gasped for air, water filling her mouth, her nose, down her throat, her lungs bursting. Those hands ripping her hair. Stop, she had to go back to the voice on the phone. Remember. The slushing tires over wet pavement, the car horns, the street sounds. No doubt the call came from a pay phone. Useless.

"Morgane blamed it on the hot-tempered amateur she'd hired," Dombasle said, pulling out a notebook from his pocket. Consulted it. "This Flèche. She said he'd threatened to take things in his own hands."

"Rounded him up yet?

He turned pages in the notebook, sucked in his breath. "You could say that. We discovered his corpse in a rented room close to Yuri Volodya's. The concierge heard a gunshot. Saw a tall female figure leave the courtyard."

Aimée shivered. The fixer?

"So make it up, Dombasle," she said. "Morgane doesn't know if the blindfold slipped, if I saw her *mec* leave. That I couldn't identity him from a mug shot."

Lie, she wanted to say. Force the truth. That's the *flics'* speciality.

"You're scared," he said, his tone changing to concern.

"No wonder you're a detective," she said. Her mind went

back to poor Yuri tied to his kitchen sink, to Madame Figuer, his neighbor, the sobbing tale of her brother water-tortured on rue des Saussaies.

Dombasle enveloped her hand in his warm ones. Calming and firm. "You're shaking."

"Going to ask me to dance?" she said.

A smile lit up his gold-flecked eyes. "Tango's more my style. I want you to meet that man drinking cider over there."

Aimée's phone vibrated. She needed air.

"Meet you in a moment, I've got to take this call."

She didn't want to talk to anyone, but it could be Saj or René. Another break-in attempt?

"Aimée, given any thought to chapter titles for my book?" Martine asked.

"Book?" Her heel caught in the cracks of the damp cobbles. She grabbed the ivy trellis for support just in time.

"The style editor's on my back."

"Right now, Martine?"

Martine blew a long exhale. Aimée imagined the nicotine rush, the cigarette's spiraling blue smoke. She'd kill for a cigarette right now.

"What's wrong? I hear it in your voice. But you can't bail on me, Aimée. Not now."

A couple hurried past her into the Breton center.

"You know you're going to tell me," Martine said.

Where to begin?

"Does this have to do with Saj running over that Serb?"

"He didn't kill him." She gave Martine the capsule version. And threw in how she'd seen Melac lip-locked with a blonde.

"Not that again! You know you were wrong before—remember, with Guy, the eye surgeon, the one I liked? He had his arm around his sister. And you were blind. Literally."

Like she could forget.

"If Melac's undercover . . . *Alors*, he's got to do. . . ." Martine's voice wavered, "what he's got to do."

"Not like that."

"*Bon*, at least René's back."

"I can't count on him with all—"

"But his tuxedo's still at the cleaners, *non?*" Martine interrupted. "He'll escort you to the wedding. The couturier alteration appointment's the day after tomorrow. Don't forget."

Aimée wanted to smack herself. The vintage blue Dior. No way could she fit into it.

"But I've gained a kilo." More.

"It'll be a piece of *gâteau* for an old pro from Patou."

"Letting out seams for a whale?" she said. "Martine, she'll have to sew me into it."

"Like Marilyn Monroe, eh?" Martine said. "By the way, *ELLE*'s sending a photographer to the wedding."

She cringed inside. The camera would add even more kilos.

"Vintage couture works at a hip wedding," Martine went on. "We'll make it the book's last chapter, of course. *C'est parfait.*"

Then it hit her. An idea that Martine, a born journalist, would eat up.

"What if I interested the oligarch's wife in an interview with you? Couple it with a fashion shoot—besides the usual magazine sidebar on the über-wealthy slum-shopping? With a photo spread?" Aimée said, thinking as she spoke. "If you got the style editor on board and suggested an ensemble piece . . . you know, a little fashion voyage you whip into an article and use in the book. Nothing wasted."

A little suck of breath. "You could make that happen, Aimée?"

"Her bodyguard likes me. Her *female* bodyguard." A little too much.

"A female Russian bodyguard? Ooh, that could work for the

shoot. I see Slavic cheekbones, toned body in a black leather catsuit."

"Picture a business suit and biceps, Martine," she said. "I'm meeting her for a drink later."

"*Bien sûr*, you're a big girl, you can handle yourself," Martine said.

"The things I do for you, Martine," she said, letting out a sigh. "She can take people down. Probably trained at the KGB."

"It's the FSB now."

The second person to tell her that today.

"Then you're interested?" Aimée paced back and forth on the dimly lit cobbles.

She heard keys tapping on a keyboard.

"Don't be silly. I'm emailing the editor right now to see if we can make this month's deadline."

"So do me a favor. Explore her husband Dmitri Bereskova's projected 'art' museum, who he owes *krysha*, and if a Modigliani would put him back on top."

Martine sighed into the phone. "Why do I think you've been angling me into getting information all along?"

Dombasle waved from inside.

"Remember Bereskova's art museum, Martine. Dombasle's beckoning. . . ."

"Dombasle as in Rafael de la Dombasle, son of the noted painter?"

Did that explain his *intello* air? "Told me he's an art cop. Got to go."

AT THE COUNTER Dombasle introduced her to Huppert. Mid-thirties, sparse brown hair, black jacket and jeans, he stood a head shorter than her, with a glass of sparkling apple cider in hand.

"This is the one I told you about," Dombasle said.

"You know I only do business at the gallery," Huppert said. No smile.

Feeling awkward, she wished they'd open a window. The close air of too many bodies coupled with the pounding feet made it hard to think. She wondered why Dombasle insisted on meeting this uninterested man.

"We won't have a chance later. You're always busy at receptions," Dombasle said.

"I've got to report on Maiwen's progress to my wife," Huppert said. "Her Breton culture's like a religion to her. Wants Maiwen to learn Breton, move to Vannes." He smiled at a flush-faced young girl, thick black hair in a ponytail, who winked back at him. "I draw the line at living near Montparnasse, that's as Breton-ville as I get. Now if you'll excuse me."

Give this man high points for rudeness. Then again, one had to respect people's privacy. But Dombasle was not going to let him go so easily.

"Show him the photo from Luebet's envelope."

There in the crowded hall, despite her misgivings, Aimée showed Huppert the Polaroid of Luebet and Yuri holding the small painting.

Huppert glanced at the photo. Looked again and set down the cider. Intent now, he put out his hand. "May I?"

She handed him the photo, and after a moment he beckoned them out the doors, past the foyer and into the courtyard.

"Why didn't the old fox Luebet mention this?" he muttered under the lamplight.

"A little late now," Dombasle said.

"I heard." Huppert shook his head, his gaze fixed on the Polaroid. "Terrible."

Aimée wanted to scream. Little good that would do now. Both men in the photo had been murdered; the Modigliani had vanished.

"How did you get this, Mademoiselle?" Huppert said.

"That's not the point. He says you're the Modigliani expert. What do you think?"

"From a bad photo?" He shook his head. "Do you know how many *faux* Modiglianis come across the gallery doorstep in a week?"

Be that way, Monsieur Expert, she wanted to say, but bit her tongue. "It's not my intention to pass anything off on you. Nor was it my idea to come here. We're wasting everyone's time," she said, reaching for the Polaroid.

She had Piotr's Volodya's letters to authenticate and give provenance. To her thinking, Yuri never intended for his wife's son to inherit the painting. But if Huppert knew and it got back to Oleg, repercussions could follow; inheritance issues, a long court case.

But Huppert didn't let go. *"Un moment."* He pulled out readers from his pocket and studied it more closely.

"What bothers me is why someone would leave a Modigliani—say it's real—in a damp cellar for more than seventy years," Dombasle said. "All of a sudden it reappears, an old man claims it's stolen but refuses to make a robbery report. He's murdered, and then after that the art appraiser. But where's the provenance, or credential of its authenticity, even some mention that this portrait of Lenin ever existed?"

Piotr's letters to his son explained some of it. Before Aimée could speak, Dombasle shot her a look to keep quiet.

"Lenin's wife, Comrade Krupskaya, hated Paris—and it wasn't just the weather. No one knows or will ever know the true story. Just background for you," Huppert said. "My research paper on *les artistes Russes* in Montparnasse touched on this."

Aimée wanted to hear something that would lead them to the painting, not an academic lecture. She was running out of time.

"Local Bolshies recounted that Lenin carried on an affair," Huppert said. "Few knew, but his wife Krupskaya guarded his reputation and fostered the myth with an iron hand. What papers she didn't burn she invalidated. Anyone whose silence she didn't trust got discredited. The comrade-wife had a stake in Lenin, she'd devoted her life to him."

Huppert paused to wave to his daughter inside.

"The reason this excites me—*faux* or not, it's a significant work. The bad quality can't mask the earth tones, that musted luminosity. So much raw energy in the set of his jaw." For a moment Huppert's voice changed, sounded far away. "To me this portrait communicates a vulnerable man, maybe even doubtful, on the cusp of something new. A man who could be in love, *non?*" He nodded to himself, studying the Polaroid. "So unlike those ragged greatcoat-leading-the-masses portraits—a powerful persona he promoted, the image Krupskaya fostered until her dying day. Lenin would have rejected this. Rumors of this painting surfaced years ago when Khrushchev visited Lenin's museum."

"What kind of rumors?"

"*Le Parisien* reporters discovered—or so they said—an old madam who counted Lenin as a client at her bordello across from the Archives Nationales. Seems he would stop by after a long day of research. Contradicts the Lenin myth, the ascetic father of the people. Why shouldn't Lenin go for the fruit of the flesh elsewhere, since his wife's mother had their bedroom and lived with them for years?" He shrugged. "But morality aside, another item came up. More serious."

Aimée realized she'd been holding her breath. She pulled her coat tighter in the damp chill.

"Twelve years ago, a descendent of Cortot, Modigliani's first dealer—that relationship was short-lived—brought papers for me to appraise and make sense of. He'd found them in the family château's attic. A job I do with annoying frequency." Huppert gave a sigh. His breath fogged in the chilly evening air. "Old collectors die and the family hopes there's a treasure stashed." He paused. "I'm straying. An entry marked 'unpaid' in Cortot's ledger lists a portrait commissioned by Lenin."

"Would that be in 1910?" Aimée asked.

Huppert thought. Rocked on his heels. Studied her for a moment. "That or 1911. Cortot couldn't collect the commission. Not surprising since Modi hated painting commissions. He refused, to all his dealers' despair. But maybe Lenin paid him with a bottle. Who knows? Cortot heard the buzz from the café crowd and sniffed money."

A couple entered the courtyard. Huppert waited for them to pass. Their laughter echoed off the stone and frightened the cat from the bushes. With the dark-blue smear of sky above the damp foliage, this once-artisanal backwater felt timeless.

When the couple was gone, Aimée asked, "Was there an exhibition of Lenin's portrait?"

"None documented. The trail dried up," he said. "Until Pauline. She posed for Modi, fourteen years old at the time, at his second dealer's. Alas, she's dead. But fifteen years ago she told me that Lenin and Modi had a known rivalry. But that could be said of all his friends at one time or another—call Modi charming and infuriating at the best of times. Cadged his meals and drinks from drawings, slept at friends'."

"All for art, you mean?" Aimée asked.

"Forget the tragic romantic," Huppert said. "Modi produced an incredible body of work. We know so much got lost—drugging and drinking to anesthetize the pain from rampant TB. He was so anxious to hide it, he'd drink even more."

Where did this lead? "You mean Pauline knew of the painting?"

Huppert expelled air from his lips. Shrugged. "Apparently Modi complained to her about Lenin. Called him a fanatic who covered up his own doubts to convince himself."

"Doubts over what?"

"Fanatics must prove something to themselves and

others," Huppert said. "He challenged Lenin at la Rotonde one night, burned Lenin's newspaper—that we know from documents."

"Some kind of duel?"

"Pauline heard him say, 'I will show the real you. I only paint truth.' And he did, she said. Lenin hated the portrait."

Again, Huppert studied the Polaroid. "He's holding what could be a booklet. At the time, an infamous manifesto against Marx's ideology circulated among the Bolsheviks. It refuted everything Lenin stood for. Who's to say he's not holding it here? Or agreed with parts of it, suffered doubts, ideological turmoil? That would have created a scandal. Maybe he recovered his zeal or had to later take power. Lead the Revolution. But here Modi slammed it in his face."

"What difference does it make today?" Aimée said. "The USSR doesn't even exist anymore."

Huppert checked his watch. As if he needed to leave but couldn't tear himself away from this Polaroid.

"Communists in Russia venerate Lenin, keep his reputation unsullied—the government pays lip service to Marxism. No poster boys left after Stalin," he said. "What's embalmed in the Red Square mausoleum isn't just waxed fruit to the older generation, or to the government who want to keep the ideology alive. The French Communists and trade unions take pride in the fact that Lenin lived and formulated his theories here. The cradle of the Revolution."

This put a new spin on things. Still, she wasn't sure how it could matter now.

"You're saying Modigliani's painting of Lenin could have had political implications?" Dombasle asked, stepping closer. "Rippling through the Kremlin, debunking the Lenin myth, tossing the textbooks or something?"

Huppert shrugged. "In 1910, Lenin was one among many exiles, no one special, banished to the edges of Paris, living on scraps among a small Russian community. Back then, Trotsky had more followers."

"So you're saying. . . ?"

"Lenin hated Trotsky. Thought he'd clawed his way to prominence, used whatever means he had to recruit followers."

Aimée still didn't buy it. "Who cares now?"

"What if this painting's implications threaten an ideology?" Huppert insisted. "Think who stands to lose if Lenin's unmasked. That's sacrilege. Of course, that's the infamous diatribe against Marx. But to know, I need to see the painting."

"You mean Modigliani sabotaged Lenin?"

"Modigliani painted the truth he saw in people. He never compromised. Wealthy patrons came out ugly and fat. To him, Lenin was a pedantic Russian nursing one drink all night. Just one man among many exiles."

Dombasle's phone trilled. He turned away to answer it. Now or never. Aimée forced herself to speak.

"Do you know the fixer?"

Huppert's brows rose. "She's involved?"

Her mouth went dry. "It's not clear," she managed. "But do you know her?"

"Very connected and out of my league," he said. "That's all I know. Ask Dombasle."

Maiwen, his daughter, appeared at his side. "Did you watch me, Papa?"

"Bien sûr, ma puce," he said, now the adoring father.

Maiwen skipped ahead and Huppert hesitated. "The art world's a deep sea: currents, whirlpools, sucking tides. Amateurs navigate at their peril."

Like she didn't know that?

"In over my head, I know. Not my choice," Aimée said, "but you're salivating even contemplating this."

His shoulders stiffened.

She'd hit home.

"You think it's real, *n'est-ce pas?*"

"Branches grow the way the tree leans," Huppert said. "Even in this bad Polaroid, such recognizable brushstrokes, the bold colors . . . it is prototypical of work from the period when he shared the studio with Soutine, in 1910. Yet this painting is so . . . so personal, unique, unlike anything else." Huppert stared at her.

"Papa, we're late," called Maiwen from the entrance.

"When you find the Modigliani, as I sense you will, may I see it? Just once?"

Aimée slipped her card in his jacket pocket.

"Connect me to the fixer," she said. "Then we'll talk."

She didn't know if they would talk. But she did know he'd scored right on one thing. She would find the Modigliani.

It didn't ride on money or prestige; it was a way to find her mother. And save her own life.

"THE *ANTIQUAIRE* SAYS tonight," Dombasle said. He lingered at his red Fiat, a two-seater that reminded her of a large insect. A sixties classic and the size of a closet. "BRB's handling logistics."

"And your role?" Aimée asked, surprised. Didn't he mastermind this?

"Let me set you straight," he said. "I'm a recovered academic, an art historian, herded into the police academy, then right into administration of the art recovery unit. Our unit assembles evidence and decides whether there's a case. I'm not often in the field."

"So chatting up art dealers and crooks at the flea market—"

"A sideline," he interrupted. "But I met you." Grinned.

"Bottom line, you're a *flic*," she said.

"Job requirement. Dinner?"

"I'm late." Her phone showed two calls from Svetla the

Russian bodyguard. Her date. "Thought you had a vernissage to go to."

"True. Hors d'oeuvres tonight by a three-star chef."

"Enjoy."

"The buy's at ten P.M. Where can I pick you up?"

Good question. "Call me."

She could have sworn disappointment crossed Dombasle's face.

Aimée checked her messages. Svetla had left the name of a bar and the time for their *rendez-vous*. It was the last thing she wanted, but when she called Svetla back, her phone went to voice mail. Great. She hoped it wasn't a leather bar. But first she had a stop to make.

MAREVNA—AN APRON tied around her waist over a T-shirt with IT'S BETTER IN THE UKRAINE—nodded to Aimée. She set down a bowl of maroon borscht with a dollop of cream topped by dill in front of an old man, the only diner at Le Zakouski, then jerked her thumb to the back. Aimée followed her into a narrow galley kitchen where an old woman wearing a babushka chopped onions.

"Cigarette break," Marevna said.

The woman, her eyes tearing, nodded without looking up.

Marevna lit a Sobranie from a black box and offered Aimée one. Tempted, she glanced at the gold band, the pink paper. She figured she deserved it. One drag wouldn't kill her.

Marevna took a long drag then passed it to Aimée. "Finish it."

The jolt hit her lungs and her brain at the same time. A moment of clarity. Then she wished she hadn't.

"So important but you forget last night?" Marevna's pink-lipsticked mouth turned down.

Like she could have helped it?

"Bad men, Marevna. Better you don't know."

Marevna took one look at her and nodded. "Right. I don't want to. But why's this so urgent?"

Aimée stubbed out the Sobranie and handed her the sealed envelope. "First we need to steam it open."

Back in the kitchen, Aimée held the envelope over the steaming pot of borscht on the stove. She wondered if it was worth using this short time she had for Marevna to listen to the recording she'd made of the diva and Tatyana. Probably just champagne-fueled ramblings. She decided against it.

The old babushka kept slicing onions, tears trailing down her wrinkled cheeks. The smell of dill and alcohol emanated from a gray-haired man snoring on a stool by the pantry.

"Who's he?" Aimée asked.

"Lana's uncle. Never called you, did he?"

Aimée shook her head, careful to keep her fingers away from the steam as she moved the envelope flap back and forth over it. "The old Trotskyist. Guess he didn't have much to say."

"But he did," Marevna said. "He knew that Yuri. Kept saying old Trotskyists never die, they just go underground. Or into the government."

What did that mean? "Care to enlighten me?"

Marevna reached above the ledge near a set of dusty red Russian nesting dolls. Pulled out a newspaper, *Socialist Daily*, dated November of last year.

"He never sober very long, but he want to show you this," Marevna said. "Said Trotsky group met underground at Saint Anne's hospital during the war."

That wouldn't help her. "I'm interested in the seventies."

"The operating room functioned in the bomb shelter then. One of the orderlies was a Trotskyist and a Jew. He hid there— many others, too. Trotskyists kept meeting there after liberation. Still do, as far as he knows. Said to tell you."

Taped to the back of the envelope with yellowed cellophane tape was a note.

"What's this note say, Marevna?"

"Lenin left in 1912 in hurry to Zurich. Entrust—that's how you say?—to him, Piotr. Made him swear on his mother's life never open or show this to anyone. Lenin say keep for me." The edges of the envelope flap curled up and Aimée pulled it away from the steam. Everything smelled like borscht here; no doubt her jacket would reek.

"Can you read this and give me the gist of it?"

"Gist?"

"A quick summary." Aimée slipped two hundred francs in Marevna's apron pocket. "I'm in a hurry."

"*Da.*" Marevna read and nodded. "On envelope say, 'In case I die.'"

Inside was a single sheet of blue paper. Marevna held the page to the light above the stove. Paused. "November 14, 1910. Very old-fashion Cyrillic. Words we don't use anymore."

Marevna read, then reread, her brow furrowed. Two long minutes. "Letter, how you say, *intime?* Private between man to a woman."

"A love letter?"

A blush spread over Marevna's face. This modern girl was embarrassed by an ancient love letter?

"Go ahead, Marevna."

"Much passion. Full of longing, wants to smell her on his fingers, feel her skin on his skin. . . . He aches that he won't see her again. Not sure he's doing right thing . . . but. . . ." Marevna's breath caught. "He loves this woman. Begs her to understand. He's consumed, thinks of her every minute. But he must do what he said. No other choice but forget his . . . how you say? Doubts. Forget his doubts."

"Doubts?" Aimée said. Huppert's words came back to her.

"This part—it's not clear." Marevna bit her lip. "Something how his beliefs, the lies, worth the price, the sacrifice. Nothing holds him back now." Marevna's voice quivered. "She's left him."

And by this hot stove in the back kitchen, Aimée sensed a presence. A spirit. As if the soul released from this missive after eighty years now hovered and breathed in their midst.

"We say a passion that shakes the tree roots," Marevna said, "happens once in a life. Makes the pain worthwhile."

Aimée knew there was an equivalent expression in French but couldn't remember it.

Marevna's hand shook. She pointed to the signature on the letter. "Vladimir."

Aimée gasped. "You mean . . . Vladimir Lenin wrote this? That's his handwriting?"

Shaken, Marevna leaned against the dishes.

Proof of what Huppert had intimated. Modigliani painted Lenin in love, a man caught between his lover, his comrade-wife, his political aspirations, his theories, his doubts before he sacrificed ideals to fanaticism.

"But who was this woman?" Marevna patted the letter, which she now held like a precious object away from the pot of borscht. "There's no name."

"A Russian woman whose role faded long ago," Aimée said. "Does it matter? She played her part in history and left. He led the Revolution, changed the world."

"No one will believe this," Marevna said, her eyes wide.

"I thought Russians were romantics, souls as deep as Lake Baikal, wide as the steppes," Aimée said. "All those things from Tolstoy. He wrote in French, Marevna. We read him in school."

"No one wants to believe this. This is dangerous, Aimée." Marevna glanced at the babushka. "Stone deaf. She refuses hearing aid. But him. . . ." She jerked her thumb at the snoring old Trotskyist. "Trouble." Her mouth pursed. "Lenin's still an icon. Old people, tourists line up all day in snow in Red

Square . . . hours to see his mummy. He is myth, but they still must believe in myth."

Aimée watched Marevna. "Does it bother you knowing he's not the Lenin you thought he was?"

"Phfft." She handed the letter back to Aimée. Stirred the borscht with a wooden spoon. "In every school we saw big letters: 'Lenin lived, Lenin lives, Lenin will live.'" But Marevna's eyes brimmed. "Okay. Inside, romantic me think it's like *Casablanca*, give up great love. But Lenin was no Rick, no hero. But it would devastate my grandma."

Thursday Evening

RENÉ WIPED HIS damp temples with his handkerchief and took a deep breath. Then another. He'd spent hours circumnavigating the firewall, disabling his safeguards, the alarm triggers he'd installed. But thank God for the thumb-drive containing his backup and the cloned token to override part of the system. Then recoding the disabler with Saj's help. Tradelert's mainframe, as designed, only allowed modification in twenty-four-hour cycles and the clock was ticking.

Now it all came down to these few seconds to stop them.

But if Tradelert had re-keyed the code, had time to install new passwords, it wouldn't work. He prayed they hadn't. Prayed they had kept the system up to show off and impress the investors who were due today, California time.

"I can keep the connection and the back doors open for two more minutes," Saj said. "Ready, René?"

Now or never.

René entered the last code. Hit the keys. Nothing.

Sweat broke out on his upper lip.

"Connection's gone, Saj!"

"Keep your sombrero on." René heard the furious clicking of keys. "One minute thirty seconds," Saj said. "Should reestablish connection within fifteen seconds." When nothing happened, he muttered, "Relay's temperamental. Weather issues cause havoc with the satellite transmission."

Please God, René thought. He was hunched over, his eyeballs glued to the screen, his fingers poised.

"Connection. Go, René."

René's fingers flew over the keyboard. He hit send.

"Done."

"We're still up. Connected. It's out of our hands now."

Wednesday Evening

LENIN IN LOVE. All the more reason for the Russian oligarch to want the painting—either to legitimize his museum or hold it over the old guard and threaten exposure.

Ten minutes later, Aimée found the bar's address behind bustling rue de la Gaîtié, studded with theaters and concert halls famous for Piaf and Georges Brassens. She'd followed rue d'Odessa past the old *bains* toward Place Joséphine Baker. It was indeed a leather bar. And she wasn't dressed for it.

Her cousin Sebastien had frequented this bar before he'd gotten clean. Run-down, she remembered, haunt of dealers and stray Bretons fresh from the train at Montparnasse, mistaking the faded leftover Breton sign for a home away from home. Looking for a buckwheat crêpe and finding the underbelly of Montparnasse.

Now a simple black door. Discreet. New owners and new clientele evidenced by the calendar of *soirées*—a menu of domination, and S-M. Tonight: *femmes et fétiches*.

Great.

A woman in a leather thong and little else, pink butterfly clips holding her blonde hair up, gave her the eye. Svetla sat at the far end of the bar. Her short hair slicked back, wearing a leather biker jacket and low jeans over bony hips, revealing a flat stomach and pierced navel. Dark shadowed eyes on the prowl. Primed for a night off.

Svetla's look played well in a lace-and-leather bar in Paris.

But Aimée needed to lure Svetla back to the Hôtel Plaza Athénée and bend the diva's ear if she wanted to learn the oligarch's plan. And hurry out before Svetla saw her.

"Didn't know you swung this way, Aimée." Cécile, a friend of Michou's, René's transvestite neighbor, was blocking her exit. Cécile wore lace bloomers held in place by strategically placed suspenders. A big pout on her *rouge-noir* lips. "You never told me."

Of all the people to run into.

"I'm meeting someone, Cécile."

"Let's make it a party," Cécile said, leaning closer to her on the bar. Smoke spiraled from her cigarette into Aimée's eyes.

"It's not like that." She wished she could make Cécile disappear.

"And pigs fly."

"*Alors*, she's a Russian bodyguard."

"Ooh, like them rough do you?"

Svetla was watching them, the edges of her mouth turned down.

"My friend gets jealous." She waved to Svetla.

"I would too, Aimée. I'm mad you never let on," said Cécile, but Aimée had already hurried past her.

"Svetla, I can't stay here. I know her."

"I noticed. Your girlfriend?"

"No way, but a little complicated." She winked. *Think. Think.* She needed to lure Svetla out. "But that party—if we don't hurry, we'll miss it."

"Miss what party?"

"*Zut!* Didn't you get my message? My friend's *soirée.* Invitation only. . . ."

"Let's have a drink first," Svetla said, unconvinced.

"And miss a Parisian leather party? Models, *les bobos chics*. . . ."

"First I've heard."

"Exclusive, Svetla," Aimée said. "I used my connections and wangled you an invite. Special, only for you."

"You mean like models, designers, Karl Lagerfeld—like that?"

"*Bien sûr.* Last time, Karl held the party. Maybe tonight too."

"Where?"

Svetla's affected disinterest didn't hide her excitement. Aimée had hooked her. Now to reel her in. And fast, without giving her time to think it through.

"They call with the address twenty minutes before—it's a flash party. But you need to change. First we'll stop at the Athénée, then go from there."

"I don't understand this."

"There's a dress code." Aimée let out a low laugh. "I want to make sure the bouncer will let us in." She had to chance it. "Or you're not interested? Shall I invite someone else instead?"

Svetla slapped down twenty francs. The notes stuck to the wet drink rings on the bar. Cécile blew Aimée a kiss as they left.

DIDN'T BODYGUARDS ROOM on the same floor as their employer—or next door? According to that hotel detective, they did. Round-the-clock protection duty. In the taxi, Svetla had revealed that the diva and the oligarch had stayed in tonight. Perfect.

Aimée glanced down the hotel hallway, deserted except for a thick blue carpet and bronze wall sconces.

"The party goes all night. Sure you're off duty?"

"On call," Svetla said.

Even better. Svetla opened the door to a suite with a dressing room the size of a studio apartment, blue velvet floor-length drapes framing the window.

"Nice," Aimée said, scanning the room for a travel itinerary, Svetla's agenda—anything that might indicate the diva's room number or her plans.

"Why don't we party here first?" Svetla said, tossing her leather jacket on the giant bed.

From behind she felt Svetla's muscular arms around her. A hot kiss on her neck. Aimée noticed Svetla's cell phone poking out from her jacket pocket on the bed.

"Think I'm easy?" Aimée arched her back.

"I can hope." Svetla's tongue licked her ear.

Aimée twisted away. "First I'll raid the minibar for champagne. Find you party clothes for later." She glanced at the marble bathroom with the huge tub. "Why don't you lather up and I'll join you."

"Promise?"

"Seduction's an art. Don't rush. Let's do it *à la Française*. We're good at that."

"World famous." Svetla grinned and began peeling off her jeans.

Aimée tried not to avert her eyes. Hoped she didn't blush to high heaven. An amazingly toned body. Svetla's muscles rippled.

"You're shy," Svetla said. "I never would have thought it."

If she only knew.

"Make the water hot for me." Aimée cringed inside, but Svetla bought it. For now. Minutes. She had minutes.

She ran to the minibar, grabbed a bottle of champagne, and then reached into Svetla's jacket pocket. The cell phone was gone. Only silver-foiled breath mints came back in her hand. She scanned the room again, noting the chair, the desk, the telephone. But fancy hotels often had phones in the bathroom.

"Chilled and perfect," Aimée said, walking in. She popped

the cork and set the champagne on the edge of the tub, beside Svetla's phone. Apparently it never left her side.

"Get in."

Aimée grinned. "I still have everything on. Champagne glasses?"

"Grab a tooth mug by the sink."

She poured, careful to spill on Svetla's phone. "*Zut . . . desolée.* Let me dry it."

Aimée reached for a towel from over the tub. "Hear that?"

But Svetla grabbed her and stuck Aimée's hand on her soapy nipple.

"They're calling me with the party location," Aimée said, a tremble in her shoulders. "Oops, let me dry this off. I'll be right back."

Before Svetla could get out of the marble tub, she'd closed the door, tied the handle with her scarf, and knotted it to the gilt chair and braced it before the door. If Svetla pulled, the pressure would jam the door tighter against it. Then she tugged the small dresser and wedged it in place.

Aimée hoped that Svetla would take a while to figure out how to unscrew the gold-plated door hinge. Figured it would hold her for fifteen minutes. Unless the scarf tore—she doubted Hermès had intended it for this kind of work. She grabbed the belt from Svetla's jeans and fastened it around the doorknob. Yelling and pounding came from inside.

"Bitch! I'm calling hotel security!" Aimée heard the whacks of what sounded like a hair dryer against the wood. Good thing four-star hotels supplied strong wood doors.

"Do that and you lose your job, Svetla." Aimée flicked on the ringer switch. Two missed calls from Marina. "What's Marina's room number?"

"You'll die, bitch."

"Try to act helpful."

"Marina calls and checks on me," she yelled. "If I don't answer—"

"Then I'll tell her she needs a new bodyguard. What did Tatyana tell Marina about the painting?"

"Painting? I don't know."

Liar. Svetla had sat beside them in the bar, in the limo—she'd heard everything. "Forget a bonus from your employer if you don't warn her. Tatyana's a fraud. Isn't your job to anticipate and avoid issues?"

"Tatyana's a wannabe, an amateur," Svetla yelled. "Marina's bored. Laughs behind her back." More loud banging on the door.

"What about the painting?" Keep her talking.

Aimée scooped up Svetla's jeans and jacket, unplugged the room phone, and threw it all in the dressing room with the rest of her clothes. She locked the door and put the key in her pocket. That should give her a few more minutes.

Scraping metallic noises came from the bathroom as Svetla worked the hinges. Tweezers from her manicure set? *Merde.* She should have taken Svetla's toiletry bag.

"Tell me about the painting," Aimée said.

"Painting for paper museum?" A laugh. "Good luck."

She wondered what that meant. "Paper museum? Explain. One more chance to tell me, Svetla," she said.

"I kick your butt first," Svetla yelled. The door rattled.

No doubt she would. In Svetla's jeans pocket, she'd found two hotel key cards. But no room numbers.

Aimée let herself out and hung a DO NOT DISTURB sign from the handle. Even with Svetla's racket, no staff would dare open it. One of the key cards opened Svetla's room. The other must be for Marina's.

She hit Marina's number. On the tenth ring, the diva's slurred voice answered. *"Da?"*

"Madame Bereskova, Svetla gave me her phone. It's important."

"What you mean? Who is this?"

"What's your room number? Svetla's gone and you're in trouble."

"You the *Parisienne* shopping girl?"

"*Mais oui.* What's your room number?"

"I don't know . . . Dmitri know."

"Where's Dmitri?"

"What trouble?"

Aimée's ballet slippers sank in the plush carpeted hallway as she tried the key card in the door across the hall. No luck. Her stomach clenched. Three doors down, the key card lit up the green light and buzzed her in.

Vases of lilies, a fruit basket, and several champagne bottles littered the suite. Some full, most empty. Marina, her smeared mascara and black sequin top clashing with her pink flannel pajama pants, sat cross-legged on the bed. She flipped channels with the remote.

"Drink Bollinger? Then we go shopping, *da?*"

"All the boutiques are closed, Marina," Aimée said.

"Dmitri make them open. He can. Opened Harrods once like for Queen."

"The way he's buying a Modigliani of Lenin for his museum?"

Marina drank a flute of champagne. Handed Aimée one. "Lenin, schmenin," she said, clinking Aimée's flute with her own.

"Tatyana's lying to you."

"So?" Her voice sounded bored.

Aimée took a sip to humor Marina. The toasty fizz slid down her throat. Not bad. "No one's telling the truth, are they?" She'd neutralized Svetla, but she couldn't count on it for long.

"Truth is flexible, Dmitri says," Marina slurred. Eyes unfocused. Drunk. "Dmitri knows. His mother died after trying to have abortion of him. His father crushed in a steel accident when Dmitri is four. Self-made, that's what you say?"

And ruthless. But she didn't care to hear Marina's drunken rant.

"*Alors*, Marina, don't tell me you trust—"

"Dmitri's good man," Marina interrupted. "Some men, they trade wife for new younger skinnier wife. Not Dmitri. Not like the others. No stick-thin bimbo for him."

For now, Aimée thought. Marina protested too much.

"We come from same village, worked in same factory," she said. "Dmitri say Tatyana no good."

"Dmitri's right. Tatyana's using you, trying to make business."

Marina waved her bejeweled hand toward the closed door of an adjoining suite. "Dmitri make business. Not me." Marina poured Aimée more pale-gold Bollinger fizz. "I no answer her calls now. Keep me company and we go shopping tomorrow?"

Poor, sad woman.

"Remember the *ELLE* magazine fashion spread I told you about?" Aimée said. "Good news. My journalist friend wants to interview you. For you to come to the photo shoot." For the first time this evening, she spoke the truth.

"Me? In the *ELLE*?" Marina's eyes widened. She clapped her hands together like a child.

And then she had an idea. "*ELLE* wants to shoot on location—in the boutiques, and in Dmitri's museum. Elegant and *Parisienne*, you know."

Marina laughed. "We find museum, no problem."

"But *ELLE* wants Dmitri's museum."

"Exist on paper."

"So there is no real museum at all? That's what you mean?"

"We rent aristocrat's *hôtel particulier*. Like private museum, okay? Dmitri do it all the time." Marina leaned over, pulled out an oversize Hermès bag and emptied it on the bed. Grabbed her checkbook. "I write check now."

A front.

Marina downed her champagne. Giggled. "Me with you, fashionable *Parisienne*. I tell them cash check after tomorrow." She wrote a figure with a lot of zeros on a check from a Swiss bank account. "Kitchen-sink banking, Dmitri call it. Everything go in and everything come out clean."

Money laundering. The proof. She'd use this somehow. Aimée grinned back at Marina.

"Dmitri's next door?" The tall double doors to another wing of the suite were closed.

"Meetings. Always meetings. About paintings and money."

And his wife too drunk to impress clients. Or he got a bit on the side.

She needed to distract Marina. Get next door. "I bet Dmitri keeps pictures of your children. A proud papa, *non?* Why don't you show me?"

Marina downed her champagne. "Children?" A sad downturn to her eyes. "Dmitri shoot blanks."

Did that explain her unhappiness, her drinking, her watching too many American films? Or that he kept to his own suite? Aimée racked her brain.

"Try on the Lolita Lempicka you bought today," Aimée said. "The one that matches your eyes."

Marina wove an unsteady path to her open dressing room. "Please to help me accessorize."

"*Bien sûr*, but let's start with that."

Aimée fingered the checkbook Marina had left on the bed, coughed as she tore a deposit slip from the back, and stuck it in her pocket.

While Marina rummaged through clothes in her dressing room, Aimée moved to the double doors. She took a breath and opened them, revealing a narrow hallway. Followed the smell of cigars to a room off to the right.

She paused at the open door. Heard the clink of glasses and voices. Should she chance going further?

"Show them and they're in," said a man's voice. Aimée edged closer.

A laugh. *"Pas de problème,* Hervé," said a man with a Russian accent. "I have it."

Two men sat in leather armchairs holding Baccarat tumblers before a fire. The one she figured for Dmitri, on the thin side with short black hair and Slavic cheekbones, wore an unbuttoned pink dress shirt, no tie. A sheen of perspiration glinted on his forehead.

The heat or nerves? she wondered.

"You said that last time, Dmitri."

Did he mean the Modigliani?

"As usual, we'll organize the funds to be available tomorrow at four P.M. Pending your bringing our new friends on board. Quit worrying, Hervé." Dmitri patted the other man's knee, almost as if reassuring himself. "Do your part."

Aimée could see Hervé's profile—prominent nose, graying brown hair that reached the collar of his pinstripe suit jacket. Then he stood. He looked familiar.

Before she could edge closer, the muted sounds of a flushing toilet came from a door behind her. Then a door handle turning. Dmitri's flunky? She had to get out. Now.

"What are you doing here?" said the chauffeur, emerging from the door and blocking her escape.

Every hair on her neck tingled.

"Madame Bereskova told me the bathroom's here."

"Why didn't you knock?" he said, arms firm across his barrel chest. The unmistakable bulge of his sidearm showed beneath his jacket. The heat and the cloying cigar smoke got to her.

"Desolée, I'm confused," she said, deliberately slurring her words and trying to edge past him.

"Who's that?" asked Dmitri. He and Hervé stood in the doorway watching her. Aimée felt like a specimen under a microscope, an insect skewered on a pin for inspection.

Her nerves jangled and the champagne rose in her throat. She hiccuped. And again. She cupped her mouth. "Too much champagne. . . ." She giggled, pretended to stagger. "Madame Bereskova's so generous, I didn't drink that much . . . I must help her with. . . ." Hiccup. "Accessories for the *ELLE* photo shoot."

"This the one from this afternoon, Rodo?"

The chauffeur nodded.

"My wife's stylist. Take care of her, will you?" Dmitri threw an embarrassed smile at the tall French man. "Women."

Rodo took her arm in an iron grip. He opened Marina's double doors.

"What you think?" Marina wobbled in strappy sandals, a beige strapless silk tent dress that hit her knees, and a purple hat.

"We need to work on the hat," Aimée said and turned to Rodo. "Out. Or do you get paid to watch?"

"You don't fool me," he said, under his breath. "We talk later."

Not on your life, Monsieur ex-KGB. He hadn't bought her story for a minute. She jerked her thumb with more bravado than she felt to get him the hell out.

With a grunt he left. Aimée locked the communicating door. He'd tell his boss. And at any minute Svetla would break out.

Better work out an exit strategy.

"Where's Pinky?" Marina's eyes wavered, unfocused.

"Your dog?"

"Bellman take Pinky for walk, why not back?"

Aimée had to hurry before the bulging-eyed, gold-collared canine returned. She sat Marina down on the huge bed. Rubbed her shoulders. "I'll coordinate accessories with what's in your closet, okay?"

But Marina's eyes closed. The next moment, she was snoring. Aimée had to act quickly.

Near the Hermès strewn on the bed, she found Marina's high-end phone. A match to Svetla's but sporting a chrome finish. She exchanged Svetla's SIM card for Marina's and put Svetla's phone—now with Marina's SIM card—in her bag. From Marina's walk-in dressing room, she grabbed the first thing she saw—a black trenchcoat. She heard the connecting door's knob turn. Svetla's phone rang. Aimée switched it to vibrate. Her damp blouse clung to her neck.

Knocking sounded on the connecting door.

Merde.

She slipped off her ballet flats to get traction in the plush carpet, opened the door, looked both ways, then ran for her life. Panting, she avoided the elevator and found the exit sign several corridors over.

She couldn't go out the front—not with the video surveillance, the chauffeur, and Dmitri on the lookout for her. By now one of them was surely calling the front desk to stop her.

Merde.

She had to find the service elevator or the back stairs. Thought back to the problems the hotel detective complained of on his night security patrol—how the laundry and linen services were behind the elevator banks by his break room instead of in the basement where they should have been—making security sweeps longer than usual.

Aimée was counting on that now.

On the ground floor, she kept to the wall, head down, until she found the door marked SERVICE. Inside, industrial-sized dryers hummed and steam escaped from a pressing machine. The woman running the press had her back turned. Sweat poured down Aimée's back.

She turned to the right, kept going and made the next right. Stacked linen and staff uniforms hung in a wardrobe area.

She pulled off the trenchcoat and jeans and slipped on a white maid's uniform, then tied an apron around her waist. She pulled on heeled boots from her bag, then stuck the bag with her clothes in a white sack at the bottom of the plastic laundry cart. Wheeled it ahead, her eyes darting for an exit sign. They must have a loading bay to receive supplies.

The woman at the pressing machine looked up. "Where you going with that?"

"I need air, it's so hot," Aimée said, fanning herself.

"Take a break but leave the cart down there," the woman said. "I'll get to it. . . ." The service phone lit up on the wall.

Looking for her already.

Aimée pushed the cart around the corner to her left, kept moving, not looking back and praying she'd find the exit. Thirty seconds later, she pushed the cart out the exit and bumped into a man smoking on a loading dock by the dumpsters. A waiter in a long white apron and a black vest.

"She wants you," Aimée said, eyeing the dim lights of the alley and the street beyond.

"You must be new." Light reflected on his shaved scalp. He gave her the up and down. "Who wants me?"

"The laundry Nazi," she said.

"Why?"

"Your apron's stained," she grinned. "I don't know. But she's ranting."

"Hold that." He handed her his burning filter-tipped Gitane and winked. "She loves me. Back in a flash."

Aimée pretended to take a hit. The minute the door closed, she tossed it, shouldered the laundry bag, and sprinted down the alley. She put every ounce of energy into reaching the next street before the former KGB—or whatever he was called—discovered her ruse in the laundry.

Praying for a return on her taxi karma, she ran through the rain-slicked cobbled streets, the laundry bag thumping against her thigh. The muscles in her calves burned. She zigzagged onto rue Marbeuf and, her chest heaving, reached broad Avenue George V.

The first taxi stopped. "Late for work?" the driver asked.

"You could say that," she said, catching her breath. "Rue du Louvre at Saint Honoré. Extra if we get there in ten minutes."

He hit the meter and took off. She hunched down in the backseat, pulled the trench coat over the maid's uniform embroidered with *Hôtel Plaza Athénée* on the pocket. Marina's phone vibrated. Six calls. She needed to think.

Two blocks past the Champs Elysées, her own phone rang. Dombasle.

"The buy's on. Where do I pick you up?" he said, horns blaring in the background.

"I'm in a taxi. Look. . . ."

"Meet me at Parc Montsouris. Café on the corner of Avenue Reille. Hurry." He clicked off.

She debated, torn. She needed to get to the office. Enlist the help of Saj—and René, if he was still around. But she couldn't chance missing the Modigliani.

"Change of plans, Monsieur," she said, and gave him the address at Parc Montsouris. "Mind closing your ears?"

"Wear these, you mean?" He held up red fur earmuffs.

"*Parfait.*"

As the taxi sped over Pont Alexandre III, she called Saj. Outside the window, globed candelabra lights lined the bridge, misted in the fog. The Seine below, a dark gelatinous ribbon, caught glints of light.

"Before you say anything, Aimée, I found what Bereskova's angling for at the trade show."

Now?

"I dug around," Saj said, excited. "His parent company manufactures guidance-system onboard electronics—"

"Hold on, Saj," she interrupted, "you mean like in airplanes?"

"All aircraft, including missiles," Saj said. "Specializing in carbon-composite materials technology needed to manufacture those wafer-thin components. He's wining and dining, aiming to seal the manufacturing contract for the Moscow parent company."

Now it made sense. "Not only wining and dining, Saj. He's got an account set up for bribes and kickbacks."

"You can prove that?"

"Shouldn't be hard with this deposit slip in my hot little hand." She dictated the Swiss bank account and routing numbers on Marina's check. "Think Rasputin can help you?"

"He hates apparatchiks like Beresekova taking advantage of the system," Saj said. "That's the plus side. Whether he agrees. . . ."

"What about René's relay and delay switch for that mainframe? Same principle, *non?*

"Worked this time, thank God," Saj said.

She allowed herself an inner sigh of relief. Clutched her bag closer on the worn leather seat. Thought as she rubbed her sore calves.

"But if you and René work out how to delay the funds transfer, Dmitri Bereskova can't pay his bribes." She remembered Hervé now from the newspapers. "At least one of the culture ministers won't get his nice cut." A patter of raindrops beaded the taxi's side windows. "Wouldn't Rasputin like to expose the oligarch's *faux* museum?"

"I'll get René on it," Saj said. "He's closer to Rasputin than I am."

But the SIM card from Marina's phone had a limited life. Before Dmitri stopped service and canceled, she needed to save the call log and numbers.

"Any ideas how I can clone a SIM card in ten minutes?"

"Got the ESN and the MIN—the electronic serial number and the mobile identification number?"

"Right here."

"You're talking to the right person," Saj said. "But it might take me a while. Say an hour?"

"Worth a shot. Meanwhile, I'll copy down the numbers that come up most in the dialed log, just in case." Budding tree branches shivered in the night wind on broad Avenue du Général Leclerc.

"What does all this have to do with the Modigliani?" Saj asked.

"Didn't I explain?"

"That you're chasing the people chasing the painting. . . ."

Until now. The buy was on. And she'd have to figure it out as it played.

"What else could I do?"

"You're the detective," Saj said. "Follow clues, question suspects, go over evidence. . . ."

She heard music in the background. Japanese. "What's going on?"

"My acupuncturist made an office call. He does massage too. René needed a shiatsu treatment."

She could use one right now as well, but the taxi was approaching the gates of the Parc Montsouris. Dombasle's red Fiat was parked on the curb. An uneasy feeling came over her.

"DON'T TELL ME," Dombasle said. "You're moonlighting as a maid? Or you're an actress auditioning for a role?"

"I like to dress up, Raphael." The smell of sodden chestnut leaves rose from the pavement.

"Undercover, that's it," he said.

"Where's the buy?"

"Postponed." He shook his head. "The *antiquaire* says tomorrow."

"Didn't you know that ten minutes ago?" Aimée said, frustrated. "Yet you insisted I come here."

He shrugged.

"What's going on?" The red taillights of the taxi disappeared in the mist. Too late to call it back.

"Come inside the café. Let me explain."

Wet and tired, she agreed.

A glass of wine later, he was holding her hand. "Don't get mad, but I wanted to see you. Hear you laugh."

And waste her time.

"During an investigation?" One that seemed to be going nowhere fast, she wanted to add. First the Russian bodyguard, now Dombasle. Was she giving off some special scent tonight? Or should she blame it on the musk and ambergris in Chanel No. 5?

But she liked this semi-nerdy *intello*, unlike any *flic* she'd met. She couldn't put a finger on why—the way he spoke about art, maybe. She sat back—wine now, on top of the champagne—at this corner table in the Montsouris café. The place was empty on this rainy night, apart from the owner reading *L'Equipe*, the sports and betting newspaper, behind the counter. Outside, on the narrow street, lamps illuminated the wet cobblestones like in a black-and-white Atget photograph.

After the rain stopped, Aimée and Dombasle walked uphill past the park shrouded in darkness, hearing the distant croak of frogs. She liked the way he asked her no questions and she told him no lies. How he kept her arm in his.

He gestured to rue Nansouty, a hilly, treelined lane of brick and timber and stone houses. Once the countryside, now exclusive and home to the wealthy. "That's my place."

A *flic* with a trust fund? "Art *flics* do all right," she said.

"My grandfather was a *mutilé de guerre, une gueule cassée*."

Aimée shivered. A "broken face"—the men disfigured in the trenches of the Sommes, in Ypres, half their faces blown away. When she was a child, the butcher's father around the corner on Île Saint-Louis wore a mask to cover his half-face, a grotesque, scarred map.

"A philanthropist built the houses for wounded soldiers and their families after the war. I grew up here." He grinned. "Last one of the original families. A unique mingling of walking war-wounded and artists. Everyone a bit crazy. My father and grandfather knew Anaïs Nin and Henry Miller, Soutine, and Dalí. All neighbors down the street. My grandfather let Braque sketch him, during his Cubist phase. That's why my father took up painting, he'd say, to find the beauty in pain. Pain lived in our house."

Part of Aimée ached to tell him of Dmitri Bereskova's paper museum. She knew she should, but held back. Not sure why.

"Huppert said you know about the fixer. Maybe if I ask with a 'pretty please' and sweeten it with. . . ."

His arms enveloped her. "With this?"

The wet wool of his coat against her cheek, a curl of his hair against her lashes. His lips on hers. She didn't want him to stop.

Bright headlights pierced the mist. For a moment she felt paralyzed, like a deer caught on a country road. What was she doing here with Dombasle? The bright light shocked sense into her. The white sign on the roof signaled that it was free.

"Taxi!" she yelled, struggling out of his arms. Brakes squealed. "I've got to go," Aimée said, and ran to the waiting taxi.

BACK AT HER apartment, the imprint of his kiss lingered. His warm lips, the way she hadn't wanted to pull away. The canopy of leaves and vines leading to his rain-freshened doorstep on rue Nansouty. The peaceful sea of foliage in the park.

Confused, she curled under the duvet, her laptop at her side and Miles Davis at her feet. Had Dombasle turned the tables on her, seduction being part of his strategy?

So far, chasing the Modigliani and her mother had only led

her to a dead end. What kind of detective would her father call her?

Something was staring her in the face, but what? Over and over, she asked herself what she was missing.

Start over, her father always said. *Go back to the beginning, reexamine every detail. Reassemble the pieces of the big picture.*

She fell asleep to the night sounds outside her mansard window—the Seine lapping against the stone bank and the tapping of the rain. Her dreams were a murky haze of running and never catching up.

Thursday Morning

AIMÉE WOKE UP to a sweet, woody fragrance wafting from the yellow and orange petals sprinkled over her duvet. Miles Davis's wet nose nudged her ears. He sported a red collar with a rosebud.

What in the world?

She grabbed her father's old wool robe and followed the aroma of coffee to her kitchen. Dozens of orange, yellow, and red roses in vases filled the counter.

"Your landline's been ringing off the hook, sleepy head." Melac, tousled hair and barefoot in jeans and a T-shirt, sipped from a steaming demitasse of espresso. Beside him was a plate of fresh-baked brioches with raspberry confiture and a slab of rich Brittany butter. Her stomach growled.

"So you raided a florist's?"

"I missed you too." He picked her up, engulfing her with his arms and kissing her neck, sweet and sticky raspberry breath in her ear.

Her heart dropped. Last night she'd almost slept with Dombasle. She felt a stab of guilt. But hadn't she seen Melac with the blonde?

This was his way of making it up to her—flowers and affection, always a man's telltale signs of guilt. He'd deny everything.

"You wasted your money, Melac. Send them back to the florist."

"But our sting op ended by the flower market. The florist's a friend." He gestured to the small green ivy topiary and minia-ture lemon trees.

"You think I've got an *orangerie?*"

"Use the *jardin d'hiver,* you've got enough room."

The old glassed-in terrace full of ancient rattan chairs she never used.

His gray eyes narrowed. "Why didn't you return my calls last night?"

"I was busy." He didn't deserve to know. "I broke my rule, never mix with *flics.*"

"Not this again," he said, moistening his thumb and picking up brioche crumbs.

"That blonde, the drunk sports star at la Rotonde," she said. "Don't deny it. I saw you."

Melac's eyes clouded. "I can't talk about it."

"Can't talk about it? You expect me to believe—?"

"A honeypot sting," he interrupted.

"And I'm Madame de Pompadour," she said.

Melac grinned. "Better. *Zut,* Aimée, she's an agent."

Of course he'd say that. "Liar, no one kisses like that. . . ."

"We needed him jealous." Melac shook his head. "The operation got more complicated than usual. Let's just say the footballer opened certain doors for us. Suzanne, the blonde, is married to my colleague. They've got three kids." He shrugged. Took the wallet from his back pocket, flipped it open to a photo: on a sailboat, the blonde, windblown and smiling with three blond children, and Melac with his arm around a man she recognized. He sighed. "That's Paul. You met him last month, remember? None of us can wait to finish this operation."

Aimée knew that look in his eyes. It had been just another day at the office for him.

"*Desolée.*" Her voice came out small. Now she hated herself for doubting him. For what might have happened if that taxi hadn't appeared.

"What's wrong, Aimée?"

Was she being that obvious?

He pulled her to him. Held her. She breathed in his citrus scent.

"Aimée, I've got a tuxedo, so I can escort you to Sebastien's wedding. I've blocked the date. They can't call me in."

She stared down at Miles Davis's battered Limoges food bowl. Should she tell him about Dombasle? Would he understand something she didn't understand herself? Could they work through this?

If she didn't, it would fester and never be right between them.

Melac picked a bottle of champagne from his sports bag and put it in her suitcase-sized fridge. "Shall we order in tonight, so you can make it up to me?"

She dropped the demitasse spoon. "Make it up to you?" Now she felt racked by guilt.

"For not returning my calls." He grinned. "Seems your cell phone's off. Saj has called five times."

Suddenly worried, she nodded. Saj was a priority. But first she had to tell him.

"*Alors*, last night. . . ."

Melac's cell phone rang. He reached in his pocket and pulled out two. "It's Sandrine. Give me a second." His daughter. "*Oui, ma chérie?*" His eyes shuttered. "Calm down, Nathalie." His ex-wife.

Another custody issue?

"What happened? You're where?" Pause. "Sandrine, in the school bus? Speak slower for God's sake. . . . How long ago?" He reached for his gym bag, his face ashen. "What hospital?"

FROM HER COURTYARD, she watched Melac pull away in an unmarked Peugeot, sirens screaming down the quai. A sliver of blue lined the zinc rooftops under a cloud-filled sky.

She stood under the budding branches of the old pear tree and prayed his daughter would make it.

Madame Cachou, her concierge, poked her head out of the round window in the courtyard loge.

"The way men come and go around here!" Her penciled eyebrows had climbed up her forehead.

"His daughter's one of thirty children injured in the school bus crash with the TGV," Aimée said.

"That train catastrophe in Brittany? It's all over the *télé* newsflash. *Mon Dieu.*" Madame Cachou made a sign of the cross. "I'll tell the *curé*. We'll say a novena."

From Melac's terse description, she'd need to say a novena and more.

Miles Davis pawed the paving stone.

"Wants his walk, the little man," Madame Cachou said, coming out with his leash. She zipped up a bright aquamarine hoodie that fit her now—she'd lost five kilos doing yoga. And looked ten years younger.

"We'll stop at the church. Shall I keep Miles Davis tonight?"

Aimée nodded. "*Merci.*" She pulled her scooter off the kickstand. Walked it over the damp cobbles. Paused. "What men, Madame Cachou?"

"*Un Russe,*" she said.

Aimée's spine stiffened. The former KGB chauffeur had tracked her down already? But how?

Madame Cachou made a sniffing sound. "Vodka seeping from his pores. Couldn't fool me. The old coot stank to heaven." She reached back behind the loge door. "He left something for you."

A Trotsyskist newspaper. It must have been the old man with the red-veined nose, drunk to the world, at Marevna's *resto*. But he'd already left one for her with Marevna.

"He said you'd understand."

Understand?

Taped to the second page was a postcard-sized blue note card. *Sainte Anne Hospital, Allée de Kafka. Friday, 5 P.M.*

"SIM CARD CLONED," Saj greeted her. He was sitting cross-legged on his tatami mat, laptop in front of him, the neck brace still on but his arm without the sling.

"Delay switch in place for the Bereskova Swiss bank account," René said, smiling. Cables and wires were draped over a massage table that had been set up by the fireplace in the office. The scent of eucalyptus oil hovered. René noticed her look. "The shiatsu masseur makes office visits, Aimée. I feel new again. You look like you could use one yourself."

Like she had the time.

"So you defused your situation, René?"

"Big time, Aimée." Maxence's eyes shone from the desk next to René's. "I'm in awe. Brilliant work. I'm designing a game based on the delay stock market option."

"Not for a while, Maxence," René said. "I want to reenter the States with my own name, and not the way I left."

"How did you leave, René?" Aimée asked.

"With a lot of luck and a drug smuggler," René said. "More your style. Hate to think of all the laws I've broken."

"And with only a sombrero to show for it," she said.

"Don't forget my clean conscience."

"What about Rasputin's take on the oligarch?"

René pulled a window up on his screen. "Interesting. Said we should ask the question: Why would a low-end oligarch create a museum in France? Tax laws in the UK favor the Russians more and they all create strings of shell companies to move their money to London. A museum in France doesn't make sense, Rasputin says. Unless the museum's non-profit, given government subsidies, tax loopholes to foster Russian relations, cultural exchanges, keep tsarist art stolen during the war or brought by the White Russians back here."

"What's in it for the oligarch?" Saj asked, clicking keys on his keyboard. "Curry favor?

"Loopholes, if you know where, exist in the regulations," René said. "Money laundering and kickbacks become donations and a perfect conduit for bribes. Financial compliance on minimal security for non-profits. Too many big fish to catch—why pursue minnows in the arts?"

"How does Rasputin know?" Aimée asked.

"It's all done through backdoor operations of hired hackers," Saj said.

René nodded. "True. He's Estonian. The best."

René caught her look.

"I didn't ask any more, Aimée. Disrespect him once and he'll never answer another email. Hired hackers set up the system to evade security nets and skirt financial compliance via loopholes. Nothing new. Done it myself."

"I don't want to know, René," she said.

"Rasputin's info checks out. Give it another eight months until an idiot talks, gets caught, and tumbles it," he said. "The exchanges of art and culture translate to a Neuilly flat for a ministry official who accepts the bid from—"

"A Russian metal cockpit aerospace firm," she interrupted. "Like Bereskova?"

René clicked and dragged a screen. "Such an easy way to move money, no questions asked. Bereskova gets the party to agree to the agenda and transfers the money to the official who happens to sit on the museum board."

"But he needs art credibility." Rays of morning light caught and illumined the blue glass vase of daffodils on the fireplace mantel.

"True. They didn't think this through or have a long-term game plan. It's all about now, while international cultural organizations go through minimal regulatory hoops. The Ministry of Culture is anxious for foreign cultural investment, so they 'spread their legs'—Rasputin's words—to facilitate a Russian cultural center, museum, whatever."

"Sounds too easy," Saj said. "Then why doesn't everyone do it?"

"The regulations are brand-new. Went into effect this year. Few know. But one glitch."

Of course. Aimée had been waiting for this. Worried, she tapped her heels.

"The time factor," René said. "The ministry's co-funding arm dries up tomorrow. But institutions who've applied are grandfathered in."

"Meaning Bereskova's paper museum's in?" she said. Maxence was listening, eyes wide with excitement. Aimée had almost forgotten he was there, he was so quiet. For once. "Then what will the Modigliani give him?"

"Credibility."

"He needs the Modigliani."

Saj nodded. "Rasputin puts the info up and promises that it will go viral in three continents within, say, three to four hours. He's dying to—"

"Put a collar on him for now," she said. "We need the timing right. I'm not sure."

"No muzzling the wild man," Saj said. "If we try, he'll take the reins and run."

René sat up. "I see the problem. If we delay the funds transaction, where's the proof? That's what you mean, Aimée?"

"*Exactement.* I need to get my hands on the painting first."

"Even if the sham museum's a front?" Saj said. "And Marina's deposit slip proves it?"

"Exposing layers like this takes time," René said.

"Time we don't have," Aimée said. She set down her bag, poured herself a warm espresso from the still-dripping machine. "If we screw up the timing. . . ."

"I've got an idea," René said.

"Like what?" Saj readjusted his amber beads.

"If it could scam Wall Street, it could scam a Swiss bank." René padded over to his desk. "But give me two hours."

"I haven't found the Modigliani," she said, feeling off her game. Was it the water torture, or those drugs? She'd felt so tired, sad, and confused after Melac left this morning. "I think I'm anemic."

"Take care of yourself for once." The skin around René's green eyes creased in concern. "Get a blood test. Iron supplements." He opened a screen on his computer. "But our girl wonder falls off the job? We'll forgive you once—but to give up?"

"Did I say that, René?"

"We're covered here."

"You mean you're staying, René?"

"If you'll have me, Aimée," he said. Then he looked down, got off his ergonomic chair. Reached for his briefcase. "But I understand if you feel otherwise. I let you down."

Three pairs of eyes stared at her.

"Not at all," she said. "I need your help, René."

He grinned, climbed back on his chair.

"What are you waiting for?"

SHE NEEDED TO go back over everything. From the beginning. In the office, while everyone worked, she propped the dry erase board against the massage table. Studied the timeline of events from the Serb's accident on Monday night, Yuri's murder on Tuesday, then Luebet. Pored over the notes she'd made at Madame Figuer's kitchen table, the details from her to-do list on Oleg and Tatyana, Damien, the concierge at rue Marie Rose.

What cracks in their stories had she missed? What wasn't she seeing? Her eye caught on her *grand-père*'s commendation from the Louvre on recovering the Degas—she could see the framed certificate just above the dry erase board.

She searched the old file cabinet for all his files. The ones she'd planned to digitize but never got around to.

Then she found it. The old investigative report on the stolen Degas. She'd been ten at the time. After her ballet lesson, he'd taken her to the art recovery unit in the complex at the *préfecture*. She remembered how huge the place felt, how musty it smelled. In a vault, he'd picked up a small bronze statue. Smiled at her. "This could be you, Aimée."

A small bronze ballerina, no taller than an uncut rose stem, her tutu suspended in midair like fluff, caught in the act of a twirl. Mesmerizing. So lifelike.

She could almost hear the rustle and swish of the short tulle skirt, the grinding twist of the leather-toed shoe on the wood stage floor of l'Opéra.

The old grande dame had been so thankful to Aimée's grandfather that she willed the ballerina to the Louvre, much to the chagrin of her heirs.

She pored over her grandfather's cramped writing on the yellowed pages in his case report—surveillance, suspects, alibis, possible motives, a diagram of interrelations.

Bon, she'd done all that. Timelined events. Followed everything step for step per her grandfather's example.

Correction—her grandfather had rechecked the alibi of the old dame's trusted secretary. The hospital nurse, who was finally back from vacation when he followed up, had never seen the secretary the night of the robbery when the secretary claimed to have been visiting her mother.

It was the little things, the details, that made 2+2 = 5, as her grandfather had said.

Aimée knew where to start.

"Let's pull up the numbers from Marina Bereskova's phone."

"Done." Saj handed her a printout. "Pretty self-explanatory. Calls to Dmitri, Svetla the bodyguard, Tatyana, a boutique. . . ."

"And this one?"

Saj shrugged. "The bank?"

She pulled out her cell phone and checked the call log.

The same number. Received two days ago at 6:10 P.M. She thought back. Damien the printer.

Her head spun. How did he connect to Marina? Wasn't she Tatyana's friend? Why was Marina talking to her friend's husband's rival?

"I've got an idea. Try Dmitri's number from one of our disposable phones."

"I just tried. Still working," Saj said.

Could it be so simple?

"BONJOUR, MADAME FIGUER," she said on the phone. "I want to send flowers to Damien's aunt, but. . . ."

"Madame Perret? She's at death's door. He's beside himself, that young man."

That answered her first question.

"Voilà. But I forgot which hospital she's in."

"Damien moved her to a nursing home," said Madame Figuer.

"Vraiment? Where?" The old busybody should know, just as she knew everyone's business. And never kept her mouth closed.

Pause. "A private one. Expensive. Near the Métro at Mouton Duvernet."

"But I thought she was too ill to be moved. Can you remember?"

"On Villa Coeur de Vey, I think," she said. "How's the case going?"

Aimée clicked her pen. "Another call, Madame, got to go. Merci."

Fifteen minutes later, she parked her scooter outside the Monoprix cornering the thin slice of an alley. On Villa Coeur de Vey, next to the charitable organization that handed out free food, she found the nursing home.

"Madame Perret?" the dark-haired receptionist said. "Too late, I'm afraid."

"She's passed away?"

"Her nephew took her home. Contacted hospice. He's following Madame's wishes."

Aimée thought back.

"When was that?"

The receptionist consulted her computer screen. "Let's see, we discharged her Tuesday to Hôpital Broussais for a CAT scan. *Oui*, the ambulance took her."

The morning of Yuri's murder.

"Her nephew accompanied her, I assume."

"He made the arrangements," the receptionist said.

Something about this bothered Aimée.

"Did you see him?"

"Tuesdays I'm off. But ambulances only transport patients."

"Then her nephew met her at Hôpital Broussais?"

The receptionist pulled the readers down from her head.

"You're a *flic, non*? I'll need to see identification, Mademoiselle."

Aimée flashed her father's police ID with her photo.

"*Alors*, a note here says the hospital's CAT scan machine was broken," the receptionist said. "Madame Perret was brought back here in the ambulance."

How did that fit in?

"Anything else?"

"We were unable to contact her nephew until late afternoon," she said. "He took care of the arrangements that evening."

"Tuesday evening?"

The receptionist nodded.

Damien told her he'd been with his aunt all day at the hospital.

"May I check that cell number against the one we have for her nephew?" Aimée mustered a smile. "It's routine."

The receptionist swung the screen for Aimée to see. She copied it down on her to-do list.

"Such a caring young man, as I remember," the receptionist said. "Very concerned over his aunt. Not many like that these days."

"But didn't one of our force question your staff?" Aimée gave a sigh. "It's about dotting the *i*'s and crossing the *t*'s for reports. We've got to follow the new regulations."

"You're the first."

Sloppy police work. And on her end, too.

SHE UNLATCHED THE gate of the printing works on rue de Châtillon. Today the courtyard lay quiet. No pounding machines or delivery *camionnette*. An older woman she hadn't seen before stood locking the warehouse door.

"Lost?" the woman asked, a frown marring her mouth.

Aimée's heels sank in the gravel. "Looks like you're closing early."

"I'm not the boss," she said.

"Where is Damien?"

"Full of questions, aren't you? Take a number."

Such helpful staff, a tradition here, she thought, remembering Florent, who'd attacked her in the truck.

The woman shrugged. "I'm off the clock. Forever. He's shut down the factory."

No wonder. It all added up.

"Everyone's gone."

Aimée saw a light upstairs at the back window.

Watching her? "I guess I'll try reaching him another way."

"Suit yourself, but I'm locking up."

Aimée walked out of the gate.

The woman locked the padlock. Without a goodbye, she walked toward the Métro.

Aimée turned into the park, following the wall away from

the *maison de maître*—the former squat she now recognized, where Yuri once held a Trotskyist banner and her mother had been arrested—to a worn path among some rosemary and lilac bushes. It ended at the back of the printing works. A scattering of metal rungs led up the crumbling masonry, rusted in places, well worn in others.

She came up with a plan while she climbed, gripping the worn rungs, testing her weight each time. At the top, she reached a ledge covered with pigeon droppings. Two stories above ground and hidden by wild lilac bushes. A perfect view of Yuri's atelier from the lighted upper floor of the printing works.

She punched in René's number.

"Any verdict, Aimée?"

"Nothing happens until I find the painting," she said. "I'm at Damien's printing factory."

"But Rasputin. . . ."

The ledge by her foot gave way. Rocks tumbled and she grasped a rock higher up. Heights, she hated heights.

"Hold on." She pulled out the phone numbers Saj had printed out. "Do you see a call to or from 06 78 90 42 30 on Marina's call log?"

"Service was cut . . . but yes, that's on the list."

"Call that number in three minutes. Use one of the throwaways in my desk drawer. Say you've got the money, tell him the plans have changed, to bring the painting. You want to meet now."

Aimée heard René swallow. "If he asks where?"

She thought quick. "Café Zèbre at Alésia."

"You're serious? Do you need me for backup?"

Too late for that now. *Merde.*

"Convince him you're the contact, your boss wants him to deal with you. Keep him talking as long as you can. Please, René. And fake a Russian accent."

She clicked off. Switched her phone to vibrate, stuck it

in her bag, and edged her way to the lighted window. Behind the bushes lay a grilled balcony invisible from the park. She climbed onto it. Stood at the curtained French doors. Silence.

She tried the door. Locked. *Merde.* Just as she was about to take out her lockpick set and get to work, she noticed another set of French doors half covered by lilacs. One of the doors was open. A fat black crow perched on the balcony ledge, eyeing her with his pinpoint yellow gaze. A sweetish smell grew stronger as she slid sideways into a semi-dark room with flickering candlelight.

She heard a phone trill. Footsteps. *Bravo, René.*

Her eyes adjusted to the light. Votive candles on the floor silhouetted a bed with a rose satin duvet. And she froze.

Lying on it was a white-haired woman in an old-fashioned lace nightgown, centime coins on her lids to keep them closed, hands crossed in prayer with a blue-beaded rosary trailing from them.

Aimée realized the source of the sweetish stench. The old woman must have been here since Damien brought her back from the clinic. Dead and decaying for several days.

The flap of the crow's wings came from the balcony. Aimée made herself move.

Damien stood in a high-ceilinged workroom that overlooked the silent printing presses below. Rays of late afternoon light glowed on the old wood, giving off a burnished honey hue.

To one side were piled boxes; on the other, paper-cutting blades and a sharpening stone were grouped on a long-gauged worktable partly obscured by more boxes. To her right were shelves with brass wire rolls and boxes of metal type.

Dotting one wall, like flypaper, hung lopsided yellowed cardboard signs with raised dots of Braille. Remnants from the turn of the century, when blind laborers worked the presses. The past clung to the dust-filled corners.

She peered over the boxes and caught her breath. To the left, in a recessed alcove, were stacked La Coalition posters; above them hung a detailed street map of the Montparnasse quartier dotted with Post-its marked with X's. On the floor sat blue canisters of propane gas, the kind available at a hardware shop. Bags of fertilizer.

Aimée froze. Good God . . . bomb-making material. And a map of the locations. Hadn't Solange, Saj's Goth-Celt neighbor, said— what had it been?—*La Coalition is militant organizing?*

Damien was leaning over something at the worktable. The phone was stuck between his shoulder and ear as he listened. Above him, on the shelf, she saw the detonators. She stifled a gasp.

"But Bereskova called me an hour ago," he said.

Merde. She'd been afraid of that.

"What do you mean?" he said. Pause. "I won't go a centime lower on the painting. He agreed on the price."

He had it. She remembered Yuri's message: "I know who stole the painting." She'd thought he meant her mother. But Yuri had counted on reasoning with Damien to return the painting.

But reasoning with someone crazed by grief who kept his moldering aunt next door? A fanatic obsessed with his political cause, bomb-making . . . Why hadn't she realized it sooner?

What if Yuri had confronted Damien about the painting, things had heated up, and. . . .

Had Damien killed Yuri? Her mind went back to the demonstration blocking rue d'Alésia—how easy for Damien to slip into the crowd and blend in. She remembered the La Coalition armband on his desk. . . .

But torture his mentor and friend?

"Change the plan, why?" Damien said.

She had to move fast. Wanted to kick herself for leaving her Beretta in her office drawer. Now she had to find a way to defend herself, a different way out. The stairs down to the printing presses were blocked by boxes. Ducking low, she moved over the slanting wood floor toward rolls of brass wire, careful to avoid the metal drums of ink, the shelves with boxes of metal type.

"We worked this out," Damien was saying. "Now . . . you're sure?"

Damien carefully slipped something in a cardboard tube, the kind used for posters. Her heart thudded. The phone still to his ear, he headed for the door—right where she stood. Stepping back, she tried to slip into a recess. Her bag fell off her shoulder and she made a vain attempt to catch it. Too late.

"You?" White-faced, rings under his eyes, he looked more haggard than before. He was still wearing the same clothes, wrinkled as if he'd slept in them.

Before Aimée could bend down for her bag, he'd kicked it into the corner. Her phone was in it. No chance of reaching the *flics* now.

Trickles of perspiration ran down the small of her back.

"The Modigliani belonged to Yuri, Damien," she said, keeping her voice even. She made herself breathe. "It's time to do the right thing. I can help you."

"The right thing? That's what I'm doing." His mouth quivered. Then a smile, and he pointed to the alcove. "They'll listen to me now."

"With propane, fertilizer . . . making bombs?"

"Don't any of you understand?"

"Understand what, Damien?" She kept her voice steady.

"La Coalition will prevent the developers from ruining the quartier."

With bombs? She didn't think so. Her shirt stuck to her shoulder blades.

"All thanks to me when Yuri finally cleaned out that cellar," Damien said. "It was me who found the painting, do you understand? I saved it." Damien set the phone down on the worktable and picked up his jacket. She could see the lighted band of numbers across the screen. He hadn't clicked off.

Distract him, keep him talking.

"You saved the Modigliani?" she said. "Why didn't Yuri tell me?"

"Yuri almost threw everything in a dumpster," Damien said. "He had no idea. He laughed at me, but I did the research. Still, he wouldn't listen."

Aimée was convinced now his aunt's death had unhinged him—she needed to calm him, keep him talking. Prayed René could hear, that the phone was still connected.

"So you took the Modigliani from Yuri's closet for safekeeping?" she said. "You knew where he hid it, but he trusted you, *non?* Just so I'm clear, it was that afternoon Yuri went out for a little while before going to Oleg's for dinner, right?" When Yuri slipped the envelope under her office door, wanting her help. "That's when you took it?"

"Good thing I did." His eyes were too bright. Too focused. "Before the grasping art dealer's thugs and Tatyana's Serb could get to it. I told Yuri over and over that it wasn't safe. Turns out he'd involved you—as if. . . ." He gave a strange smile. "So many depend on me, it's the right thing I'm doing. We can continue our work."

Crazed all right. And delusional.

"By making bombs? That's destruction, not preservation."

"Only a means to an end, I explained that to Yuri. Over and over. But he wouldn't listen."

She edged closer to the phone on the worktable. Praying René could hear. "I know you meant to protect Yuri. He helped you run this printing business—all that encouragement. You told me, remember?" she said, moving closer. "He regarded you like a son, *non?* You were there when we hit his car."

"More of a son than Oleg," Damien said. "Even if we aren't

related by blood. Or marriage. All Oleg cared about was money. When Yuri boasted about the Modigliani, Oleg and Tatyana buzzed like bees to honey."

Aimée kept her hand behind her, moving forward with small steps. She needed to reach the wire, or something heavy. . . .

"Stay back . . . stay right there." Damien watched her with glittering eyes.

"*Reste tranquille*, Damien, we're just working this out," she said. "Tuesday morning your aunt went for a CAT scan and Yuri called, just as you told me he did."

She felt something long, wooden with sharp points. Her fingers traced the sharp edges. Metal. She coughed to cover the sounds of it.

"Damien, I know you meant well."

He nodded.

"Didn't you, Damien?"

He nodded again. She needed him to talk. Needed to keep him focused.

"Then tell me what happened," she said. "I know you're upset after your aunt's death. But I need to understand to help you."

He glanced at his watch. She was losing him.

"Didn't Yuri want the painting back for the art dealer's appraisal?" she said. "Then things got out of hand." She approached him cautiously. "*N'est-ce pas?*"

"I don't have time for this." His voice was different. Harder.

"But you took the time to strangle Yuri with his own tie, to torture and drown him. Why, Damien?"

"You want to know why?" Damien's voice rose to a shout. "I found the painting, dusty and stuck in the back corner. Yuri promised me whatever it was worth."

"Of course, Yuri was generous to a fault, he would have shared with you," she said. "But there's history behind it. Modigliani gave Lenin's portrait to Yuri's father in friendship. His father knew Lenin as a young boy."

"Generous to a fault?" Damien snorted and grabbed the phone. "I counted on that money. But he'd cut me out. Yuri already had a buyer."

"So do you—millions from the half-bit oligarch who's as greedy as you are." Now more pieces fit. Tatyana was paranoid for a reason—he'd followed her. "You have the Modigliani in that tube to sell via Tatyana."

"Tatyana?" The muscles in his jaw twitched. "I didn't mean to. . . ." His gaze flicked to the corner by her bag.

Alarmed, she stepped forward, for the first time noticing a dark maroon footprint, the red trickle veining the grooved wood floor. The metallic smell of blood she could almost taste. Behind the boxes, under the worktable—a slumped Tatyana, her snakeskin scarf ending in a pool of blood. Her eyes were rolled up in her head.

Aimée gasped.

"She showed no respect for my aunt. She kept yelling, demanding . . . I never meant to. . . ."

"Like you never meant to murder poor Yuri?" Aimée said, shaking. "Or shove Luebet on the Métro tracks?" The hypocrite. "But torturing him? The same way Madame Figuer's brother was tortured, to cover your tracks. . . ?"

"That old busybody? Such a joke, that old story of her brother."

Cruel as well as unhinged.

"But Yuri turned on me. Wanted no part of La Coalition," he said. "The bank refused me credit to keep this damned place going. How else can I keep funding the cause, making change happen? Look at Lenin. . . ."

Lenin? "You think printing posters and making bombs funds a revolution?"

"My aunt told me I deserved it. I do and now I will."

"Your aunt's beginning to smell as bad as your ideas," she said. "You fired your staff and shut the doors. Old news. Try something fresh, like admitting the truth."

"Yuri had already sold the painting—it never mattered what the appraiser valued it at."

Aimée shuddered. "You mean to the fixer?"

Damien grabbed the cell phone, shoved the boxes at her, and ran. But she'd darted back, ready, and batted at him with the typeset roller. He ducked and tripped on the scattered boxes, dropping the phone and the tube, which skittered across the floor. Pieces of the rust-encrusted roller fell apart in her hands. Rust flakes spun in the air.

Damien hobbled to his feet, grabbed the paper-cutter blade from the worktable. "You're like the others," he shouted. "You won't get away."

The phone lay on the floor. She had to reach René. "Tell Rasputin now, René. Now!" she shouted, hoping to God the phone was connected, that he heard.

Damien swung the paper cutter. Her back was up against the wooden boxes, nowhere to go. Shaking, she couldn't stop shaking. She scrambled sideways, grasping for the floor—which, in her terror, seemed to tilt away. She heard the blade rip her jacket. Cold air whooshed up her blouse.

An Yves Saint Laurent vintage jacket. Now she was angry.

From one of the boxes by her elbow, she grabbed the first heavy thing her fingers closed on, a letterset bar of sharp, raised metal letters. She pulled it out and whacked him in the jaw. Damien cried out, spun, blood dripping from his cheek. He came back at her waving the blade. Darting left, she swung again. Hit his rib, heard a crack. The metal letters A and S clattered to the floor. But the sharp-edged letterset bar had pierced his T-shirt and was embedded in his chest.

Damien collapsed, moaning in pain. His bloodstained fingers scrabbled to wrench it out. She bound his ankles and wrists with the wire before she pulled the bar out. Then she found the phone.

"René . . . René?"

"Funds delay done three minutes ago," he said. "And Rasputin's one happy camper now."

"Took you long enough," she said. "Partner."

"I've missed you too, Aimée."

AIMÉE HEARD THE crow flapping in the next room. Managed to shoo it away from the old woman's face. She'd leave it to Dombasle to call the health department, but he wasn't answering his phone. She left the rue de Châtillon address on his voice mail. Let him figure it out. It was time she got out of here.

Going out the way she'd come, she paused on the ledge and took the crackling canvas from the tube. Not much bigger than a large atlas, missing and unmissed for so many years, and now the cause of so much greed and death. In the fading sun, the lilac leaves brushing her arm, she unrolled it.

It took her breath away. A man almost alive looked back at her. The curve of his cheek, the thin mustache, the almond-shaped nut-brown eyes. So vulnerable, so in love, it shone. Warm with an appetite for life, a hunger to experience. Flecked with doubt, maybe, but a fully fleshed-out human being in an ingenious assemblage of deft brushstrokes. The earth tones and still-vibrant green of the jacket, the patched elbow, the hands holding a booklet.

Painted on the back, in quavering letters: M o d i g l i a n i for my friend Piotr.

She took the photocopied letters from her bag, rolled them up with the painting, put them all in the tube, then stuck the tube in her bag. She'd let history decide what it meant.

AIMÉE WALKED IN the twilight with the Trotskyist paper rolled under her arm, hoping the Sainte Anne appointment would lead somewhere. Did these old Trotskyists stick together somehow? She'd recovered Yuri's *patrimoine* from his father, but too late. Melancholy filled her. Yuri had hired her to recover his Modigliani. There were even four thousand francs and change left to prove it. Dombasle . . . the rest . . . she didn't know.

She turned into 64 Boulevard Arago, the walled Sainte Anne psychiatric hospital—*la maison des fous*, the madhouse, as people called it. Built over the Catacombs and quarries honeycombing the quartier, the hospital was, in the seventeenth century, a farm under the patronage of Queen Anne where *les fous* worked for their keep. The grounds never failed to make Aimée uneasy. The bars on the rain-beaded windows reminded her of La Santé a few blocks away—another kind of prison. For a moment she wanted to turn around and leave this wet, damp place.

Years ago, she'd accompanied her grandfather here to visit a woman he called Charlotte.

That cold, sleeting February afternoon flooded back to her: Charlotte's pink peignoir, her little barking laugh, the intense look in her wide eyes; the sad expression on her grandfather's face, the way he'd told Aimée to smile at Charlotte and act polite; how afraid Aimée had felt when Charlotte stroked her cheek with her bandaged wrist. "Why did we go see that lady, Grandpa?" she'd asked him in the café afterward over a steaming *chocolat chaud*. He'd shrugged, his shoulders slumped in resignation. "People shouldn't be forgotten, Aimée. Not even the broken ones."

The caramel-colored stone pavilions, each named after a writer or thinker, seemed at odds with the mix of nursing staff and hospital-gowned patients who strolled in the gardens and greenery between them. No security cameras, lax supervision. Didn't they worry the patients would get out? Or maybe the serious cases never saw the light of day.

Half an hour early, she found the visitors' café, a glassed-in affair with plastic chairs that gave one the illusion of sitting outdoors. Before she could order an espresso, a tall man in a green bloodstained gown joined the line. A doctor? But those weren't scrubs. Her craving for espresso evaporated and she edged out of the line. No one looked twice at the man.

At Allée de Franz Kafka, she sat down under the pillared pavilion on a wood bench framed by green metal. Now she wondered what to do. Her Tintin watch, its face clouded with moisture, had stopped again. Great.

Muffled moans, a sob. Aimée cocked her head forward to see a woman seated further along the bench. Her face was buried in her hands, and she was rocking back and forth. Alone.

Sometimes she felt like that too. Forlorn, adrift. But this was no time to read her own story in the woman's suffering.

"It can't be that bad," Aimée said, feeling inadequate the moment the words came out. Banal and patronizing. "I mean . . ." She hesitated. "Can I help you?"

"Only if you weren't followed," came a reply. But the voice issued from behind her, by the entrance to the old underground operating rooms. Struck by the accent, the inflection, she turned around. Alert.

"No one followed me," she said.

In the shadows stood a tall figure. A woman in a doctor's coat. Aimée mounted three steps to the glass overhang.

"You're the fixer?" Her throat went dry.

Aimée felt her hands being grasped, squeezed in the warmth of another's. And she was enveloped in a hovering *muguet* scent. Familiar, so familiar. She felt a jolt like electricity as her eyes fixed upon the unlined face of the woman looking back at her: the chiseled cheekbones, the dark brows and large eyes, the carmine lipstick. She'd always thought she'd know her mother the moment she saw her. Feel a connection like molten steel, the bond resurfacing. But she wasn't sure.

"*Maman?*" Warmth emanated from this woman.

"Curious, always so curious," she said. "When you were little, you asked questions day and night."

Aimée felt a sob rising at the back of her throat. A weight pressing into her. Her breathing went heavy. It couldn't be . . . but it was.

Her mother lifted Aimée's hands to take a look at them. "Ink stains on your palms," she said, her American accent tinged by rolling *r*'s. "You had crayon marks on them the last time. Even your father. . . ."

"Papa?" she said. "You know he never got over you."

Her mother glanced away.

"The company lied. As usual."

The CIA. "You work for them. A hired killer. . . . ?"

"Not any more, Amy. "

Aimée's throat caught. She hadn't denied it.

"I've led a double life. Done ugly things." A shrug. "Dealt with devils. Paying the price to keep you safe," she said. "Now I'm rogue and I can't protect you. I counted on the wrong people. There's no one left to trust now. But years ago I saved Yuri's life." A cough. "He thought selling his painting through my channels, the contacts I knew, would buy my freedom."

"You're a fixer. Make things happen. Buy time."

A twist of her mouth. "I don't have much, Amy," she said. "Yuri shouldn't have involved you." Footsteps sounded and she stepped back in the shadows. Silent. Then a whisper. "Let me say what I need to."

Everything bubbled up—the hurt, the cold afternoon, the

empty apartment she'd come home to when her mother abandoned them. Never a word in all these years.

"Every day after school I looked for you." That eight-year-
old's whining voice came out; she couldn't stop it. Did the
shared blood coursing in their veins mean nothing? But Aimée
didn't know this woman. "Why did you leave?"

"I was protecting you," the woman said.

"Protecting me?" The words rose like a tide. "But I wanted
you. My mother." She looked down, her shoulders heaving.

Warm fingers stroked her cheek. Rested on her chin, and
with a feather softness raised Aimée's face to hers.

"You think I didn't want to be there? To be with you?"

The moment of silence was filled by the shooshing sounds of
wet leaves running in the gutter. Her mother's eyes darted back
and forth. Watchful. For the first time, Aimée noticed a metal
door standing ajar on the side of the building.

"I don't care if you sold arms and traded with terrorists,"
Aimée said, her insides wrenched. "But now you come back
and say this? What do you expect?"

A deep cough. Her mother's face stayed in shadow.

"Not everyone deserves to be a mother." A little sigh. "But
I've followed you for years."

"Through Morbier, non? But why lie?"

Her mother opened her palm to reveal Aimée's old charm
bracelet. Hadn't she lost that years ago?

"Your first tooth, a lock of your hair," her mother said. "Don't
make my mistake. Find the right man, have babies."

"That's rich coming from you. You found a wonderful man,"
she said, her voice shaking. "You had a baby." No way would
Aimée have babies. Sometimes she'd wake up at night terrified
that she'd do what her mother had done. Couldn't face the
responsibility. "So why would you reappear now? Don't tell me
you feel guilty."

"I wanted to see you once. Selfish, you're right." Her eyes

darted around, checking to be sure they were alone. Then bored into Aimée's. "Everything you've said is true."

"*Mais non*, you wanted the Modigliani—a painting people have been killed for. You planned on it to finance more dirty deals."

A small shrug. Her mother's thin shoulder bones stuck out in the white coat. "You have no reason to believe me. But maybe you'll take my advice. Learn to cook, quit criminal work," she said. "There's an account set up so you won't need to worry for a while. Travel, live life, find a man, do something else. . . ."

Cold wind sliced through this hospital enclave, a web of pavilions and old boiler buildings. Aimée felt anger well up.

"Throw away Leduc Detective? After everything *Grand-père* and Papa worked to build?" she said. "What right do you have?" Aimée trembled with deep, raw hurt. "You're just a stranger who's walked back in the door. Not part of my life. You'll leave again." She bit her lip. "But for once I'm doing the leaving. You don't know me—how I feel, what I want, what drives me."

Her mother receded in the shadows. Sighed. "Amy, you're like me. Please don't make my mistakes."

She said her name the American way, "Amy." Just as she had when Aimée was a child.

And then Aimée saw Dombasle in conversation with a nurse at the far end of the *allée*. The nurse pointed in the pavilion's direction. Another man joined Dombasle.

Merde! It had been only twenty minutes since she'd left rue de Châtillon. Dombasle, in cahoots with the BRB, must have had her followed. Probably all along.

He wanted the Modigliani and the fixer.

"The *flics*? You turned me in?" Her mother's conflicted expression, the look in her eyes seared Aimée. Turn her in, a wanted terrorist on the world security watch list who'd been expelled from France years ago—that's what Aimée should do.

This woman who abandoned her, now full of regret. Should she? Could she?

Footsteps pounded, echoing under the archway by the war memorial to the fallen hospital staff.

"*Non*, you're my mother. Get the hell out of here. You're good at that."

Her mother hugged her. For a moment, that scent of *muguet* brought her whole childhood back to her. "I love you. Stay safe, little mouse."

Aimée heard the creaking of a steel door and they both looked toward it. "*Vite*, Sydney!" The old drunk waved his arm to hurry her along.

Aimée choked back a sob and thrust the tube under her mother's arm.

"Go."

Saturday

EVERY PEW IN the Marais's Armenian church was filled. White floral sprays covered the altar and Serge's twin boys, for once, stood still in their short pants. Each held a lace pillow, transfixed by the wedding rings tied to them.

"Melac won't show up, will he?" René asked, adjusting his silk cravat in the church vestibule. When Melac never returned her calls, René stepped in as an escort. "You're sure he's not coming?"

Staying at the hospital in Brittany, from what Paul at the *Brigade Criminelle* had told her last night: after twelve hours for the emergency crew to extricate Melac's daughter from the bus, she remained in a coma. Critical. His ex-wife complicated events with a nervous breakdown and attempted suicide.

"Melac's on leave from the force," Morbier said.

Aimée's knuckles whitened on the bouquet. And his friend Paul hadn't told her? "How do you know, Morbier?"

"Watch the *télé*," he said. "He's a little busy. No promotion."

"The *télé*? You know I don't have one," she said, realizing Melac wouldn't be coming back.

The other bridesmaids filed in with their escorts. The soft tones of a flute echoed under the Gothic struts. As maid of honor, she had the distinction of having two escorts, Morbier and René.

"Ruining his career," Morbier muttered.

"So that he can be with his family?" Aimée whispered

sharply. "Maybe he doesn't see it like that, Morbier. That's why
he has a family." *Unlike you.* But she kept that back. For the first
time, she became aware that her family was standing right here.

"You didn't fall for Dombasle, Leduc, did you?"

The rat who used her as bait for the Modigliani . . . for her
mother? And to think she almost did. She shook her head.

"*Bon,* never trust an *intello,*" Morbier said.

"We need to talk about my mother, Morbier."

His eyes shuttered. "Not now, Leduc. This is a happy occa-
sion."

Regula, the bride, resplendent in white lace and trailing
whiffs of gardenia, winked at her from behind the rectory door.

"Aimée, love that Dior," she said.

Determined to wear this Dior no matter what, she'd used
safety pins to let out the seams as much as possible. Even more
than the couturier had been able to that morning.

"Gained a little weight, *non?*" René said. "Color in your
cheeks, healthy for once."

"I'm anemic," she said, tired of repeating this to the world.
"Just awaiting the lab results so I can start iron supplements."

"Could have fooled me."

And then her cousin Sebastien appeared. He looked dash-
ing in a black tuxedo, gardenia corsage, and trimmed beard.
Aimée hugged him tight. "I'm so proud of you, little cousin.
Bursting with pride."

He'd turned his life around. Found a wonderful woman, a
gourmet chef who loved him to bits.

"You said you'd be the maid of honor if you could wear
chiffon," he said, hugging her back. "But bursting the chiffon
seams?"

Already? *Merde.* She looked down at the shredding fabric.

"No wedding cake for me," she said. "Or just a sliver."

Her cell phone rang in her matching beaded clutch.

"Turn the damn thing off, Leduc," Morbier said.

"Won't take a moment. I need the lab results so my doctor can fill my prescription today." She answered in a whisper.
"*Allô?*"

"We've got the test results, Mademoiselle Leduc," said a lab
technician, "*Excusez-moi*, is it Madame?"

"*Mais non*, Mademoiselle, but that's not important right
now," she said, feeling the tug of Morbier's arm. René's darting
looks. The opening organ strains of the bridal march sounded
in the front of the church.

"Last minute?" the lab technician said. "Better late than
never, eh?"

"What? Look, just send on the results to my doctor so I can
fill the prescription."

"Prescription? You mean prenatal vitamins?"

"Heads up, Leduc, we're next," Morbier growled.

The second bridesmaid walked up the aisle. In a moment it
would be their turn. The organ swelled.

"For the iron supplements. The blood test shows I'm anemic . . .
wait." She punched up the phone's volume. "What did you say?"

"You're pregnant, Madame Leduc."

"But there's some mistake." She spoke loudly over the organ,
which struck a loud chord and then paused between verses.

"No mistake. You're pregnant," the lab technician shouted,
his voice blasting in the suddenly quiet stone vestibule.

The phone and the flowers fell to the stone floor. "Pregnant?"

Everyone turned.

René swooped the bouquet back up and tucked the phone
into her beaded clutch. He pulled her down and kissed her. "I'll
plan the baby shower."

The organ strains rose, filling the church.

Beads of perspiration popped on Morbier's forehead. He
took her arm and turned her toward the chapel. "*Alors*, Leduc,
pregnant? You listened to me for once."

Now he wanted to claim credit?

"A baby? Me, barefoot in the kitchen?" she shot back in a whisper as her two escorts led her down the aisle. "I don't think so."

Morbier smiled. "You'll do it your own way, Leduc, like you always do."

Acknowledgments

MY HEARTFELT THANKS belong to so many: Dot; Max; Barbara; Jean Satzer; Grace and Lillian; Mary and Susanna von Leuven; Keith Raffel from the Valley; Dr. Terri Haddix, medical pathologist; Jean-Luc Boyer, Commandant de Police Chef de la Documentation; Corinne Chartrelle, Commandant E.F. Chef Adjoint of the DCPJ-OCBC (*Office Central de lutte contre le trafic des Biens Culturels*); Stéphane Thefo and Jeanette Kroes of the Criminal Intelligence Office, Works of Art Unit, Drugs and Criminal Organizations Sub-directorate I.C.P.O. at INTERPOL; Catherine Driguet, retired veteran of the *Brigade Criminelle*; Arnaud Baleste, veteran of the *Brigade Criminelle*; Thomas Erhardy of the BRB, *Brigade de Repression de Banditisme*; Andre Rakoto, *Chef de Cabinet,Service historique de la Défense, Château de Vincennes*; Olga Trostiansky, *adjointê Maire de Paris*; the brilliant collector Peter Silverman; Adrian Leeds; Carla Bach; Benoit Pastisson; Jim Haynes for sharing his kitchen, his friends and his heart; Natalia Rublevko; Madame Fauvette; Karen Fawcett; Cathy Nolan and Emilie la chat; Svetla; Valeria Pavlova; Julie McDonald; Ariane Levery; encore Naftali Skrobek; Sarah Schwartz, who insisted I write about her 'ood'; Agnes Varda on rue Daguerre; Alice Barzilay; Gilles Thomas.

This book wouldn't have been written without the help of plotmeister James N. Frey; Bronwen Hruska, my wonderful publisher, and everyone at Soho; my editor extraordinaire, Juliet Grames; and the support of Jun and my son, Tate.